ALL THE WANDERING LIGHT

ALL THE WANDERING LIGHT

HEATHER FAWCETT

BALZER + BRAY
An Imprint of HarperCollins*Publishers*

Balzer + Bray is an imprint of HarperCollins Publishers.

All the Wandering Light
Copyright © 2018 by Heather Fawcett
All rights reserved. Printed in the United States of America.
No part of this book may be used or reproduced in any manner whatsoever without written permission except in the case of brief quotations embodied in critical articles and reviews. For information address HarperCollins Children's Books, a division of HarperCollins Publishers, 195 Broadway, New York, NY 10007.
www.epicreads.com

Library of Congress Control Number: 2018938417
ISBN 978-0-06-246341-8

Typography by Sarah Nichole Kaufman
18 19 20 21 22   PC/LSCH   10 9 8 7 6 5 4 3 2 1

First Edition

ALL THE WANDERING LIGHT

PART I
HOME

ONE

I WAS LOST.

The wind lashed my face with snow lifted from the mountainside. Drawing breath was difficult, seeing my way near impossible. I forced myself to put one foot in front of the other, to replace my hood when the gusts blew it back, though I noticed little difference in warmth. I noticed little of anything. Even the wind's claws against my face, carrying ice so sharp my fingers came away spotted with red, had faded from my awareness.

Another step. Another.

Behind me, Azar-at was silent. At times, the wind and blown snow seemed to dissolve the fire demon's tenuous, wolflike form, and all I could see were eyes the color of fired coals gleaming through the swirl of white. Even when I didn't look, though, I knew it was there. Azar-at's presence was a weight that dragged behind me like a heavy cloak.

Biter croaked in my ear. Lusha's raven familiar was nestled in the crook of my neck, the weather making flight impossible. Clouds swirled around us, spilling snowflakes the size of coins. Despair washed over me. When I had left Raksha's summit, the wind had been rising, and I was too exhausted to make it down the rock wall I had scaled before. It had seemed possible to descend the precipitous slopes to the east, then traverse back to the plateau where I had left Tem, Lusha, and Mara two days ago.

Possible. Now that I was actually descending, I was discovering how little resemblance "possible" bore to "advisable."

Narrowing my eyes against the howling wind, I drove my ax into the mountain again, focusing on what mattered most: Lusha and Tem.

Their names, repeated in my mind, were the fire that kept me going, though every muscle screamed at me to stop, to give in to the hungry pull of the earth below. Were my sister and my best friend all right?

I pictured Tem, pale and haggard. He had been badly injured in the avalanche that almost swept him and Mara off the mountain. Lusha could barely walk after breaking her ankle on the Ngadi face, a treacherous wall of ice. Neither of them would last long in this environment. If I didn't make it back—

I shook myself. I couldn't dwell on *ifs*. I had to focus on finding Lusha and Tem, and after that, figuring out how to save Azmiri from the witches' inevitable attack on the Empire. As the closest settlement to the witches' lands, Azmiri was vulnerable.

But what could I do? I hadn't been able to stop River from lifting the binding spell at the summit of Raksha, and restoring the witches' powers—how was I going to protect my village from an army of creatures who could take any form they chose, and control the darkness itself? I couldn't begin to answer that, but it didn't matter. First, I would get us off the mountain. Then I would come up with a plan.

"It's all right," I said. My throat was raw from the cold, and I barely recognized my own voice. "We just have to keep going." I wasn't sure if was talking to Biter or myself.

The raven croaked again, a low sound like the purr of a cat. He was exhausted too—there was no shelter on this side of the mountain, no ledges to rest upon. Twilight was falling. I had been descending since morning.

Occasionally, the wind dropped and the snow cleared, revealing a glimpse of the vastness before me. Each time, I choked back a sob. It wasn't because I was thousands of feet in the sky, clinging to a slope so steep that one wrong step would send me tumbling into the clouds. It was because the view never changed. I could have been standing where I was an hour ago. How was I going to find my way back to the others?

Which brought me, again, to Azar-at.

I glanced over my shoulder, locating the glowing eyes in a heartbeat. I knew the fire demon was still there. I looked because part of me hoped it wasn't.

When I had made my contract with Azar-at, I had been

desperate. My body was bruised and battered from the ascent to the summit, and the thin air made it difficult to think straight. Azar-at's power seemed like the only way I could get myself off Raksha, let alone help anyone else. Yet I had discovered that, impossibly, I had scraps of strength left. I hadn't used the fire demon's magic yet—or paid its inevitable price.

Biter let out a cry. He launched himself into the air, leaving behind a small patch of warmth on my neck.

"Biter!" I tried to grab at his tail feathers. The raven flew a few yards down the mountain, settling into a hollow I could barely see.

After an interminable time, I reached the narrow shelter. It was only a few feet high, curved like a halved egg. It looked as if a chunk of the mountain had loosened and fallen away—recently, if the thin layer of snow was any indication. I was too exhausted to consider the danger—I tucked myself into that tiny pocket of space within the vastness of snow and sky, and something inside me wilted. I removed my pack and dropped my head onto my knees.

Azar-at crouched above me, the strange furnace of its body singeing the snow. It dripped down the rock, freezing in icicles like jagged teeth.

Why do you struggle, Kamzin? its voice murmured in my thoughts. *Friends need you. They wait for you, worrying. You should not let friends worry.*

"I'll find them." Not for the first time, I wished I could shield my mind from the creature's sinuous voice.

Fast is the wind over the mountain, Azar-at said. *Faster still could you reach friends if you use your magic.*

"It isn't my magic," I snapped. "It's yours. I will borrow it when I have no other choice—and only then. Don't you remember what I said?"

I remember.

"Then don't ask me again." I couldn't use Azar-at's magic without giving the fire demon part of my soul. That was the only currency it would accept.

We are friends now, Azar-at said. *I will do anything you want.*

I suppressed a shudder. Biter nipped at the flap on my pack, and I shooed him away. I carefully tucked the pack into a crevice in the rock where the snow wouldn't settle on it. I knew that the small creature inside could no longer feel the cold, but I couldn't bear the thought of Ragtooth's body being swallowed by the snow, becoming a frozen feature of the mountainside. Loyal to the end, my familiar had challenged Azar-at on the summit, and Azar-at—who had then been bound to River—had broken him. I felt fury at River rear up again, followed by grief that ached in my bones.

No tears came. I had none left.

I didn't realize I had fallen asleep until I opened my eyes and found that the night was still. I blinked, uncomprehending, shaking off the snow that covered me.

The blue-black sky hung before me like a vast, unraveled scroll. Countless stars flickered, forming constellations both familiar and strange. And across them streaked something I had never seen before.

Thousands of shooting stars. So close to where I sat, in that pocket of sky, that I felt I could touch them, and so bright my eyes watered.

"Azar-at," I whispered, equal parts fearful and awed, "what is this?"

The fire demon—crouched above me in the shadows—shook itself. Little drops of melted snow speckled my *chuba*.

It is River, Azar-at said.

Terrified, I shrank back as if the stars would burn me. They streaked across the sky in fiery bursts, tinged with red and yellow and blue. It was as if the night was tearing itself apart. I half expected the sky to give a shudder and fall to the earth in shards, revealing some strange otherworld hidden behind it.

"River?" During that long day, I had beaten back all thoughts of him, my fury subsumed by the simple need to survive. He had lied to me, betrayed me, and left me. He was not the person he had pretended to be—the emperor's favorite, his trusted advisor. Or, rather—even worse—he was those things, and he was also a witch who had been working against the Empire from the very beginning. He had stood at the summit of Raksha, in the witches' abandoned city, and unleashed their powers. Even the sound of his name seemed to settle in my chest like a small, cold weight. "What do you mean?"

They tell stories, Azar-at said. *River made an end. An end and a beginning.*

"Stories," I murmured. The stars told stories, certainly, for those—like Lusha, or Yonden—skilled enough to read them.

What had my sister once said about star showers like this? That they were rare, so rare the last one had faded from living memory. And that they marked significant events. Turning points in the course of history.

I watched the sky. In spite of myself, I was awed. River had done this—altered the fabric of the world. But he hadn't acted alone.

I bit my lip so hard I tasted blood. I had helped him, guided him to Raksha. And everything that happened as a result would be my fault. If I couldn't warn Azmiri of what was coming, if I couldn't get back to the village before the witches attacked—

"Biter," I said, wincing as I shifted position, "we may not have another chance like this."

The raven, who had returned to the crook between my neck and shoulder, croaked sleepily. He shook his wind-ruffled feathers and took flight, winking past the burning trails of the stars. But though the gusts had lessened, they never completely abandoned this exposed crag. After being beaten back against the mountainside twice, Biter flapped back to the shelter, landing inelegantly with wings askew.

"That's all right," I said, even as dread unspooled within me. "We'll take it slow. At least we can see now."

I forced myself to my feet. The pain in my ankle had dulled, but I knew it was just because everything was dulled, and that this was a dangerous thing. I leaned against the snow-caked mountain for a moment, then I drew on my pack and began descending again. The burning sky provided enough illumination to make out the shape of the mountainside.

I stabbed my ax into the ice, using it as an anchor as I craned to look in all directions. This couldn't be right. I had been bearing west all day, and by now, I should be close to the rocky plain where River and I had evaded the ghosts. And yet I could see only snowy slopes, impossibly sheer. I would have to turn back and find another route down.

I punched at the snow. How could this have happened? My sense of direction was normally unerring. As I contemplated my worsening prospects, Biter called out a warning, sharp in my ear.

I turned. To my right, the terrain rose to form a treacherous cornice, wreathed in mist. My breath caught in my throat.

A figure perched on the cornice, silhouetted against the blaze of shooting stars. He was tall and slender, clad in an expensively woven *chuba* tugged by the wind. His hood was up, and I couldn't see his face. It didn't matter. I would have known that *chuba* anywhere.

"River?" I croaked.

The figure's head tilted. Even his stance was River's—one foot propped carelessly against the lip of the snow as if nothing but solid ground was beyond it; elbows bent over hands thrust into pockets. Graceful and nonchalant, and equally unknowable, a shadow in the night.

How could he be here? When I had last seen him, he had been descending the mountain faster than any human could move.

Fury rose again, dwarfing the surge of hope that had risen, unbidden, at the sight of him. After all that River had done, he would dare return here? And for what purpose—to gloat? I crept toward him, raising my second ax. But before I could get any farther, he took a single step forward and plunged into the abyss.

"River!" I cried.

A moment of mad scrambling brought me to the cornice. The ice groaned ominously beneath my weight. To my astonishment, there were no footprints in the snow. And there was no sign of River. The mountain fell away in a sheer drop of perhaps a hundred feet, and at the bottom was—

I gasped.

The exposed rock of the mountainside curved down to a shallow plateau, and a mound of rock where a cave had collapsed. The very cave where River had trapped the dead explorer Mingma and the other ghosts, what felt like weeks ago.

I hadn't been traveling in the wrong direction after all. I just hadn't gone far enough.

I sank onto the snow, weakened by relief. To think that I had almost turned around, when I was only a few hours from Lusha and Tem! Biter, catching my excitement, flapped in a circle around my head. The wind tossed him against my pack, which gave a shudder.

And then another shudder.

My heart leaped into my throat. I wrenched the pack from my shoulders, fumbling with the flap with half-frozen hands. I reached inside, my fingers grasping at soft—and surprisingly warm—fur. There came a quiet whine.

I eased Ragtooth out of the pack and tucked him inside my

chuba. My vision dissolved as tears streamed down my face.

"I thought you were gone." One of the tears caught on his whisker and hung there like dew. "I'm sorry."

The fox stirred. One eye was sealed shut from the swelling and dried blood. His back was bent at an odd angle, his limbs stiff and cold. I held a finger in front of his face, and he gave it a weary lick.

I cradled him to my chest. Ragtooth made a sound deep in his throat and burrowed his head into my *chuba*.

I knew that I should say something, but the words didn't come. Ragtooth had been at my side since before I could remember, his uncanny presence a constant in my life, through my mother's death and my father's absences. His green eyes gleaming in the dark had comforted me as a child afraid of monsters. And after all our time together, this would be how it ended—in this cold and barren place, far from home.

Silent as falling snow, Azar-at settled beside me.

No help for death, it said. *No use for tears. Tears will not bring back friends.*

"He's hurt." It was stupid to deny what was happening. But still there was a part of me that refused to accept it. "He isn't—"

I stopped. Slowly, I turned to face Azar-at. "Can you heal him?"

I? I do not interfere in human business. But you could, Kamzin.

I stared. The creature gazed back at me, its eyes as unfathomable as the stars, or the darkness between them. I turned back to Ragtooth. His chest rose and fell, rattling with each breath. But still he managed the faintest of growls.

"Don't start," I snapped, dashing my tears away. "I don't care if you think it's a good idea. It's my decision." Losing Ragtooth had felt like a wound that would never heal clean. If there was even the smallest chance that I could save him, I would take it, no matter the cost.

I turned back to Azar-at. "All right."

The creature almost seemed surprised. Almost—it was eternally hard to read its emotions, if it even possessed them. *Are you prepared?*

Nausea rose in my throat. "Never mind that. Are you sure this is possible?"

Yes.

"Then do it. Quickly." I leaned back, bracing myself for pain worse than I had ever felt. I pictured Ragtooth opening his eyes, alive, healthy. But the fire demon merely sat there, motionless. The seconds slid past.

"Well?" I said. "Is there—?"

Ragtooth let out a ferocious growl. He leaped to the ground, and suddenly there was no trace of injury anywhere on his body— even his fur seemed healthier, gleaming faintly in the starlight. He growled again, his gaze fixed on Azar-at.

My cry of delight was cut short by a force that knocked me onto my back. To call it pain would be a mistake, for this was something beyond pain, a searing heat that bloomed in my chest and radiated through every inch of me. And with that agony was a strange sense of something being torn from me so quickly I couldn't place what it was, leaving behind a haunted feeling, as if I had awoken from a nightmare that evaded memory.

Then it was gone, and my weariness returned tenfold. Shakily, I sat up. I didn't feel any different—at least, I didn't think I did. Was this what River had experienced each time he used Azar-at to cast a spell? How could he have borne it so many times?

Ragtooth nipped me. With a shaky laugh, I wrapped him in my arms and buried my face in his soft fur. He struggled, but only halfheartedly. Azar-at watched us. The fire demon's gaze burned, but its expression was the same—frozen in a wolf's grin, tongue lolling.

"Ragtooth, no," I cried as the fox writhed out of my grip and scuttled close to Azar-at, growling and snapping. I knew all too well what had happened the last time he challenged the fire demon.

No need to fear, Kamzin, Azar-at said. *I would not hurt friends.*

I shook my head. I didn't have time to make sense of Azar-at's loyalties, which seemed to shift as easily as the smoke off a campfire. I gathered Ragtooth back into my arms, risking a kiss on his furry snout. A star soared past the mountain, so close I heard the air crackle, with a smaller one trailing in its wake.

Lusha. Tem. The stars seemed to blaze even brighter, echoing my determination. I would find them, and then—somehow—I would find a way to stop what I had helped River unleash. I settled Ragtooth around my shoulders and lowered myself over the edge.

TWO

River

HE SOARED ABOVE the earth, an owl silhouetted against the stars as they arched and burned. He tried to race them, and when he tired of that he flew to the ground, owl dissolving into leopard. He tried on a dozen different animals in quick succession—hawk, dragon, tahr—reveling in the magic. The binding spell had been cast long before he was born, and his powers were new—everything felt new. He tried transforming into shadow, folding himself into the darkness as witches were said to do in stories, but either the stories were exaggerated or it was a skill that required practice. He eventually gave up the effort.

As the night deepened, River assumed his familiar, human form at the edge of a stream shining with ice and crowded with glacial boulders. He threw himself onto the ground, exhausted but jubilant. The emperor's spell was broken, and he had the powers that should have been his from birth. He no longer had to rely on secondhand magic from Azar-at. As he gazed into the sky, he felt that even it was too small to contain him.

As if echoing his mood, shooting stars painted the night with fire. The sky was so bright it could have been lit by three moons. No doubt there was some mystical reason for it—something dull and prophetic, as those things often were.

He had descended the tallest mountain in the world, then covered fifty miles of ground in a single day. The Arya Mountains were still visible to the west, their sharp, snowy peaks faded to dusky gray. Raksha loomed over the rest like a dark threat. As he traveled, he had the sense that the mountain was watching with an odd combination of menace and regret. He shrugged off the feeling.

While witches could assume the shape of almost any animal they chose, the stories said that most used only one regularly: their secondskin. Changing shape was tiring, particularly when it involved taking the form of an animal you felt no affinity with. Yet he didn't feel tired, and all the shapes he tried felt easy and natural, though he perhaps preferred the leopard he had first chosen, with its sleek grace and deathly silent paws.

The land before him was familiar, though the trees were sparse, nothing like the heart of the Nightwood, the witches' forest. A hint of smoke hung in the air, another taste of home. At his current pace, he would be there within a day.

He held out a hand and let the shadows play over the water, creating ripples and waves. For more than three years, home had been a patch of grass in the wilderness, the oilcloth of a tent flapping in the wind, the howl of wolves. Or it had been the ridiculous spectacle of the emperor's court, where even the spoons were inlaid with jade and you could die of boredom were it not such a commonplace sensation that one grew inoculated. There had been no River Shara—he had invented him. But there was something appealing in that—in becoming a person he had created, rather than one constrained by things he had never chosen.

Now that their powers were restored, he supposed that the witches would attack the Empire. Or would Esha, his brother, wait for a more opportune moment, perhaps when the emperor was distracted by a barbarian invasion?

It doesn't matter.

River didn't care about the Empire. He didn't care about revenge, which had always struck him as a wasteful concept. His years as an explorer had taught him how fine the line was between life and death, for the powerful and powerless alike, and he had no intention of wasting time constructing elaborate plots to wreck the Empire. His thoughts had been occupied by one thing: breaking the spell. Now it was done, he would not stay in the Nightwood for long—he would not stay in any place for long. He would leave the Empire behind, and go wherever he liked.

He had always wondered what strange lands lay east of the Nightwood. Or perhaps he would travel south, all the way to the great lake that the stories said was made of liquid salt and stretched to the edge of the world.

The shadows had begun to drift. He lifted his hand, and they darted back to him. It was surprising how easily the darkness responded to his command. He focused, and the shadows swirled together, spinning like a dancer over the water. Shapes rose from the darkness. A fish. A rhododendron bloom. A palace on a hilltop. His eldest brother, Sky, his grim face caught in one of his rare smiles.

The shadows spun faster. Sky, Esha, and Thorn—each of his older brothers was ruthlessness personified, a knife edge in the night. He had only missed one—Sky, the eldest, quieter and more deliberate than the others. To most, that deliberation only added to his fearsomeness, for he had been a large, imposing man, given to deadly flashes of temper. There had only been one person who was spared that temper, and that was his youngest brother. But Sky was dead—he had taken his own life soon after their mother had.

River pictured his brother's brow furrowing as he recounted the story of his years at the emperor's court, Sky balancing his chin on his hand as he did when lost in thought. River would have told him about the banquets, the impossible luxury juxtaposed with the harrowing expeditions to distant lands. His mood darkened.

He glanced over his shoulder. "What do you think . . ."

No fire demon gazed back at him. The place where Azar-at would have sat, tongue lolling and coal eyes glittering, was empty. He had left Azar-at behind, as he had left Kamzin and the rest of his expedition.

He was suddenly very aware of the expanse of land around him, the whisper of the icy stream. River dashed his hand through the shadow, shattering the shapes he had summoned. He lay down, expecting sleep to find him quickly.

A steep, snowy slope, and the pull of the earth far below. His hand clenched on his ax as it bit into the mountain, his fingers aching with cold. Before him loomed the col that joined Raksha to its neighboring peak, sharp against the starry sky. He took a deep breath and raised the ax again—

He bolted upright.

He glanced down at his hands, half-convinced he would find his ax. But they were empty, and he had abandoned the ax, along with most of his other possessions, in the cave below the summit of Raksha.

He was uneasy. The dream had been strangely vivid—so vivid he could still feel the chill wind against his face. He had left Raksha behind. But Kamzin hadn't. Was that why his thoughts had strayed there?

When he had reached the summit of Raksha, he could taste the magic in the air. He had known he was close to breaking the binding spell that had weighed on him like a chain of iron since the day of his birth.

He felt a stab of something like anger, but colder, more fundamental. Kamzin had nearly succeeded in stopping him. A human girl with no magic whatsoever, just an impossible stubbornness. He wouldn't have harmed her, yet she had looked him in the eye, her gaze cold as an avenging spirit, and sent him to what should have been his death.

Through the anger came a strange pang of longing. He pushed

Kamzin from his mind. Thinking of her brought about an uncomfortable tangle of emotion, and he didn't have the patience to sort through it.

A flash of motion from the corner of his eye. A fox scuttled out from beneath a boulder and paused in the starlight. Green eyes gleamed as the creature turned to look at him, head cocked playfully.

River froze.

Every sense told him that the fox was Kamzin's familiar. But it was impossible. There was no way it could have followed him from Raksha. He dashed the sleep from his eyes, and when he opened them, the fox was gone.

First he was imagining himself back on Raksha, and now he was seeing Kamzin's fox. Next he would be imagining Kamzin herself lurking in the shadows, her large eyes, framed by their dark lashes, narrowed with fury—the way she had looked when she tried to kill him.

His urge to linger on that quiet bank had vanished. Now he wanted to move, to watch the miles dissolve beneath him. He changed back into an owl and launched himself into the air, silent as a ghost.

THREE

THE CAVE WAS quiet and still, shadowed in the early morning light. Nothing stirred on the snowy plain, and I saw no footprints. Given the wind last night, I told myself, that wasn't unexpected.

"Stay back," I ordered Azar-at. "Remember—"

You wish to keep secrets from friends, the creature said. *I remember.*

I stopped short. "That's not—"

I understand secrets, Kamzin.

"I bet you do," I muttered. Azar-at crouched behind a drift of snow, tail wagging. I left it there and headed for the cave. Ragtooth trotted at my side, light enough to tread atop the snow. I wished that Biter was still with me, but the raven had soared off somewhere as soon as the winds had died, and hadn't returned.

No smoke rose from the cave. Surely that was to be expected too, given their low supply of firewood.

"Lusha?" I called. "Tem?"

Silence.

My pace quickened. Despite my weariness, I was almost running. Ragtooth reached the cave first, peering inside with a plaintive sound. I was right behind him.

The cave was empty.

Strewn across the floor were the ashes of the fire, scattered by the wind. An empty satchel lay on its side, dusted with a fine layer of snow. The cave looked as if it had been abandoned months ago.

I backed out, panic rising in my throat. The blushing sky, still streaked with shooting stars, seemed oppressive, as did the mountain. It was all too vast, too silent.

"Tem! Lusha!" I yelled. My voice didn't echo—the wind carried it off, dead, as soon as it left my mouth. I was almost too exhausted to shout. "Mara!"

Find Lusha and Tem. The words had been an endless refrain as I descended the mountain. They now took on a mocking quality. *Find Lusha and Tem. Save Azmiri.*

Ragtooth had his snout to the ground, sniffing around the mouth of the cave. I saw myself and River finding it, staggering inside after an exhausting day. We had talked for hours that night, until I drifted asleep, feeling warm and safe. And then, after Lusha's expedition followed ours, and River abandoned us all, my sister and I had sat here holding a statue of our mother, an explorer many times braver than me.

That brought me back to my senses. If something terrible had happened to Lusha and Tem, why would they have taken the trouble to gather up their belongings?

"Kamzin?"

I whirled.

Behind me was a thin figure, his *chuba* torn and stained with blood, his normally smooth, chin-length hair a dark tangle. Yet he stood upright, and his cheeks were flushed from exercise. His eyes, as they met mine, were filled with an undiluted joy that almost stopped my heart.

I was in his arms before either of us could draw another breath. The dragon perched on Tem's shoulder gave a chirrup of alarm and leaped into the air. Tem's shoulders shook, and I realized he was laughing. I began to laugh too, a wild sound that took my breath away and made me fear I would never stop.

We drew apart. I could barely believe my own eyes. When I had last seen Tem, he couldn't lift his head, let alone walk. Yet apart from the weight he'd lost and the shadows under his eyes, he seemed almost *well*.

"I thought—" we both began at the same instant. I laughed, but the humor had died from his eyes.

"You look . . ." He stopped, and I felt a shiver of alarm. Did he know about Azar-at? If so, how? Could he somehow see the missing piece of my soul, like a hole in a piece of cloth?

"You look like you've been through something," he finished. He touched my face, and I was surprised by the whisper of pain it brought. Of course—the driving hail last night had cut me, and I was covered in bruises.

I eased back slightly. "Lusha?"

"She's fine," he assured me. "Mara too. We recovered the tent yesterday and pitched it on an outcrop nearby. Lusha wanted to be somewhere with an unobstructed view of the sky."

The notion that Lusha was prioritizing astronomy over a warm place to sleep surprised me for about half a second. Tem's brow furrowed. "Your ankle."

"It's nothing." I tried to balance my weight more naturally, even as my ankle seethed.

"I doubt that. But it will be, after an incantation or two." He coughed—a slight cough, far different from the frightening rattle that had plagued him throughout our journey to Raksha. "Mara wanted to go back down, but Lusha refused. We didn't know what sort of shape you'd be in. We thought you might need our help to get off the mountain. Lusha was planning to go after you, if the weather held today."

I shook my head. "Tem, I thought you'd need *my* help! When I left, you were—" *Dying*, I almost said.

He nodded. "I know. But a day's rest made a big difference. I slept for hours, and when I woke yesterday morning, I felt better. Stronger. I tried using my magic again, and I was able to heal my broken leg. And my ribs." He tapped his side, wincing slightly. "I'll be sore for a few days. Then I got to work on Lusha's ankle. She's practically as good as new, or so she says. You know Lusha: she wouldn't complain if she was being burned alive."

I was astonished. "All that, from a day's sleep?"

"Apparently." I could see that it had surprised him too. "I was using my magic too much. Once I was forced to stop for a while, it just . . . came back."

I had never heard of a shaman regaining their powers so readily—overusing magic to such an extent should take weeks to recover from. But then, Tem's powers had never been ordinary, or predictable. "Well, thank the spirits for that. Now I won't have to carry you down to base camp." *Or have Azar-at float you there.*

Tem seemed to read something of my thoughts in my face, for his eyes grew solemn again. "Kamzin, what happened?"

I turned away, feeling a stab of guilt. "Let's find Lusha. I'd rather not have to tell this story more than once."

We came upon them at the edge of the plateau, where they'd pitched the tent behind a boulder. The dragons spotted us first, and soon they were circling, chirruping their excitement at the arrival of a potential new food source. They were hungry, that was clear—their blue lights were barely visible, and flickered within their scaled bellies.

I paused. For a moment, the view struck me as strange: Mara and Lusha alone, framed against the sky. Part of me had expected more people to be there. But Dargye, one of our assistants, had been left at base camp to guard our supplies. And our other assistant, Aimo, as well as River's personal shaman, Norbu, had died shortly before River and I set out for the summit.

Mara glanced up. When his eyes met mine, he reached out to grab Lusha's shoulder. She was seated in the snow, bent forward as she peered through her small telescope. Of course she had brought the telescope, regardless of how much food she had to leave at base camp to compensate for the added weight. I wondered what she was looking at—it was too light to see any constellations, though the shooting stars were still visible, faintly.

Lusha blinked at me. She turned back to the pile of scrolls on her lap and calmly added a note. Then she stood.

"Lusha," I began, alarmed by the look on her face as she approached, "I tried to stop River, I swear, but he—"

She wrapped me in a fierce hug, smothering my words against her shoulder. To my surprise, hot tears welled in my eyes. They flowed down my face, dampening the collar of her *chuba*. I hadn't realized I'd been holding them back until now.

She stepped back and placed her hands on my shoulders. "So," she said without preamble, "River broke the spell?"

I swallowed, brushing the tears away. I quickly recounted everything—leaving aside my contract with Azar-at. How I had followed River, and watched him shatter the spell. What I had found on the summit. The witches, who were not bound to human form, had lived there once, and built a city of shadow among the clouds. This sky city had been abandoned long ago, though some of the witches' magic still lingered among the ruins. The place had had an uncanny, watchful quality about it.

I felt, again, the full weight of my failure. When I finished, there was a small silence.

"You were right," I said. "I never should have trusted—"

She made a gesture, and the apology died on my lips. Lusha

had always had that way about her—she could silence the General of the First Army with a glance.

"Preventing River Shara from getting his way was always a long shot," she said. "What's done is done."

"Azmiri . . ." I stopped. The village filled my thoughts—the neat stone houses, the slopes dotted with flowers and snow, the terraces cut into the mountain like a staircase to the sky. For the first time, I understood how fragile my home was, how small, tucked into a wilderness at the edge of the Empire with the witches' forest at its back. "It's so close to the Nightwood."

She nodded, her expression grim but thoughtful. "We need to warn the village."

"How?" Mara said. "It will take us days to reach Azmiri. Weeks."

Lusha held out her arm. For a strange moment, I thought she was trying to cast a spell without a talisman, but then there came a fluttering sound, and Biter settled on her wrist, his enormous talons curling gently around her sleeve.

"Biter!" I said. "I thought I'd lost you."

Lusha bent to retrieve a scrap of parchment and scrawled a message with a bit of charcoal. Then she furled the note and tied it to Biter's leg. The raven kicked once, but Lusha murmured something I couldn't catch, and he stilled. Once Lusha had the note secure, he took off. The beat of his wings lifted wisps of snow from the ground, and then he was gone.

"He should reach the village by tomorrow morning," Lusha said. "At least—at least they'll know what's coming."

27

Mara and Tem were staring at her. Even I felt a stab of disquiet, and I was long used to Lusha's familiars, their uncanny ability to understand her every whim. I knew, on some level, that this was how most people must feel about Ragtooth, though it was impossible for me to experience any awe when I thought about the creature who had trailed after me like a small, scruffy shadow since I was a baby.

"It isn't enough," I said. "We have to get back to Azmiri before the witches attack. We have to help them." My mind was on Azar-at's magic. I wouldn't use it unless absolutely necessary, and saving Azmiri fell into the category of absolutely necessary. Would the witches attack the village before striking the Three Cities, or would that come later, after the emperor's armies had been defeated? Azmiri was next to the Amarin Valley, one of only two corridors between the emperor's lands and the Nightwood.

My frustration surged. It was impossible to know what the witches were planning, or if they planned at all. I felt a sense of dislocation at the idea of River taking part in an attack on Azmiri, as if I were trying to force a key into a lock it didn't fit. I shoved that feeling away. River was a witch. He was capable of anything.

I pictured Father striding through the village on one of his nighttime rounds, the stars gleaming crisply, the houses dark save for the occasional flicker of dragonlight. I saw the shadows begin to stir, to coalesce, figures taking shape from the darkness, surrounding him.

I would use Azar-at's magic to defend the village. No matter what it cost me.

"If the witches have truly regained their powers, all hope is lost," Mara said. He was looking at Lusha. "We know they'll take revenge on the Empire. There's no reason to believe it won't be brutal and swift."

"So we should just abandon Azmiri?" I snapped. "Stay here with the ghosts?"

"I'm merely stating that—"

Lusha held up a hand, and we both fell silent—Mara, with an understanding nod; me, with a mutinous glare. "What do the bells say, Tem?"

Baffled, I watched Tem open his pack. He withdrew the *kinnika*.

"How did you—?" I took a step forward. "River threw them off the summit."

"Biter," Tem said. "He brought them to us an hour ago. They're all right—only one broken."

"The witch bell?"

"No."

I couldn't look away from the *kinnika*. I thought of the city on the summit, and the remains of the dead witch king. River, wreathed in shadows.

"That bell is the best weapon we have," Lusha said.

"It's the *only* weapon we have," I said. "According to Chirri, the *kinnika* are one of a kind."

"Tem thinks he can amplify the magic."

I stared. "What?"

"It's just something I was experimenting with," Tem said, flushing.

"Not 'just,'" Lusha said. "It's brilliant."

Tem, who was rarely on the receiving end of praise, least of all from Lusha, looked vaguely alarmed. He handed me one of the bells, a small, plain one with a notch in the rim.

"I've imbued it with the same power held by the witch bell," he said. "Or rather, altered the magic it held before. It's a form of transmutation—at least, I think it is. The Janyim scrolls describe it in detail. You remember—Chirri assigned you an essay on them."

I gazed at him blankly. I vaguely recalled Chirri lecturing me on the Janyim scrolls, one of the ancient shamanic texts, but I must have discarded the information, like most of what she had taught me. Tem sighed.

"If we can create more of these talismans, we can protect the village," Lusha said. "You said it yourself: River was overcome when you rang a single bell. Think what we could do with a dozen, or more."

I turned back to Tem. "And you can do this?"

His face was pale. "I think so."

"Then we take the *kinnika* back to the village," I said. "Before the witches attack."

Mara was shaking his head. "Given the distance, I'm not sure that's possible."

"We'll make it possible," I said. "I won't let him—them—" I

couldn't finish. I didn't have to. I could see my fears reflected on Lusha's face.

"We're at least two weeks from Azmiri," Mara said. His voice was quiet and carefully steady, as if he thought to calm me. "That's if the weather's fair, and if we walk from dawn to dusk—"

"I'll walk from dawn to dawn if I have to," I said. "The rest of you can follow behind."

"Kamzin—" Tem began.

"But first," I interrupted, "we have to get off this mountain."

I didn't look at Tem. I looked at Lusha. I waited for her to argue with me, to call me impractical and headstrong.

But Lusha merely held my gaze. I thought I saw the barest hint of a smile cross her face. After a moment, she nodded and turned to gather her things.

FOUR

River

THE NIGHTWOOD WAS a labyrinth of smoke and shadow.

The trees were blackened, sharp-needled things, so dense the smallest animals could barely slip through—not that many did. The only living creatures who dared dwell among the twisted boughs were red-eyed mice and hooded crows, and the odd half-starved fox. The only way to move easily was to follow the mazelike passages—witch paths—that crisscrossed at sharp angles. Branches knitted together overhead, at times resembling a cage, at others melting into something as solid as a roof. Smoke rose from the ground, which was bog-like in places, and strangely hot. Ghosts flickered among the branches, darting away as soon as they drew your gaze.

River leaned against a tree, his hands shoved in his pockets. He felt suffocated in that dense forest, as he always had, and wished himself elsewhere—anywhere. He stood in the Great Hall in the heart of the Nightwood, which was not a hall in the human sense, a place of carved stone and tapestries and dragon perches. It was merely a part of the forest—the deepest, darkest part—a cavernous place of column-like trees the width of several arm-spans. It was so dark that a human would have perceived only a shifting maze of shadow—there was no illumination in the Nightwood, save for the occasional shaft of sunlight that struggled through; witches needed neither dragons nor torches to see their way. When River had been a child, the Great Hall had been an empty, desolate place.

Today it held several hundred witches. All waiting for River's brother Esha to be officially named emperor.

Some stood in the shadows, conversing in small groups, or hovered in anticipatory silence around the boulder that formed a rough dais in the middle of the hall. A few—those that had already mastered their powers—perched high in the boughs as birds or monkeys, virtually indistinguishable from the darkness. There were more witches than River had ever seen in one place, a crowd so large it was unnerving, even to him. He could only imagine what a human might feel, gazing at that sea of strange faces.

"River." A white-haired witch appeared before him and clasped his hand. The man—who River thought was called Sonpa—said nothing beyond that, merely bowed his head before turning away. River, who had only experienced such displays of deference in the emperor's court, briefly expected to hear himself addressed as *dyonpo*.

It wasn't the first gesture of respect he had been paid since his return yesterday. But not everyone had welcomed him back. There were those who simply stared at him, distrust on their lean faces. They knew he'd broken the binding spell, but they also knew that he had been one of the emperor's most trusted advisors, an instrument of the hated Empire.

Let them think what they wanted. River had long since discovered that was easier—and in some ways, more advantageous—than explaining himself to anyone.

A girl was watching him. *Dawn*, he recalled, one of Thorn's friends. Growing up, River didn't think she had ever even looked at him, but now she smiled when she caught his eye. Her face was soft and pretty, framed by a waterfall of dark hair. She reminded him of Kamzin.

River looked away, pushing Kamzin from his thoughts.

He summoned a yew tree's shadow and pooled it in his palm, letting it spill through his fingers like water before catching it in his other hand. The branches stirred beside him, revealing his second-eldest brother, Thorn.

"Looking forward to this?" Thorn said in his cool voice, gesturing at the dais.

"Immensely." River had spent more than enough time on stages in the emperor's court, presiding over endlessly dreary royal ceremonies. "Will they cheer me or kill me?"

"Both appealing options." Thorn was smiling slightly, but it wasn't entirely clear that he was joking. Unlike most witches, Thorn always looked neat—he regularly stole clothes from human villages, or perhaps scavenged them from Esha's victims. He collected other things too: human trinkets. Salt candles and spirit statues; jade earrings and panes of colored glass. It was unnatural—witches had no possessions; ownership was not part of their world. It had taken River time even to get used to carrying supplies on his expeditions. But Thorn had always had a fascination—if not obsession—with the human world.

Thorn ran a hand through his dark hair, an absent gesture that River recognized in himself. He was closest to River in age as well as appearance. They were like blurred mirror images: Thorn's eyes were the same mismatched brown, a trait inherited from their mother, but Thorn was densely muscled where River was slim, his nose broken in some forgotten quarrel. Otherwise, they could have passed for twins—long a sore point for both of them.

"Esha says you're leaving tomorrow," he said.

"Yes." River had promised Esha he would stay for the coronation. His thoughts flashed to open skies and crisp mountain air. He wished he were already gone.

Thorn cocked his head, amusement flickering in his eyes. "Always so impatient. Where will you go?"

"I don't know." In truth, he did know where he would go—everywhere. He just didn't know where he would go first. He had spent his childhood fantasizing about escaping the smoke and strangled sky of the Nightwood, of traveling to distant and bizarre lands. He had had a taste of it after joining the emperor's court, though there, he had gone where he was bid.

"You don't know." Thorn's amusement seemed to grow. "You haven't changed. You never think ahead, do you? I still find it hard to believe that you of all people were the one who broke the spell."

Thorn's voice had a lazy quality River distrusted, though his face gave nothing away. It rarely did. Thorn had always been the quietest of the four of them, his thoughts like a lightless pool at the heart of a mountain. River and Thorn had never been close. Thorn and Esha were a pair, just as River and Sky had been a pair. Esha had barely noticed his younger brother at all—when he had, it had been to torment him. He was the cause of most of the scars River bore, more than all the glaciers he had scaled and wild beasts he had faced combined.

"Is there any point to this?" River said. "Other than stroking Esha's ego."

"Inheriting the Crown is a great honor."

"And you think Esha deserves it?" The Crown wasn't a physical object—witches didn't rely on human symbols to convey their standing. Centuries ago, before the emperor cast the binding spell, the Crown had been a magical gift, passed down from one ruler to the next. It marked them as separate from other witches. Some said it also instilled respect—and fear. Since the binding spell was cast, the Crown had lain dormant. Esha, the eldest descendant of the woman who had last held it, was naturally the one the Crown had chosen.

River didn't say what he truly felt: that Esha shouldn't be the one standing there. It should have been his mother, or Sky. Something sharp rose inside him. He had never been good at naming his emotions, and it had only grown more difficult since he had met Azar-at.

Thorn gave him a strange look. "I suppose so. Though I wouldn't have minded being chosen myself."

"Esha's next in line."

"That doesn't always matter."

River rolled his eyes. Thorn was dreaming. The Crown was almost always inherited by the eldest child. Sometimes, there were exceptions. If the emperor was murdered—which had happened—it sometimes passed to the assassin.

The Crown can be fickle, his mother had once said. *It doesn't like weakness, and it will seize any chance to escape a weak ruler.*

But Esha was the eldest. And while he was many things, he wasn't weak.

Something rustled the leaves. River started as a small, pointed face thrust through the branches behind Thorn's feet. The creature bared its teeth at the sight of him.

It was, unmistakably this time, Kamzin's fox.

River barely had time to process this before the creature slid back into the forest, pausing only to snap at Thorn's heel. His brother shifted position slightly, frowning.

River's hands clenched into fists. What was the fox doing, trailing after him like a bedraggled shadow? Was it spying on him? He had always thought there was something strange about it, though

Kamzin had never seemed troubled by its odd behavior.

Murmuring swept through the forest. River turned to the boulder, where his eldest brother had emerged from the shadows, eyes blazing. Esha's eyes were always bloodshot, irritated by the smoke and haze of the Nightwood. His hair was an unkempt scraggle, and he was painfully thin, but not in a way that suggested frailty—his every movement hummed with a fierce vitality, as if some dark flame burned at the heart of him.

River's gaze drifted to the boulder beneath Esha's feet. His thoughts flashed to the times Sky had raced him to that boulder, a convenient landmark for games. River had won every time, drawing even with Sky at the last moment, then surging past his eldest brother's wide-eyed amazement. He had thought himself the fastest runner in the Nightwood. It wasn't until he was older that he realized Sky had been letting him win.

"River." Esha's voice was calm and carrying.

River's fists, he realized, were still clenched in his pockets—with an effort, he loosened them. He didn't bother to wait for the crowd to part, merely strode forward, requiring everyone to get out of his way. They did. Murmuring swelled through the hall as he strode to the dais and, uninvited, stepped onto it. Irritation flickered in Esha's eyes.

"Welcome home, brother," he said.

River gazed into the sea of faces. He recognized a few, here and there—Rohna, his mother's cousin, who stared at him with a hungry sort of pride; Kalden, an ancient witch who had often quarreled with Sky over raids on the Empire's villages, his creased face filled with suspicion. Others he might never have seen before—Esha had summoned witches from even the farthest reaches of the Nightwood. Shadows swirled, and the air was electric with magic. He hadn't meant his comment to Thorn as a joke—witches were unpredictable, and there were certainly those in the crowd who hated him for joining the Empire, even given what he had done for them. He kept his expression opaque.

"You've surprised us," Esha said. "The spell was already failing, it's true, but you hastened its demise. For that, we are grateful."

River smothered a smile. It was clear that the effort of paying his youngest brother a compliment was, for Esha, near to torturous. He was beginning to enjoy himself.

Esha turned back to the crowd, and River wondered if he was about to dazzle everyone with a display of magic. The witches gazed at him worshipfully. River knew that few of them regretted Sky's death. As a flame draws moths, Esha had always attracted admirers—he was like fire himself, enticing yet dangerous, warm with some and vicious with others. He was the opposite of quiet, brooding Sky, who had always been respected, but rarely liked. Any witch, if asked who they would have chosen to lead them, would have said Esha—and Esha knew it. He had spent his life hating Sky, never having forgiven him for the crime of being firstborn.

But rather than unleashing his powers, Esha merely gestured to two witches standing near the dais.

"Bring them," he said. The witches slipped away through the trees.

Excited murmurs swept the hall like wind. No one knew what Esha had planned, and they were enjoying the mystery. Even River felt a stab of anticipation. Something rustled in the trees behind him. Probably a ghost—the forest was full of them. Any creature that died in the Nightwood tended to stay there—something about the forest was *sticky*, and held on to the spirits of the dying like spiderwebs. They were humans mostly—merchants, soldiers, village children. Esha was responsible for many of them. River's brother had never discriminated between soldiers of the Empire and her children, something River found distasteful. There were also animal spirits, those of livestock stolen from the mountain villages. River had encountered more than one yak ghost, which was always unpleasant. Many animals mistrusted witches for their ability to assume their shapes, but yaks, for some reason, had particularly disliked him. It was an antipathy they seemed to retain in spirit form.

There were no witch spirits. Witches didn't become ghosts.

River felt something inside him go out, like a flame in a gust of wind. He would never see Sky again, in this world or any other.

The noise came again, louder this time. It wasn't rustling—it was whispering. Sharp, staccato whispers that rose and fell, as if carried on a breeze—

The wind howled. The snow fell thick and fast, blotting out the landscape. Lusha's hand held his arm. Tem, beside him, clutched at the kinnika, *his head bent as he murmured an incantation. His shield was failing.*

Lusha nocked an arrow, her eyes narrowed as she searched for a target through the raging snow. She turned to him.

"Kamzin—"

"What are you doing?"

River came back to himself with a start. He was in the Nightwood, beside Esha on the dais. Esha was staring at him—he had stumbled slightly, and now stood blinking in the darkness.

Kamzin. That was Kamzin's mind. Kamzin's thoughts.

His vision swam. For a moment, he thought he would be pulled back to that snowy world, where the cold burrowed beneath his skin in a way it never had before.

It wasn't possible. It didn't make *sense*.

And yet he couldn't deny what had happened. It had been real, as real as the murmur of the nearby stream and the taste of smoke. He had been enspelled. But by who? Some small, detached part of him was impressed by the tidiness of the magic—most spells left traces, but he could sense nothing.

She had been frightened. River felt a brief urge to lash out—not at Kamzin, but at whatever it was that had been threatening her. He tried to probe the memory, but it was like pushing against a door that only swung one way. He couldn't find his way back to Kamzin's thoughts. What she had been thinking in that moment wasn't enough to piece together an explanation.

Two things were clear: one, he had been enspelled. And two, he couldn't reveal it to anyone. It was a clear sign of weakness.

"Don't look so concerned, Esha," River said. "I just climbed the highest mountain in the Empire. If you want me to stay awake, don't drag me to tedious ceremonies."

Esha's scornful look returned. "I apologize for expecting you to take this seriously. I should have known I'm still dealing with a child."

The two witches had reappeared, each dragging a captive. The captives were clothed in finely made *chubas*, light in color, and they stood out against the surrounding shadow. River started.

The *chubas* were made of tahrskin.

The explorers—one man and one woman—were led to the front of the dais. Horror dawned on their faces as they beheld Esha looking down at them. River felt a stirring of unease. He didn't recognize the man, but the woman he had met before. Her name was Malay, a member of the nobility and one of the emperor's favorites. River had once sat beside her at a banquet, where they had traded jokes and stories about their separate travails in the Drakkar Mountains.

Malay's gaze drifted from Esha to River. She seemed to freeze, her face whitening. River, unconsciously, had taken a step forward. Esha was already speaking.

"These two were found in the Amarin Valley," Esha said. His voice remained low, but it carried across the Hall, which was eerily silent, despite the number of witches present. "Empire spies."

That raised a low hiss from the gathering. Malay looked over her shoulder, as if startled by the number of voices she heard. In such darkness, she would be barely able to see.

"It's said that, in ancient times, every coronation ran red," Esha said. "The stories say the Crown is strengthened by blood."

The murmurs were approving. A enormous hawk alighted on a lower branch closer to the dais, as if to seek a better view. A bear growled from the trees.

Esha raised his hands, and the darkness began to stir. It snaked over the two explorers. The man struggled before growing still, his mouth round with horror. The shadows twined about his wrists and ankles, lifting him into the air.

Malay did not move—her gaze was fixated on River, her graying hair stirred by the shadows. Her eyes had a glassy quality, as if she was too shocked to comprehend what she saw. Even as the man began to scream, as the shadows pierced his skin, she stared at him.

After a moment, the man fell silent. River didn't even glance at him. The shadows moved to Malay, sliding over her body and lifting her into the air. She jerked in alarm, breaking eye contact with River at last.

He was moving before he knew what he was doing, leaping off the dais, summoning the shadows that wrapped around Malay. To his surprise, they obeyed him without hesitation, spooling at his feet like thread. The explorer hit the ground hard, and River crouched beside her. She was unconscious, though her eyelids fluttered as he touched her face. Her mouth was still open, as if she had carried her terror with her into sleep.

River was so relieved to find his friend still alive, still breathing, that he didn't immediately notice how quiet the hall had become. Even the wind seemed to hold its breath.

He looked up. Esha's jaw was slack with shock. Thorn's eyes were narrowed, absent their characteristic amusement. And hundreds of witches stared at him with a hungry fury in their eyes.

"I take it back," Thorn said. "Everyone definitely wants to kill you."

River ignored him. He threw himself down on the throne, folding his ankle over his knee. The great rock, situated in a clearing on the brow of a hill some distance from the Great Hall, was stained with blood at the base, evidence of innumerable battles and assassinations. River's thoughts flashed to the emperor's immaculate, gilded throne. How many times had he seen Lozong seated there in precisely the same posture?

Esha was pacing. He hadn't spoken a word to River since the scene in the hall an hour ago, when he had ordered the witches to disperse, barely a heartbeat before they tore River to pieces.

"What's wrong with you?" There was no anger in Thorn's question, only bafflement. He stared at River as if he were a stranger.

"I know her." River heard the strangeness of his own words. He felt a sense of futility, as if he were trying to communicate with his brothers in a language they didn't speak. Malay was part of the Empire—she had, in all likelihood, come to the Nightwood to spy on them. But still . . . she was his friend. He wasn't going to watch Esha harm her.

"Is that sentiment?" Esha turned to face him. "For one of the emperor's slaves?"

"She's no more his slave than I was," River snapped.

"I think I know what this is about." Thorn peered at River as if he were slowly coming into focus. "I told you he hadn't changed, Esha."

Thorn's tone made his meaning clear. Scorn replaced the shock in Esha's gaze. "Is that it? You had a relationship with a human?"

River almost laughed, and not because he saw any humor in the situation. There was no point in attempting to explain himself to his brothers. Let them think he had baser feelings for Malay. It was certainly simpler than explaining his true motivations, which he wasn't sure he could even explain to himself.

"I thought that you might have matured in the years you spent in the Empire's service," Esha said. He clearly had taken River's silence for an admission of guilt. "But I see now that you're the same irresponsible child you were when you left."

Esha came forward into the light, though he didn't leave the shadows behind; they swirled at his back like a cloak. River suppressed the urge to lean away. Esha's magic smelled of soot and things that grew in dank places.

"You've given the others a very good reason to distrust you," Esha said. "As if they needed the encouragement. I don't know if I'll be able to protect you forever."

Now it was River's turn to stare at Esha. "Protect me?"

"As it turns out, I need you." Esha turned away. "A star fell in the Ash Mountains two days ago. Several witnessed it."

River watched him, perplexed. He couldn't fathom why Esha was bringing this up now. "And?"

"I want you to retrieve it for me."

For a moment, River was too surprised to reply. "You want me to—"

"Retrieve the star, yes." Esha watched him. "You can do it? You are a celebrated explorer, after all."

River looked from Esha to Thorn, whose expression showed no surprise whatsoever. He knew little about fallen stars—he knew that the emperor sought them, and that they possessed an ancient magic. He didn't know what kind. The shamans of the Three Cities told stories about them, all fantastical and contradictory. Some said they killed any who touched them. Others that they could level cities.

"Why?" he said.

Esha began to pace again. "There are barely three hundred of us left alive. Do you know how many soldiers Lozong has at his command? How many shamans? Their numbers are in the thousands. We can't destroy the Empire as we are. We need the star. They say there is nothing more powerful."

River felt a surge of frustration. Esha would never be dissuaded from attacking the Empire. Like most witches, he had breathed fantasies of revenge his entire life. Yet River knew it went beyond that for his brother. Esha finally had what he had always dreamed of: authority. The chance to be a leader. He now needed to prove what he had always believed to be true: that he, not Sky, was the one who deserved the title of emperor.

"So that's your plan?" River said. "Find the star, then attack the Empire? You don't even know what powers it will give you."

The corner of Esha's mouth quirked in something that wasn't

a smile. Though he wasn't afraid of Esha anymore, as he had been as a child, that look still gave River a chill. He had seen Esha wear it before he tore people apart. Literally. River had witnessed what he had done to a group of Empire traders who had strayed into the Amarin Valley.

"The attack has already begun," Esha said. "I've sent raiding parties to the border villages of the Empire. We will lure the emperor's armies away, spread them thin. Then, with the star, we'll invade the Three Cities and reduce them to ash."

River didn't know why Esha's words would fill him with an odd, cold feeling. Perhaps because it was such a brazen plan that it was difficult to imagine it actually working. He eyed Esha with distaste. It shouldn't surprise him that his brother had already constructed an elaborate plot to destroy the Empire. Esha had always been the cleverest among them, and plotting was his specialty— one of his least appealing traits, in River's opinion. He wondered what other plans Esha had laid, for surely there were others. Esha's plots were like loose threads in a tapestry—pull at one, and three more tumbled free.

River flicked a speck off his *chuba*. "So you need me, do you? I thought I was just a child."

Esha's eyes narrowed. "We can reach the Ashes in three days. We'll take a small party, to travel as quickly as possible."

"My mistake," River said. "An *irresponsible* child."

"Can you do it?" Thorn said, anger cutting through his customary coolness. Esha placed a hand on his shoulder, surprisingly gentle. But then, Esha had always been gentle with Thorn, as he was with all his hangers-on. It was all the more startling given the purity of his viciousness toward his enemies. Despite himself, River felt a twinge of jealousy.

He leaned back into the throne. "Fallen stars are almost impossible to catch. They don't stay earthbound for long—a few days, at most. The emperor sent me after a star shortly after I was named Royal Explorer." He recalled the long journey to the unexplored lands south of Dawa Lake, days tearing through hot, dense forest and nights of torrential rains that flooded his tent. Even Azar-at had seemed fed up. When they reached the place the royal seers had described, all they found was an empty crater. "It wasn't my most successful expedition."

"You have your powers now," Esha said.

River pondered it. Absently, he twined one of the shadows about his fingers, pooling it in his palms as he had before. He had to admit, the idea intrigued him. It irritated him that he had never succeeded in catching a star, something other explorers deemed impossible. Wouldn't it be enjoyable to test the limits of his powers, to watch the impossible shatter like ice beneath his boot?

"You helped Lozong," Esha murmured. "Yet you won't help us? The Empire killed Mother. They killed Sky. Have you forgotten?"

"No." River's anger flared. He saw his mother, hair tangled with dirt and twigs, raging. Sky had been the only person who could steady her, but there were times when even he couldn't guide her through the wilderness of her imaginings. The binding spell had affected all witches differently—most felt it like a weight that accompanied their every movement. But for others, it was a mental, not a physical one. Some broke under that weight. His mother had been one of them.

When River had last seen her, she had been on that throne. It had been one of her rare moments of clarity, and she had known who he was and that he was leaving. She had touched his chin, as she had when he was a boy, and wished him luck in an oddly wistful voice. Had she known it would be the last time they would see each other?

His thoughts darkened. He might not care about revenge, but that didn't mean he didn't hate the Empire. If Esha wanted River to bring him a fallen star, he would do it. He could disappear afterward.

"Tell me where it fell," he said.

FIVE

THE SUN HAD set by the time we finally reached base camp, a small, elevated plateau nestled in the lower slopes of Mount Ngadi. We had descended Raksha in a day, painstakingly lowering ourselves down the treacherous ice wall as the sun and wind chapped our skin, then traversing the icefall of towering, groaning seracs. Though I was exhausted, I felt little relief as we stumbled toward the tents. I wouldn't feel entirely free of the mountain until we left its shadow.

The yak grunted excitedly as we approached. She was huddled behind a rock, head lowered in a morose posture. I held out a hand and she nosed up to me, pressing her forelock into my neck with uncharacteristic enthusiasm. She was untethered, which surprised me. But then, she would know better than to stray too far from her only food source in miles. The dragons we had left behind lay in a tangled heap by the tent. They murmured sleepily at our approach, too cold to stir.

"It's been out for a while," Tem said, examining the small fire-pit. A layer of snow covered it. Wordlessly, Mara began assembling kindling.

"Dargye?" Lusha called, approaching the tent. The flap, which Dargye had failed to secure, rustled in the breeze with a gentle *shhh, shhh.*

I collapsed on the ground, too tired to care that Dargye had fallen asleep when he should have been watching for our return. Tem might have healed my ankle, but the rest of me was spent. I let my pack slide down my shoulders with a sigh of relief.

"Tem," I said, "do you know a spell to make our dinner prepare itself?"

He chuckled, the smile breaking through the weariness on his face. "No. But I can help Mara start the fire." He pulled out the *kinnika,* which gleamed in the dying light.

Something nagged at me as I watched Tem caress the bells almost lovingly. *Stolen magic,* River had called them. Imbued with witch magic, like every talisman used by the emperor's shamans. "Has their power weakened?"

Tem looked thoughtful. He lifted one of the bells, muttering something. I jumped as one of the scraps of kindling in the firepit exploded into flame.

"I don't think so," he said.

"I can't understand it," I murmured. "If the talismans are sto-len magic—magic that returned to the witches after the binding spell broke—shouldn't they be powerless now? River said—"

"Clearly, River isn't right about everything." There was an odd note in his voice. I bit my lip and made no further argument.

Lusha strode back to us. "Dargye isn't here."

"What?"

"Tent's empty. His pack's gone." She began setting up her telescope. "I'll see if I can find any evidence of his trail."

"Where could he be?"

"Hunting, I assume. He took the bow."

Mara eyed the sky. "Light's long gone. He should have returned by now."

"We should go after him," I said. Despite my exhaustion, I moved to retrieve my pack from where I had dropped it.

"No," Lusha said. Just that word.

I felt a prickle of irritation. "Lusha—"

"This terrain is too dangerous to navigate in the dark," she said. "We should all stay close to camp tonight."

Mara was nodding. "That's certainly the safest course."

I fell mutinously silent. I had been the leader of River's expedition, and I still saw myself in that role, broken and diminished as our group was. At the same time, it was abundantly clear that Lusha viewed herself in the same light. It was unlikely that the idea of a different hierarchy would even occur to her, or to Mara. Even Tem watched Lusha expectantly as she bent over her telescope.

I gazed into the gathering dark. Nervousness twisted in my stomach. The thought flitted through my mind: *Azar-at could find Dargye*. I shoved it away, but not before I imagined I saw the fire demon's eyes gleam in the shadows. The Aryas pressed into our backs, while before us lay the enormous glacier that flowed down from Raksha, riven with cracks and ripples that gleamed a ghostly blue in the dying light. To the south, the ground fell away—a constant decline covered in mountain rubble and patchy snow. Far in the distance was a landscape of low hills, crowned with black trees that marked the edge of the Nightwood—the witches' lands.

After a moment, Lusha looked up and shook her head. *Shhh, shhh*, went the tent flap.

There was nothing else to do but prepare for the night. Mara and Tem did the cooking, and within minutes, the smell of fried *sampa* filled the air, lifting everyone's spirits. It had been days since any of us had eaten a proper meal, and I had to stop myself from scooping the half-cooked porridge from the pot with my fingers. To distract myself, I set up the second tent and fed the dragons and the yak. Lusha didn't stir—her face was buried in her telescope again, but the instrument was pointed at the sky now.

After eating, we took turns bathing in the stream that trickled down the mountainside a short walk from camp. The surface was crusted with ice, which had to be smashed to reach the frigid water below. I scrubbed myself quickly from head to toe, my teeth chattering. I dunked my head under and rose with shards of ice tangled in my hair. Finally, when I was unable to feel my hands or feet anymore, I dressed in the clean clothes I had left at base camp and staggered back to the fire.

"I could kiss you, Tem," I groaned unthinkingly as he handed me a bowl of butter tea. He smiled, but a flush started on his cheeks. My thoughts flashed back to the last night we had spent here together, the feeling of his lips against my skin and the warmth in our small tent. I felt a prickle of guilt—I knew that Tem had feelings for me that I didn't share. I had known then, and yet I had almost let us go down that road again, which wasn't fair to him. I looked away, swallowing the tea so quickly I burned my throat.

The night was clear, and the stars blazed with their cold light. The yak was asleep, her rump turned toward the fire, the dragons burrowed contentedly in her fur.

"How are you feeling?" I asked Tem. As Mara had pointed out, we were at least two weeks from Azmiri, though I hoped to reduce that by setting a punishing pace. Tem was the one I was most concerned about—he had stumbled several times during the descent.

"I'm fine." He wasn't looking at me. "Don't worry about me, Kamzin."

Mara sat across from us beside the fire, head bowed over a map. He rubbed his nose absently, smudging it with charcoal. I craned my head, and found a painfully familiar rendering of our abandoned camp on Mount Raksha staring back at me. Mara was not mapmaking, but drawing, the image bordered by lines of dense characters. I would have thought it impossible that such a sensitive rendering could belong to someone as cold and high-handed as Mara, was I not seeing it pour from his hands.

"That's beautiful," I said.

Mara started. He muttered something that sounded like "thanks" but was accompanied by an unpleasant look in my direction.

"You're still recording," I noted. "No one would blame you for stopping. You aren't exactly River's chronicler anymore."

Mara shrugged. "Some habits are hard to break."

I watched him, wondering. If it was merely habit, why had he seemed so absorbed? The look on his face reminded me of the one Tem wore when he bent over a scroll detailing some ancient incantation, or Lusha's as she arranged her telescope before settling in for a night of stargazing.

"You must be one of the greatest chroniclers in the Three Cities," I said.

He swiped the charcoal over the page in rapid, precise lines. "Not *one of*. Why do you think I was chosen to accompany the Royal Explorer on his expeditions?"

"But you don't want to be the Royal Explorer's chronicler," I said. "You want to be in River's place."

"And I will be." Mara's voice held a deep satisfaction. "Can there be any doubt? I'm the most experienced of the emperor's explorers by far. Once River's betrayal is known, the court will turn to me."

I made no reply. I thought of all I had heard of Mara's reputation, not to mention what I had seen from him. He may have traveled to the farthest reaches of the Empire, but it had not made him a great explorer. Would the emperor truly turn to him, when other candidates existed?

I watched, engrossed, as the mountain grew beneath his skilled hands. Mara captured not only the look of landscapes, but the *taste* of them. And he was certainly a natural storyteller—I had read over his entry from yesterday, which wove details together so skillfully that I had seen the images rise in my mind. It struck me as strange, almost sad, that Mara couldn't content himself with what he was good at. Yet it seemed to be a fixture of his character, to care most for what he couldn't have.

"I haven't seen Ragtooth since morning," Tem said.

"He's probably skulking around the stream, looking for fish."

Tem was frowning. "He's been going off by himself a lot lately."

I felt a flicker of worry. But Ragtooth had seemed perfectly healed, and in any case, his wanderings were as familiar to me as the stars over Azmiri. "He'll turn up."

Tem looked like he was about to say more, but Mara, his face still buried in his scroll, said, "No doubt precisely when you need him."

I blinked at him, surprised. "What does that mean?"

"There's an explorer in the emperor's employ who travels with a familiar," Mara said, leaning back slightly from the sketch to examine it. "A man named Tsering. I traveled with him once. His familiar is a brown panda. It had an uncanny ability to locate game and forage when our supplies were low."

"Is Tsering's familiar as bad-tempered as Ragtooth?" I said.

"No," Mara said. "Tsering is a steady sort of man. A familiar's temperament seems to reflect that of its master."

Tem seemed to smother a snort. I glared at Mara, replying in a dignified voice, "I haven't heard that to be the case."

He shrugged. He was in an uncharacteristically communicative mood, as if his work had loosened something inside him. "They're interesting beasts. Some have magical abilities, which must be spirit-granted. They seem to arise in response to the master's need."

This amused me. "Magical abilities? Can Tsering's panda fly?"

Mara gave me the same puzzled look he turned on the yak when she made a sudden sound. "As I said, abilities that meet the *master's need*. Tsering's familiar could understand every one of his commands—even when Tsering spoke in the barbarian dialect. He once retrieved a satchel of maps Tsering had left back at the palace. At the time, we were weeks from the Three Cities. We never did figure out how he did it."

"I've never known Ragtooth to be capable of anything like that," I said dubiously. "Though he did fetch my mittens once. Well, after he gnawed holes in them."

"From what I've read, a familiar's capabilities are also proportionate to those of its master."

"From what you've read." Clearly, initiating any sort of conversation with Mara had been a mistake.

"Yes." Mara stretched, furling the scroll, then he moved to Lusha's side where she sat by the telescope.

Tem seemed to be on the edge of laughter. "Kamzin—"

"Oh, forget it." I was too tired to get worked up over Mara's remarks. He and Lusha rustled through the star charts, murmuring. Their voices melted together with the wind's, which was calm tonight, playing gently over the oilcloth of the tents.

I leaned back on my hands. For a moment, seated next to a warm fire with a full belly, my fears for Azmiri, and the dangerous journey ahead, seemed like little more than the fading wisps of a nightmare. It struck me for the first time that I had climbed Raksha and made it back alive.

The peak of the great mountain gleamed white in the moonlight. I had stood there—it felt impossible now, looking up at it. And I had done it without the help of a fire demon, or any aptitude for magic. I dug my fingers into the earth, excitement sparking inside me—the sort of feeling that had lain dormant for days. The realization that I had been the only human to set foot on that peak filled me with determination. If I could climb Raksha, could I do other impossible things? Could I protect Azmiri from the witches? Could I face River again?

A cold, familiar weight settled in my chest. I saw River on the summit of Raksha, the fierce wind pulling at his hair and *chuba*. He hadn't hurt me, even when I tried to stop him. Would he hurt Azmiri?

I thought of the evenings we'd sat together after a long day's march, watching the stars wink into existence. His mismatched eyes sparkling as I teased him, or for no reason in particular— River often seemed at the threshold of laughter, which rippled over his features like sunlight on water.

I didn't know what River would do. I didn't know him—the face he'd shown me had been a lie. All I knew now was that he was my enemy. I drew my knees to my chest, an odd sort of loneliness washing over me.

"Can you really do what you said?" I asked Tem. "Amplify the magic in the witch bell?"

Tem touched the *kinnika*. He had strung them on a new cord, and they rested in their familiar place around his neck. His face, as he held the witch bell, was slightly troubled. "Yes."

I wanted to feel relief. Our plan, meager as it was, hinged on Tem's magic—his ability to use the *kinnika* to defend Azmiri. But something made me uneasy.

"I thought about what you said about amplifying talismans," I said slowly. "I do remember Chirri mentioning it. But it wasn't anything like this—the Janyim scrolls deal only with healing spells."

Tem nodded. "I know. But magic is magic. I can do it, Kamzin. I know I can."

I bit my lip. It wasn't that I didn't believe him. It was that, sometimes, I didn't want to. Tem's knack for magic was something I had never understood. This had become even more true since we left Azmiri. Tem had been forced to call on spells he had never used, and magical talents he had never explored. And, in a few weeks, he had exceeded anything even Chirri was capable of.

"What will you do if we get through this?" I said.

Tem blinked. "I don't really think about it."

"All right, I'll go first," I said lightly. "I'll sleep in every day until noon, and spend the rest of the time stuffing myself with Aunt Behe's spiced bean cakes."

Tem laughed. "You'd do that for a day, and then you'd be so bored you'd go charging off to Mount Karranak to chase feral dragons."

I laughed too, because he was right. We were quiet for a long moment. The *kinnika* tinkled faintly.

"I'd go to the Three Cities." Tem's voice was so quiet I could barely hear him. "I'd take the Trials."

"The Trials?" It caught me by surprise. The Trials were the examinations taken by all those seeking to apprentice to the royal shamans. I had never heard Tem even mention them. But then, there were many subjects Tem didn't speak about, most of them pertaining to himself.

"I mean, if I could do anything," Tem said quickly, as if he regretted having spoken. "But my father would never allow it."

"Your father doesn't have to matter," I said. "You're almost seventeen."

"It's just a thought I had." Tem turned back to the *kinnika*. "It's not something I would actually do."

I bit back a response. I wanted to tell him that I thought he would pass the Trials in record time. That he could probably best the emperor's shamans, let alone their apprentices. But I knew Tem well enough to recognize that he wouldn't be pushed to say anything more on the subject. He leaned over the *kinnika*, muttering an incantation I didn't recognize.

"I thought you already cast the warding spells," I said.

Tem's brow furrowed. It was a moment before he was able to focus on me. "Actually, I was looking for River."

It was as if the cold weight shifted an inch closer to my heart. "River?"

"I know he's gone," Tem said. "I just can't figure out why that bell's still sounding." He tapped the bell absently, which was small and seemingly unremarkable, an outlier next to its shiny, gaudier neighbors. It made no sound. It only sounded in the vicinity of someone, or something, who meant harm to those who bore it. I pictured the *fiangul*, dark shapes gliding toward us through the blizzard. It had sounded then, a harsh peal.

"Remember how it kept whispering, during the journey to Raksha?" Tem said. "I thought it was because of him—I noticed that it went quiet when the two of you left for the summit. But ever since you returned, it's been doing it again. At first I thought he could be following you. But that doesn't make sense—why would he come back?"

As if on cue, the black bell gave the tiniest shiver of sound, then fell silent.

My heart pounded in my ears. "Ever since *I* returned?"

Tem smiled. "I didn't mean it like that—obviously, it isn't because of you."

"Obviously," I echoed faintly. "What about the other bell—the one that sounds when a witch is near?" *Shadow-kin*, the engraving on the bell said. "We know that one responded to River."

"It's been quiet." Tem sighed. "Maybe you're right. Maybe when the binding spell broke, something happened to the *kinnika*. To all the talismans. Their magic feels different."

"You mean weaker?"

"No—not exactly." Tem rubbed his eyes. "I can't explain it. But it's harder sometimes to work the spells. It's as if the talismans don't want to cooperate anymore."

I set my butter tea aside—the smell, so enticing only moments ago, now made me queasy.

Could the black bell be sounding because of me? I thought back to the stories of those who had used the magic of fire demons—power-hungry shamans who lost all sense of anything beyond their own ambition, and were slowly driven insane. Would that happen to me too? I shifted closer to Tem, drawing comfort from the familiar timbre of his voice. As I did, the black bell gave another quiet shiver.

SIX

I STARTED AWAKE before dawn the next morning. I rolled over in my blankets, trying to pinpoint what had woken me.

Voices. Lusha's and Mara's. I glanced over at Tem, but he was still snoring on the other side of the tent, his sleep-tousled hair the only visible part of him.

I rose, or tried to—before I got halfway, I encountered a lump of fur and claws, weighting me to the bed. Ragtooth, it seemed, had decided to fall asleep on my hair.

The fox growled, clearly under the impression that I was going to remain where I was. Rather than try to coax him, I simply sat up, sending him rolling onto the ground.

I riffled around in the darkness, searching for my socks. I knew I had a clean pair in my pack—where had they gone?

Ragtooth hopped back onto the bed, the socks clutched in his jaws. He dropped them on my lap. They were wet with drool, and the left had a hole in the toe now.

"Thanks," I muttered. Ragtooth gave an insouciant stretch, then curled himself into a ball atop the warm pillow. I gathered up the blankets and flung them over him. A flurry of growls and snarls erupted as the fox tried to writhe his way out, only succeeding in entangling himself further. Smiling darkly at my victory, I tossed my *chuba* over my shoulders and stepped out into the chill air.

Lusha paced by the blazing fire, scattering our camp with shadows. She and Mara had clearly been awake for some time.

"Are we packing up?" I said. We had planned to set out early, but not this early—we needed daylight to see our way around the glacier's crevasses.

"Dargye didn't return last night." Mara's face, shadowed by his graying beard, was grave. He looked twice his thirty-one years. "We did a thorough tally of the food, and there's too much of it."

"Too much?" I swallowed. "That means—"

"He's been gone longer than we thought," Lusha finished. "Days."

I wrapped my arms around my chest, feeling chilled despite the warmth of the fire. "That doesn't make sense."

"We'll start the search as soon as it's light," Mara said.

I scanned the sky. The sun, still behind the horizon, painted the massing clouds a lurid orange.

"I know." Lusha nodded at my unspoken concern. "Hopefully we can find some evidence of his trail before the storm reaches us."

"We should send the dragons ahead," I said. "They might be able to sniff him out."

But Lusha was already shaking her head. "If the storm hits, and they get lost, we'll be in a bad spot. We need them."

"So does Dargye," I said, but Mara was talking over me.

"We should take weapons," he said. "Just in case."

They began running over our supply of weaponry, paying me no further heed. Again I chafed at Lusha appointing herself leader of our group, despite the fact that I was the most skilled navigator. Not to mention twice as good at tracking.

I swallowed my anger, or tried to. Dargye's safety was what mattered. Lusha's insufferable self-assurance was something I could deal with another time. Just yesterday, I had been so relieved to be reunited with Lusha. Now, a tiny, dark part of me fantasized about a world in which I had left her on the mountain.

Ten minutes later, we were walking south through the frosty dawn, trailing behind Tem as he murmured to the *kinnika*. Even in that short span of time, the wind had risen, lifting the loose snow from the ground and dragging it along as a sharp mist. Mara had his dagger unsheathed, while Lusha's bow was slung over her shoulder. I felt uneasy without a weapon of my own, though I knew full well that, if we encountered witches, neither dagger nor bow would be of much assistance.

Without comment, Tem gave a wide berth to the crevasse where Aimo had fallen. It was covered with snow, as it had been when we came this way, with only the faintest furrow to mark its presence. I didn't want to think of Aimo, trapped down in that dark place, but once the image arose I was unable to think of anything else. The water whispering deep beneath the glacier had seemed peaceful before. Now it seemed hungry.

It was awful that we were going to leave her there. Yet that was the fate of most explorers, eventually—they weren't cremated and put to rest beside their ancestors, in a temple where their family and friends could visit their spirits. They rested in dark mountain passes, or on precarious summits, with no company but the wind and snow. I thought of the bodies River and I had found on Raksha. That could have been my fate. It could still be my fate, if I became one of the emperor's explorers—not that I was thinking of that now. The future I saw before me—before all of us—was dark and clouded.

"I'm sorry," I whispered to the crevasse.

Tem stopped, waiting for us to catch up. He was frowning, his eyes fixed on the *kinnika*. "His trail is fading. I don't understand it."

"It's too old," I said, my teeth chattering.

Tem sighed. He shook the *kinnika* roughly, and the bells sang in protest. "They aren't cooperating again. I'm not sure I can trust what they're telling me."

"Let's follow this course for a while," Lusha said. "If we see no sign of him, we'll return to camp and plan our next move."

"What is there to plan?" I said. The thought of abandoning Dargye was terrible. But we had to return to the village. "We make for Azmiri as quickly as possible."

"We're not going anywhere with this storm bearing down on

us." There was a note of finality in Lusha's voice that raised my hackles.

"It may swing south," I said. "Even if it doesn't, I can keep us on the right course."

"Through a blizzard?" Lusha gave me a stern look. "I want to reach Azmiri as much as you. But we won't be any help to the village if we end up dead on the way."

My eyes narrowed. It wasn't so much what Lusha said that angered me, it was her calm certainty, the dismissiveness with which she greeted my words.

"I can navigate a storm," I said. "You've seen me do it. That time we visited the spring market with Father, and a squall overtook us on the way home. I led us to safety while you were in the wagon hiding under a blanket."

It wasn't entirely fair, given that Lusha had been ten at the time, but I felt a flicker of satisfaction at the sight of her cheeks reddening.

"We can't just go charging off into a blizzard," Mara said. "The wiser plan is to go back to camp and wait it out."

"Oh, shut up, Mara," I snapped. I knew I was being unreasonable, but I didn't care. All the anger and fear I had been holding back since I had stood on the summit of Raksha seemed to swell, overwhelming me. "We all know the real reason you're taking Lusha's side. And it has nothing to do with *wisdom*."

Mara looked as if I'd struck him. "If you're implying—"

"Kamzin." Tem's voice was strange. He lifted something out of the snow, where it had been partially submerged.

Dargye's bow.

Silence fell. Tem didn't seem able to tear his gaze from the weapon. Mara turned slowly on his heel, scanning the terrain with the gaze of a wary animal.

Lusha broke the spell, marching to Tem's side and seizing the bow. She kicked at the snow, unearthing a quiver of arrows where it lay a few feet away.

"We're going back," she said. As she strode past, she dumped the bow and arrows in my arms.

"I don't know how—"

"You're the only one without a weapon," she said without breaking stride. Mara fell into step behind her. Swallowing hard, I followed, slinging the quiver over my shoulder.

Clouds thickened around the mountains as we walked, blotting out the sky entirely—at our elevation, the trailing edges swept over the ground, veiling our surroundings in white fleece. Snow swirled, tangling in our hair.

Mara paused. He gazed around at the suddenly unreadable landscape. Even Lusha looked confused.

"Camp's this way," I said, taking the lead.

"Are you sure?" Lusha said. She sounded uncharacteristically hesitant.

"Yes." I didn't have the energy to add a retort. Tem was already heading in the direction I had indicated, and Lusha shot him an irritated look. He gave me a small smile that I returned gratefully. After a moment, there came the satisfying crunch of Lusha's and Mara's boots behind us.

One of the *kinnika* rang out—a sudden, sharp sound that raised the hair on my neck. It took me a moment to realize why. Only one bell sounded like that.

The black one.

It chimed again—it wasn't whispering now. My mind flashed back to the time I had last heard it sound like that. My eyes met Tem's, and I saw the same realization reflected there.

"No," I murmured.

"What is it?" Lusha said. Even as she spoke, she was lifting an arrow to her bow. Her gaze flicked from my face to Tem's.

Neither of us answered. I felt again the storm in Winding Pass, the wind suffocating and sharp with snow. The figures who had loomed out of the mist, surrounding us—

"How much time do we have?" I asked Tem.

As if in response, the black bell rang out again, more insistently. *Ching. Ching. Ching.* The sound was dolorous, and cut through the moan of the wind, the muffling swirl of the snow.

"I don't know." Tem's voice was uneven. In that moment, he seemed more like the old Tem—unsure, self-conscious. His hand shook as he brushed the bells.

I pulled an arrow from the quiver, but when I bent it to the bow, it felt ungainly. Father had taught me how to shoot, but the skill had never come naturally. "Can we make it back to camp?"

"Won't matter." Tem stood up straighter, and seemed to pull something into himself. He unclasped one of the bells and handed it to me. "This will be more useful than that bow."

I stared at the talisman in disbelief. "You're joking."

"You know the incantation." He unclasped another bell. "Besides, weapons won't be any use against them."

"We'll see about that," Lusha said. She tapped the obsidian point of her arrow.

"It isn't witches," I said. The black bell was sounding constantly now, and I had to raise my voice to be heard. "They don't travel in storms, Lusha; it's—"

In the distance there came a ghastly cry. It sounded like a bird, or rather, it sounded more like a bird than it did anything else. The sound seemed to float on the wind, eddying.

Lusha whirled. "I've heard that before."

"With Mother." I touched her arm. Lusha's face was paler than I'd ever seen it. Her hand shook slightly on the bow. "The storm in the pass. We were attacked. You remember?"

She nodded. She looked thirteen again, her age when we accompanied our mother's expedition in search of a new route through the Arya Mountains. "We never saw them," she murmured. "We never saw what attacked us."

"We're about to." I handed the bow and arrow to Mara. "Stay close to Tem. Whatever you do, don't step beyond his shield."

No one spoke. We formed a ragged circle, each facing a different direction. Tem sounded the stout bronze bell that usually hung in the middle of the chain. As he did, I felt a warmth spread over us and radiate out.

For a long while, there was nothing. Just the sweep, sweep of the wind, and our breath rising in clouds that were quickly funneled away.

They appeared slowly.

At first, as faint black shapes glimpsed through the snow, shapes that might not have been living at all, but the silhouettes of dead trees. A gust of wind tossed a veil of snow between us, and they were gone. When they appeared again, it was from another direction, closer than before.

The *fiangul* came like pillars of dark fog. They did not walk—the wind swept them toward us, hovering over the snow. Their wings were open but motionless, like hawks riding the thermals. All-black eyes fixed upon us, in faces that were half vulture, half human—something grotesquely wrong, but impossible to look away from.

"Spirits," Lusha murmured. "The stories are true." Mara's eyes were as round as full moons.

"Kamzin," Tem said, his head still bent over the *kinnika*.

"Sorry." I loosened my grip on his arm. "Do you see them?"

"I don't need to. I can feel them." He raised his head and shouted a single word in the shamanic language, sounding the bell rapidly before silencing it against his hand.

A warm breeze played through my hair. I felt, rather than saw, Tem's shield spread out to surround Lusha and Mara where they stood a few steps away. It shimmered, a gentle flickering that had, the last time we fought the *fiangul*, reminded me of fireflies, but now made me think of a wall of glass—not fragile, but heavy and thick. The *fiangul*, only yards from us now, began to shriek. My hands flew to my ears in a vain attempt to block out the sound, which was at once hateful and wretched, a desolation so complete it made my bones shudder. Lusha, with an incoherent shout, loosed an arrow at the closest creature. It passed through Tem's shield, but missed its mark—the *fiangul* darted aside with a motion as light as a sparrow's.

"Don't." Tem's voice was quiet but commanding. "It weakens the barrier."

Lusha shifted position, helplessly craning her head to watch the *fiangul* circle Tem's shield. They didn't attempt to throw themselves at it—they merely prowled its perimeter, black eyes searching for a way in. When their wing tips brushed against the shield, they chittered sharply and fell back as if it pained them.

"They're stronger," Tem murmured. "I can feel it."

"Stronger? How is that possible?"

"I don't know—could be the binding spell. Maybe they had some connection to it, through the witches. They're said to be allies."

I closed my eyes briefly. "Can you hold them off alone?"

He met my eyes. The barest hint of a smile tugged at his mouth. "I think so—the spell's easier than last time. I don't understand it."

I fell silent. Whether it was easier or not, the strain on Tem's face as he muttered the incantation was obvious. I exchanged a look with Lusha. She seized my hand.

Time passed. It was difficult to gauge how much. We huddled close together, aching with cold as the snow billowed and the *fiangul* circled like the contorted specters of a fever dream. I began to feel trapped in a cage. How long would the storm last? Minutes?

Hours? Tem's face grew paler, though his voice never faltered as he chanted the spell. Somehow, impossibly, the spell held. Hope began to blossom inside me. The winds were dropping, and the snow no longer blew sideways.

"Mara!" Lusha shouted. "What are you doing?"

I whirled. Mara was outside Tem's shield, moving with a strange, unsteady gait toward the nearest *fiangul*.

"Mara, get back here!" I cried. What was wrong with him?

"I can't." Mara's voice was faint. "They— I can hear—"

Ignoring Lusha's shout, I surged forward. Tem's spell, as I crossed it, brushed against my skin like insect wings—a soft, harmless thing that somehow held back the *fiangul* with the strength of iron.

Mara was on his back now, sliding across the snow. I couldn't make sense of it—then there came a gust of wind, and the snow parted, revealing the grotesquely thin, hunched figure that dragged him roughly by the hem of his *chuba*.

"Mara, fight!" The chronicler was barely struggling, though his *chuba*, as the creature dragged him along, was so taut against his neck that he seemed to be choking. It didn't make sense.

In that moment, I was overwhelmed by a cacophony—not the *fiangul*'s birdlike cries, but voices. Rasping, contorted whispers that filled my ears and crowded out all thought.

We will guide you safe, they said, a hundred voices repeating the same words, like the drone of bees. *Safe. Guide you. You are safe.*

I stopped, wondering suddenly why I was worrying about Mara. The *fiangul* hovered calmly, their black eyes fixed on me.

Did they truly mean to harm us? Or were they here to guide us through the storm?

Safe now. Come, we guide you.

"Kamzin, don't listen to them!" Tem shouted. Somehow, he was maintaining the spell, even as he gripped Lusha by the arm. A dozen yards separated us—enough that the swirling snow blurred his outline. If I had gone any farther, I wouldn't have been able to see him at all.

His voice cut through the din of the *fiangul's* murmurs, returning me to my senses. I reeled, and saw Mara react in the same moment—he gave a hoarse shout and struggled against the creature's grip. The whispers surged again, but Mara's steady stream of bellowed threats drowned them out. I dashed toward him. As I neared, I saw something spill from the folds of the creature's torn *chuba.*

Talismans. Worn around the *fiangul's* neck, they winked in the faint light—some made of gold, others encrusted with gems. A sickening realization overwhelmed me.

"Norbu!" I screamed. "Norbu, stop, please—"

At the sound of my voice, the creature faltered. It turned briefly to gaze at me. It *was* Norbu, the abstracted Three Cities shaman who had traveled with River during his time as Royal Explorer, and been part of our expedition to Raksha. After attacking us at base camp, he had vanished with the other *fiangul.*

Mara slammed his arm into Norbu's, breaking his hold. I reached his side and helped him to his feet as he gasped and coughed, and together we staggered back to the protection of

Tem's shield. He expanded it to embrace us as two *fiangul* swooped down.

"I could tell they were stronger." Tem's voice was grave. "But this is new."

The whispers rose again. It was as if they were pounding against my skull, seeking a way in. Tem grabbed me, shouting my name. Somehow, I had lurched forward again, almost to the edge of his shield.

"Can't you hear them?" I stared at him, dazed, as the whispers wormed through my thoughts. *Guide you. Safe, safe.*

"I can hear," Tem said. "But it doesn't affect me. Perhaps the *kinnika*—"

Mara shouted. It was Lusha who was in danger now—she had staggered just beyond the shield. Mara hauled her back as one of the *fiangul* reached its taloned hand toward her billowing hair.

"Lusha!" I yelled. All my former anger was forgotten in an instant—I wrapped my arms around her, pinning her in place with all my strength. She continued to struggle, but I only tightened my grip, grateful for my stockier frame. I wasn't going to let her go anywhere.

"Azar-at," I whispered. "Where are you?"

I am here.

I looked around. I thought I caught a flash of ember-colored eyes, somewhere just beyond Tem's shield.

"I need your help," I said into the storm.

Yes, Kamzin. If I hadn't known better, I would have thought its tone was almost dry.

I swallowed. "Wait until I give the word."

"It's weakening," Tem said. Despite the cold, sweat stood out on his brow. "The spell—I can't hold it."

"Drop the barrier, then," Mara said. His hair was tangled with snow, and a bruise darkened the side of his face. He strung an arrow to Dargye's bow and took aim at one of the *fiangul*. "Let's fight—I'm sick of this cowering."

"We'd lose," I snapped. "They'll order us to lay down our weapons, and we'll do it. Tem—what about that snow spell of River's? It worked on them last time."

He shook his head. "I don't—I don't think I have the power to cast something like that."

But I do. I bit my lip and tasted blood. Tem needed me. His spell wouldn't hold much longer. I remembered the torment I had experienced after healing Ragtooth—yet it wasn't that which gave me pause. How much would it cost me to drive the *fiangul* away? Terror twisted my stomach into a knot. Yet the wind was still dropping—the storm was beginning to lift. Could Tem hold on?

Suddenly, one of the *fiangul* dove toward Tem's shield with a ghastly cry, wings folded. It struck the barrier and hovered there, writhing, while Tem shouted a new incantation. The air shuddered—and then the creature fell through the shield, sending up a spray of snow as it landed. Lusha buried an arrow in its chest before it could rise again. Crimson blood spilled onto the snow—a jarringly human color.

Tem sounded the *kinnika* furiously. But the *fiangul* now seemed barely hindered by the spell—one flew toward us, its wings beating rapidly as if approaching through a fierce headwind. Another lunged at Lusha. Tem grasped a different bell, and a blast of wind knocked the *fiangul* on its back. Mara slashed his dagger across the creature's throat, and the snow bloomed redder still.

It had taken only seconds. Tem's shield had fallen.

Lusha grabbed my arm and shoved me between her and Mara. "Back-to-back!" she shouted.

That's not back-to-back. My mind seemed to be working in slow motion. The *fiangul* glided toward us like a dark tide. Norbu was among them, but there was no hesitation in him now—his eyes, black and staring, could have been fixed on any one of us, or none.

"All right," I whispered. "I'm ready."

You must picture the spell in your thoughts. Azar-at's voice was as calm as always, even as Lusha loosed another arrow, and another. *Give form to the magic.*

Give form to the magic. My mind went blank. Chirri had never taught me any defensive spells—which, in her caustic opinion, were too dangerous for someone of my abilities, more likely to kill me than my target.

You must decide, Kamzin.

Lusha screamed. One of the creatures had seized hold of her hair as it was tossed by the wind. Mara slashed at the *fiangul* with his blade, and the creature retreated, black strands tangled in its fingers.

Tem rang another bell once, sharply, shouting a different

incantation. It seemed to knock the *fiangul* back like a physical blow.

An idea struck me.

"Tem," I said, "try River's spell. The one he used on the *fiangul* in the pass."

He blinked, struggling to focus on me. "I told you, I—"

"Just try," I urged. "You can re-create it, can't you?"

"Kamzin—"

"Please, Tem." I gripped his shoulder, squeezing until he flinched. "Trust me."

He swayed, seeming on the edge of unconsciousness. Lusha's bow twanged. A glimmer of recklessness dawned, in his eyes. I could see what he was thinking—what did it matter? If we were about to die, why not die fighting with every ounce of strength we had?

"All right," he said.

He ran his hand over the *kinnika* almost absently, his fingers hovering over two bells—one small and bright and intricately carved, the other larger, tarnished, and bent. He began to sound them in unison. He spoke the incantation quietly, which gave me a little start. Some spells were cast this way; that wasn't what surprised me. It was that Tem, who had never cast such a spell before, would sense its characteristics instinctively.

"Azar-at," I whispered, "get ready."

The winds shifted. I realized that Tem had chosen not the spell River had cast in the pass, but the second, more frightening spell. A funnel cloud formed above us, snatching at the *fiangul's* feathers and spiraling the snow.

The *fiangul* screamed. But just as it seemed the cloud was gathering momentum, it faltered and dissolved. Tem's forehead beaded with sweat.

"*Now*, Azar-at." I stepped forward and pressed my hands into Tem's chest. I pictured Azar-at's magic flowing through my arms and into Tem—into the spell he was casting.

Tem made a quiet sound of surprise. For a moment, I thought it wasn't working—I couldn't feel anything. Then my hands began to tingle, a sensation that radiated up my arms and into my chest.

The wind rose again. The funnel roared to life, reaching down to the ground, where it caught at the snow and flung it into the air. Lusha ducked as an enormous sliver of compacted ice soared past. The *fiangul* were screaming again. The creatures nearest to the funnel tried to flee, spreading their wings and darting with uncanny speed toward the mountains.

But another funnel was there, spilling to the earth like water. It wrapped the *fiangul* in its cloud of displaced snow, and drew them in. The first funnel whipped around us, barely stirring my hair, devouring the remaining creatures. It spun once around the second funnel, and then they collided with such force that the ground shook. The *fiangul* had gone silent. Slowly, the enormous cloud lifted off the ground, and then it was sinking back into the sky. The clouds, once dark and menacing, began to thin and break apart.

It was over. But I had no time to feel relief. The agony

overwhelmed me, and I fell forward with a cry. Tem caught me in time, gathering me in his arms.

And then the pain was gone. It had been briefer than last time, but just as intense. I felt off balance, unsteady, as if I had drunk a barrel of *raksi*.

"What did you do?" Tem was pale with shock. "I felt . . ." He didn't seem able to put in words what he had felt.

"I'm fine." Was I? For a moment, I felt a *difference*, something that didn't quite fit anymore, like a shutter swinging on a loose hinge. But then it faded.

I sighed. "Azar-at, you don't need to hide now."

The fire demon stepped out from behind a snow drift that should have been too small to conceal it, and came to my side. It sniffed at Tem's *chuba*, then licked my hand before I could draw it away. *You are safe. Friends are safe. This is good.*

Lusha stood up. Blood flowed from her scalp where the *fiangul* had torn at her hair. Her eyes narrowed.

"Lusha," I began, "I can—"

She struck me across the face.

SEVEN

ONLY A FAINT mist lingered as the sun sank behind the mountains. The clouds formed circles over the Aryas, whirlpools shaped by the fierce winds that scoured the peaks. Here, though, the world was calm.

Too calm.

We had set up camp under the overhang of an enormous boulder twenty miles south of base camp. Twenty miles closer to Azmiri. It wasn't enough—we would have to move faster tomorrow. It had been a long, difficult hike over the ice before finally, at midafternoon, we had left Raksha's glacier behind. As we set foot upon solid ground, I felt a sense of release, as if Raksha's power had swung shut behind us like a gate. The great mountain was no longer fully visible, its massive bulk hidden behind its crenellated neighbors.

A streamlet trickled down the mountainside and past our camp, trapped beneath a layer of ice. Lusha was perched, as usual, in front of her telescope, maps and star charts spread about her and weighted with rocks. She hadn't spoken to me all day. Mara sat next to her, pretending to ignore me. He kept darting glances in my direction, then acting as if he were only scanning the landscape for the hundredth time.

"Ragtooth?" I stepped outside the firelight. "Dinner."

I peered into the shadows, hoping for the familiar spark of green eyes. But nothing stirred.

"Ragtooth," I called a little louder, in case he had fallen asleep somewhere.

Nothing.

Frowning, I returned to Tem's side. He handed me a steaming bowl of rabbit stew. Mara's afternoon hunt had been successful, though the game this far north was scrawny, more fur and bone than meat. I gave Mara a nod of thanks. He looked at me as if I had drawn a weapon on him.

"I don't know why he's so jumpy," I muttered to Tem. "He spent three years with River, and he never attacked him."

"Just ignore him," Tem said.

Distracted, I spooned the stew into my mouth so quickly I burned my tongue.

"Are you all right?" I said. Tem's eyes were red.

He didn't answer right away. "Do you think I killed him?"

For a moment, I didn't know what to say. "Tem . . . Norbu was already—"

"I know." He swiped at his eyes. "I know. But before, there was a chance. If I killed him—"

I bit my lip. Tem had spent more time with Norbu than any of us—the shaman had taken him under his wing during the weeks-long journey to Raksha. And though Norbu had ordered Tem about like a servant, the man had also seemed to trust him, in a thoughtless sort of way. I felt a pang as I realized that the consideration Tem had been shown by the stuffy, pompous shaman was more than he received from most of the villagers in Azmiri, including his father.

Tem stirred his dinner for so long I wondered if he'd forgotten about it. I examined him, taking in the tightness of his mouth, the slight furrow between his eyes. "It's not just Norbu, is it? You're angry."

"I'm not angry." He returned my gaze, but there was a shroud over his expression, and I couldn't read him. When had I not been able to read Tem?

My eye, already showing the imprint of Lusha's fist, gave a throb. It had been a while since she had hit me, and neither her aim nor her forcefulness had diminished. "You don't trust me now."

"Did I say that?"

"You don't have to." I set my bowl aside—my appetite had vanished.

"You saved us," he said. "I don't like the decision you made. But I understand why you did it."

He sounded, to my ears, as if he was mouthing words he had

rehearsed in his head. I wanted to shake him until the mask fell away and he showed me what he really felt.

"This is my fault," he murmured.

I stared. "Your fault?"

"I should have tried a different spell." His gaze drifted back to the fire. "I should have reserved my strength for when it really mattered. Then you wouldn't have had to . . ." He didn't finish.

"Tem," I said quietly, "Azar-at is the only one able to fight the *fiangul*. You know that."

"I could have done better." He coughed and set his own stew aside. "From now on, I'll do better. You won't have to use Azar-at's power anymore."

"How can you make a promise like that?" I said disbelievingly. "The reason I did this was because I knew that none of us has the power to keep Azmiri safe. That's what we have to focus on: protecting Azmiri."

"We don't know the limits of Azar-at's power," Tem said, "and we shouldn't trust anything a fire demon says. Kamzin, when you cast that spell, when you"—he stumbled over the words— "touched me and gave me Azar-at's magic, I felt what it was. It's nothing like shamanic magic. It's a magic like fire, that burns as it's expended. It's dangerous—and *wrong*. Magic shouldn't change you; it shouldn't make you *want* to use it. No wonder every shaman who joins with a fire demon ends up dead. That sort of power is addictive."

"River used Azar-at's power for years," I argued. "He ended their contract when he chose."

"River isn't human. It may have been different for him—we can't know for sure."

"So what will we do if the *fiangul* attack again?"

"I'll stop them." Tem sounded so completely certain that I almost believed him. Almost. But the strain on his face, the grayish tinge of his skin, belied his words. The magic he had used today had cost him dearly. His cough, which had been lessening steadily, had worsened. He was in no position to protect anyone.

He pressed my hand between his own. "Promise me you won't use Azar-at's power again."

Tem's mouth was a hard line. He *was* angry, I realized, but not with me—with himself. As ridiculous as it was, he blamed himself for what had happened. And so he had decided that it was his responsibility to fix it, even if it killed him.

I felt my own anger rise. I looked at Tem, his face pale with concern, and wanted to run away. I knew he was right about Azar-at, and the decision I had made—that wasn't the point. I was angry because it had been *my* decision. And now he was taking that away from me and making it his.

I pulled my hand free. "I won't promise anything. If I need to use Azar-at to protect myself, or anyone I care about, I will."

Tem's expression clouded. "How can you say that? You haven't read the stories of what happens to shamans who abuse a fire demon's magic."

I laughed humorlessly. I knew exactly what the magic did to shamans. I had felt it—twice. Suddenly, my anger went out like a snuffed flame. Lusha wasn't speaking to me. Mara looked at me like I was liable to curse his head off at any moment. And now Tem—his gaze was hard. The anger that had been turned inward was now directed at me. Something in that made me feel oddly satisfied.

Because he should be angry with me. Hadn't I been the cause of all this? Our lives were in danger because of me and the decisions I'd made. Didn't he realize that I deserved the fate I had chosen?

I turned away. I liked this cold, empty feeling. I didn't need to be hurt by what Tem thought, or anything else for that matter. "I made my decision. It was necessary—I had no other choice."

Tem gave me a strange look. "You sound like River."

I blinked. "What?"

"That's how he used to talk," Tem said. "Necessary. No other choice."

"Fine," I said, my voice cold. "Then I sound like River."

Tem was staring at me. "It's already changing you. Since when do you give up so easily on an argument?"

I faltered. I thought about what River had said about Azar-at making it more difficult to feel. Was this strange coldness what he had meant?

Tem stood. His expression was closed again. "All right. We'll talk about this later."

"Now *you* sound like Lusha," I muttered. I turned away, pretending to occupy myself with the fire, which was blazing healthily. Tem let out his breath, and he seemed about to speak again. But then his footsteps moved away.

I forced myself to eat, keeping my gaze on the fire. Lusha drifted off to her tent, followed by Mara. I wondered idly who that arrangement was more uncomfortable for. It would have made more sense for Lusha and me to share a tent—but then, to suggest that, I'd have to talk to her. My eye gave another throb.

In order to reach Azmiri in a fortnight, we would have to cover twice as much ground as we had today, which meant finding every possible shortcut and avoiding bad terrain whenever possible. As the most skilled navigator, I would be the one choosing our path, and scouting for water and safe campsites. A shiver of loneliness traced its way down my back.

With a start, I realized that I missed River. Not the person he had turned out to be, but the person I had thought he was. The River who used to sit with me as our campfire died down, helping me plan our next adventure. The River who would challenge me to a game of Shadow, and then laugh with pure delight when I beat him. The River who had been my friend. Not just because I had thought I loved him—even before that. I had always felt like an outsider in Azmiri. Traveling with River had been the first time I'd felt like I belonged somewhere. I wondered if I would ever feel that way again.

I drew my *chuba* up to my chin and inched closer to the fire. Its warmth did little to dislodge the chill inside me. An idea occurred. Hesitantly, I held out my hand to the flames.

Give form to the magic, Azar-at had said.

I pictured the fire growing larger, hotter. Almost as soon as I had the thought, the flames leaped into the air, their warmth expanding.

I felt a whisper of pain, gone in a flash—I barely had time to wince.

I loosened my *chuba*. I was much warmer now, and pleased that I hadn't needed to use more of our firewood. Tem would be upset, but I was still angry enough to find satisfaction in that. Compared to what I had done to the *fiangul*, surely a minor spell like that was nothing.

A small shape crept out of the shadows and sniffed at my bowl. Finding it empty, the creature let out a growl.

"Ragtooth!" Relieved, I scooped the fox up, holding him beneath his front legs so that his plump tail hung to the ground and his green eyes were level with mine. "Where have you been?"

Ragtooth consented to be held for only a few seconds before starting to squirm. I stood, tucking him under my arm. "No more skulking around for you. It's time for bed."

To my surprise, the fox allowed me to carry him. He seemed tired, and his fur smelled smoky, as if he'd been sleeping next to the campfire.

I paused next to our jumble of supplies, hoping to find some *ruhanna* bark to lessen the throbbing in my eye. I remembered using most of the healing herb on Raksha to treat Tem's injuries, and so was surprised to see an entire satchel of it, full to the brim.

"That's odd," I murmured. Shrugging, I popped a piece of the soft bark into my mouth, then ducked inside the tent.

Tem lay in his makeshift bed. He had succeeded in removing only one of his boots before falling asleep, and his blankets were half-trapped underneath him. I removed the other boot and drew the blankets up to his chest. Then, unthinkingly, I smoothed his hair back.

The planes of Tem's face were sharper now from days with little food. He was even handsomer in sleep than he was awake, when he often used his hair as a shield. He looked like one of the ancient heroes painted on silk scrolls, all broad shoulders, knife-sharp cheekbones, and wind-tousled hair.

I drew back. I wasn't blind—it was natural that I might occasionally think of Tem that way. But there was nothing underneath it. Even if there had been, I didn't think it could exist again. That part of me that had felt something for River, something deep-dwelling but full of light, had been irreparably damaged. Broken. I felt it even now, as I drew my blankets up to my chin: a weighted darkness that pulled at my thoughts when I didn't think of River, and ached like a burn when I did.

Ragtooth nestled against me, making a small noise in his throat. I buried my face in his smoke-scented fur and waited for sleep to take me.

My dreams were strange.

I stood in a dark forest of smoke and rustling branches. Someone was speaking to me, but I was distracted. I wanted to escape—

The scene shifted. Now I was flying, soaring over the forest, which thinned to snowy planes punctured by black trees. I was searching for something. I had searched for it before and been unsuccessful. The sky was a tumult of stars, and I was among them, the wind lifting me higher and higher until I was certain their light would burn me—

I woke with a start.

Snow tapped against the tent like fingertips, a soft, soothing sound. I lay there listening, warm in my blankets. I guessed by the light that it was near dawn. Oddly, the dream didn't fade as dreams usually did, but hovered in my mind, bright as a new memory.

Someone was rustling around outside, clinking pots and tossing items onto the ground. The yak grunted, and a dragon chittered. I pushed myself up on my hands. I needed to get up, and to wake Tem, who was still snoring in his blankets, so that we could get moving. But I was disoriented. I could still feel the wind buffeting as I soared over those dark trees—

I alighted on a branch. Esha and the others were far behind. None of them had mastered their shape-changing abilities yet, a fact I enjoyed, at least where my brother was concerned. I ruffled my feathers against the wind, my owl eyes scanning the terrain. Then I swooped to the ground and reassumed my human form.

Thorn was the first to catch up. His secondskin was a langur, which could travel almost as quickly as a bird through the trees.

He landed next to me, transforming from langur to man with only the slightest hesitation. Thorn had almost mastered his secondskin, though he hadn't succeeded in taking on other shapes yet.

"Anything?" he said.

"I can barely make out the Ashes from this distance," I pointed out. "Let alone a fallen star."

"It's a star," Thorn said. "They're visible at greater distances than this."

"Didn't I tell you how my last star-hunting expedition went? We were eaten alive by insects and half-drowned by rain. And all for nothing." That frustrating expedition was still vivid in my memory. Mara had been insufferable—the damp kept getting into his scrolls, and every day brought new complaints about the impossibility of working in such conditions. I had eventually tossed his scrolls into a stream, just to quiet him. The chronicler had assumed they'd been swept away by the rains.

"You'll find it," Thorn said. "You are, after all, the greatest explorer in the Empire."

I looked at him but saw nothing mocking in his expression. He returned my gaze calmly.

"You're better at changing shape than anyone else," he said. "I'd like to try an owl. You go first, and I'll watch."

I shrugged, stepping back. But suddenly, the leaves rustled behind us.

Esha stepped into the clearing. His secondskin was an enormous boar, his hair as ragged as in his human shape. His tusks were long and sharp, his frame heavy—every inch of him conveyed menace. He melted into his human form with none of Thorn's grace—it was a jerky, uneven transformation, so that he briefly seemed both human and boar, an abomination that reminded me of the fiangul.

His eyes fixed on me, and for a moment I could still see the animal gazing out from behind them. The shadows stirred as the others *emerged from the forest, some in animal form, some human, others melting into the darkness itself—*

I fell back against my blankets. For a moment, I had no idea where I was, or who. All I could think of was that monstrous boar, the boar that wasn't a boar, but a *witch*.

I found my voice and screamed.

EIGHT

SOMEONE WAS SHAKING me, repeating my name. I pushed them off, terrified that it was the witches holding me down—there had been at least a dozen of them in that forest. The hands tightened again, and I struck out with feet and fists.

"Hit her," a voice said.

"Don't you think there's been enough of that?" replied the person holding me. The first made an irritated sound, and there was a pause. Then a blast of icy water slapped me across the face.

It was so unexpected, and so painfully cold, that I screamed again.

"Helpful, Lusha," the nearest voice said.

My eyes flew open. Tem's face, drawn with worry, gazed down at me. Lusha was behind him, crouched at the foot of my bed.

She looked more wary than concerned. In her hand was a bowl, empty now.

"What happened?" I demanded, gazing around desperately. I was back in the tent, but how? Was I safe? Was I *me*?

"You had a nightmare," Lusha said. "You attacked Tem when he tried to wake you, so I did it myself."

I stared at her. "How?"

"Would you like another demonstration? I can get more water."

"No, how did I get back here?" I stood quickly, and just as quickly fell over as my vision swam. "I was in the Nightwood."

"Kamzin—" Tem began, but I was already pulling on my boots. I staggered out of the tent.

Dawn drenched the scattered clouds in oranges and pinks. Fat snowflakes drifted down, catching the light like flakes of gold.

My relief was overwhelming. I was where I was supposed to be. And yet I knew with an awful certainty that I had just been somewhere else.

I gazed down at my hands. They were mine, familiar and stubby-fingered, but for a few moments, they had been someone else's. I knew those hands well—the fingers long and aristocratic, except for two on the left hand—

Mara sat beside the fire, oiling one of the dragons, who crooned and preened in his lap. He glanced at me, his face illuminated by the flickering green light.

"Bad dream?" he said, in the sort of tone you would use with a tiresome child.

"River," I murmured. "That was River."

Mara's expression changed. "River was here?"

I didn't reply. I was still gazing at my hands, though I no longer saw them. How was this possible? Had River cast a spell on me? I thought back to the last time I had seen him, cloaked in magic on the summit of Raksha. Why would he do that?

"She said she saw River," Mara said to Lusha, who had followed me out of the tent.

"Not here. He was in the Nightwood," I said. "At least, I think so. He's looking for something, something his brother thinks can destroy the Empire." I thought back. Unlike a dream, the memories remained perfectly intact. "A fallen star."

Lusha's furrowed brow was almost a mirror image of Tem's. "What in the name of the spirits—"

"I wasn't dreaming," I said, silencing her with a frustrated gesture. "I saw his thoughts. It's like I was watching from—from behind his eyes. I can't explain it, but it was *real*. I know what they want. The witches." My mind raced frantically. My heart felt ready to burst through my chest. I felt terror, certainly—but with it came a dark excitement. Because I knew now what River wanted.

And that meant I could take it from him.

I saw River saving my life. I saw him laughing by the fire. I saw him abandoning me on the summit of Raksha. I could take the star and prevent him from hurting anyone. From hurting Azmiri. For a moment, I wasn't certain what I wanted more: to take the star from River, or prevent the witches from using it. They were the same, and yet they weren't.

"We have to head north," I said. "We have to find the star before the witches do."

They all stared at me. A long moment passed, during which the only sounds were the hiss and pop of the campfire.

Mara spoke first. "She's lost her mind. That creature—it's done something to her."

"This has nothing to do with Azar-at," I snapped.

The fire demon, perhaps responding to the sound of its name, appeared at the edge of my vision. It could have stepped out from behind the tent, or simply summoned its wolfish shape from the air. It settled on its haunches, tongue lolling, ember eyes taking us in.

"Go through it again," Lusha said, "slowly. In your dream, you saw River's thoughts?"

"It wasn't a dream." I had to restrain myself from shouting. "He's looking for a fallen star in the Ash Mountains. I don't know what it does, only that it's powerful. I guess it can be used as some sort of weapon? His brother wants it—I think his brother is their emperor." For as long as I had been alive, the witches' ruler had been named in fireside tales as the *shadow empress*, a creature made of bones and darkness. But now, if my vision had been true, River's brother had taken his mother's place.

Lusha started. "The Ashes?"

"Yes." I gazed at her. "What is it?"

For a moment, she didn't reply. "There *was* a star that fell in the Ashes, during the shower. I tracked its trajectory—fallen stars are rare."

"You see?" I turned to the others. Mara's expression was skeptical, while Tem looked queasy, or perhaps he was still recovering from the kick I faintly recalled landing in his stomach. He hadn't said a word during the entire argument. "I'm not delusional."

"I'm not convinced of that," Lusha said. "Do you really expect us to go chasing after a fallen star because you had an unusual dream?"

Mara made an irritated sound. "Do we even need to debate this? It's nonsense."

"Did River know?" Tem said quietly. "Did he sense you?"

Mara stared. "Don't tell me you believe her."

Tem ignored him. He kept his gaze on mine.

I thought back. "No. I don't think so. I didn't realize it myself until I woke up. It was like I was seeing everything from his eyes. Like I was *gone*." A shiver traveled down my back, and I had that odd sensation again, of being not quite moored to my own body. Being inside River's mind had been unsettling, to put it mildly. Not least because of the power I had felt at my command, like an untapped reservoir of unfathomable depths. I felt almost drunk from the memory alone. How did River focus on anything else, with that much magic at his disposal? Was he even fully conscious of it?

Tem's gaze turned inward. I recognized that look—he had worn it often enough in the elder's library in Azmiri, poring over shamanic scrolls. Lusha glanced from me to Tem. She still didn't believe me, I could tell, but Tem's reaction had given her pause. Through my anger, I felt a flicker of surprise. Back in Azmiri,

Lusha had barely spared Tem a glance. She had that in common with most of the villagers, who saw Tem as the shy sidekick of the elder's daughter, if they noticed him at all. But the last few days had altered something in her perception of him—and Mara's. The chronicler seemed to be waiting for Tem to speak.

"What?" Lusha prompted impatiently.

"I think Kamzin's mistaken," he said. My stomach dropped. "I think this has everything to do with Azar-at."

I blinked. It was the last thing I had expected him to say. "What do you mean?"

"Well, Azar-at connects the two of you. River may have ended their contract, but Azar-at still has part of his soul—maybe the better part of it, for all we know. And now—"

"Now he has part of mine." The world seemed to shift. I had thought I'd known what I was getting myself into when I agreed to Azar-at's offer. But now it seemed there were entire worlds of consequences that I couldn't have imagined.

The fire demon was silent throughout our exchange, its tail stroking the snow. The flickering orange glow of its wide eyes seemed to take us all in at once.

"What are you saying?" Lusha's face was pale. "Have you heard of this sort of thing happening before?"

"No. It's rare for shamans to bind themselves to a fire demon," he said. "And for two people to bind themselves to the same one—I doubt it's ever happened. But what Kamzin is describing is plausible, given the laws of shamanic magic, at least. When you give away a piece of your soul, it doesn't die—a soul *can't* die, even if it's divided. It lives on in whatever vessel you choose to hold it. I suppose it's possible for two souls, cut off like that, to jumble together, at least slightly."

Mara was now looking at me as if I had contracted something horribly contagious. "Does that mean—could it work the other way? Could River be here now?"

I felt faint. I looked at Azar-at. "Is he here?"

River is gone, the fire demon said. *He left.*

"What does that mean?" I demanded. "*Was* he here?"

The creature shifted position, wavering in the breeze. *River is gone.* There was an odd note in its usually flat tone.

"How long did your vision last?" Tem said.

"A few moments." My throat felt very dry.

"And can you see his thoughts now?"

"No."

Tem nodded. "It's probably the same for him. Or perhaps he can't see into Kamzin's mind at all, given that he's no longer tied to Azar-at. Perhaps it only works one way."

I felt faint. "I'd prefer that it didn't work *any* way."

"But if this is true, it could be useful." Lusha seemed to be thinking out loud. "It could give us a window into what the witches are planning."

I glared at her. I wasn't sure I appreciated being referred to as a useful window.

"Well, you're all right, aren't you?" Lusha said defensively. "Now that you've calmed down."

"I'd like to see how calm you would be, in my shoes."

"I will never be in your shoes, Kamzin." Lusha's voice was ice. "Because I would never be foolish enough to trust the word of a fire demon."

"I'm still not convinced," Mara said. "Dreams can be vivid— isn't that the most likely explanation? Besides, I can't imagine River would allow Kamzin to use Azar-at's power, if this sort of thing was possible. I doubt he would be happy sharing his thoughts and plans."

"River doesn't know about my contract with Azar-at. He was long gone." I was frustrated. "If I'm imagining this whole thing, if it was just a dream, how is it I know that River led an expedition to look for a fallen star before, and that you were with him?"

Mara's expression grew scornful. "He could have told you that himself."

"So now I'm delusional *and* a liar?" I narrowed my eyes. "Apparently it rained the whole time, but that wasn't as bad as your complaining. And your scrolls weren't carried off by the floods, you know. River threw them away when you weren't looking."

Mara opened and then closed his mouth. Any response he might have given, though, was forestalled by the sound of wing-beats.

"Biter!" Lusha called. The raven circled our campsite, then landed with a thud on Lusha's shoulder. She winced, while the bird crouched low, clearly relieved to rest his wings. His feathers were in disarray, and he managed only a low *crrk* when Lusha stroked his beak.

"You made it," she said, her voice gentle. Biter held out his foot, and she removed the scrap of parchment tied there. The bird burrowed into her hood.

"That's not your note, is it?" I said.

"No. He reached Azmiri."

"What does it say?" I crowded around her before she could respond. The note, once unrolled, was short. The sight of Father's handwriting brought tears to my eyes. The paper smelled like home, of Aunt Behe's cooking and Father's incense. He would have written it at the table in his bedroom, his shoulders hunching to bring his eyes as close to the paper as possible—Father's sight was terrible. I swallowed against the tightness in my throat.

The message was simple enough—there had been no sightings of witches in Azmiri, and as far as anyone could tell, the Nightwood was quiet. There had been an attack on one of the villages in the Southern Aryas—the signs suggested a barbarian force. The emperor had sent his Ninth Army to investigate, which would certainly get things under control. Father would have guards stationed around the village, and any animals or birds who strayed within its boundaries would be shot on sight with obsidian arrows. Chirri would cast all the warding spells she knew, and he would send a messenger to the emperor to request an army to protect Azmiri. In short, he wrote, we were not to worry about the village, but were to return home as quickly as possible, where he would expect a full account.

"I didn't give him many details," Lusha said. "About River, or what happened on Raksha. He would have blamed himself."

She folded the note gently, careful not to tear it. River's

deception, and my own role in breaking the binding spell, loomed large in my thoughts. "We'll have to explain it all eventually."

"Eventually. After we get home and he sees that we're safe."

"Can I look at that?" Tem said. Lusha handed him the letter. He unfolded it, muttering something about the Ninth Army.

"Can't we reply?" I said.

Lusha touched Biter's beak. The raven barely stirred. "He wouldn't make it. It will be days before he can fly again."

My chest ached. I wanted nothing more than to follow through on our plan—to make for Azmiri as if the *fiangul* were chasing us. But—

"Lusha, we have to find the star," I said. "I think the witches need it—why else would they hold off on attacking the Three Cities? They despise the emperor more than anything. If they could destroy him now, they wouldn't hesitate."

Lusha didn't meet my eyes. Her gaze was fixed on the ground, but it seemed distant.

"If you truly saw a glimpse of River's expedition to the southern rainforest, you should know how ridiculous your idea is," Mara said. "Fallen stars are impossible to retrieve, because they don't *stay* fallen—they return to the sky within days."

"If you say so," I said. "I don't know anything about them, besides what River was thinking in that moment. I don't even know what they do."

"The ancient shamans used them," Tem said, glancing up from the letter. "To what purpose, I don't know. It's not something Chirri ever asked you to study—probably because they're so rare."

We all looked expectantly at Lusha. Of all of us, she would know the most about fallen stars, having been apprenticed to Yonden, the village seer, for more than five years.

Yonden. I realized that Father likely wasn't the only person on Lusha's mind as she turned to gaze in the direction of Azmiri. I bit my lip and refrained from pressing her.

Finally, Lusha said, "Fallen stars convey power over death. The power to kill—and the power to raise the dead."

"That's impossible." Even I knew that life and death were beyond magic. Shamans could wound, certainly, and they could speed healing, but they couldn't stop someone's heart or bring back the dead. There were resurrection spells that could, if wielded by a skilled shaman, rescue a life that hovered near death—Chirri used them on clutches of dragon eggs that had been abandoned by their mothers. But even those were useless past a certain point. Some things, Chirri had always said, were bigger than magic.

"No," Lusha said, "it isn't. Shamans have raised the dead before—Yonden has traced their stories. Such magics are dangerous and unstable. They were banned long ago, and in the early days of the Empire, it was against the law even to mention them. A fallen star can raise the dead, but they're not—they're not *right*. They're different than they were in life."

The hair on my neck stood up. "How?"

Lusha looked at me. "The few accounts I've read refer to the process as 'unspeakable.' The dead are enslaved by the shaman who raised them, twisted and corrupted. Shamans used them to evil ends, but it's just as evil to inflict that sort of suffering on the dead."

We were silent. The wind rustled over the snow—it sounded like distant footsteps. "What would the witches want with a resurrection spell?" Tem said finally.

Mara looked grim. "That's not a difficult question. Their numbers are greatly diminished since the days before their powers were bound. The Empire has killed thousands of them."

"Surely they couldn't bring them all back."

Lusha was shaking her head. "A fallen star isn't like a talisman. Their power is difficult to exhaust. They could raise an army. They could destroy the Empire," she finished, her voice tight, "with one strike."

I felt frozen, shocked into silence by the horror of it.

"Then we need to do as Kamzin says," Tem said. "We find the star. We take it to the emperor—perhaps his shamans know a way to destroy it, to prevent the witches from ever—"

Lusha let out her breath in a sound that wasn't quite a laugh. "The emperor won't destroy it."

"Certainly not," Mara agreed. "He has sent numerous explorers after fallen stars."

"Why? Does he want to raise the dead?" I said. "Or does he seek the power to kill?"

"He already has that power," Tem said. "He is emperor, after all."

"Fallen stars can grant the power to kill without weapons," Lusha said. "Without armies. A wave of your hand, and your enemy falls by the hundreds, while your forces remain intact. Imagine it."

I didn't want to imagine it. "But he's never caught one?"

Mara shook his head. "Not for lack of trying."

"But he did catch one," Lusha said. "Once, over two centuries ago. I helped Yonden trace that story. The emperor used the star against the witches."

"How? By killing them?"

"He tried. But it didn't work." Lusha's brow was furrowed, and she gazed at the stars clinging to the western horizon as if to center herself. "Something went wrong—as I said, these magics are often unpredictable. Using the star gave the witches a kind of living death—it didn't kill them, but they were no longer fully alive. In the stories, witches carry magic in their bones, in their blood. That's why they don't need talismans—magic is part of them. The spell the emperor cast didn't take the breath from their bodies—it took what they *were*."

It took me a moment to work out what she was saying. Tem arrived there before me. "The binding spell."

I drew in my breath. Mara looked as if he had been struck. "Then it wasn't truly a binding spell. Was it?"

"It wasn't meant to be." Lusha's expression was dark. "It was meant to destroy them. In a way, it did."

A shudder ran through me. I had never thought much about the spell that had been cast on the witches long before I was born. It was simply a fact of life. Necessary, and right—a check on the witches' dark powers. Yet in a way, the spell Lusha described was as terrible as raising the dead, even if the witches' crimes had warranted the half-life the emperor had given them. Was that how the witches had felt—damaged, not quite alive? Was that how River had felt?

"Then the binding spell could be recast," Tem said, "if we can find the star."

"And Azmiri will be safe." I set my jaw, forcing back my unease. "All the more reason to set out for the Ashes. Now."

"I agree," Mara said. "It will be a perilous journey. But surely in this case, risk is warranted."

We were all staring at Lusha again. She turned to us finally, her face very pale.

"It's wrong," she said. "Trapping fallen stars is wrong. All seers understand this. The stars are apart from the human realm. Their power isn't meant to be held in human hands—or, for that matter, in the hands of witches."

I shook my head. "Lusha, we don't have the luxury of worrying about some seers' code. The witches will destroy the Empire, and Azmiri."

"If they catch the star," Mara said. To my complete unsurprise, his certainty was wavering in the face of Lusha's hesitation. "It's possible it's already returned to the sky."

"I need to think," Lusha said abruptly. She strode to the edge of the stream, seating herself beside the water. Mara drifted after her, clearly of the opinion that his presence could only help her thinking.

Tem was watching me. His expression was difficult to

read—there was concern there, but also something like wariness. It seemed to soften as I met his eyes.

Suddenly I was sick of the tension that lay between us, all the sharp, unspoken words. I just wanted Tem on my side again.

"You don't have to say it," I said. "You were right. I won't use Azar-at's magic again. There's too much we don't understand about it." I paused. "And one visit to River's mind is quite enough for me."

Tem's face broke into a smile so genuine that it warmed me like sunlight.

"I can protect us, Kamzin," he said, his voice low and fierce. "I promise. I won't let you down the way I did with the *fiangul*."

I gazed into his drawn face, which looked even thinner in the wan light of morning. The shadows under his eyes were almost as dark as the bruise that bracketed mine. I forced myself to smile back.

Tem took my hand. "Tell me everything."

It was no easy thing, describing what I had seen, because I hadn't just seen it, I had *lived* it. The visual impressions were all jumbled up with scraps of River's thoughts, and snippets of memories and emotions that I couldn't interpret, being absent of any context. It was a bit like rattling around in someone's messy drawer, trying to make sense of the odds and ends of things. By the time I finished speaking, Tem's gaze was miles away.

"So they're still a distance from the Ashes," he murmured. "And not all of them have mastered their shape-shifting powers, which means they're probably not traveling much faster than human speed. I assume it would take them a while to find the star."

"*River* has mastered his powers." I pictured the enormous black cat on the summit of Raksha, felt again the ghostlike flight of the owl. "We can't assume anything."

"How far are we from the mountains?" Tem said. My own trepidation was mirrored in his eyes. It was one thing to contemplate traveling to the Ashes—it was quite another to actually undertake the journey. The Ash Mountains, which ran perpendicular to the Aryas to the northeast, were said to mark the edge of the world. No one—not even the emperor's explorers—had ever traveled beyond them. Time was said to move strangely there—the nights lasting days, the daylight as short as minutes. *The twilight mountains*, they were often called in the stories.

"Three days, maybe," I said. "But I don't know where to look."

"Lusha does."

We both turned to watch her. But she and Mara were no longer perched on the stream bank—they had moved to a small rise. They seemed to be gazing at something to the south. Lusha's hand was pressed against her mouth in an uncharacteristic gesture.

I squinted. Rising from one of those distant mountains, whose foothills were hidden by the horizon, was a column of smoke.

My breath caught. The column was thick and towering, so great that, even at this distance, I was surprised we hadn't already smelled it. As if in response to my thought, the wind rose, carrying with it a hint of ash.

"That's Mount Zerza," I murmured.

"And that," Tem said grimly, "is witch fire."

I swallowed. The smoke was dark—unnaturally so. So dark it seemed mixed with shadow. It twisted strangely, plumes reaching toward the sky like grasping hands. There was only one possible source of that smoke—the sole village on this side of the Aryas, where, mere days ago, Tem and I had eaten and drunk and danced by firelight.

"Jangsa." I felt a chill deep in my bones. "Jangsa is burning."

The Elder of Jangsa had welcomed us, had given us shelter and aid when we desperately needed it. I remembered the smile of the healer who had treated Norbu, the faces of the villagers we had met. I remembered something else too: River's hand on my waist as he spun me through the dance at the Ghost March, his voice murmuring in my ear. The elder had welcomed us, not knowing that among our expedition was someone whose true mission might destroy us all.

I dashed away the tear that slid down my cheek. "We have to help them."

"How?" Tem looked as if he had been struck. "It would take days to reach the village. By then—" He didn't finish his sentence. He didn't need to.

By the time we reached Jangsa, there wouldn't be a village left to help.

"Why?" I said. "Why attack them? Jangsa isn't even part of the Empire. It doesn't make sense."

Tem fingered the letter Biter had brought from Azmiri. "It does if you want the emperor's attention."

I waited.

"The Ninth Army," he said. "Your father wrote that the emperor sent them to the southern villages. He also wrote that he was requesting an army to protect Azmiri."

My heart slowed. "And Jangsa—"

"The emperor will send soldiers," Tem said. "That smoke will be visible for miles. Jangsa might not be part of the Empire, but the emperor will want to know if there's been an attack on his border."

"And if there are other attacks," I said, "on other villages—"

"The emperor will send soldiers there too." Tem's voice was grim.

"Leaving the Three Cities weakened." My throat was dry. "Vulnerable."

"Why fight the entire Empire," Tem said, "when you can just cut off its head?"

I slid slowly to the ground. The snow was soft, almost comforting. I gazed at the pillar of black smoke and tried not to think of Azmiri. The witches had burned it too, hundreds of years ago—it had almost been destroyed. Would they do so again? I saw black smoke wreathing the village, blanketing the whitewashed homes and narrow lanes, devouring the stand of pines where Tem and I had played as children—

Lusha was coming toward us. Her face was pale, her mouth set in a hard line, but her eyes were blazing. I had seen that expression before, countless times—at the age of six, when she had accosted one of the village boys who had been teasing me; on Raksha, when she had confronted River. I knew, with a sinking heart, that it would be impossible to sway Lusha now. If she had made up her mind to go straight to Azmiri, that was what she was going to do.

"Pack everything up," she said as she strode past. "I want to be halfway to the Ashes by sundown."

NINE

Chirri

THE DAWN REACHED her hut before any other, nosing its way through the shutters. Chirri was already awake, hunched over a pile of talismans that would have seemed a hopeless jumble to a casual observer. Bronze, bone, wood—each had its own purpose, but could be combined to weave spells as complex and multitoned as a symphony. She wasn't casting a new spell but strengthening one that already existed, laid down decades ago by the last village shaman, her aunt.

It wasn't enough. She groaned at the realization that she would have to stir from her cross-legged position on the floor—the process of getting up and down was something she tried to keep to a minimum these days. Small Nuisance, the one-month-old dragon sleeping at the foot of her bed, stirred and yawned. He was the last of the baby dragons who had been unwanted guests in Chirri's hut. She had sold the others, mostly to traveling merchants who often remarked on the quality of the dragons bred in the mountain villages. For some reason, she had turned down their offers for Small Nuisance, despite the fact that he was the most troublesome of the brood, sharpening his claws on her furniture and taking an extraordinary amount of time to understand the practicality of doing his business outside.

By the time Chirri finally lifted herself to her feet, she was light-headed and out of breath. The downside of a long life, she had often thought, was that you had to spend as much time in an old body as you did a young one.

Undaunted, she took up her staff and stepped outside. The clouds below her hut were woolly and gray with rain, partly obscuring the village. A whitewashed home here, a lane strung with laundry there—the rest was tucked under the cloud. Mount Imja to the north, separated from Azmiri by a thinly forested valley, was clear, its white peak glittering in the early light. To the north and south stretched the Aryas, towering and blanketed with snow. The sky was a vast canvas, richly blue.

Though Chirri never had any shortage of responsibilities, she always paused to look at that view.

A wisp of cloud hovered not fifty feet below her hut. Chirri slowly descended toward it, leaning on her staff, beating her way along the precarious trail worn by her own boots. She had fallen only once, during her overly excitable youth, in a hurry over something she couldn't remember now. Chirri never made the same mistake twice.

Small Nuisance followed her down the slope. He didn't try to settle on her shoulder, knowing he would receive a rap on the snout for the impertinence. The light in his belly was just beginning to darken—it would be a rich emerald when he was fully grown. Chirri, who still told herself she intended to sell the beast eventually, tried to ignore the fact that his presence made it easier to navigate the shadowed path.

Upon reaching the finger of cloud, which was tangled in clover and grasses, she removed a vial from her *chuba*. Gently, she blew part of the cloud into the vial, then stoppered it. The cloud appeared to dissolve once placed in the vial, but that wouldn't affect the magic.

Some magics were older than talismans, Chirri knew. Talismans were useful, though most these days were imbued with a dark magic, a stolen magic, and they were now beginning to falter. But shamans had existed before there were talismans, and while their magic then had been of a quieter variety, they could not truly be called weak. Unlike most shamans, Chirri had been taught those magics.

She climbed back to her hut and started a fire in the pit outside her door. Once it was hot enough, she tossed the vial into the flames. The glass began to char, and then to melt, glowing as it warped and stretched. Chirri spoke the incantation, and the trapped cloud rose out of the flame, invisible but for a flicker of silver here and there, like metal catching the light. The wind rose, scattering the cloud over the village, where it broke apart, vanishing.

The wards protecting the village seemed to shiver. Chirri closed her eyes and felt them knitting together, their threads tightening, sealing any gaps worn by weather or time.

Chirri settled herself on a grassy ledge with a sigh of relief. Small Nuisance perched beside her, and she fed him scraps of *balep* that, for some reason, she had stored in the pocket of her *chuba* after last night's dinner. He devoured them, snorting in an exuberant way that might have been intimidating had he been larger than a kitten.

Chirri waited.

An hour passed. The sun crept higher, and the clouds dissolved. Finally, they came.

It was difficult to distinguish them at first—they could have been ordinary shadows, perhaps cast by tree branches tossed by the wind. But these shadows were not attached to a tree or anything else, and the sunlight did not disperse them. They crept up the mountainside, gliding like dark snakes, moving with no particular hurry, but with a clear purpose. Chirri could see it all from her high perch.

Would the wards hold?

The shadow-figures paused at the edge of the village and seemed to recoil. Chirri thought she caught the edge of a cry, twisted and barely human. The shadows melted together, and then they surged, throwing themselves at the wards.

The wards held.

The shadows dissipated, as if the wards themselves had vanquished them, but Chirri knew better. It was not the first time the witches had come to Azmiri in recent days, nor would it be the last. But Lusha's letter, carried by her exhausted raven, had given Chirri the warning she needed. Not five minutes after Elder had thrust it into her hand, Chirri had been at work, strengthening the wards surrounding the village, visiting each house and farm to teach their inhabitants a few basic incantations to defend against witch fire. She should have taken such precautions long ago, she knew. If she had been younger, with fewer aching bones, she might have done better. If she had been gifted with a halfway useful apprentice, who had not spent most days trying her patience. But "if" was the least practical word in existence, and Chirri quickly cast such thoughts aside.

Yet there was one "if" she could not overlook. The witches hadn't attacked in great numbers, but in small parties more suited to a quick raid than a full-scale assault. What was holding them back? If they came to Azmiri in full force, Chirri would not be able to bar them. One of the emperor's armies was on its way to the village, but would the soldiers arrive in time?

She rose, accompanying the movement with such a heartfelt flurry of curses that Small Nuisance flitted away in alarm. She wandered back to her hut, muttering to herself. Where she stopped.

Perched on an open windowsill was the fox.

"Hello, old one," Chirri said. "Back again, are you? And what is it this time?"

Ragtooth bared his teeth. He was thinner than when Chirri had last seen him a few days ago, and his fur was matted. But his eyes were as bright as ever, a green glitter like the dew on spring leaves.

Chirri propped open the door of her hut and rummaged through the shelves. The last time, he had come for *ruhanna* bark, a potent painkiller—she hadn't wanted to think too hard on the reasons for that.

Ragtooth stretched in a sunbeam. He sauntered to one of the cabinets at the back of the hut, where cobwebs hung thick in the shadows.

"Really?" Chirri followed with some trepidation. Small Nuisance's light flickered against the cabinet, sending a few spiders scurrying away. Chirri tugged at the first drawer, which groaned open. It held several vials, some half-empty. Each contained a dark powder that sparkled like glass. A poison—but not one meant for humans or animals.

She settled a full vial on the floor. "This won't stop them. Not now that they have their powers back."

Ragtooth only gazed at her. Small Nuisance fluttered close, thinking to make a new friend. The fox snapped at his tail, sending the dragon scurrying behind her legs.

"You'd best be careful," she said sternly. "Going back and forth like this—it will wear you down, even an old one like you."

The fox took the vial in his jaws and slipped out the door. Chirri was tempted to go to the window to watch, to try to pinpoint the exact moment when he vanished, folding himself into a gap between mountain and sky. But it was a juvenile impulse, and the shaman quashed it.

What are those fool children up to?

Lusha and the others had been gone for weeks. The elder believed they were on their way home, but Chirri was less certain. It wasn't just Ragtooth's visits, or Yonden's vague pronouncements. Chirri had no doubt that, given the opportunity, her bumbling apprentice would seize upon some new quest of great importance. But would it be a quest that helped the Empire, or caused even greater harm than what had already been unleashed?

Chirri adjusted her shawls and began making her way down to the village. She would visit the farmers, those whose fields were closest to the Amarin Valley, and task them with laying animal traps among their crops. Then she would speak with the elder and reassure him that, once again, the wards had held. They were holding—for now.

For now. Chirri squeezed her staff and continued on her slow, careful way.

PART II
THE ASHES

TEN

MY HANDS ACHED with cold, and my arms shook, but I hauled myself onto the top of the boulder. There I lay on my back, unmoving.

My breath rose in clouds above me, muting the bright of the moon. The sun had set early—too early. We should have had another hour of daylight.

The twilight mountains. I tilted my head to look at them. They bristled out of the horizon like blades of darkness that sliced away the stars.

We had been traveling north for two days, over an increasingly barren landscape. Two days of marching late into the night, yet we still hadn't reached the foothills of the Ashes. The problem was the terrain, which was stony and pitted and caked with frost, making for dangerous going with the yak. I was beginning to despair.

We knew where the star had fallen—at least, Lusha swore she did—but could we reach it before River? Before a creature who could take any shape he chose?

I shoved the question from my mind, because it wasn't a question. We had to reach the star before River did.

I forced myself to my feet, squinting into the darkness. I had left the others to set up camp for the night in order to scout the terrain. Nothing stirred among the shadows, either animal or witch. My heart sank—the landscape before us was even more rugged, strewn with boulders and gouged by glaciers that had once dragged themselves across the land. The earth was held together by ice—we had left behind trees and grass—but in places, hills sagged into loose debris that would be impossible for the yak to scale. I could see no clear path.

I examined my hands. The last finger of my left was an unhealthy white, and bending it was difficult. I cleared my mind and focused.

Warmth spread through my hand, as if I had doused it in a bath. The color returned to my skin, and my fingers felt limber again. I paused, waiting for the flash of pain to subside. As long as I restricted myself to small spells, it was bearable. Small magic had a small price.

I put my glove back on. I had made use of Azar-at's magic several times since our battle with the *fiangul*, always for similarly small spells. Whenever I did, I took care to hide it from Tem and Lusha.

I pushed the guilt aside. I had promised Tem I wouldn't use

Azar-at's magic, and for the most part, I had kept my word. I doubted that Tem would want me to develop frostbite.

Something stirred the air above me. Just a bird—probably. There was no way to be certain anymore. The fire Tem had lit, though it burned low, was like a beacon among all that snowy dark.

I hurried to descend the boulder, suddenly nervous. I didn't like leaving Tem and Lusha alone.

Mara had gone south. Alone, despite the danger—though, as he had pointed out, in his dismissive way, danger couldn't very well be avoided, as it lay in every direction. He would go to Jangsa to see if there were any survivors. Then he would continue south to the Three Cities and tell the emperor what the witches were planning.

I hadn't thought I was capable of feeling admiration for Mara. He hadn't spoken a word of complaint, despite the fact that he had poor odds of surviving the long journey without the protection of a shaman. When he set off, Lusha followed at his side for the first few paces. They had stopped together briefly, speaking in low tones. Then Mara had carried on, growing smaller and smaller until he passed the brow of a hill and was gone.

Now we were only three.

I tried not to dwell on that as I marched back to the campfire. Eight of us had left Azmiri on a mission to save the Empire. And now it fell to Lusha, Tem, and me to finish it.

The ground beneath me gave a shudder, and I leaped back. But it was just the snow settling, not a crevasse opening to swallow me as it had swallowed Aimo.

My heart pounded. I didn't trust the snow fields as I had before—now, whenever they groaned or shifted, I saw the blackness of the crevasse, Dargye's face as he clutched the torn scrap of Aimo's *chuba*. Death came so quickly in the wilds—it was something I had never understood before, when I used to run heedless with Tem over the slopes of Azmiri. Without warning or ceremony, it could snatch away someone you had known your entire life.

Our camp nestled between two boulders, which leaned drunkenly together, forming a natural shelter from the wind. I hurried toward the fire, shivering. The climb had warmed me, but it was still bitterly cold, particularly with the wind running its claws over the earth. At the edge of the light, I stopped.

Three figures sat around the fire, huddled together in conversation, their backs to me. Tem and Lusha—I would recognize either of them from a mountain summit—and someone tall and slender, with disheveled black hair.

He wore a tahrskin *chuba*.

My breath caught. I was surging forward, my heart in my throat, when Tem saw me. His expression was wary, but not alarmed. The man turned.

With a start, I recognized the heavy, brooding brow, the stiff posture. The light fell on his tahrskin *chuba*—the garb of one of the emperor's explorers—revealing it to be old-fashioned in style and cut.

"Mingma," I breathed.

"Kamzin," the ghost said drily. The light glinted strangely off his skin, as if he were made of water. "I gather you aren't overjoyed to see me."

My mouth seemed to have stopped working. When I had last seen Mingma, he and his terrifying companions were attempting to drown me in a glacier-fed mountain pool, all acting under the power of a spell laid down centuries ago by the witches. I felt again the agonizing chill of the water, the thin fingers dragging me below the surface—

"He's been following us since we left the Aryas," Lusha said. "He won't hurt us."

"I'm sorry about that business on Raksha," the ghost said. "As you know, I didn't have much choice in the matter."

"That business?" My terror was giving way, slowly but surely, to fury. "That business?"

"Kamzin," Lusha said in a quelling voice. "Mingma has offered to help us locate the star—as you know, he spent more time in the Ash Mountains than any explorer."

"He tried to kill me," I said, emphasizing each word through my teeth.

"I also saved your life," Mingma said. "You'd be a mound of snow on that mountain if it weren't for me."

I froze. I saw a figure silhouetted against a sky blazing with shooting stars, *chuba* rippling in the wind. I had been desperately lost. And like a familiar star, he had pointed me home—to Lusha and Tem.

I had thought it was River that night. Then, later, my own delirious imagination. But it had been Mingma.

"He didn't have to stay," Lusha said. "The other ghosts crossed over when the spell holding them on the mountain broke."

"I thought you could use my help," the explorer said, scanning the landscape with that clear, intelligent gaze, as if he were comparing his surroundings against a memorized scroll. "Though Kamzin less so, perhaps. I kept an eye on you as you descended Raksha—I don't think I've seen a climber so skilled. You'd make an excellent explorer."

In spite of myself, I felt my face warm at the compliment. I hid it behind a stony glare. "How did you free yourself from the spell? How can we be certain this isn't some kind of trick?"

"When River broke the binding spell, he also shattered the one holding us on Raksha," Mingma said. "I doubt he intended it, or even knew it had happened. The breaking of a powerful spell like that often has an effect on other, nearby spells, particularly one as old and brittle as that which bound us to the mountain."

I glanced at Tem, who, as usual, had been quiet, listening as the conversation played out, his expression partly shielded by his hair. "What do you think?"

"It's true that he isn't under the witches' spell anymore," he said thoughtfully. "I was able to detect traces of it, but that's all that's left—traces."

The wind played with Mingma's hair—I found myself staring at it, marveling at how he could at once be *there* and *not there*.

"We'd be foolish not to accept his offer," Lusha said in a pointed tone. "He knows the terrain. He's *mapped* the terrain. He can help you navigate."

"I don't need help. I can find the way."

"The nights are long here. Can you find the way in the dark?" Lusha sighed. "Kamzin. We need Mingma. We can't move nearly as fast as the witches, but this gives us a chance."

I felt backed into a corner. Even the sound of Mingma's voice set me on edge, but what could I say? I thought of his maps of Raksha, which had guided me safely almost to the very summit. And Lusha was right—we needed to move fast. We'd already lost too much time.

"Lusha showed me where she believes the star landed," Mingma said. "I can get us there by sunset tomorrow. I know a valley that will take us through the foothills."

"Why are you still here?" I said.

He gave me a smile that was so easy and open I couldn't help staring. In that moment, he was an entirely different person from the man I had met on Raksha, twisted by bitterness and a lifetime trapped in that bleak, inhuman place. Something in his expression had dissolved, like frost under the spring sun.

"I thought I'd have one last adventure" was all he said.

I gave him a long look. He returned it mildly. "Fine," I said. "Just you. None of your . . . friends."

I didn't know what I would do if he didn't agree—he was a *ghost*, after all—but Mingma took me seriously, nodding and gesturing to the map in Lusha's hands. "I can show you the route now."

I came closer, trying not to think about what I had just agreed to—being guided through a twilight landscape with witches lurking nearby, by a ghost who, only last week, had attempted to kill me. Mingma laid the map on the ground by the fire, sketching out the details of tomorrow's hike. It would be grueling, but it seemed doable. I avoided leaning too close to the ghost as he gestured at the map.

"Have you ever tracked a fallen star, Mingma?" Lusha said. I gave her a dark look. I strongly suspected that her too-easy acceptance of the explorer was a veiled barb directed at me. We had spent much of the day arguing—despite my designation as navigator, Lusha remained largely incapable of adjusting to a situation where she was not in charge. She had challenged every change of course, every conclusion I drew from the maps. My musings about Tem's knowledge of silencing spells had not been well received.

"Emperor Lozong sent me on several expeditions for that purpose," the ghost replied. He was settled comfortably on the ground, leaning back on his hands, as if he had been a member of our party from the beginning. In a way, I thought with a little shiver, he had been. "I never came close."

"Then the emperor has always coveted them."

"The emperor covets many things," Mingma said.

"Lusha," Tem said, "can you tell us anything else about their powers?"

Lusha frowned. She was perched cross-legged on a blanket, a dragon's light spilling across her star charts. Her hair was in uncharacteristic disarray, and her eyes were shadowed. She had spent most of the previous night by the fire, poring over the charts. Despite her initial skepticism about my plan, she seemed

to have dedicated herself—with her customary decisiveness—
wholeheartedly to finding the star.

"As we all know," she began, "shooting stars are said to be the
spirits of ancient heroes."

"As well as great villains," Mingma said.

Lusha nodded. "Anyone who has had an impact on the course
of history—for good or ill. Star showers like the one a few nights
ago occur because someone on earth has changed that course.
Altered the world somehow. When that happens, it's said that the
spirits of those heroes rejoice and dance across the sky. Some fall
to earth. Those that do can be captured."

"Isn't that dangerous?" I said. "If it's the spirit of some vicious
barbarian lord?"

"There is that risk," Lusha said in a chilly tone. It was a tone
that had become more frequent since we turned north, always
directed at me. At first I had thought Lusha was angry about
my contract with Azar-at, but she hadn't mentioned the creature
again, or seemed to take any interest in its presence.

"Risk?" Tem repeated.

"It matters little," Lusha said. "A captured spirit is bound to
you and must do what you ask of it."

"Like Azar-at?"

"Not really. For one thing, the star isn't really a *being* anymore—
it's closer to a talisman than a person, and can be used as such."

My brow furrowed. A captured star didn't sound like a talisman at all—it sounded like a ghost held prisoner against its
will. I looked at Mingma, but he was gazing into the fire with a

fascinated expression, as if he had never seen one before.

In spite of my best efforts, my thoughts strayed to River. I saw him by the campfire, laughing. I saw him on the mountain, after the serac had fallen an inch from me, his face rigid with horror. In some moments, I was able to convince myself that it had all been feigned, but my conviction didn't last. What would I do if I met him in the Ashes?

I drew my legs up and rested my chin upon my knee. The answer was simple enough, on the face of it—I would have to kill him. Or watch Tem do it.

A mountain pass, deeply shadowed under a dark sky—

I jerked my head up. Beside me, Tem murmured, "What is it?"

I crouched on the edge of a sheer promontory, rolling a handful of pebbles across my palm. Before me stretched a vast valley tucked between jagged mountains, blanketed with drifts of snow a hundred feet deep. A shooting star blazed across the night. I selected a single pebble—it was icy, coated with flecks of frost. Under my gaze, it began to smolder like coal, enveloped by fire that could burn any material, even solid stone.

Once the pebble grew bright enough, I casually tossed it over the cliff. It illuminated the valley as it descended. I ignited another pebble and launched it in the other direction.

Nothing.

I grimaced as I imagined Esha's reaction when I came back empty-handed again. I stood and leaped off the cliff, my arms dissolving into owls' wings—

"No." I wrenched myself free of the vision.

Lusha and Mingma hadn't noticed—their heads were bent over Lusha's star charts. Tem's grip was the only thing holding me upright. His face was bloodless. My hands tingled, as if River's magic had coursed through them. The flame he had lit seemed to brush against my palm, feather soft.

"What did you see?" Tem said.

"They've reached the mountains. But they haven't found it." I swallowed against the nausea rising in my throat. "He—he's still searching."

Tem's eyes narrowed. "How much time do we have?"

I shook my head. There had been a moment of freefall, before River transformed, and I felt that sensation now.

"Very little," I said.

ELEVEN

River

THE LANDSCAPE GREW starker the farther they traveled. Trees gave way to snowy plains scoured by wind that stirred up an omnipresent, icy haze. Now they were in the foothills of the Ash Mountains, farther north than River had ever been as Royal Explorer.

It was not for nothing that the Ashes were called *the twilight mountains*. The stories of a land of perpetual night were exaggerated, but it was still a strange place. Dawn and dusk were longer here, and the stars never faded completely—River could see them now, faint behind the cerulean sky. It was as if the spirits that had once haunted the place had cast a net and drawn the stars closer.

The Ashes themselves were smaller than either the Aryas or the Drakkar Mountains to the west. But they were sharper, wilder, the winds having weathered them to dramatic points of snowy rock. They rose like the tines of a comb, their slopes close to sheer. In the foothills, subterranean springs melted the snow, creating pools of star-strewn water brushed with clouds of fog. It was a world of sky, above and below.

Though he would never admit it to Esha, River was enjoying himself. He sat atop one of the hills, examining the vertical terrain before him, which bristled with rock and ice. He felt the same stirring of excitement he always had when he visited a new place as Royal Explorer. It was a relief to be away from the Nightwood. River had forgotten how much he hated it.

He was going to find the star. He could feel it in his bones, a pulse of anticipation. He didn't care much about the star's mysterious powers—mostly, he just felt a juvenile urge to hold in his hands something that had eluded hundreds of explorers before him.

He held a bundle of string, twisted and stretched to form a pattern. He let the wind loosen several strands, and a new picture emerged.

"I don't know why you bother with that," came a voice behind him.

His concentration shattered. Without turning, he said, "What do you want, Thorn?"

"The same thing I wanted yesterday." He sat beside River, carefully arranging his *chuba*. "We're not going to find the star if you keep wasting time worrying about the weather." He motioned to the divining strings.

"It's more than that," River said. "You should know. Sky used to read them."

Thorn shrugged. Suppressing a sigh, River said, "They pick up disturbances in the atmosphere. Storms. Magic. Stars falling out of the sky."

River pulled a small telescope from his pocket—a gift from the emperor, and one of the few things he had kept from his former life. He scanned the mountains. After a welcome moment of silence, Thorn gave a loud yawn.

"What does River Shara, Royal Explorer, need with divination?" His voice was lazy. "What about those celebrated instincts?"

River twisted the strings once more around his fingers. Thorn gave him a sweeping look, taking in his well-worn boots and tahr-skin *chuba*, which, for reasons River didn't fully understand, he was still wearing. The other witches, with the exception of Thorn, were barefoot and cloaked in rags. Thorn had made several barbed remarks about River's human appearance, despite the fact that he was dressed in a similar manner. It didn't trouble River, for he understood the source of Thorn's antipathy, which was not disgust, but envy. He had long been fascinated by the pomp and finery of the emperor's court, and was known to kidnap merchants from the Three Cities who strayed close to the Nightwood—not to torment them, though he no doubt enjoyed that as well, but to add their wares to his collection of trinkets.

There was a hardness in Thorn's eyes, though he still smiled his languid smile as he stood. In his tall, polished boots and black *chuba*, he could have been a visiting aristocrat in the emperor's court. "My lord dislikes being kept waiting. Why is this taking so long?"

River suppressed a grimace at the "my lord." Thorn had always trailed after Esha when they were children—now that he was emperor, Thorn was practically kissing his feet.

"I'm flattered Esha places such confidence in me," River said. "That he would think I could locate a fallen star in a vast mountain range within a matter of hours."

Thorn made a low sound of disgust. River ignored him. He wasn't trying to irritate his brothers—which wasn't to say that he didn't enjoy it. When the emperor had sent him after a star before, he had been given precise coordinates by Lozong's seers. He didn't have that now—he had nothing more than a vague description from the witches who had seen the star land somewhere in the Ashes. River might be able to move like the wind, but that was of limited benefit if he didn't know where to go.

"Esha will not—"

"If Esha wants the star found more quickly, he can kidnap a seer," River said. "As I've told him, I'm no expert in astronomy."

River's words stirred up a memory. Kamzin's sister was a seer, a talented one—she had guessed things about River's identity that not even the emperor's seers had discovered. No doubt she would be able to track a fallen star. He wondered if they were still on Raksha, or if they had made it off the mountain and were now heading back to Azmiri. Either way, they wouldn't be far—not for him. Lusha would have little interest in helping them, but River had no doubt Esha could find a way to convince her.

He gazed thoughtfully at the mountains. It wasn't as if River had warm feelings for Lusha—quite the opposite. She had tried to sabotage his expedition. She had nearly destroyed everything he had been working toward for over three years. He felt nothing for her but animosity.

"Unfortunately, seers are in short supply in these parts," Thorn said drily. "You're the best we have."

River pressed his lips together. He bent his head over the strings again. "So it seems."

"We've had another one take ill," Thorn said. "It doesn't make sense. Esha was furious."

"Yes, I'm sure she fell ill to spite him." The illness that had afflicted several of their company had slowed their progress further. Oddly, it resembled the symptoms of obsidian poisoning, once a common weapon used against the witches by Empire soldiers.

"He was furious because he thinks someone's working against us."

"Who?" River gestured at the vast, empty landscape. "Esha's only grown more paranoid over the years. More likely, they've been overusing their magic. I've seen shamans sicken from that."

Thorn leaned back on his hands. He was watching River again. "What's he like? The emperor."

"Arrogant. Vain. Given to tormenting his brother with impossible tasks."

Thorn actually laughed. "I meant Lozong."

River pulled at another string. "They're rather alike. Though

Lozong's chief preoccupation these days is his banquets and festivals. I doubt anyone would invite Esha to a banquet. He'd eat the guests."

"We're fortunate the empress is no longer alive," Thorn said. "She was more attentive to the security of the Empire than Lozong, wasn't she?"

"So they say." River had never met Empress Iranna—she had died decades ago, having refused to allow her life to be lengthened unnaturally by magic, as the emperor's had been. By all accounts, she had been a fearsome ruler, with a sharp tongue and a sharper mind, and more than a match for the emperor. It was clearly a quality that appealed to him, for he was said to have been wholly devoted to her. River found it hard to believe, as the only person he had seen inspire devotion in the emperor was himself. Yet it was true that he had never remarried.

"Esha wants to speak with you," Thorn said, standing. "He's in a foul mood."

"Does he have other moods?"

Thorn laughed again and strode off. River found himself wondering idly how it would have been between him and Thorn had it not been for Esha. Sometimes they were almost capable of getting along.

River set the divining strings aside and scrubbed a hand through his hair. The problem wasn't just the interruption. He had enough difficulty sitting still, let alone fiddling with bits of string.

He pictured Sky hunched over his hands by firelight, plucking at the threads as intricate patterns took shape. He made it seem so effortless—as a child, River had sometimes fallen asleep watching him. Sky would sit beside him, a bulky, comforting presence, explaining the patterns in his calm voice.

Thinking of Sky brought about that hollow feeling again. River shoved his thoughts away. Discarding unpleasant thoughts was easier than it had been before he'd met Azar-at—another reason to be grateful for the fire demon's companionship.

The wind whispered over the hill, rustling the water of the nearest pool so that the stars seemed to melt together. River reached for the telescope—only to find it gone.

Claws scraped against stone. He turned.

Gazing back at him was Kamzin's fox, the telescope clutched in its jaws.

For a moment, River could only stare. The fox stared back, green eyes narrowed with what River could have sworn was amusement. The creature scampered down the hill, moving with uncanny speed.

In a blink, River transformed into a black leopard and surged after the fox. But within a few yards, its trail disappeared. He pawed at the snow, perplexed.

Was the rat to blame for all the other things that had gone missing since they'd left the Nightwood? The maps, the compass?

River felt an uncharacteristic prickle of disquiet. For a moment, Kamzin's presence was almost tangible. He half expected to find her standing behind him, chin tilted and arms crossed in that stubborn posture she so often assumed, her large eyes flashing like starlight. The visions of her had been disquieting, though he'd had none recently. Kamzin had no magic, and in a way, seeing the world through her eyes had felt like stumbling around with his hands tied behind his back. Yet he hadn't felt weak. He had felt bold, and heedless, and full of a jangling energy.

If he ever figured out who had placed the spell on him, he would kill them.

He found Esha in the shadow of an enormous boulder from which a rare pine grew, jutting out of a crevice like a warning hand. He stood with his arms folded, gazing down at the girl who knelt before him. River thought her name was Ivy. She was thirteen at most, clad in a torn and overlarge *chuba* that had no doubt been stolen from one of the mountain villages, perhaps by her parents. She had the characteristic raggedness of most witches, her frame too thin and her bird's-nest hair tangled with leaves.

She was shaking. River wondered how long she had been there, and what she had done to displease Esha. He had a contemplative look that always foreshadowed something unpleasant.

"Brother," Esha said without turning, "what have you found?"

Ivy's eyes swung to him. She wore a hopeless expression that only deepened River's sense of foreboding.

"I've narrowed the search area to three mountains," River said. "We should be able to locate the star within a day or two, if the skies stay clear."

He had no idea if this was true. But given the mood Esha was in, River felt no inclination toward honesty.

"A day or two," Esha repeated. "That was your estimate yesterday, I recall."

"Oh, was it?" River abandoned any hope of quickly extricating himself from the conversation. Esha's tone was calm and deliberate. It was a bad sign. It was how he had spoken before he had driven a boar's tusk through River's shoulder when he was five years old, after they had quarreled over a game. Sky had nearly killed Esha for that, and afterward, Esha had been careful not to injure River in ways that left obvious marks. River knew that Esha had enjoyed tormenting him in part because he was Sky's favorite, and though Esha felt little warmth toward Sky, his resentful temperament made him view Sky's allegiance to their youngest brother as a personal affront.

"It's difficult to travel quickly, with so many ill," River said. "Whatever it is, it's almost as bad as obsidian poisoning—"

"It *is* obsidian poisoning," Esha said. "A scout found traces of it at the edge of the last stream. Any ideas how it ended up there?"

River's thoughts flashed to Kamzin's fox. But that was impossible. Wasn't it?

His head was beginning to ache. "Why are you asking me?"

"Why am I asking you? Was that your customary response when you faced a challenge as Royal Explorer?"

"No one tried to poison me before I took up with you, Esha."

Esha smiled. "Tell me about the sky city."

River blinked. "What?"

"The city you found on Raksha. Tell me about it."

"I already did." He had recounted his last expedition to Esha and Thorn. Why was Esha bringing this up now? His labyrinthine mind was as much a mystery to River as it had been when they were children.

"A city of shadow, you said." Esha rubbed absently at one red-rimmed eye. "Towers made of darkness that disappeared when the light touched them. But what did you *feel* when you were there? Did it feel alive?"

River didn't want to think about the sky city. It had been a haunted place, tucked into the wind-scoured summit. He still found it difficult to believe that anyone had ever lived there—not because it was impossible, but because it was so unpleasant, the sky close and confining. He had felt little connection to those long-ago witches who had abandoned it. Yet he had felt *something* when he stood there. A watchfulness that seemed to seep from the ruins themselves.

"I suppose so," he said. "Why?"

Esha didn't reply. He merely stood there with his arms crossed, gazing thoughtfully at the girl who still crouched before him on her knees, shaking.

"One of our scouts found her halfway back to the Nightwood," Esha said finally. "What would you do, River? I've heard stories about what the Royal Explorer would do."

River regarded Ivy, who seemed as frightened of him as she was of Esha. He had indeed encountered deserters in his service to the emperor. Some people were simply incapable of dealing with the hardships that accompanied his expeditions. Though River, as Royal Explorer, had acquired a reputation for executing deserters, the truth was that he generally let them flee. In the harsh wilderness, revenge was a luxury. But this girl wasn't some shirking assistant—she was just a child. No doubt Esha had chosen her for the mission on the basis of her shape-shifting ability.

"I would let her go," River said.

Esha considered him. River wished that he would rant and pace, unpleasant as that was. Esha's calm was like the coiled tension of a viper—you knew that when he did lash out, it would be brutal and without warning.

"Apparently, she planned to rejoin her sister beyond the Nightwood," Esha said, turning back to Ivy. "She wasn't content to serve her emperor."

With that, River understood. While most witches had rallied to Esha's cause, eager to strike at the Empire, some had slipped quietly away once their powers were restored. They had left the Nightwood behind, journeying east or south to unknown lands. Not everyone was eager for revenge—nor did everyone wish to be ruled. Though their numbers had been small, their departure had inspired a fury in Esha that River had never seen before.

"Is that true?" Esha asked the girl, his voice almost gentle.

Ivy was biting her lip hard enough to cut it. Yet even in her terror, she gazed at Esha with something close to awe. It wasn't the first time River had seen that look. Even standing there, motionless, there was something about Esha that drew the eye, something fiery, larger than life. Emperor Lozong had the same quality, an aura of predestination. Yet Esha hadn't been destined to rule—Sky had.

"Yes, my lord," Ivy whispered. "It's true."

Esha turned back to River. "I've been thinking of what you said the other day, about what you called my *impatience* to find the star. You recall our conversation?"

"Vaguely." It had ended when Esha summoned a gust of wind that had flung River against a tree, hard enough to topple it.

"Your lack of respect is troubling. I am your emperor now, after all. The Crown is said to increase wisdom."

"I wonder how that works," River said, "if the bearer is starting from a deficit?"

He regretted it instantly. The corner of Esha's mouth quirked in that expression that was not a smile. River braced himself for an onslaught of unpleasantness. He thought that if worse came to worse, he could become an owl and escape. Despite the powers bestowed on him by the Crown, Esha was oddly clumsy when it came to shape-shifting.

"Perhaps you need motivating," Esha said. And he turned and struck Ivy across the face. It was not a slap, or a punch—it was something that snapped her head back, her neck bent at an odd angle. She fell onto her back and moved no more.

River was still. He felt as if his breath had turned to ice inside him.

"There," Esha said, absently rubbing the side of his hand, which was bloodied, perhaps where it had caught on the girl's teeth. "Does that inspire you? Don't think that because you're my brother I won't deal with you harshly if you disappoint me."

"She was a child." River's voice was quiet. He didn't know why he said it. But it was the only thing that rose to his lips.

"And?" Esha's blank look wasn't feigned. He had known how River would react to this, though he didn't understand the reason. "There will be more deaths like hers—you should get used to it. The Empire sees us as monsters, and we will give them every reason to do so—fear is, after all, our most potent weapon. When we step out of the shadows, we mustn't disappoint expectations."

River had no doubt that Esha was a monster. He wasn't sure about himself. He stared at the girl sprawled across the snow, a single smudge of red upon her mouth.

Esha touched River's face, his fingers cool and dry against his cheek. He seemed pleased with himself, and with River's reaction. "Happy hunting, brother," he said, and strode away.

Snow speckled Ivy's body—it wouldn't be long before it covered it. River shook himself. He changed shape as effortlessly as shedding a cloak, lifting off the hill as an owl with pale wings that dissolved against the landscape. Then he soared into the sky— neither knowing nor caring his direction, desiring only to be away.

TWELVE

I ROSE QUIETLY the next morning and pulled on my boots. Lusha slept beside me, her breathing shallow. She had been late to bed again, having stayed up talking to Mingma by the fire, and I doubted I would wake her if I shouted. Tem, on my other side, was snoring.

The air was frigid, even in the tent. Not thinking much, I invoked the same spell I had used on my hands last night, creating a small cloud of warmth around my chilled feet. I gritted my teeth until the pain faded. I then wrestled one of the dragons out from the blankets—the creature kept trying to burrow down among the folds—and stumbled into the dark. Beyond the shadows of the boulders, the snowy landscape was silvered and still.

Ragtooth, sleeping on a blanket next to the embers of the fire, stirred at the sound of my boots. He made a querying sound, then rose with a stretch and followed me.

I took the bow, because I needed a reason to be up if Tem or Lusha woke. There was little game here, apart from the odd pika or snow quail, and neither made for much of a meal. But our rations were meager, and if I saw an opportunity, I would take it.

"Can't sleep?" said a voice behind me.

I whirled. Mingma perched on a pitted boulder that had definitely been vacant a moment ago, his eye pressed against a telescope. My heart thudded. "You startled me."

"Sorry," the ghost said, lowering the telescope. "I believe I saw a burrow by the spring to the south. Would you like some company?"

"No," I said a little too quickly. "That's all right, I'm— I won't go far."

He sat with one leg crossed over the other, entirely at ease. His immaculate tahrskin *chuba* was open, one side rippling in the breeze. "I'd avoid the hills. Rockslides are inconvenient things to encounter alone," he said in his dry way.

I nodded. Mingma looked down at the map in his lap—it was one he had drawn fifty years ago, when he was still alive. A little uncanny shiver went down my spine.

"He's back, I see," the ghost said, motioning to Ragtooth. "He disappeared for hours today."

"He does that."

"If it were my expedition, I wouldn't travel with a creature like that," Mingma said. He adjusted the telescope thoughtfully.

"Traveling with those who have their own agendas introduces complications."

I glanced down at Ragtooth. The fox's familiar eyes glittered in the darkness. His fur was matted and unkempt, and he needed a bath worse than I did. I couldn't imagine what sort of agenda Mingma thought he had, but I knew some people didn't trust familiars.

"I doubt that," I said. "In any case, it isn't your expedition."

A sharpness must have entered my voice at that, for Mingma glanced at me. "No," he agreed, his tone mild. I turned to go.

"Kamzin?"

I paused. In the starlight, Mingma's hair was the gray of cobwebs.

"Keep an eye out for witches," he said.

"Oh." I gave a slight shrug. "The *kinnika* haven't made a sound all day."

"You should stay on your guard," Mingma said. "When they come upon you, it will be without warning—don't ever forget that. Take it from someone who's traveled with them."

That stopped me in my tracks. "You traveled with them?"

He lifted the telescope, pointing it toward the mountains. "Happy hunting, Kamzin."

He gave no hint he was aware of the curiosity his casual statement had roused—yet I had the strong suspicion that it was an act, and that, judging by the tightness of his lips, as if he were suppressing a smile, he was fully aware that I was standing there with my mouth open.

Well, I wasn't going to take whatever bait he was offering me. I wondered briefly what Mingma thought he knew about me, from our brief encounter on Raksha. I headed toward the spring, Ragtooth trailing behind. Once I reached it, I walked along its bank until I was out of sight of the tent. I settled on the ground, crossing my legs.

The spring was like others we had passed—the water was hot, almost scalding, and misted in the chill air. The moisture settled on my cheeks, warming them. The mist undulated over the water like wisps of cloud.

Ragtooth huffed at the water, clearly unimpressed. I let the dragon loose, and it skimmed over the pool, delighting in the feeling of warm mist against its scales. Its light ghosted off the surface.

I drew a deep breath. "Azar-at?" I said quietly.

Yes, Kamzin.

The fire demon stepped forward, as if it had been behind me all along. The creature's eyes glowed in the darkness, while its smokelike form was a smudge, barely visible.

Ragtooth didn't start at Azar-at's presence, as I had—he seemed, for the most part, to ignore the creature, as if Azar-at was beneath his notice. Of course, Ragtooth responded that way to almost everyone.

"I've seen River's thoughts twice now," I said. "I want to see them again. Can you tell me how?"

The fire demon's tail swished over the snow. It seemed to consider.

It is a strange connection, Azar-at said. *Unexpected. I have never seen it before.*

"I'm sure you would have warned me if you had," I muttered.

There is no "how," Kamzin. It will happen again, if you wait.

"That isn't good enough," I said. "I can't afford to wait—I need to know where he is. What he's planning. I need to be a step ahead of him when we reach the Ashes."

The fire demon gazed at me. *I do not control these visions. They are a result, not a deed.*

I was becoming impatient. "But surely you know how they work. How I can—I don't know, turn them on and off?"

I can show you River's mind, Azar-at said. *I can send you into his thoughts, so that they become yours, and you can control the words he speaks, the decisions he makes. I can take his memories, and give them to you, so that it will be as if he has no past, and cannot recognize friend from foe.*

A shiver trailed down my back. "No, that's—that's not what I'm asking. I want to look into River's mind. I want to understand what he's doing. Don't you see?"

The fire demon's tail wagged faster. *You wish to understand River.*

"Like I did before," I said. "Can you tell me how?"

Close your eyes.

I didn't move—or blink. "Do you understand what I'm asking?"

Yes, Kamzin.

"I don't want to take anything from him," I said. "I just want to see through his eyes."

I understand.

Trepidation washed over me. I couldn't shake the feeling that I was talking past Azar-at somehow. But didn't it always feel like that? And wasn't it essential to understand what the witches were up to? My heart thudding, I closed my eyes.

Think of River.

I thought of River. I saw his mismatched eyes, so jarring at first glance, the hint of a smile at the corners. His messy hair, the scattering of freckles across his nose, which in some lights made him look younger than he was, boyish. I couldn't picture River as a boy. It seemed impossible that he hadn't simply stepped fully grown from the shadows, capable of unerring navigation in whiteout conditions and moving like the wind over the most treacherous terrain.

That was the last thought I had before everything dissolved.

I stood in a forest clearing. The trees were blackened, twisted— many almost leafless. They knitted together overhead like a cage, and the air was heavy with smoke that seemed to emanate from the ground. It was dark, so dark.

I knew immediately that something was wrong. This was not like the other visions I had experienced. In those visions, I had *been* River. The connection had been seamless. Now I saw the world from behind River's eyes, but there was a distance. And I was very much myself.

"Esha!" River shouted, and I started. River's voice was different—he was young, possibly six or seven.

I wasn't seeing the present. I was seeing the past.

Part of me began to panic—this wasn't what I wanted. Azar-at had tricked me. Another part of me watched in awed fascination.

River continued walking, pushing through sharp underbrush, shouting his brother's name. His voice was hoarse—how long had he been out here, lost? For clearly he was lost, judging by how often he paused to study the stars through the thicket of branches. Something darted past, something that whispered like a ghost. But River, perhaps accustomed to their presence, didn't look, so I couldn't either. Though I had only been there a few moments, I hated this place. The burned trees were alive, but in a ghoulish, unnatural way.

"Esha!"

It was strange. I saw through River's eyes, but I could only see flashes of his thoughts. River wasn't cold, barefoot as he was, but he was hungry and tired. Esha had brought him here, promising a game—they had walked for hours. Then Esha had hid himself, which had been part of the game, but this, he knew, was not. River stopped to examine the sky again, then readjusted his course. Part of me marveled at it—there were only a few stars in the scrap of sky visible through the branches. Even I couldn't have found my way by them.

Something was moving through the forest, making little effort to conceal itself. A young man stepped out of the trees.

He was tall and broad, with a frowning face and lank hair that hung past his shoulders. He would have been handsome, in a coarse sort of way, but for the fierce glint in his eyes that made me want to take a step back. When he saw River, his expression lightened.

"Thought I'd have to walk all the way to the headwaters before I found you," he said, in a voice that was surprisingly gentle for such an intimidating man. "And what are you doing out here? Don't you know the wolves have returned to this part of the forest?"

"I'm not afraid of them," River replied. Beneath his confidence was a surge of relief. It wasn't relief that Sky had found him—it was relief that someone had been looking. River wasn't used to being noticed, and felt momentarily overwhelmed. And now, he thought happily as he ran to his brother's side, he would have an entire afternoon alone with Sky.

"I caught something," River announced proudly, displaying the mangy crow he had been carrying. Its wings were splayed and hardening—it must have died several hours ago. "You won't have to go hunting today."

"I see." Sky's nose wrinkled slightly. But he added, "Well done. You'll be catching hares and geese in no time."

"I'm faster than them." River's thoughts were full of his brother's praise, and he needed to prove himself worthy of it. "Quieter too. I snuck up behind him and snapped his neck. He didn't see it coming. I'll bet I could sneak up on a wolf, if I tried. I could sneak up on one of the emperor's soldiers. They wouldn't—"

"Don't speak of that." Sky's voice was sharp—it cut through the background murmur of the forest like a knife. "If you see a soldier of the Empire, you will not go near them."

River was startled. He searched for a way to correct his mistake. "I didn't—"

"River." Sky knelt so that he was at River's eye level. "If you see a soldier—or an explorer, or anyone else of the Empire, you will run. Is that clear?"

River nodded, relieved to have been given a way to make things right. He didn't point out that Esha bragged about having once killed a soldier. Esha had led him here, and then abandoned him. Esha had once threatened to kill him for following him and his friends. River would do what Sky wanted. It wasn't even a choice.

The scene changed.

River was still in the forest, crouched on the bank of a lightless stream. He looked down at the water, and I let out a silent gasp at the sight of River's reflection gazing back at me.

At least, I thought it was silent. River glanced up, his brow furrowing. After a moment, he shrugged and returned to the water.

He was older—fourteen or fifteen, perhaps. It wouldn't be long before he joined the emperor's court. Was he thinking about it now? I didn't know. His mind was like a lightless well. I only knew that he was wrestling with something dark.

Shall we discuss the plan, River? a voice said, and I bit back a scream.

Azar-at stepped out from the shadows, as if it had been there all along, and I felt a moment of déjà vu. River didn't turn his head, nor did he speak.

You are doubtful, Azar-at said after a pause. There was a question in the creature's voice that surprised me. I hadn't thought it capable of uncertainty.

River let the silence drag on another moment. When he spoke, his voice was quiet. "I wouldn't have traveled to the farthest reaches of the Nightwood in search of your kind, Azar-at, if I had any doubts."

No doubts. The fire demon's tail wagged. Looking at Azar-at was eerie. I had just been speaking to the creature on the shore of a northern spring. *Fear, then. Fear is strong. I am stronger.*

"No." River launched a pebble into the water, shattering his reflection.

Anger. You are angry.

"Is this part of our contract?" River said. "You will badger me until I confess my every thought? I don't recall that clause."

Azar-at cocked its head. *Definitely anger.*

River let out a short laugh. His mood lightened so abruptly I felt dizzy. "I'm beginning to suspect you have a sense of humor, you strange little monster. That's something, I suppose."

He watched the ripples settle on the water. "Do you really want to know what I was thinking?"

Yes, River.

He tossed another pebble. "I don't want to leave."

Why? The fire demon's usually remote tone held an unexpected note of curiosity.

River stood, sliding the remaining pebbles from one hand to the other. "Because I'm not sure what will happen to them without me."

You will make things right, the creature said. *You will help family.*

River's eyes drifted away from Azar-at. Curious, I tried to peer into his thoughts, but they were too unsettled; it was like trying to pick out a face in a crowd viewed through dirty glass. I wondered if even he could make sense of them.

Something crashed in the distance. River was on his feet before the first echo died, scanning the forest. Then he plunged into the trees.

Branches slapped his face. River was light on his feet and navigated the twisted woods as skilfully as a deer, seeming to intuit the position of rocks and roots a step in advance. He was soon bursting into a clearing, which was cast in a lurid glow.

A woman crouched in the center of the clearing. She looked up, revealing a thin face framed by graying hair. Her eyes were River's eyes—one dark, one light, and her skin was heavily freckled. Even if I hadn't read it in River's thoughts, I would have known she was his mother.

Around her, the forest was burning. It wasn't witch fire, but it burned just as fiercely—as River watched, a branch broke from a tree and fell to the ground in an explosion of sparks. Several struck his mother, singeing her hair. Yet she made no move to shield herself. Instead, to my astonishment, she rolled onto her side and lay motionless among the sparks and blown embers.

River darted forward, dodging another branch. The woman looked at him, and in her eyes there was no recognition whatsoever. River dragged her to her feet and swept her up in his arms. She was taller than him, but she weighed as much as a child, being little more than skin and bone.

"Azar-at," River said, lifting his hand. Obligingly, the fire leaped out of the way, forming a path to safety. River plunged along it, a stray spark striking his temple. I felt it as clearly as if it had struck my own face, heat sharp as a needle. It was soon joined by a familiar pain, difficult to locate but no less sharp, as Azar-at took what it was owed—

I let out a cry. It was not my face that had been burned, it was my hand. I had fallen forward, my palm plunging into the heated water of the spring. I leaped back, burying my hand in the snow.

My head spun. I touched my face, my hair. I was myself again. River was gone—the reflection gazing back at me was my own.

"What was that?" I searched for Azar-at, and found it, unsurprisingly, sitting behind me, slightly too close. My heart was thudding. "You showed me River's *memories?*"

I gave you what you asked for, Kamzin. The creature's voice was unperturbed. *As I always do.*

"No, I—" I sagged forward as the pain overwhelmed me, a sharp spear. It was the second time I had felt it in as many moments—the first through River's eyes; the second through my own. For a moment, I could almost see the invisible thread connecting us—a thread made of fire and pain.

There is much more, Azar-at said. *Would you like to see? I could*

156

show you River's time as Royal Explorer, his triumphs and failures.

There was a different note in the creature's voice, an eagerness I had never heard before. It reminded me of how Azar-at had spoken of River before. As if it regretted his leaving. Almost as if it *missed* him.

"Azar-at," I said slowly, "do you—do you wish you were still with River?"

Its tail stopped wagging. There was an odd sort of pause.

River was different from the others, it said finally. *He did not wither and fade as they did. Eventually, they came to curse me. Then they forgot who I was.*

I was shivering. "And River never did."

River left, Azar-at said.

The creature's eyes burned, as unreadable as ever. It was madness, I told myself, to imagine that there was anything like sorrow there. To see Azar-at as some sort of dog abandoned by its owner. It might look like a wolf, but it was anything but. It was ancient, its power vast as the darkness beyond a campfire. The creature's tail was wagging again.

Ragtooth sinuously interposed himself between me and Azar-at, who was still too close. He snapped at Azar-at's leg. To my astonishment, the fire demon fell back a step. Ragtooth gave a satisfied growl and placed a paw upon my knee.

I can show you more, Kamzin, the fire demon said.

"That isn't what I want," I said. "And you know it." My anger flared and then faded, leaving behind that eerie, cold feeling. My thoughts were full of what I had just seen—it was too much.

River's family, the Nightwood. How his mother had looked at him, as if in that moment she had been unable to recognize her youngest son. With her height and uncanny grace, she would have been a fearsome person to encounter, in another state of mind. As it was, there had been something childlike about her. Childlike and *broken*.

River had said she had died a year ago. He would have been at the emperor's court, or roaming the wilderness far from the Nightwood. I couldn't imagine what it would be like to lose someone like that. When my mother had died, I had been with her, along with Lusha and Father. To have been far away, unable to say good-bye—

But why was I wondering about any of this? It didn't matter what River felt, then or now. What mattered was learning his plans.

Azar-at had vanished. I looked in all directions, but saw not even a hint of its glowing eyes.

I thought of River perched at the edge of the stream. He might have had regrets about what he was doing, but he hadn't let those regrets interfere with his plans.

I rose. I would load our supplies onto the yak and go over the maps again with Mingma. We had to reach the star first—the Empire would fall if we didn't. But that thought, over the last few days, had grown increasingly tangled up with something else: a desire to beat River, as if we were back in the Aryas, playing a game of Shadow. I didn't fully understand it—this wasn't about me and River. Yet part of me couldn't stop thinking about how satisfying it would be to reach the star first, and be gone before he even knew I was there.

Motioning to Ragtooth, I turned my back on the water and hurried back to camp.

THIRTEEN

Mara

FINDING HIS WAY to Jangsa required neither map nor compass. He simply followed the smoke.

The plume towered before him. Sometimes he was breathing it, depending on the direction of the wind, and his throat burned. Witch fire had a peculiar scent—or perhaps it was not the fire itself, but the materials it burned. Things that had no business burning—soil and rock and waterlogged wood. Mara moved quickly, stopping for only a few hours each night to sleep. As he neared the foothills of Mount Zerza, the single black plume became three, then a dozen. More. Mara clambered to the top of a frost-rimed hill, sweating in the midday sun. There he had his first view of the village.

What remained of it.

He had come to survey the damage and offer assistance on his way to the emperor's court, but Mara guessed there were few left to assist. Before him was a landscape of ash and smoke. He would not have thought there had been a village here, but traces of it lay like a skeleton halfway unearthed. The buildings that dotted the lower slopes of snowcapped Zerza were scorched and roofless. Where once there had been green—grass or crops or the stunted poplars that grew at this altitude—now there was only burned earth. The fires were out, but still the village wept black into the blue purity of the sky.

Mara had never visited Jangsa. Kamzin had described it in almost fantastical terms—a village of old stone huts slowly sinking into the green hillside, where spirits were worshipped obsessively by furtive-eyed villagers. For his part, Mara thought it must have been a lowly place, judging by its size, and no wonder—there could be little industry in an isolated village like this. His father, who had made his fortune in the dye trade, would have thought it a place not even worth marking on a trading route.

The towers of black smoke rising off the ruined village made for such an unearthly sight that Mara's fingers itched for his charcoal and parchment. He paused to jot down a few observations, along with a cursory sketch he would tidy later.

"You there," he said to the first villager he saw, a stocky man with an ash-smeared face dragging a cart of blankets. "I've come on an expedition from the Three Cities. The emperor will want a full report of this attack. I wish to speak with your elder—does he live?"

The man stared at him. He seemed to put his full effort into the action, lowering the cart to the ground and facing Mara.

"I'm sorry for your losses," Mara said, "but I have little time."

The man continued to stare. After a long, uncomfortable moment, he ducked into one of the scorched dwellings. Two voices murmured within.

Mara waited, but the man didn't reappear. The thought of entering that collapsing black ruin, which loomed jaggedly like a monster's maw, put him ill at ease, so he walked on. As he passed the man's cart, he realized it wasn't loaded with a jumble of blankets—beneath a sheet of rough cloth was the still body of a woman.

Mara's hand went to the talismans in his pocket. His magical skills were passable—better than most, in his estimation—but he was out of practice. His thoughts turned to the witches who had abducted him in the Amarin Valley, their feral strength and grace. It was the memory that River had taken from him two years ago, after River had rescued him and revealed his own identity in the process. For two years, Mara had been enspelled, part of his memory suppressed by River.

River. Mara's hand tightened around the talismans. He had always resented River. How could he not resent someone who, at the age of fifteen, had strolled into the emperor's court and stolen the title of Royal Explorer, which should have been Mara's? It was ludicrous how everyone at court had swooned over his every exploit. Mara had never trusted River, not even when he saved Mara's life, as he had done on several occasions. In fact, looking back, Mara seemed to recall that he had once or twice wondered if River had some connection to the witches. Perhaps he had even confronted River about it, and River had removed those memories too.

One thing was certain: he would enjoy revealing River's identity to the emperor. He imagined doing it in front of the entire court, their faces paling as they realized the depth of their favorite's betrayal.

Mara entered a square of stone houses that seemed to have escaped the inferno. Two men and a girl of perhaps thirteen were lifting another body off a cart and placing it in a row with several others. The cloth that covered it slipped, revealing an arm blistered with burns.

Mara cast a cool look over the bodies. "I am sorry to interrupt your rites," he said, keeping his voice calm but authoritative, "but I'm looking for your Elder. I was sent from the emperor's court."

"Really?" the girl said in what might have been a dry tone—Mara couldn't read her. None of the others smiled. The girl stood, absently wiping bloody hands on her dress. "We've received more travelers from the Empire in a month than we normally do in a year. Are you from Kamzin's expedition?"

Mara paused, surprised. "I— In a sense. She is—"

"This way." The girl strode past him without a backward glance, stepping calmly over a body.

Mara followed her up a narrow lane, where there were several more intact dwellings. The witches had destroyed most, not all, of the village. He felt a stab of foreboding. If they had attacked Jangsa in revenge, they would have taken care to ensure that nothing—and no one—survived. No, their aim had been to burn the village quickly, sending smoke billowing into the sky like a beacon—a beacon to draw the Empire's eye.

The elder was seated in a bed over which a healer leaned, murmuring. He was a stout man with a round face within which his small, dark eyes seemed almost lost. When he saw Mara, he dismissed the healer. He motioned the girl forward, and she whispered something in his ear. She bowed herself out.

"Welcome, explorer," the elder said. "Atyu tells me you are with Kamzin's expedition. Yet I don't remember your face."

"We traveled to Raksha in separate parties," Mara said, still wondering at the appellation. It had been River Shara's expedition that had stopped here—Kamzin had merely been his guide.

"I see." The elder did not seem to require additional clarification. He regarded Mara for a long moment, taking in his ink-stained hands, his tahrskin *chuba*—worn by all the emperor's explorers. Mara regarded him in turn. He didn't see any obvious sign of injury. Then the man shifted position beneath his blanket, and Mara saw that his hands and arms were horribly burned. The skin was coated in a resinous salve that would numb the pain and prevent further damage, but the man would bear disfiguring scars for the rest of his life.

The elder noted Mara's gaze. "There was a child trapped by one of the fires. I managed to extract her, though her parents were not so lucky. Is your friend recovered? The one caught in the storm."

Mara's thoughts darkened at the mention of Norbu. He had known the man for years—traveled with him, respected his vast knowledge of shamanic lore. He knew his wife too, a noblewoman of ancient lineage with a ready smile. Sarven.

The elder gave a heavy sigh. "I'm sorry. Our healer did her best. But I see we were too late."

"Yes." Mara doubted it had been too late—no doubt the healers of this isolated place had inferior skills. "I'm afraid I must share something with you. The witches have their powers back because of one man—the Royal Explorer. You gave him shelter here."

The elder looked puzzled. "Ah," he said, after a pause. "You mean the young prince? Yes, I'm not surprised he was responsible for this. He takes after his mother. I saw that the moment we met."

Mara stared at him.

"You knew what he was," he breathed. "How?"

The elder gave a quiet laugh. "I used my eyes."

Mara thought about the stories he'd heard of Jangsa, the mysterious village at the edge of the Nightwood that refused to pay tribute to the emperor. It was said that many of the villagers had witch blood, and that some of their shamans could work spells without talismans. Mara looked into the man's small black eyes and shivered.

"Why did you invite him into your village?" he said. "Because of him, Jangsa has been destroyed."

"Jangsa will never be destroyed," the man said in the patient voice one might use when teaching a child. "We will rebuild, as we have done before. You southerners don't understand—you thought the war between the witches and the Empire was over. You grew too comfortable in your polished city guarded by the emperor's useless shamans and well-fed soldiers. You came to regard the witches as little more than myths, monsters you hear about in fireside stories. In Jangsa, we know better."

Mara felt uncomfortable beneath the elder's gaze. It was as if the man were not merely looking at him, but *inside* him.

"Your people should leave this place and seek protection from the Empire," he said. "Are you not afraid the witches will return?"

"Oh, no," the man said. "They have what they came for."

Mara waited, but the elder didn't continue. The healer entered and busied herself with a jar of salve. Mara, relieved to have an excuse to leave, bowed himself out.

"I invited him in because that is what a host does," the elder said. Mara turned, at the edge of the doorway. "There are some laws older than any conflict. Hospitality. Justice." He paused. "Your emperor stole something that didn't belong to him. Something he didn't understand. Now we will all feel the consequences of his arrogance."

The elder said it mildly, as if remarking on the weather. The healer handed him a glass of some dark liquid, and he smiled at her, his gaze leaving Mara at last. Shaken, the chronicler left the room.

Mara walked a short distance, finally pausing beside a shrine that leaned into a patch of singed hillside. One of the music bowls hummed gently in the wind.

Mara thought of the letter from Azmiri. The attack in the Southern Aryas, the emperor sending the Ninth Army to investigate. The Ninth Army was usually stationed close to the Three Cities.

You came to regard the witches as little more than myths, the elder had said. He had been right. Mara doubted that the emperor viewed the witches as creatures who could think and plan. Intelligent enough to lure his armies away, one by one, and leave his capital defenseless.

Mara's fists tightened. It was up to him. He had to warn the emperor—not just of River's betrayal, but of the witches' plot. The Empire's security rested on his shoulders. Mara turned, intending to seek out fresh provisions. He was unsurprised to see one of the Elder's attendants hurrying down the hill toward him.

"He says to give this to Kamzin's young friend," the attendant said without preamble, shoving something into Mara's hand. Then he kept walking, clearly on some business elsewhere in the village.

Mara stared. It was a talisman—a small bronze bell like the *kinnika*, engraved with an intricate pattern of flowing lines that reminded Mara of water. "Wait," he called. "What is this?"

"A talisman," the man replied, as if he genuinely believed Mara to need this clarification. "For the dark fire. It's how we put it out."

"Don't you need it?"

"We have several. They're very old. Be careful with it—Elder expects it to be returned one day."

Mara shook the bell. It made no sound—none that he could hear. Giving Mara a patient look, the man took the bell. When he shook it, it sang out with a clear, high tone. He handed it back to Mara. The bell, vibrating with its own echoes, stilled instantly against his skin.

"It responds to blood," the man said. "It won't obey you. It's for the boy—should he and Kamzin have need of it."

This made little sense—how did Tem's blood have any connection to the people of Jangsa? Mara tucked the bell into his pack, reddening at the realization that he was being asked to deliver a gift to a yak herder from a village most people in the Three Cities hadn't even heard of.

"Very well," he said. "If I survive the journey back to the emperor's court, I will do my best to see that Tem gets it. There are no guarantees. The terrain between here and the Three Cities is treacherous."

The man gave him a blank look. "No guarantees," he agreed politely. "The elder thinks it likely you will perish in Winding Pass. He hopes this is not the case, and wishes you luck on your journey." Then, with the air of someone doing something he has never done before, but knows is expected, he clapped Mara on the shoulder and strode away.

FOURTEEN

I STABBED MY ax into the ice, reaching back with my other hand to help Tem up the slope. The narrow ridge fell away on either side, two clean sheets of snow that faded into shadowed valleys punctured by spurs of rock. It was a world of sharp peaks, deep caverns, and unnaturally long nights.

We had reached the Ashes.

After leaving our camp between the boulders, we had hiked all day—with Mingma's unerring directions, we had quickly located the shortcut through the foothills. The valley had been blanketed with a dense snowpack that covered any treacherous scree, and we made rapid progress, despite our exhaustion. I felt, at times, like I was sleepwalking.

The unnamed peak we scaled jabbed out of the earth like a fang. Lusha was certain—she said she was certain—that the star had fallen here. But the moon was behind the mountains, and the shadows were thick.

"Kamzin!"

I looked up. Lusha perched on a fluted shelf tucked into the mountainside, only visible by the cobalt light of the dragon on her shoulder. We each had one, though mine kept trying to burrow into my *chuba*, rendering its light useless.

I gritted my teeth and urged my feet to move. It took an age to climb that short slope, as I had to pause to help Tem every few steps. He stopped to cough into his hood, and I gripped his shoulder until the fit subsided, afraid he would pitch over the side.

When we finally made it to the shelf, Lusha and Mingma had already set up the tent.

"I'll keep watch," the ghost said, and promptly disappeared. For a moment, I simply stared at the place where he had been. I didn't think I would ever get used to him doing that. I supposed I should have been grateful for Mingma's presence—without him, it would have been impossible to reach our destination so quickly, giving us a chance at beating the witches to the star—but I still felt uneasy around him.

Tem and I dove inside, and Lusha handed us a flask of water and some dried yak meat. We wouldn't be making a fire tonight— the wind whipped violently over the mountainside, and it would be impossible to get anything burning. The walls of our tent flapped so loudly I had to shout into Tem's ear.

We should have been on top of the star right now, if Lusha's calculations were correct. But either Lusha's calculations weren't correct, or we had missed it in the darkness. Or, worse, the star had already returned to the sky.

Lusha's head was bent over one of her star charts. Her dragon rested on her lap.

I raised my hood, trying unsuccessfully to block out the noise. I had no idea how Lusha could concentrate through that racket, but she gave no sign of being troubled by it. Tem said something in her ear, and she shook her head once, without taking her eyes from the chart.

The frown between Lusha's eyes had deepened since yesterday. She had barely spoken in hours. I could tell that Tem was nervous and confused by her behavior. But I understood.

Lusha was doubting herself.

It was rare, but I'd witnessed it before—when Father fell ill three winters ago; when torrential rains hit Azmiri, drowning most of the crops. Each time, she had confined herself to the observatory, barely speaking to anyone, trying to glean the way forward from the stars.

Still, her obsessiveness now went beyond anything I recognized. Despite our grueling journey, Lusha insisted on staying up late into the night, poring over the charts and maps, checking and rechecking her calculations. The shadows under her eyes were so dark they looked like bruises. If anyone interrupted her with a question, she bit their head off—particularly if the interrupter was me. Her iciness toward me had not thawed—if anything, it had deepened.

I hunched into my *chuba*, frustrated. We needed to find the star soon—every hour we delayed was an hour that brought the witches closer to finding it themselves. Tem seemed occupied with thoughts of his own, absently running his thumb over the *kinnika*. I looked instinctively for Ragtooth, but he had vanished. I didn't normally worry about Ragtooth's whereabouts, but given the weather, it made me uneasy.

It was a bleak night. Despite my exhaustion, I could only doze, starting awake during the loudest gusts. My dreams were flashes haunted by *fiangul*. Judging by the absence of Tem's snores, he was having the same difficulties I was. I distracted myself by examining the wear on my boots, running my hands over them in the darkness. In a place like this, even the smallest thing could make the difference between survival and death. The left heel was loosening, which would affect my balance in a minute but potentially dangerous way. I focused my thoughts, summoning Azar-at's power, and the flaw vanished.

I let out a quiet gasp. The pain this time had felt like a paper cut—sharp and stinging. I felt a wave of unease—it had never felt like that.

About an hour before dawn, the winds died. I rose and left the tent.

Even with the cold stinging my face, I felt calmer outside—more at home among the elements than I had in the relative comfort of the tent. The sky was clear, the stars blazing. I lit a fire in a crevice in the rock, using only a few small pieces of wood. Tem had mastered a spell to make wood burn more slowly—the fire licked at it just as hungrily, but each piece took hours to turn to ash. I settled on the snow. We were partly protected here, tucked into an amphitheater in the mountainside.

Mingma sat across from me, making me jump a foot in the air. He had a habit of doing that, merely appearing in your field of view with none of the customary warnings, such as footsteps or rustling clothes. "Sorry," he said.

I tried to calm my breathing. "Where do you go, when you disappear like that?"

"Somewhere . . . else," he said. "I can't always be with you. It's too tiring. But I try not to stay away for long."

"Oh." I hadn't realized that the expedition had been difficult for Mingma too. He hadn't spoken one word of complaint.

"This was always my favorite time," he said. "The moment before dawn."

I gazed at the eastern horizon. A star clung to it, twinkling defiantly against the gathering light. "I always preferred the opposite. Just after sunset, when everything is violet and black, and the stars are just starting to show."

He smiled. He was handsome when he smiled—it lightened the brooding set of his eyebrows and gave his eyes a teasing light. "That's not surprising."

"Why?"

"Night is when wild animals prowl the shadows," he said. "When criminals go about their work, and dark creatures stir. Night is danger. That suits you."

I shivered. I heard the Elder of Jangsa's voice in my mind again—he had said something similar. It felt like a very long time ago now—a different time. Or had *I* been different? I added another scrap of wood to the fire, wondering absently if Mingma could feel its warmth.

"I don't think it does," I said. "I'm just as frightened as anyone else. If we can't find the star before the witches do, my village could be destroyed. I don't relish the thought of the people I love being in danger."

"I'm not saying you do. But it does seem that, wherever danger happens to be, you're always there with it." He turned back to the horizon. "I led three expeditions to these lands. *The twilight mountains*, they're called. I call them a great bother. Never could work out a way through. That's the most frustrating thing an explorer can encounter."

"What?"

He looked at me. "Walls."

I tugged absently at a pebble poking up through the snow. "I used to think that. I used to think that if I could just get away from Azmiri, if the emperor would hire me as an explorer, I would be happy. That it would be all I needed. But I don't believe that anymore."

"Why?"

I swallowed. I saw Aimo's face. Norbu's. Dargye's. I felt the pain of River's betrayal. I had helped the witches achieve their goal, and Azmiri could be destroyed because of it.

"Because it's all gone wrong," I said. "All I've found out here is death."

"Well, death is a given," Mingma said in a conversational tone.

"It's everywhere, in so many varieties. My mother was killed on a hunting expedition—a friend put an arrow in her back while aiming for a pheasant. Unfortunate business. My father used to say that if she had stayed home that day, she would still be alive. But my mother loved hunting. Choosing to lock yourself up in a life that doesn't suit you is its own sort of death, wouldn't you say?"

I tossed the pebble away. "But what if the choices you make hurt others?"

Mingma shook his head. He stretched his hands out to the flames, answering my earlier, unspoken question. "I asked myself the same thing. Up on that mountain. I led fourteen men and women to Raksha, didn't I?"

I gazed at him. I couldn't imagine what it must have been like, trapped in a forsaken place like that, along with all those he'd led to their deaths. It was too ghastly to consider—and yet it had been Mingma's lot for fifty years.

"What answer did you find?" I asked.

"I stopped looking. Some truths aren't meant to be found, even by the most determined explorers. I know one thing, though—your coming to Raksha freed me and my companions. Perhaps terrible things will result from the choices you made—perhaps good. You can't know for certain before all's said and settled. And you certainly can't blame yourself for the paths that branch off from the one you've beaten, even if they lead others to dark places."

I drew my legs up, hooking my arms around them. Even now,

after all that had happened, I felt a familiar shiver of anticipation as I gazed at the unexplored landscape stretched out before me.

I wished that I believed what Mingma was saying. But I didn't know if I could.

A thought occurred, and I laughed, surprising myself. "What?" Mingma said.

"I never thought I'd be sitting here with you, having this conversation."

He smiled. The wind tossed a lock of hair onto his forehead, and he brushed it back. "Nor did I. When I set out for Raksha, I expected to be back within a month or two, with a few stories to tell. Now I'm heading for the Ash Mountains with some strange girl years after I should have died in my bed, my head full of gray hairs."

I glared at him, but the corner of my mouth twitched. "I'm not strange."

"I didn't say it was a bad thing."

I laughed again. I felt oddly refreshed, even after a night of little sleep. It was odd—Mingma had tried to kill me. But the Mingma I had met in the caverns of Raksha seemed an entirely different person—somehow, I knew this was the same Mingma he had been in life, not the bitter creature he had become.

My eyes drifted. Mingma was right about one thing: I had chosen the path I was on. Everything that I had done had been my choice. Just because I had chosen badly once, given my trust to someone who didn't deserve it, didn't mean it always had to be so.

"Why do you want to be an explorer?" Mingma said.

I frowned. It was like asking why the sky was blue.

Mingma smiled at my expression. "I felt the same way once. I grew up in a small village, and I wanted adventure. But there's more to being an explorer than adventure."

"Like what?"

"One day, your story will be written in the stars," he said. "It's up to you to choose what they'll say. You have the power to reshape the world—for better or for worse."

I was quiet. I remembered my mother, hugging me the night before she left on an expedition. She had pointed to the stars winking in the sky and told me that her story was already being written there, and that one day we could look up and read it together. I had been fascinated. I knew that the lives of famous heroes and leaders were written in the stars, and I had felt proud that one day, my mother would join them.

The best explorers make the night a little brighter, she had said. *Not just because they do great things, but because they do good things.*

I watched the bright tapestry wheel slowly across the sky. My mother had died before she had a chance to make her mark on the world. Now here I was, following in her footsteps. But would the world be brighter because of what I had done, or darker?

"You said before that you had traveled with them," I said, my voice quiet. "Witches."

"Once." Mingma's gaze grew distant. "She offered to guide me through Winding Pass—on a whim, I think. Though I had just saved her life."

I waited for him to continue, but he only smiled at me. "That's a long story. Perhaps for another time. But I had dealings with them before that. I mapped the southern half of the Nightwood, after all."

"Dealings," I repeated. "In the stories we're told in Azmiri, the only 'dealings' you can have with a witch don't end pleasantly."

"And who are the storytellers? People who spend their entire lives in one place, never daring to see what lies beyond their borders. You should know better, by now, than to trust such stories."

"Then what are you saying?" I felt my anger rise. "That the witches are innocent? They once tried to burn my village to the ground."

"What I'm saying is that I've had dealings with them," he said calmly, as if failing to notice my anger. "Some helped me. Most tried to kill me. Make of that what you will."

I bit my lip. "So what's your opinion? The stories say they're evil, every one."

"Well, I don't find evil to be a very useful word. It's true they don't have much of a conscience, on the whole. They think nothing of lying or cheating—or killing—to get what they want. Some are worse than others, in that respect. Those that have spent time among humans often seem to possess a rudimentary understanding of right and wrong, though it's not what you could properly call a conscience, being more learned than instinctive. But they can also be exceedingly loyal to those they care about. And fairness is important to them."

"Fairness?" I said, surprised.

"Their definition of fairness tends to vary," he added. "But if you do them a good turn, they'll return the favor." His gaze grew distant again. "The opposite is also true."

I hadn't known anyone to speak this way about witches—they were unfeeling and without mercy, in the stories. Darkness in human form. Something inside me shifted ever so slightly as I considered Mingma's words. "Can they feel love?"

Mingma was silent. When I glanced up, he was giving me a sympathetic look I wanted no part of.

"I think so," he said. "In their way."

My thoughts were a tangle. I needed to move, to leave the heat of the fire, which now felt suffocating. And I was suddenly very aware of the darkness, and the thought of the witches prowling the mountains, drawing ever nearer to the star. I stood. "I'm going to look around—we don't have any time to waste. Can you keep watch here?"

Mingma nodded. He leaned back, looking for all the world as if he were relaxing on a shaded bench in the emperor's gardens, not sheltered on a precarious slope high in the sky.

I moved cautiously over the uneven ground, glancing up at the sky to orient myself. Few constellations were familiar here, though I found one, the ancient hero Khana-rok, her bow drawn to slay the ice demon. I followed the direction of the bow, which always pointed west.

I didn't know what to make of what Mingma had told me. I had thought—foolishly, it turned out—that River had been the only witch to have any contact with the Empire. Were there other explorers besides Mingma who had dealt with them? Who had been shown something other than cruelty? I thought of the way Mingma's gaze had clouded as he spoke of the witch who had guided him. Something in his face, a trace of longing, had stopped me from questioning him about her.

I caught a flash of movement out of the corner of my eye, the flicker of glowing eyes, but when I turned, there was nothing there. I wondered, not for the first time, if Azar-at would be able to locate the star. I suspected so—the creature's powers weren't constrained by any limits that I could see.

Azar-at hadn't shown itself since our encounter by the lake. At first I had appreciated this, but now I found myself wishing I knew precisely where the creature was. The notion that I might turn my head at any moment and find its ember eyes fixed on me produced a faint but constant dread.

My thoughts drifted. Now that we had reached the Ashes, the temptation to use Azar-at's magic had been strong. I knew that it could lead me to the star—but I also knew that it would be big magic, bigger than warming my hands or repairing a tear in my *chuba*.

And yet.

I had only to put my will behind the thought, and Azar-at

could lift the star from whatever valley or snowbank concealed it, and place it in my hand. I could tell the others I had stumbled upon it. Why wouldn't they believe me?

But would Azar-at even give me what I wanted? I thought of the jarring visions of River's memories. But if I phrased it clearly enough, and left no room for interpretation—

Snow crunched behind me. Tem staggered into view, clutching his ax in one hand and a sleepy-looking dragon in the other.

"Tem, what are you doing?" I grabbed his arm as soon as he was in reach—the ground wasn't stable.

"Pairs, remember?" He frowned. "You're not going off on your own, are you?"

"I thought I'd have a look beyond that ridge."

"I'll come along," Tem said. He lifted the *kinnika* by way of explanation.

I refrained from pointing out that Tem was likelier to need magic to save himself than me. By coming along, he was giving me an additional variable to worry about. The thought surprised me, and brought about a twinge of guilt. I nodded, and we set off.

"Are you sure you should be using those so often?" I said, gesturing to the *kinnika*. "Remember what happened last time. You wore yourself out."

"I'm fine," Tem said.

I gave him an assessing look. His face was pale, but he was clearly in better shape than he had been on Raksha—and he had used his magic more often, on the journey to the Ashes. "The magic doesn't seem to tire you the way it used to."

"No."

"What do you think that means?"

Tem gave a weary shrug. I could tell from his expression that it was a question he had asked himself, likely more than once.

Once we made it to the ridge, the wind dropped. I tapped my ax against the ice, considering. The ridge was almost sheer, but I knew I could climb it easily, and hopefully find a vantage point. I examined the jagged silhouette of the mountain. If Lusha's calculations were off even slightly, we could be a great distance from the star.

"Don't move while I'm gone," I warned. The snow beneath our feet was solid ice.

Tem nodded. I readied my ax and began to climb. As I went higher, the wind quieted to a whisper. I glanced down at Tem, who had his head bent, murmuring to the *kinnika*.

It didn't take me long to reach the top—without Tem to worry about, I moved as easily as a shadow. Treading carefully, I moved to the lip of the ridge, hoping against hope that I would see a sign—any sign—of the star.

My heart sank.

The moon peeked out from behind one of the neighboring mountains, providing enough light for my starved eyes to see clearly. The mountain descended steeply beyond where I stood in a series of cliffs and buttresses, all the way to the basin of the glacier far below. Another mountain reared up to the north, separated by a narrow col, but it was in silhouette, dark and unknowable. What

I could see was empty. A vast series of snowy slopes, unmarked and unblemished.

I took out the unusual pocket-sized telescope I had rescued yesterday from Ragtooth's jaws. It was expensive-looking, and emblazoned with the emperor's symbol—I could only assume that the fox had stolen it from Mara's pack, as I had never seen it before. I held it to my eye, sweeping the landscape.

A cry pierced the night.

Instantly, I was running—back the way I'd come, abandoning caution. My heart stopped as I saw that the narrow ledge where I'd left Tem was empty. Then I spotted the tip of an ice ax wedged into the snow. Tem had slipped, but somehow managed to swing the ax into the ledge.

I didn't think. I just leaped.

The drop was at least thirty feet, but I managed to slide half the way in a breathless glissade and end the descent in a crouch, not a sprawl.

"Tem!" I cried. Below me, he looked up, his face the color of the snow. With one hand, he clutched at his ax; with the other, he fumbled desperately at the *kinnika*.

"Kamzin—" His hand slipped, and he was falling.

I did the only thing that made sense. I dove forward, driving my ax with all my strength through the fabric of Tem's *chuba*, anchoring him to the mountainside. Unfortunately, I also drove it through a piece of his arm.

Tem shouted. He reached for the blade, trying instinctively to lift his weight off it. I had his ax in my hand now, and managed to anchor myself to the ice while I pulled him back onto the ledge. We collapsed against the mountain, breathing hard.

"Sorry," I murmured, examining his wound. Fortunately, it was only a deep scratch.

"It's all right." He pressed his hand to his arm, wincing. Awe flickered in his eyes. "You're fast, Kamzin. I didn't even get through half an incantation in the time it took you to reach me."

"Magic's too slow for some things. Maybe that's why I never had any patience with it."

He let out the ghost of a laugh, his eyes drifting shut. We leaned against each other. One of the *kinnika* whispered in the wind, and Tem absently stilled it with his hand. I frowned at the talismans. I hadn't been joking—magic often *was* too slow, in a place like this, where the line between life and death was as thin as a hair. I remembered how River had nearly fallen from the ice wall on Raksha—River, who had more power than any of us. But incantations and spells were useless when death came for you faster than you could think. Only instinct could save you then.

"I don't know what I'm doing here," Tem said.

"Here?" It took me a moment to realize that he didn't just mean the mountain. "Why?"

He drew a breath that caught, making him cough, and gave me a weary smile. "Have you ever seen someone more poorly suited to an expedition like this?"

I felt another stab of guilt—Tem was echoing my earlier thoughts. "That's ridiculous," I said in a cajoling voice. As if I could cajole him as I had when we were little and I wanted him to join in one of my ill-planned adventures—hunting for spotted pheasants in Bengarek Forest, or a race to the highest ridge of Mount Biru. "Tem. Our firewood would be gone by now if it weren't for you. Lusha would never have found the map she misplaced at our last camp, and Mara would have lost his ear to frostbite."

"Everything you just described could be accomplished by a halfway competent shaman," Tem said.

"If you're going to pretend you're only a halfway competent shaman, I don't know what to say to you," I snapped.

Tem was quiet. He leaned his head back against the ice.

"Would you rather be back in Azmiri?" I said. "Helping your father with the herds?"

Though spoken without rancor, the words themselves held a sharpness that I hadn't intended. Tem flinched. I thought of what he had said about the Three Cities, and the Trials, and felt a wave of guilt.

"No," he said. There was a weariness in his voice that matched his expression.

"You've forgotten the *fiangul*," I added quickly, recognizing that I had gone wrong. "You saved our lives twice. Could a halfway competent shaman have done that?"

"Maybe not." He gave me another smile, but it felt false, as if he was agreeing for the sake of ending the argument.

"I need you," I said, my voice quiet. "That's why you're here."

"Do you? Sometimes I get the impression that you don't need anyone."

His tone wasn't angry, but it held an odd mixture of admiration and sadness that was somehow worse.

"You're wrong," I said. "You only think that because . . ." My voice trailed off. Because why? Because Tem didn't understand me? Tem had always understood me. And yet it felt true. A distance had been growing between me and Tem since Raksha—perhaps even since we left Azmiri—and I didn't know how to close it. Sometimes it felt as if Tem was receding beyond a horizon like daylight, even when he sat beside me, warm and close.

Tem was watching me. We were close, our heads together. For a moment, he seemed about to lean toward me—but then he drew away, flushing.

"We don't have to talk about this now." He seemed to force a smile. "What did you see?"

I shook my head. Tem didn't need to ask what I meant—my expression said it clearly enough. Nothing.

Something nagged at me. "Where's the dragon?"

Tem gave a start. "She was asleep on my shoulder when I fell."

In unison, we scrambled to the edge. Far below and to the west, a light gleamed against the slope of the mountain.

No. Not one light—two.

I squinted. One of the lights was pale blue and seemed to be hovering in midair, fluttering back and forth. The other was a tiny gleam. I would have mistaken it for the moon glinting off the snow, but the quality of this light was different. It had an almost yellowish tone that put me in mind of an animal's eyes glowing in the dark. It seemed to rest on a narrow terrace of ice.

"Do you see that?" I said.

"I think so." He stopped. "Wait—could that—"

We stared at each other.

My heart pounded frantically against my ribs. The light pulsed slightly, so faint that it would have been difficult, if not impossible, to see if the brighter light of the dragon hadn't drawn my attention to that precise spot. I watched it for a moment, then turned my attention to the surrounding terrain, mapping every rock and feature in my mind in order to commit them to memory. It was a trick I knew well—if bad weather struck, and I had to navigate my way back through limited visibility, I wouldn't get lost.

I whistled. The dragon, who had been fluttering around the light as if fascinated, began to move toward us.

"We have to tell Lusha," I said, standing so quickly I almost pitched over the side. "We can't reach it from here. We'll have to rappel down the ridge, then climb back up—"

Tem's grip on my arm pulled me back down. "Are you forgetting something?"

"What?"

"Well, if that's the star . . ." Tem swallowed. "Then where's River? I thought he might have found it already."

A chill ran through me. I pictured River leaping from the precipice—how far away had he been? The Ashes stretched over many miles.

I thought back. River had told me once that he had no use for astronomy—that meant that, unlike us, he wouldn't know where to look, even if he was capable of traveling more quickly.

"Lusha led us right to it," I said. I felt triumph stir. River would come to this place and find it empty. All his searching would be for nothing. We would take the star to the Three Cities, and there the emperor's shamans would bind his powers once again.

The dragon reached us. I stuffed her into the hood of Tem's *chuba*, smothering the light. Suddenly it was much too bright.

"From now on, we keep the dragons covered," I said. "We get the star, and we leave. I don't want River to even know we were here."

FIFTEEN

Mara

HE CLAMBERED OFF his sweating horse, wincing as his muscles protested. He hated horses. But when the Elder of Jangsa had offered him one of their few surviving beasts, it had been impossible to refuse. The animal had been of little use to him east of the Aryas, but once he made it through Winding Pass, the terrain opened up, glacial boulders and frost-painted pebbles giving way to grassy meadows. He had traveled straight through Bengarek Forest, finding the old trail created decades ago by the emperor, which was now little maintained but still preferable to scrabbling around in the underbrush. He had ridden hard, pushing his horse to the breaking point. He had no time to waste.

He gazed up at Mount Karranak, its broad summit capped by three massive glaciers. He was well south of Azmiri now, and only a few days' ride from the Three Cities. The soldiers who had greeted him at the outskirts of Lhotang village had been skittish, one nearly running him through with an obsidian dagger when he appeared in their midst. Mara, unaccustomed to disrespect from common soldiers, had given him a verbal thrashing. Their captain had apologized, though Mara was still in an ill humor over the incident. He had not traveled all this way, defying peril these soldiers could barely comprehend, to die in a clumsy accident.

In fact, Mara's journey had been astonishingly uneventful. He had braced himself for an attack in Winding Pass—had even prepared for it, composing a lengthy farewell letter and leaving it in his pack so that if any traveler happened upon his abandoned supplies, they would know his fate. But the weather had remained fair. No storms threatened, supernatural or otherwise. He wondered if the Tem's spell had driven the *fiangul* into hiding, at least temporarily.

The soldiers were impressed by him, though he gave them only hints of what he had been through, wanting to save the full story for the emperor and his court. One of them followed at a respectful distance as they entered the village, sweating a little under Mara's pack. The man kept eyeing Mara's tahrskin *chuba*, which wasn't surprising. The emperor's explorers were venerated by the common people, and welcomed into every village they visited. Mara nodded to two villagers who bowed low upon sighting him. After the unsettling reception he had received at Jangsa, such signs of normalcy were heartening.

Mara's gaze swept the village. Lhotang was a picturesque place, straddling the banks of a roiling river, its stone bridges like stitches crisscrossing the misty rapids. Whitewashed houses and well-maintained spirit shrines dotted the rocky terrain. There were no roads—they were unnecessary; carts and yaks easily traversed the smooth rock. The river's source was a waterfall that thundered down Mount Karranak, looming over the village— sheer, icicled falls alternating with vivid blue pools. But Mara recognized a change in the place that had nothing to do with the presence of so many soldiers. There was an uneasiness in the faces of the usually jovial villagers. Several of the shops Mara passed were shuttered.

"Mara," the General of the Fourth Army said in greeting, bowing his head slightly. He stood at the edge of the village square, conferring with one of his soldiers. Mara bent his neck the same amount. Mara, as one of the emperor's explorers, was equal in rank to any general save the woman who led the First Army.

"I understood you to be in the north, with River Shara," the general continued.

"I wish I had time for pleasantries," Mara said, "but I'm on urgent business for the emperor. What is the news here? This is not the customary deployment for the Fourth."

"No." The general's eyes, heavily lined from decades of squinting against sun and weather, swept over the village. "The emperor recalled us from our campaign against the western barbarians after he received an urgent request from the Elder of Lhotang. It seems there have been sightings of witches."

Mara could hear the man's skepticism in his voice. "When?" he asked, as a chill settled in his chest.

"They come at night, they say." The general paused as his captain came forward to murmur in his ear. She stepped back, clearly waiting for the general's interview with Mara to end. "Some in shadow form. I haven't seen them myself. The Elder's house was swarmed by a flock of birds who pecked at her shutters all night and tore apart her dogs. Half the yaks in the village have gone missing, some found later, in pieces. No human deaths, however." He scratched his side idly, under his armor. "The mountain villages tend toward superstition. Unusual occurrences are often attributed to spirits or witches."

"You must believe it." Mara's voice was firm. "The witches' powers are unbound. I must deliver the news to the emperor."

The general stared at him. "Then you have seen them?"

Mara briefly considered telling this man the whole story, if for no other reason than to witness his amazement. But no—the emperor must hear it from him firsthand.

"I have seen them," he said, though in truth, he had only seen one. "It is as I've said. The spell that contained the witches has broken, and they are preparing an attack on the Empire."

"Then why bother with the villages?" the man demanded. Mara bristled at the doubt in his voice, and tried to remind himself that the man's skepticism was natural—the witches had been a dormant threat for years, now primarily invoked to frighten naughty children. "Why not strike the Three Cities directly?"

Mara gave him a grim look. "Can you not think of a reason? Yours is not the only army to be drawn away from the Three Cities and stationed far away on the outskirts of the Empire. Is it?"

The general's face paled. But he was a soldier well into his sixties, and had seen much, and he only took a moment to master himself. "Then you are saying—"

"Gather your soldiers," Mara said. "Make for the Three Cities without delay."

"I can't. Not without the approval of Emperor Lozong."

Mara bit back his frustration. Of course it was as the man said—the emperor had sent the Fourth Army here, and the general could not simply ignore his orders on the word of one man, even if that man was one of the emperor's explorers. He thought of other villages even more remote than Lhotang, days from the Three Cities even if every soldier traveled on horseback. It took days, weeks even, to move an entire army from place to place. Mara doubted they had that long.

The general was gesturing to several of his soldiers. "I will assign you an escort to the Three Cities. You will have a fresh horse and depart without delay. The Fourth Army will remain here to await the emperor's decision."

Mara nodded, and the general strode away, speaking quickly with his captain.

Mara gazed over the village, its small homes nestled in the chilly embrace of the glacial river. Smoke wound from several chimneys, mingling with the mist off the water. Mara breathed it in—a clean, honest smell, unlike the smoke that had hovered over Jangsa. A knot of villagers stood at the edge of the square, watching him, and he wondered whether they had overheard his conversation. Mara thought of shadows moving in the night, of dogs torn apart by unseen claws.

His mind turned to Lusha, as it often had during his journey south, and the fallen star. Mara didn't doubt Lusha's abilities, but their mission was near impossible. It was his view that the only hope of saving the Empire lay with him—if he could reach the Three Cities in time, and convince the emperor to recall his armies. . . . Now, though, he found himself wondering whether Lusha could succeed, against all odds. For if she didn't, if the witches found the star and gained the power to smash the Three Cities with one blow—

Mara swallowed. River and the other witches had laid a perfect trap, which was now beginning to close. It was possible that their only hope now rested on Lusha's shoulders, and the impossible mission she had undertaken in the Ashes. Shaking his head, Mara strode off, snapping instructions at the soldiers hurrying after him.

SIXTEEN

"YOU'RE SURE ABOUT this?"

"Positive."

"But I don't see anything."

I handed Lusha the coil of rope. "It's there."

She gave me a suspicious look. She'd been giving me suspicious looks since I had shaken her awake that morning, after returning to the tent with news that Tem and I had located the star. Now, after hours of hard climbing and a risky traverse, we stood at the base of an icy crag on a precarious outcropping of rock, gazing up at the ledge I had memorized. I wished that Mingma was with us—the ghost could have reached the ledge in a heartbeat—but he hadn't shown himself since last night.

The light from the star seemed even fainter in the early twilight than it had at dawn, and I wasn't sure if I could see it at all, or if the light on the snow was playing tricks on my eyes. I hid my doubts from Lusha—not that it did any good.

"According to my calculations," she said, as the wind whistled around us, "we're too far west. There's a reason we didn't search this area."

"Lusha." I clasped her arms and spoke slowly. "Your calculations are probably correct. I may have imagined what I saw, and right now, I'm wasting time. I'm good at that. But there's a chance the star is up there. And I find it hard to believe that you wouldn't want to eliminate every possibility."

Tem glanced up from the *kinnika*. "Are you sure you don't want me to come?"

I was sure that I didn't want to worry about Tem while climbing up the icy rock. "Yes. You can keep an eye on us from down here."

"My calculations *are* correct," Lusha said, but she was already tethering us together. "I've gone over them a hundred times."

"Then you must be dying to prove me wrong." Without waiting for a reply, I turned to the crag and began to climb.

I set an easy pace, making sure to keep enough slack in the rope for comfort. The mountainside wasn't perfectly sheer but leaned into a series of terraces, each set farther back from the next.

Lusha climbed well, though more slowly than me—she was overly methodical, in my opinion, thinking through every step three times before making it. And her late-night obsessiveness had left her even more tired than Tem, though she hid it well. I paused on the first shelf until she caught up with me, rising to her feet in one smooth motion, not even a hair out of place. She had ignored the hand I offered her.

"Go slow," she said. "We don't want to frighten it."

"Can a star be frightened?" I kept my tone light, though I felt a shiver. When I had faced River at the summit of Raksha, I had been alone. There had been something appealingly simple about that. Now, with Lusha climbing behind me, and Tem waiting below, there were more variables.

I've never had much use for variables. River's words came back to me, his voice pitched low for the intimate space of the cave. It was as if he was speaking in my ear.

I froze, terrified that the memory would herald another descent into River's mind. But I remained myself.

As I climbed, I tried not to think of what had happened early that morning, after I returned to the tent. Tem and I had fallen onto our blankets, intending to rest only a few moments before planning our route to the star. Something had altered in me since discovering it—I felt tired and faint, as if whatever barrier had been holding me back from sleep before was gone. I slept without meaning to, deeply, waking an hour later with a start, a dream lingering. In it, I had been searching for Azar-at, intending to offer the rest of my soul in exchange for the star. But he was nowhere to be found, no matter where I searched, and I was frustrated and frightened. Somewhere between sleep and waking, I looked up and found a girl leaning over me.

A scream strangled in my throat. The girl was stout and not overly tall, though with the suggestion of strength in the set of her shoulders. Her long hair was loose, framing large eyes and high cheekbones. On her face was a look of confusion, and she reached toward my face with familiar hands—frighteningly familiar. I met her eyes.

The girl was me. I started fully awake, surging upright, convinced someone was truly there. But the tent was empty and still, save for Lusha's quiet breathing.

"How does this work?" I said as Lusha and I came to the second ledge. "Will it try to attack us?"

Lusha paused. She was breathing heavily now, her face red. Lusha didn't redden in blotches as I did—her cheeks flushed a rosy pink that emphasized the luminous dark of her eyes. "Of course not," she said coldly, as if it was obvious. As if anything about what we were doing was obvious. "We have to catch it. Once caught, the star will bend to our will."

"And how will we do that?"

"I'm not sure," she said, after a slight pause. Her tone was stiff, as it always was when she felt backed into a corner.

"Seers are so helpful," I muttered.

Lusha shot me a look, then turned back to the climb. Her hands, I noticed, trembled ever so slightly. Despite her calm demeanor, Lusha was nervous. I should have recognized the signs before—the slight tension in her shoulders, the inward-focused gaze. Lusha disliked situations she couldn't control, things that couldn't be planned or foreseen, and this went beyond that. Yet, in spite of this, she turned her steely gaze back to the rock face, put one hand in front of the other, and kept going.

I thought about Lusha setting out for Raksha to stop River from finding the witches' talisman. She and Mara had snuck away during the night, gathering what they needed for a long journey and attempting to sabotage River's own expedition all within a few short hours. That too had been a journey into the unknown, fraught with danger and the likelihood of failure. Few people, I knew, would have taken it upon themselves to attempt what Lusha had attempted. Yet Lusha hadn't balked, hadn't assumed that the Royal Explorer's dark plans were someone else's responsibility, though she was merely the Elder-in-waiting of a small village with little contact with the royal court. She had seen danger written in the stars, decided that something needed to be done, and then she had done it. Was that an admirable display of courage, or astonishing arrogance?

I gazed at the back of her head as she climbed steadily up the mountain, neither hurrying nor delaying. Her determination had an inexorable quality that put me in mind of a force of nature. I shook my head, shoving away the grudging admiration that stirred inside me. Perhaps for some people, words like "courage" and "arrogance" simply didn't make sense—any more than trying to assign a color to the wind.

We reached the ledge some minutes later, both red-faced and out of breath. Lusha sat for a moment, her legs dangling over the cliff we had just scaled, her head bent over her knees. I forced myself to my feet.

The ledge was narrow—perhaps half a dozen paces at its widest point—and roughly triangular, nestled between two perpendicular planes of the mountainside. I stood slowly, testing the grip of my boots.

"Look," I said, grasping Lusha's arm so firmly she made a small noise of protest.

Behind us, the snow and rock split apart like a sword slash, little furrows on either side. And beyond that was a dark stain.

Lusha moved forward, shaking off my arm. The stain was roughly circular, and revealed itself, on closer inspection, to be a gash in the mountainside. Bits of rubble were strewn about, stark against the snow. Judging by their position, the mountain hadn't merely crumbled here—it had exploded.

I knelt next to Lusha, who seemed to be hesitating. This was no time for caution, in my opinion, so I set my jaw and reached into the gash. I dug out several broken shards of the mountain, which Lusha examined closely, as if they held vital information. I reached inside again, and my fingers closed on something rounded and smooth. But when I drew it out, it was only a gray rock.

I expected Lusha to toss this aside too, but she didn't. She rose to her feet, staring at the bit of rubble as if lost in thought.

"Nothing." I brushed my hands against my *chuba*. "But this is where the star landed."

"So it seems." Her voice was strange.

I looked at the gash in the mountainside, where there was certainly no glittering star, or even a fragment of it. "We must be too late. I don't understand—it was here only a few hours ago." I turned to Lusha, expecting to see my own disappointment magnified in her expression. But her face was pale, blank.

"Lusha?"

She held the rock out to me. "We're not too late."

"What?"

"Take it."

I did, still confused. "I don't—"

"Look at it."

I looked from her to the rock, nonplussed. What I held was a lump of stone about twice the size of my fist. It was no shape in particular, a nonshape, rounded on one side and squarish on the other, with haphazard lumps in between, and its texture was a tangle of smooth planes and rough angles. It was, in short, the most ordinary rock I had ever seen, as cold as the mountain from which it had been drawn, and gray as gray could be, lifeless, dead.

"Be careful," Lusha snapped as I transferred the rock to my other hand. She took it back, holding the thing as if it were a precious gem, and stuffed it into her satchel.

"Um, Lusha—"

"Let's go." She was already turning, already walking away.

With one last glance at the broken part of the mountain, where perhaps a fallen star had lain, I followed. Lusha moved like someone possessed, lowering herself back down the mountain without even waiting to see if I was keeping up—which, given that we were tied together, was inconvenient. I hurried after her, trying to match her pace before she dragged me over the edge on my back. I alternated between terror that Lusha would put a foot wrong and pitch down the slope, and a grim satisfaction at the prospect of her own arrogance being the cause of another broken ankle.

"Slow down," I admonished, as a careless step caused her to lose her footing. I wrapped my hand around the rope and hauled her back against the mountainside just in time.

She gave me a fierce look. "I will not *slow down*. We have to get this to Tem."

I wanted to ask what she expected Tem to do with a lump of rock, but kept quiet. Lusha was already behaving recklessly enough, and I didn't want to distract her further with an argument. We continued in silence, barely any slack in the rope between us. When we reached the bottom of the face, Lusha stumbled. Mingma appeared out of nowhere, steadying her, Tem close behind.

Lusha handed Tem the satchel. "Seal this."

"Seal it?"

"Yes. Cast a spell to contain its power."

"She thinks the rock is going to make a run for it." I leaned against the mountainside, out of breath from the frenzied descent.

Lusha was panting too, and swaying slightly, but that didn't dim the determination in her eyes.

Tem dug the rock out of Lusha's satchel and eyed it curiously. He brushed a hand over its surface, murmuring something—an incantation, or perhaps a question.

"That's it?" Mingma said. His tone changed as Lusha's gaze turned to him. "It's—ah, unexpected."

"It's a joke," I said, no longer constrained by any worry for Lusha's safety. "The star's gone. After all this searching, all this time, we've ended up with nothing. There's no hope of recasting the binding spell now."

"Yes, there is." Lusha's normally cool gaze was fierce. "This is the star. We have to bind it so that it doesn't escape."

Tem glanced up, frowning. "I don't sense anything. I suppose I could try a spell to search for traces of hidden magic."

"Lusha, open your eyes," I said. "What I saw was glowing. That looks like what Aunt Behe uses to grind *yerma*."

"What do you know about this, Kamzin?" she said in that now-familiar icy tone. "I've read the accounts of fallen stars. I can recognize the signs."

"You're seeing what you want to see," I snapped. "If Tem doesn't sense anything—"

"I'd like to have a look at the impact site," Mingma said. "Perhaps some fragment of the star remains."

Tem was turning the rock over in his hands, looking thoughtful. "Maybe if I tried—"

It was all I heard.

The wind sang, the mountain unfurling below me as I rose out of the shadow of the valley. The sky was a patchwork of stars and clouds, but the fading light didn't hinder me, for I knew where I was going. I had seen it, though not with my own eyes.

I wrenched back to myself. The others hadn't noticed—Lusha was opening her mouth to interject something.

"Tem—" I managed, before I was pulled back again.

I let the air currents lift me high above the mountain. They were difficult to make out, at that height—small specks of darkness against the snow. Four figures standing on a ledge, one smaller than the others, unmistakable—

"Kamzin."

I opened my eyes, which I had unwittingly clenched shut. It hadn't made a difference—the vision had been painfully clear. Tem peered back at me.

"Did you see—"

"He's here," I said. My voice sounded strange.

"What?" Lusha's hand went to the ax she had slung from her belt.

The chill wind dug into my bones as I tucked my wings in and dove—

Tem was shaking me. "Kamzin."

"It keeps happening," I said. I held on to Tem's arm as if it could anchor me to myself. Was it because River was close? "I can't—"

Lusha cried out. She pressed me behind her as my focus

sharpened on the sound of rustling feathers, faint against the murmur of the wind. We watched, frozen, as the owl alighted on the snow, wings outstretched as it found purchase, and then in one fluid movement dissolved into River.

SEVENTEEN

HE LEANED AGAINST the mountainside, one hand gripping the rock. He shook his head, blinking, as if to clear his vision.

"What—" His eyes found mine. "What did you do?"

Tem reached for the *kinnika*, which, in his surprise, he had dropped in the snow. But the shadows moved, and suddenly River was there, tossing the *kinnika* aside and shoving Tem hard against the mountain. The bells sang out as they fell into darkness.

Lusha brandished her ax, but River merely gestured, and a violent gust of wind sent her sprawling, limbs akimbo, across the snow.

I fell back before the look in his eyes, certain he was going to toss me into the air as easily as Lusha, but he stopped barely two paces away. For a moment, I was disoriented—I had looked out from behind his eyes, lived his thoughts, and now he was here in front of me. The world seemed to fracture before sliding back into place, subtly changed.

I stared at him—I could count the freckles on his nose. He was both familiar and unfamiliar—his mismatched eyes were the same; his unruly hair, which had an echo in the owl's ragged feathers. But the powerful impression he gave off now, of being cut from the night, or perhaps the cold, unfathomable sky, was new and frightening. I could almost see the magic coiling through the air.

Looking past this, though, I could see that there were smudges under his eyes, and the line of his jaw seemed sharper, as if he hadn't rested in days. He still smelled the same—a stark, clean smell like the wildflowers that grew above the snow line in Azmiri, mixed with something close to campfire smoke. It wasn't a *human* smell, and now I knew why.

River's gaze hadn't left my face—it roved from eyes to mouth to chin and back again, as if he was trying to locate something he'd lost.

"What," he repeated, "did you do? You cast a spell, didn't you? Something that's causing these—these visions."

Realization struck. A moment ago, I had felt like I was crumbling. As if I couldn't hold myself together, so rapidly had I shifted back and forth from River's mind. I felt whole again—now—but the sense of displacement remained. "You felt it too, didn't you?"

He made no reply.

His words hit, and I let out a breath of laughter. "*I* cast a spell on you? Is that what you think? I'm incapable of magic."

A flicker of a smile crossed his face, startling me. River's moods shifted as easily as the wind. "Kamzin. You're not incapable of anything. If someone dared you to climb the mountains of the moon, you'd find a way."

I flushed, and for a moment I was confused. Then bitterness rose again. Everything I had done to reach this point had come to nothing. River would never let us continue searching for the star. The sense of loss ached in my chest. "How did you know we were here?"

"You know how. It was your spell that connected us." He glanced over his shoulder to where Tem stood murmuring over a bronze talisman he must have dug out of his pocket. "Or was it Tem's?" He made a careless gesture, and a tendril of shadow wrapped itself around his mouth, silencing the incantation. Tem pulled at it, but his fingers passed right through.

"I know you sent your familiar to spy on me," River said, turning back to me. "You can't deny that."

I stared at him, nonplussed. He thought I had sent *Ragtooth* to spy on him? Was he mad?

"Well?" he said. I recoiled. The shadows around us seemed alive—they swayed and undulated like branches in the wind.

That was when the *kinnika* rang out.

River fell back, his face a mask of pain. Mingma stepped out of the shadows, sounding a single bell—the bell marked *shadow-kin*, an old term for *witch*.

"Kamzin," Mingma said, but before I could run to his side, River fixed him with a murderous look and uttered a single word—

"Stop."

The bell fell silent. Mingma stood as if frozen, his knuckles white as he gripped the *kinnika*.

I looked from Mingma to River in disbelief. Lusha, who had drawn herself to her feet and now leaned heavily against the mountainside a few yards away, looked as baffled as I felt.

"Surprised?" River said. "Don't be. He still carries traces of the witches' spell that tied him to Raksha. His will hasn't been fully his own for fifty years. It still isn't. I'll take those." Mingma handed him the *kinnika*, hesitating only briefly. His gaze, fixed on River, was as bitter as it had been on Raksha. He was trapped, just as he had been there.

River grimaced, holding the *kinnika* between his thumb and forefinger, as if they were something he'd fished out of a swamp.

"Shamanic magic," he said, "has a terrible smell. Like something left out to rot. I've always been amazed how humans don't notice it. Oh well." He placed the *kinnika* around his neck. The witch bell let out a shiver, and he grimaced. "I'll have to hold on to these. I don't relish the prospect of you sending me over a cliff again, Kamzin. And as for you . . ."

He turned to Mingma, his expression dark. "I'm growing rather tired of running into you. Were you not already dead, this would be much more entertaining. Fortunately, though, that old spell provides an alternative."

"River, don't—" I began.

"Begone." River slashed out his hand. Mingma was flung back, or so it appeared—a gust of wind seemed to lift him, and winnow

him like grain. His outline seemed frozen in midair, and then it too dissolved, and was gone.

I stared at the place where Mingma had been. "What did you do to him?"

"I sent him away. He won't bother us anymore."

"Where?"

"Where?" River could not have sounded less concerned. "Far away, I hope."

"How could you do that?" My voice was shaking. "Hasn't Mingma been through enough?"

River gave me a look of frank disbelief. "Do you truly feel for him? He tried to kill you."

I remembered voices luring me from the safety of the cave on Mount Raksha. Cold hands dragging me beneath colder water. But that thought was subsumed by the image of Mingma sitting by the fire, easy and smiling. For the first time in fifty years, he had been happy.

"He didn't have a choice," I said quietly.

River shrugged, his mood shifting again. "You're very forgiving. That's good. It will make this easier."

"We're not giving you the star." My voice was fierce with determination.

"I thought it was a rock?" He picked it up from where it had landed in the snow. "I was here for part of that argument. Lusha? You said you knew the signs. Are you still convinced?"

Lusha let out such a vicious string of insults that I half expected the snow to melt between them.

"I'll take that as a yes." River held the rock up to the sky, his brow furrowing. "I've never seen one before, so I'll have to trust your judgment."

I met Lusha's gaze. Her hand was pressed against her shoulder where it had struck the stony ground, and there was a jagged cut on her chin. Through the pain, her expression was fierce, almost pleading. And suddenly, I realized why.

Lusha was utterly convinced that we had found the star. If we had, and it was now in River's possession—

I swallowed. Lusha was pleading with me to trust her. Because I was now the only one with the power to help us. It would be big magic, costly magic—but what choice did we have?

"Azar-at," I murmured.

The fire demon moved to my side, emerging from some unseen place behind me. *Hello, River.*

River started. "What in the name of the spirits are you doing here?"

"Azar-at is with me," I said. "And I can't think of a better use for its power than blasting you back to the Nightwood."

River stared at Azar-at. His gaze went from shock to amazement. Then, to my astonishment, he began to laugh—so hard he had to lean against the rock for support.

"I should have known you would convince him to help you," he said, once he had caught his breath. "You're nothing if not resourceful, Kamzin."

"Azar-at isn't difficult to convince," I said grimly.

"Ah, but that's not quite true." River eyed the fire demon. "Is it, my friend? Azar-at only helps those he deems worthy of his attention."

I shook my head. I wasn't going to let him distract me. I pictured the clouds descending, swirling over that exposed crag, dragging River into the air. "*Now*, Azar-at."

The fire demon whined low in its throat. Its glittering gaze was fixed on River.

I stared at it. "What are you waiting for? I said, *now*."

Not right, Kamzin, the fire demon said. *Not good. You forget my promise.*

"What are you talking about?" My voice was shaking again, fury rearing back up. "You're always so eager for me to use your magic."

You made me promise, on Raksha. I do not forget promises. The fire demon settled back on its haunches, tail stroking the snow. *You cannot use magic against friends.*

I felt like screaming. "River is *not* a friend."

"Don't bother trying to make sense of it," River said. "I gave up long ago. Fire demons follow their own laws."

He turned the star over in his hands. Lusha was staring at me so hard her eyes could bore holes in my skin. I met her gaze. She reached into her *chuba* and drew out a rock.

Not a rock. The star.

The breath left my body. Lusha had somehow, in the few seconds before River appeared, snatched up a stone of similar size to the star, then pretended to drop it. Lusha moved to my side, limping. She was either a very convincing actor or was genuinely hurt.

River paid her no heed. She wrapped her arm around me, as if to comfort me. Then she slipped the star into my pocket. I froze, my heart thudding in my ears.

River's expression was distant. "The magics contained in fallen stars belong to neither witches nor shamans. But I should be able to sense *something*. Maybe you were right, Kamzin. Maybe Lusha is imagining things."

My heart was in my throat. Lusha murmured something, but it was too low for me to hear. "Tem couldn't sense anything either," I said, my voice even.

River's eyes swung to me, and instantly I knew I had made a mistake. River could read me too well. I kept my expression carefully blank, but it was too late—his eyes were narrowing, and he was turning to Lusha—

Who had drawn her bow and fired an obsidian arrow.

I let out a cry—of surprise, or fear, I didn't know. River, who must have reacted to the sound of the arrow leaving the bow, had moved more quickly than I could follow. He pressed his hand against the arm of his *chuba*, then drew it back. There was no blood. The arrow had cut fabric, not skin.

Lusha nocked a second arrow, but a wave of shadow crashed at her feet and spilled up her body. She was flung back against the mountainside and pinned there.

River paced toward Lusha, his expression stormy. She stood immobile, trapped by shadow. She didn't flinch, merely leveled him with a cold look.

"No!" I cried, surging to my feet. But River merely plucked the bow from her hand and turned back to me. He seemed to notice my expression.

"I wasn't going to hurt her," he said.

I stared at him. Given the tumult inside me, I hadn't thought I was capable of surprise as well. "Why?"

"Why?" River looked puzzled, as if he had only just considered the question, and the answer was as much a mystery to him. When he spoke again, he sounded uncharacteristically hesitant. "She's your sister."

"I don't believe you," I said. "You're capable of anything. You want to use the star to destroy the world."

"Is this world worth saving? Perhaps for you. It wasn't for us."

He stood there in that familiar *chuba*, gazing at me with those familiar, mismatched eyes, and all I wanted to do was run at him, pound my fists against him. I wanted to lift my ax from where it lay in the snow and drive it into his chest. I withdrew the star from my pocket.

River's eyes narrowed. He seemed to guess what I was thinking. If I threw the star off the mountain, could he find it? His powers hadn't helped him find the star before. There was no longer any possibility that we could escape with it—the least I could do was keep it out of the witches' hands.

My hand, suddenly, was *hot*. The star was burning; I felt it through the wool of my glove. What was happening? Startled, I stumbled back—onto the talon of ice at the edge of the spur.

Which promptly gave way.

Shouts followed me through the air. Acting on pure instinct, I lifted my ax and drove it into the mountain. It arrested my descent, and I swung my body onto a narrow ledge. It held for a moment, then crumbled beneath my feet. Gasping, I slid down the mountain, which curved outward slightly, before landing in a heap on an outcropping several yards below. I was on my feet in an instant.

Through my fear and fury rose a sudden, desperate hope. The clouds swirled around me in thick sheets. Could I somehow conceal myself and the star from River? Could I lure him on a wild-goose chase, then make my way back to Lusha and Tem, and escape?

It seemed impossible. And yet I had to try.

I leaped again. The rock wasn't quite sheer, and I slid at a terrifying speed before catching hold of a crevice in the mountainside. My wrist wrenched painfully, but I didn't pause. From there, I lowered myself rapidly to a spur of rock we had passed hours earlier—it had taken that long to climb the area I had just descended. The mountainside fell into shadowed mist beyond the spur, tinged with silver and gold from the setting sun. It was a dreamlike sight that took my breath away. Yet I knew the mist hid certain death—I was thousands of feet above the ground. Beneath the spur there was only air.

I hurried along the rock to the cave I knew was tucked within a fold in the mountainside. The clouds swirled around me, cold and damp. Ice crystals formed around my eyes and nose, but I didn't care—the clouds were my cloak.

I reached the cave, which was difficult to spot at first, for it was as if a light shone inside it, erasing every crack and crevice. No, not a light.

The cave had no shadows.

I stumbled back. Around me, the shadows were being pulled back like a retreating tide. Clouds swirled over a landscape that was harsh and jagged, almost painful to look upon. I turned, drawing the dagger from my *chuba*. I couldn't see River, but I could see where the shadows were gathering—at the edge of the cliff, where it seemed a figure stood shrouded in darkness.

Anger beat in my veins. River had found me. River had access to power I couldn't imagine. It was unfair, and I hated it.

I threw the dagger.

The shadows gave a shudder. I had no time to see if my desperate shot had hit the mark, however—I turned and ran, making for a rubbly ledge of ice. The ground shook strangely beneath my pounding boots. The rubble seemed to dissolve, and I realized that beneath it was nothing but air.

"Kamzin!" River shouted. His voice was distant. I was falling.

Chunks of snow and rock struck my face as I tumbled with them through the air. My ax was gone, spinning from my hand and into the shadows. The shadows—

They swirled around me, tugging at my cloak. One alighted on my shoulder, small as a bird. It clung to me, digging itself into my *chuba*. Other shadows grasped at my hem and sleeves. Slowly, impossibly, I felt my descent slow. I was no longer tumbling head over heels. I was on my back, just below the cloud cover, hovering over a snowy valley. I opened my mouth to scream, but no sound came out.

The tiny shadows began to lift me through the air, rippling like wings, so quickly that I flailed and thrashed instinctively. I rose back into the cloud, gliding toward the spur where I had fallen.

When I reached the edge of the rock, River was there, grabbing me by the back of my *chuba* and hauling me onto solid ground. The little shadows dissolved. I sagged against River, and for a moment, I felt his heart thudding against mine. Then I shoved him back and slid away from him.

River leaned against the rock, his hand pressed against his shoulder. Blood seeped through his fingers. We gazed at each other across a small distance. For a moment, the only sound was the moan of the wind across the upper slopes of the mountain.

"So," I said, aiming for a dismissive tone, which was difficult with my heart throbbing in my ears, "it doesn't take an obsidian blade to hurt you."

He regarded me warily, as if he suspected that at any moment I would toss myself over the cliff again. "It won't kill me, even if you drove it through my heart. But yes, being stabbed does hurt, thank you."

I leaned my head against the frigid rock. "You don't need to look at me like that. I'm not going to run again." My voice was bitter. "It's clear that there isn't any point."

"I don't know about that." He seemed amused. "You can move

faster than any human I've met. If it wasn't for the snow, I don't think I would have found you."

"The snow?"

River pointed to the spur stretched out behind us, where, unmistakably, there was a trail of footprints.

I cursed inwardly. Lusha would never have made such a mistake. Anger rose again as I looked at him. His dark hair fell haphazardly across his forehead, speckled with snow, and for some reason that angered me too.

"It would be easier for you if I did run again," I said. "Wouldn't you rather collect the star from my broken body, if I were to fall?"

"You wouldn't fall," he said. "I wouldn't let you."

I let out my breath. River's voice was annoyed, as if it irritated him to state something he viewed as self-evident. And it was true that he had saved my life, even after I had thrown a knife at him. I didn't understand him at all. My eyes roamed his face as if I could find some way back into his thoughts.

River shifted slightly, wincing. He sprawled against the mountain in his familiar, casual attitude, one leg dangling over the ledge. But his body held a tension that was not usually there, and I knew he hadn't lied about the pain he was feeling.

Casually, I removed the star from my pocket and tossed it between my palms.

"What's wrong?" I wasn't above taunting him, even when there was nothing to be gained from it. "You don't seem as eager to change your shape as you usually are. Don't you want to turn into an owl and carry the star away in your talons?" I paused. "Or perhaps a yak, to tear it from my hand?"

River looked repulsed, as if I had said something unimaginably filthy. "No."

"So, being injured makes it harder for you to change shape." Because some tiny shred of hope remained, I ran through all the possibilities this created. Each was wilder and less plausible than the next.

"Not harder," River said. "But it becomes unpleasant. The injury doesn't vanish, you see. It has to change its shape too. If I changed form now, it would feel like being stabbed several times over."

Some small part of me was intrigued by this—with their powers restored, I had imagined the witches to be nearly invincible. The larger part of me was filled with fury and despair. Then it was as if those feelings crumpled, leaving a cold emptiness in their place. I gripped the star.

"This is it, then," I said. "You'll take the star and create an army. You might not care about the Empire, but what about the spirits of the witches you'll raise from the dead? Don't they deserve their rest?"

River gazed at me blankly. There was a small silence, and realization dawned in me.

"You don't know what the star's powers are." My voice was low.

"I don't care what they are. It's my brother who wants it, not me." But his expression was troubled. "I doubt it has that power. Nothing can raise the dead."

"Fallen stars can," I said. "In a way. They can bring a person back to life, though they aren't the same. Haven't you heard the stories? The ancient shamans who raised the dead and kept them as slaves?"

"I've heard the stories. That's all they are."

"Why would I lie to you?" I was frustrated. "How was I to know you didn't want this?"

"Esha wouldn't do that." River seemed to speak half to himself. "Not even him."

"Why did you *think* your brother wanted the star?" I snapped.

River didn't reply immediately. "It grants power. He didn't know what kind. I didn't think he even cared, so long as it hurt the emperor. He said—" He stopped.

I didn't understand his reaction. His expression was distant and uncertain, and for a strange moment, I was reminded of the boy who had followed his brother into the woods and become lost. But it didn't matter. From the moment he had appeared, all hope was gone.

"Clearly, I can't escape." My voice was hollow. "And I can't fight you. So take it and go."

River blinked. Uncharacteristically, he seemed at a loss for words. He gazed at me as if I were a riddle whose solution had long eluded him. His gold eye gleamed in the fading light, while the black was all shadow. Despite myself, my heart gave a strange skip.

A tremor ran through the shadows surrounding us. River looked up, and his face darkened.

"Esha."

My heart seemed to stop. I dragged myself to my feet, turning to look at the creature who stood slightly above us at the very tip of the spur, the darkening sky at his back.

River was already standing, moving with that disconcerting speed. In another instant, he was at my side, plucking the star unceremoniously from my hand and then—to my confusion—shoving me behind him.

"You followed me." River's voice was flat, almost dismissive, but a tension had entered his body.

"Of course I followed you," Esha said. "You don't think I'd let you take the star?"

He came forward, stopping only a few feet from River, and I let out a choked gasp. Esha was just as I remembered—thin, pale, but with an eerily forceful presence. He reminded me of a cadaver unnaturally returned to life. I saw nothing of River in him, except perhaps in the grace of his movements, or the shape of his mouth, that slightly upturned corner. He wore dark rags, and his feet were bare.

I fell back a step, or perhaps River moved forward—I wasn't able to focus on anything beyond Esha's presence.

"Take the star?" River held it loosely in his left hand, as if it were nothing at all. "I don't want it. This expedition was your idea."

"Do you take me for a fool?" Esha began to pace, like an animal with too much energy. "You've been sneaking off every chance you get, to search alone. Did you think I wouldn't work it out? I know

221

you convinced the others to flee the Nightwood, to undermine my authority."

River let out a disbelieving breath of laughter. "I didn't convince anyone of anything. Those people left of their own accord. Not everyone wants to be ruled."

I gave a start of surprise. I had always thought of the witches as a collective—fearsome and single-minded. But were there some who disagreed with Esha's plan? Who wanted no part in his attack on the Empire?

"Then you deny you want the throne?" Esha's voice was soft.

"The throne?" River's brows knitted. "It seems I have an endless variety of secret plots. I thought I wanted the star."

"Your magic is stronger than mine." Esha came to a stop, his hands clasped behind his back. His red-rimmed gaze had a feverish intensity. "Haven't you noticed?"

"I've noticed that I'm holding the very thing you sent me all this way to find. And that you still haven't thanked me."

"All right." Esha held out a hand. "Prove your loyalty. Give it to me."

"River, don't." I lurched forward, placing myself between the two of them.

I couldn't have said, afterward, what drove me to do it. It certainly wasn't wisdom. Esha looked at me as if I were a mouse he was about to crush under his heel, while River's face went blank with astonishment.

"River," I said, "please. Don't give him the star."

"What's this?" Esha said. "A shaman? Have you allied yourself with the enemy?"

I didn't look at Esha. I only looked at River. I didn't know what I was doing. All my senses told me to run as quickly as I could. But there was a small voice, so small it was barely audible, that told me to stand fast and hold his gaze.

I didn't move.

"Kamzin," River said. His voice was barely above a whisper. His gaze held a rare emotion—fear. I had seen it only once, days ago—on Raksha, after I had narrowly escaped being crushed by a falling serac.

"He's going to use it to destroy everything I know," I said. My voice was raw and honest—I put aside anger, fear, betrayal. There was no time for any of them. "To kill people I love. He's your brother, so you're helping him. I understand that. But you don't have to do this. You have your powers back. What more do you need?" I swallowed. "I helped you. So you owe me this."

My words hung in the air, as strange to my own ears as they must have been to River's. He was frowning, and I couldn't interpret his thoughts. But I had lived his thoughts, if only for a few moments. I had seen a boy running through smoke and fire in a dark forest.

Esha let out a low chuckle. It occurred to me, an edge of hysteria in my thoughts, that if Lusha was wrong, I was about to be killed over a lump of rock.

"She says you plan to use the star to raise the dead," River said.

His voice was even, almost conversational. "Is that true?"

"And if it is?" Esha said. "The emperor has killed so many of us. It will be a reparation, of sorts."

"He's killed hundreds," River said. "Surely you can't mean—"

"To bring them all back? Yes, I do, every one. The star's power has no limit."

River's face was pale, his freckles standing out in stark relief. "How could you be that stupid? You won't bring them back—you'll only turn them into monsters."

"As I keep reminding you, River," Esha said, "that's what they always were. It's what we are."

The shadows stirred behind River. Something—someone—seemed to be emerging.

"River!" I cried. That was all I had time for. Suddenly the shadows were on fire, surging hungrily toward me. The flame was strangely dark—

"*No.*" River darted between me and the witch fire. It passed harmlessly over him and was extinguished, smoke leaping into the sky. He shoved me against the mountain, scraping my cheek against the cold rock, keeping himself between me and Esha—and the second figure who now stood at Esha's side.

Unlike Esha, it was clear from a glance that the second witch was River's brother—he had the same eyes, the same unruly hair. They looked so alike, in fact, that I was momentarily disoriented. But his build was heavier, his posture menacing. The same amusement hovered around his eyes, but his amusement was cold. He wore a finely woven *chuba* that I recognized, with a shiver of disgust, as being like those worn by the elders of the mountain villages.

"You *are* allied with her." There was a strange edge of delight in Esha's voice. "Did you see it, Thorn?"

"I'm not allied with anyone," River snapped. I couldn't see his face. "She has nothing to do with this."

"You protect humans now, in addition to deserters?" Esha's expression could not have been more appalled.

"I've been saying it for years," Thorn said, shaking his head. "There's something that isn't right about him. Sky never listened to me, of course. He wouldn't hear a word against his precious River."

Esha, who had seemed as incurious about the presence of a human in this forsaken place as he might be about an unusual insect, examined me properly for the first time. I shuddered, for it was like being examined by a raging storm—with a gesture, he could toss me from the mountainside.

"Is she from the emperor's court?" Esha demanded. "Did you bring her here to spy on us?"

"Who cares?" Thorn sounded almost bored. "Let's get this over with."

"Get what over with?" River said. In the same moment, an enormous hawk soared over my head, its talons narrowly missing me. I cried out. The shadows around Esha and Thorn began to move. At least three more witches were there, though I could make out only the barest hint of their outlines. A black jay darted past, ruffling my hair, its form melting into that of a barefoot woman, her hair a tangle that hid her eyes. She was at once physical and ethereal, flesh and bone and something bloodless and breathless, like night. In that sense, she reminded me of River—in every other, she was a monster from a nightmare.

Esha was eyeing River with an expression that was half-wary, half-calculating. "Did you think I'd let you keep the Crown, River?"

River's expression was as confused as I felt, though my confusion was dwarfed by dread. I wanted, increasingly, to put distance between myself and him—all of them—but moving would only draw Esha's gaze. "The Crown—"

"I didn't inherit it, you see." Esha turned away slightly. "Nor did Thorn. That leaves you. You were so quick to master shape-shifting, weren't you? And the shadows obey you without hesitation."

"Esha, you're mad," River said. "The Crown always passes to the eldest child, unless . . ." He stopped. An awful expression dawned on his face. He seemed to take in the witches circling in the shadows.

"River." My fingers dug into his arm. It was clear to me what Esha's intentions were, even if I didn't understand anything else. We had to get out of here, now.

"Unless," Esha murmured. "'The Crown can be fickle'—is that not what Mother always said? It may have abandoned our line entirely. But perhaps—*perhaps*—it's fickle enough to pass to the least deserving member of the family."

"Esha," River said, his voice very quiet, "what really happened to Sky?" The shadows at his feet, as if sensing his agitation, were trembling. A chill settled in my chest as I realized what River meant, and I looked at Esha with new repulsion.

"Ah, you guessed that," Esha said. "No matter. I knew the binding spell was breaking, and I knew it would be harder to get rid of Sky after the fact, when he came into his powers. With Mother's death, and you off gallivanting around the Empire, Sky was distracted."

"He always did have a talent for moping," Thorn said, in the sort of tone you might use while examining your nails. I wondered distantly if anything had ever shaken the look of smug malice from his face. "Esha and I were more than a match for him."

"He didn't deserve it." Esha's voice was twisted with an old, bitter anger. "Sky never had what it took to lead us. He wouldn't have had the courage to attack the Empire."

"This has nothing to do with courage," River said, so low I could barely hear him. "Unlike you, Sky wasn't obsessed with revenge at any cost."

"In fact, I couldn't care less about revenge," Esha said. "This is a preemptive strike. Do you truly think that the emperor won't attempt to bind our powers again? Lozong *despises* us. He will take our magic, and then he will hunt us to extinction. The only way to ensure our survival is by reducing the Empire to ash. What I'm doing, everything that I'm doing, is for our people. Sky never would have thought that far ahead, because he wasn't a leader. And neither are you."

"I see." River's voice was almost as conversational as Thorn's, though the shadows' agitation had only grown. They were like living serpents at his feet. "So there *was* a reason you followed me here."

Esha lifted his hand—in almost the same instant, River seized me and pushed me out of the way. But I was tired of being flung around, so I clung to him, and we rolled together down the slight slope as behind us the mountainside exploded, a tremendous crater opening as projectiles of stone soared in every direction. River was on his feet in an instant. In one smooth motion, he removed the *kinnika* from his neck and tossed them at me. I had only a second to marvel at this, though, before everything dissolved into chaos.

In a whirl of shadows and cloak, River was gone. The others vanished too, including the hawk, folding into the shadows that cloaked the narrow crag. The shadows became a tangled swirl, stirring my hair and *chuba*. I staggered back until I was pressed against the mountainside as the animate darkness surged and spun, churning up the snow.

"Wait," I murmured to no one in particular. I had seen something, somewhere among the shadows. The star—River had dropped it, and it lay against the mountainside among the broken shards of rock. But to get it, I would have to plunge into that blizzard of darkness, and where would I go after that? I doubted the witches would remain distracted long enough for me to escape.

That was when a mad idea struck me.

"Azar-at," I whispered. "Are you there?"

Yes, Kamzin, the creature murmured into my thoughts. It appeared at my side, tongue lolling.

"I need your help with something. Something big."

Remember my promise.

"I don't want to hurt River," I said. "This won't touch him in any way."

That is good. The fire demon settled on its haunches. *Friends should not fight.*

I shook my head. Then I dove into the shadow.

It was a strange sensation. The shadow flowed over my skin like wind, but something about it was solid, almost tangible. It felt like a thousand wings brushing past my face.

I wove through the darkness, finding my way to the star. I picked it up, and it was as dull and lifeless as it had been when I first touched it. I plunged back into the darkness, reaching Azarat's side just as I heard the cry.

I turned. River had appeared, as had Esha. They stood at the edge of the spur, framed by the stars. They were at the center of the swirl of shadows, which had slowed to a menacing dance. River was clutching his side. He pulled something out, something that gleaned darkly in the starlight.

An obsidian dagger.

"River!" I screamed.

River sank to his knees. Dark blood spilled over his fingers. He gazed at Esha, his expression filled with a hatred so intense it seemed to vibrate through the air. Esha leaned forward and placed his hand on River's face—a gesture of affection so utterly incongruous that I started. Then he took the dagger from River's hand and drove it into him a second time. Esha turned away as River fell.

I felt oddly disembodied. For a moment, it was as if I could see through River's eyes, but it wasn't because of our connection this time—it was a memory. I was back on Raksha, hunched in the snow, watching as River left me behind, broken and defeated on the summit.

I wasn't defeated now. I had what I had come here for, and this time, I wasn't giving it up—no matter what. I choked back the tears that ran down my cheeks and pinged against the rocky ground, already frozen.

Esha turned to look at me, his head cocked—a brief pause, before he unleashed some merciless spell in my direction. River followed his gaze. For a moment, our eyes met. His face was paler than I had ever seen it, and his eyes seemed to struggle to focus on mine.

Azar-at settled at my side, the creature's smoke-fur melting the snow from my boots.

"Azar-at," I said as I thought of Lusha and Tem with all my might, "take us to the emperor."

PART III
THE THREE CITIES

EIGHTEEN

AZAR-AT GAVE NO warning.

The mountain vanished, the snow crumbled underfoot, and the stars went out like snuffed candles. All was black and still, the stillness of dead things and snow-cloaked forests. I was dying but unable to die, to breathe, to move. I felt—something. Countless shapes moving, rustling against my bare skin.

Those were the only impressions I had before I tumbled forward onto the floor of a forest.

I lay on my back, winded, as if I had fallen from a great height. Had I? I had a strange image of myself falling from the peak of that unnamed mountain in the Ashes, into a forest that didn't exist that far north. But here, it was day, an ordinary afternoon. The light of an overcast sky spilled through the trees.

I pushed myself up onto my elbows, head spinning. Lusha

groaned a few feet away. Wind played through the leaves, and it was gentle, almost warm, with none of the sharp edges it had in the north. A stream flowed over a bed of moss.

Where are we?

I didn't have time to wonder about it. For in that moment, the world dissolved again, obscured by a veil of agony.

Someone was screaming, some distant part of me noted. Everything was distant—it was as if, in that moment, I was reduced to a kernel of pain, every other thought, memory, and sensation stripped mercilessly away. It was a pain that was everywhere, and nowhere, and it went on and on.

Then, without warning, it stopped.

"Kamzin." Someone was touching me—a hand on my face, another on my shoulder.

I blinked, my eyes coming open. Tem knelt over me, his face pale. With his other hand, he grasped at one of the *kinnika*, as if readying to cast a spell. But there was no spell that could help me.

The pain was gone, though in its place was a bone-deep weariness. I drew myself half-upright as my vision swam.

"River—"

"It's all right." Tem's voice was low. "He's not here. What happened? We saw you fall . . ." The way he touched me was strange, his hand light and tense, as if he was torn between restraining and comforting me. Mixed with the concern in his face was something harder, like anger.

I saw River's face, half in shadow. The blood staining the snow. Something twisted inside me, sharp as a knife. The pain clouded my vision, as sharp one of Azar-at's spells but somehow deeper.

Tears streamed down my face. They didn't freeze here, but fell against the grass like rain. Tem held me. It seemed impossible that River could be dead. He had defied death so many times as Royal Explorer—how could be be defeated by a shard of glass? My palms tingled, as if remembering the fire River had summoned days ago.

"Can you stand?" Tem asked when I had calmed.

"I don't know." The world tilted again as exhaustion rolled over me like heavy fog.

Branches rustled as Lusha strode into the glade. There were leaves tangled in her hair and a smear of dirt on her cheek. Her chin was stained with drying blood. Yet despite her disheveled appearance, she radiated a self-righteous fury that put me in mind of the warriors depicted on my father's tapestries. I cringed away in spite of myself.

"What happened?" Her voice was quiet, which was never a good sign.

I recounted it all, speaking rapidly—Lusha's gaze was like a carpet of hot coals I wanted to escape as quickly as possible. She showed no reaction as I described River's part.

"Next question," she said. "Where are we?"

I looked around. "Azar-at?"

The fire demon appeared, a tendril of smoke unfurling from the greenery. I suppressed a shudder of revulsion. The creature was as calm as ever, watching me with its patient, fiery gaze.

I have done as you asked, Kamzin.

"I asked you to take us to the emperor." My voice shook. Had what I just endured been for nothing? "And you've done what? Returned us to his lands? That isn't the same thing. We should be in the Three Cities right now."

The Three Cities are close. The creature's tail began to wag. *Shall I take you there?*

"*No.*" I felt dizzy with anger and betrayal, and horror at what I had done. I had sacrificed part of my soul, and abandoned River— and for what? Azar-at had deceived me. How had I not suspected it? I thought of how accustomed I had become to the creature's power, all the small spells I had cast. It had made me trust it.

The rage that had been building flickered and died, leaving something cold in its place. I tried to grasp at the anger, to summon it again. But it slipped through my fingers—just as River had said.

"You were right," I murmured, leaning into Tem's shoulder.

He didn't need to ask what I meant. Hatred blazed in his eyes as he looked at Azar-at, as if this was all its fault—but, of course, that wasn't true.

Lusha pressed her hand against her eyes. "What were you thinking, Kamzin?"

I swallowed against the nausea rising in my throat. "I was thinking that I would save our lives."

"And this is how you chose to do it?"

"I wanted to take us to the emperor," I said, my voice rising. "To bring him the star, so that he could recast the binding spell. Why is that hard to understand?"

"Perhaps because neither the emperor nor his shamans seem to be nearby. And there's one other small problem with your plan." Lusha's voice still held that threatening calm.

I gazed at her blankly. When I recognized the meaning behind her words, I started so violently I elbowed Tem in the chest. I rooted around on the forest floor, my hands catching at stones, earth, leaves—but not the star. It was gone.

I cursed. "How is this possible? I *had* it—"

"And now you don't." Her voice was vicious. An almost tangible heat flared between us, melting Lusha's icy demeanor. "You didn't think to specify that Azar-at should bring the star along?"

"I—"

"You didn't think," Lusha repeated, turning away. "You never do."

I stared. "I never think?"

"It was all for nothing." She paced back and forth, kicking at stray pebbles and roots in an uncharacteristic display of frustration. "All we've been working for since we left Raksha—you've thrown it away with another reckless decision."

I felt as if she had slapped me. "Another reckless decision? How have I been reckless?"

"Do you really need me to say it?" Lusha stopped. "You made a contract with Azar-at, didn't you? As a result, River was able to track us to the star."

"I didn't know—"

"You didn't know. Because you didn't think. Just like you didn't think before you trusted River. And we've seen how that turned out."

I flushed. For a moment, I couldn't speak. The pain in my chest seemed to twist, several knives instead of one, as River's face rose before me again. Did the pain mean that I still loved him, after everything? I didn't know. But I knew I couldn't bear to think of the possibility—the likelihood—of his death.

"That isn't fair, Lusha," Tem said quietly.

"I'm not really concerned with fairness at the moment." She began pacing again. "We could have used the star to save the Empire—and Azmiri."

"Are you saying I don't care about Azmiri?" My shock was slowly giving way to fury. "How can you—what gives you the right—"

"Because it's *my responsibility*." Lusha's voice was like a lash. "It always has been. You wouldn't understand that, because you've never taken your responsibilities seriously. Who else is going to protect the village, if not me? Father has no way of dealing with the witches now that their powers are unbound. I went to Raksha to save Azmiri. Now I'm here in some spiritsforsaken forest, hundreds of miles from the one thing that could have helped us. The village is defenseless, and I can't protect it. I can't protect it." She came to a stumbling halt. Her face was flushed, and she was breathing heavily. With her *chuba* askew and the dirt on her face, she suddenly looked very young.

My own anger had crumbled. For a long moment, we stood in silence, the twittering of the birds the only sound.

"No one expects you to save Azmiri alone," I said finally, but I heard the emptiness in my own words. Everyone in Azmiri looked up to Lusha, in the same way they looked up to Father. Though only nineteen, she was seen as more than an elder-in-waiting; she had already taken on many of the elder's duties. And the first and most important duty of any elder was protecting the village.

"I'm sorry," I said, my voice trembling. "You're right, Lusha—I don't always think. I know I've made a mess of things."

Lusha let out a quiet laugh. She leaned against a tree, looking even more exhausted than before. "We both have, haven't we?"

I shook my head. "No. You've been right from the beginning. You tried to stop River."

"I tried." Lusha gave me a rueful look. "But I couldn't have followed River to that peak. Even if my ankle wasn't broken. You're the only one who could have done that, Kamzin."

I shook my head. "But it was for nothing. If I hadn't trusted him—"

"I shouldn't have said that." Lusha's voice was quiet. "I should have told you what I read in the stars. I just—" She shook her head slightly, as if marveling at her own words. "I didn't really think you'd follow me."

I didn't know what to say. The silence stretched out. Lusha seemed to have returned to herself, the color leaving her cheeks and her expression calming. Her gaze, as she regarded me, was not exactly warm, but it no longer held the chill of the last few days. I thought of Father, and Azmiri, and felt a surge of despair. How were we going to protect the village now?

Tem grasped my arm—hard. "Kamzin."

Ragtooth trotted out of the bushes. He moved with an oddly

lumbering gait, as if off balance. He was carrying something in his mouth.

The star.

Lusha let out a strangled sound. The fox dropped the star into my hand without protest—covered in drool, naturally—but he *did* protest when I gathered him tightly into my arms. He nipped my ear, and I let him leap to the ground.

"Where did he come from?" Tem said. He eyed Ragtooth with an oddly suspicious expression.

"Azar-at must have brought him with us," I said. "Thankfully." The thought of Ragtooth being stranded in that bleak place made me ill.

Tem's brow was furrowed. "Kamzin . . . Ragtooth wasn't with us on the mountain."

"What are you talking about? Of course he was."

"No, he wasn't. The last time I saw him was on the glacier."

"He was obviously following us."

Tem shook his head slightly. "Did you hear what River said? He thought Ragtooth was following *him*. Why would he think that?"

I didn't want to talk about anything River had said—the thought of him was like a knife twisting inside me. "River also thought the yak was scheming against him," I said roughly. "Here—it still looks like a rock to me." I handed Lusha the star, drool and all. I felt lighter immediately. That fragment of rock was responsible for what had happened to River. I didn't want anything to do with it.

Without replying, Lusha marched into the forest. She plucked a branch out of the deadfall.

"Tem, can you light this?" she asked.

He dragged his gaze from Ragtooth, who was calmly washing between his toes. "Why?"

"Just do it."

Tem gave her a puzzled look. He selected one of the *kinnika*, and murmured a word. The leaves at the end of the branch flickered with flame. Lusha settled the star on a rock and pressed the makeshift torch against it.

A painful glimmer flooded the forest. Instinctively, I turned my face away. The light was white-hot, radiating in a way that reminded me of a pulse. Lusha drew the branch away. As it cooled, the star dimmed, until it looked like an ordinary gray rock again.

I blinked away the spots that floated across my vision.

"Do you believe me now?" Lusha said.

Tem gingerly lifted the star. "Kamzin's right. We have to take this to the emperor's shamans. It's the safest place for it."

"Azar-at," I said, my voice cold, "where are we? If you'll be so good as to share that small detail."

Sasani Forest, the creature replied calmly.

"That's only two or three days north of the Three Cities," Lusha said. She reached for her pack, which was lying on the forest floor—all our things were there, scattered around the glade at random intervals, even our tents. "I have a map."

She bent her head over it. I became aware, suddenly, of how quiet the forest was, how still. The only sound came from Tem as he sorted through the *kinnika*, muttering about a wayfinding spell. The gentle tinkling of the bells seemed painfully loud.

The hair on my neck stood up. Slowly, I reached out and stilled Tem's hand. I turned around.

The trees were broad-chested here, dark-needled pines mixed with birches and oaks. The forest was dense enough to dim the light, but not extinguish it—I could see well enough between the trunks. Something stirred at my back, and then, soft as the rustle of a leaf, came the sound of an exhaled breath.

My mind leaped to witches—Esha, stepping out from the trees, his eyes alight with menace. Had he somehow followed us here?

"Run!" I shouted, grabbing Tem's hand. Lusha looked up just as chaos erupted.

Horses' hooves thundered, voices shouted, arrows flew. People dressed in scaled armor and glittering silver helms charged us from what seemed like all sides. Tem and I dodged a man coming at us with the butt of his sword raised—Tem stumbled, but I caught him and dragged him on, still staggering.

"Lusha!" I yelled. She turned toward me, our eyes locking across the distance, and I realized she was surrounded by a ring of soldiers. She raised a hand.

It was covered in blood.

I let out a wordless cry. Then there were hands on my shoulders, shoving me into a tree so hard my vision blackened briefly. Other hands seized Tem, striking him across the face as he opened his mouth to shout something. I clawed ferociously at the person restraining me, earning the satisfaction of a muffled curse.

The butt of a sword was driven into my stomach, and I stumbled, gasping and choking. I couldn't breathe—

And then there was an arrow in my shoulder.

I stared at it. I was aware, distantly, that someone was shouting something, that soldiers were pouring into view, surrounding us with drawn bows, that Tem was staring at me with a look of horror I had never seen on his face.

He pulled me down just as another arrow sailed by overhead. That was when I felt the pain blossoming in my shoulder.

The arrow made it hard to focus on anything. So I reached up and pulled it out.

The cry caught in my throat and came out as a broken groan. It hurt, it hurt, it hurt—but not as much, it seemed, as the spells I had cast with Azar-at, nor was the pain as deep. I would be fine. Though those spells had not been accompanied by this strange floating feeling.

"Don't worry," I muttered. "I barely felt it."

Tem, crouched at my side, was saying something. He was pressing against my shoulder. His hands were red.

"That's a lot of blood," I told him. It seemed important that he know this.

One of the soldiers pulled him away from me, but Tem, seemingly oblivious to the weaponry pointed our way, made a gesture that blasted him backward.

A man shouted something in a carrying, commanding voice, and another soldier moved to Tem's side. And beyond them, everything was growing dark.

"River?" I murmured. My mind was a haze. The thought of River brought a surge of relief. It meant he wasn't dead, wasn't lying in a snowy wasteland where I could never talk to him, or kiss him, or curse him, ever again.

Shadows gathered over the stream. In the forest, more shadows stirred, sliding onto the bank like animals seeking a drink. The soldiers gazed about, wide-eyed. For some reason, they had fallen back from Tem, who stood alone at the center of a swirl of shadow.

More shouts, and an arrow flew toward Tem. I opened my mouth to scream, but a shadow darted out, and the arrow went wide. A soldier approached him, sword drawn, but a skein of darkness wrapped around his ankle, and he fell with a clatter of armor. Realization hit like a shock of ice water.

The shadows belonged to Tem.

"Seize him!" a woman shouted, her voice hoarse.

"No," I said, as chaos erupted on all sides. One of the soldiers had made it through the shadow-cloud to Tem, who seemed to have sagged forward. Lusha was yelling. The soldiers were yelling. Everyone was yelling. Shadows skittered back to the forest.

"No," I repeated, louder this time.

I didn't know what I was denying—everything, I supposed. Everything was wrong. Well, I wasn't just going to sit there. I was going to do something about it.

I dragged myself to my feet, and that was when the world tilted violently, and the ground came swooping up to greet me.

NINETEEN

HANDS WRENCHED MY shoulder back, pressing something cold against it. I felt a shock of pain, then a spreading
numbness that almost made me weep with relief. A voice chanted
an incantation. I must have slipped back into unconsciousness, for
the next thing I knew, the hands were gone.

I opened my eyes.

I lay on my side on the forest floor, a dark figure looming above
me. I felt a moment of panic and disorientation. When I raised a
hand to my shoulder, I encountered dry bandages, no blood. All I
could see, at that angle, were the hooves of a massive horse. When
I shifted position, there came a shaft of pain that made me wish I
hadn't opened my eyes.

"Who did this?" a cold male voice said. "The general said *capture*, not maim."

"Apologies, my lord," a woman's voice murmured.

There came a curse, and then a pair of leather-clad feet landed on the ground not two paces from my head. A man, tall and armored, his face half-hidden by a gleaming helm that covered his eyes and wrapped around the sides of his neck, knelt at my side and passed his hands matter-of-factly over my body. I paid him little heed. My stomach felt as if it had been rearranged by the blow it had taken, and my shoulder throbbed beneath the salve. My breath came in wheezes.

"Get away from her," snapped the familiar voice of the person beside me.

"Lusha," I managed. It came out as two words. I pushed myself upright with my good arm, then wished I hadn't, as the world tilted. The knot of soldiers surrounding us visibly tensed. Lusha didn't look injured. There was a smear of blood across her palm, mixed with earth—she must have fallen.

"Tem—"

"He's alive," Lusha said. "No thanks to these cowards."

"Cowards?" the tall man repeated as a little shiver traveled through the armored figures gathered in the glade. There were six of them, and most had arrows trained on us. "We are soldiers of the emperor's Fifth."

I felt a chill. Each of the emperor's ten armies was renowned— or notorious—for its own specialization. The First Army was the largest and most powerful, and was often sent out to fight the fearsome barbarian tribes at the farthest reaches of the Empire. The Fifth was smaller—it kept close to the Three Cities, patrolling the forests and plateaus through which the Empire's major trade routes threaded, searching out the bandits and thieves that preyed upon unwary travelers. Once caught, those bandits were dispatched with casual brutality and left where they had fallen as a warning to others. Father had spoken of the blackened bodies he had seen at the side of the road during his last visit to the Three Cities.

"I don't care if you're the emperor himself," Lusha replied, her voice icy. "You attacked a group of unarmed travelers without provocation. What is the difference between that and banditry?"

The air cooled further. I contemplated clamping a hand over Lusha's mouth. But though her hands on my shoulders shook slightly, her gaze was iron. She knew what she was doing—knew that it wasn't suicide, as much as it appeared that way. With an almost painful effort, I forced down my objections. Lusha's gaze was fixed on the man who had examined me for injuries.

He was silent for a long moment. Then, to my astonishment, he let out a bark of laughter. Instantly, the mood lightened. Soldiers shifted position, their armor clinking.

"Unarmed travelers?" I sensed rather than saw that the man's entire focus was on Lusha. "You are witches."

"No," Lusha replied, reacting more quickly than I would have thought possible to that incomprehensible statement. "We're flesh and blood. You've seen that for yourself."

"And your friend?"

Lusha was silent. What was the man talking about? It couldn't be Tem—and yet Tem was the one missing. Where had they taken him?

"Tem is not a witch," I said. The very idea was ludicrous.

The man made a dismissive sound. "I do not doubt what I see with my own eyes. He can control the shadows. Only witches can work such magic."

The tangle of memories from those chaotic moments of the attack began to sort themselves into patterns. I remembered the shadows, how strangely they'd behaved. Tem had thought my life was in danger. Somehow, that realization had allowed him to draw on a power I'd never seen him use before.

"No." I said it even as I remembered how the shadows had responded to Tem's commands. How his powers had seemed to grow after the binding spell was broken.

The spell's easier than last time.

I couldn't accept it—my mind balked. Tem was familiar; Tem was *home.* I knew everything about him—his expressions and mannerisms, his quirks and habits.

"Kamzin." Lusha's expression held a warning, but there was little of my own disbelief reflected there.

My thoughts churned. No one knew who Tem's mother was—no one except his father, Metok, and the ill-tempered man had always refused to speak of her, even to Tem. I had grown so used to thinking of Tem as a boy without a mother, but of course that wasn't true.

It was as if the world had shifted, rearranging itself into new patterns.

"He's always been good at magic," Lusha said, so quietly only I could hear. "Too good."

Tem had witch blood. *Tem.* My amazement was dampened by a surge of fear. What had the soldiers done to him?

"You're telling me that you didn't know your friend was a witch?" The man's voice was flat with disbelief.

Lusha merely looked at him, as if sizing him up in turn. I knew better, though—the blankness of her expression told me that Lusha was uncharacteristically lost for words. My stomach sank as I realized why. These soldiers had little reason to keep us alive after what they had seen.

"We are innocent travelers," Lusha said finally. "If we were witches, your soldiers would have endured more than a few cuts and bruises for attacking us."

The grove became quiet.

The man let out a breath that was not quite a laugh. "Is that a threat?"

Lusha didn't waver. "It's a fact."

The man seemed unable to take his gaze off Lusha. "Witch or not, you're an odd creature to stumble upon in a place like this—a ragged girl with a face like the dawn and eyes as bright as fireflies."

"We're here on the emperor's business," Lusha said.

The man raised his eyebrows at that spectacular statement. "The emperor's business?"

Someone was approaching the glade—or rather, multiple someones, mounted and on foot. My heart sank. Were we to be surrounded by the entire Fifth Army?

A woman in a crested helm came forward, followed by two soldiers who had a chronicler-ish look about them, clothed in leather armor with packs slung over their shoulders. The tip of a scroll peeked out of one.

"General." The tall man drew himself to attention with a lazy sort of formality. The woman's gaze swept the glade.

"Well?" she said, that small word so crisp with command that it set my heart pounding. She was perhaps forty, with hair of pure silver cropped at her ears, giving her the appearance of wearing a second helm. Her features were sharp and uneven, as if carved by a rough blade. She was short—about my own height, and more than a head shorter than the man, yet when she spoke, every gaze snapped to her.

"Three witches claiming to be innocent travelers," said the man, with a glance at Lusha. "Several dragons, and one confused yak."

It took a second for this to sink in. "Azar-at," I muttered, knowing the fire demon, wherever it had gone, could hear me, "you brought the *yak?*"

You said "us," Kamzin.

I closed my eyes briefly.

"Innocent?" The general turned her sharp eyes to me and Lusha. "Two soldiers with broken bones. Gunril is still unconscious."

"You attacked us," Lusha said, her voice low. "We had no idea who you were, or—"

"I am Jinsang, General of the Fifth Army," the woman said. Her voice rasped, as if she spent a great deal of time shouting, but it carried. She spoke with the air of one who routinely announced her title to people on their knees, and had grown bored with it. "This is my captain, Elin. You will state your names and purpose here, or he will cut you down."

At that, the tall man removed his helm. He was younger than I had guessed from his voice, twenty-five at most, with a face so handsome my breath momentarily caught in my throat. At least, "handsome" was my first impression, taking in the sleek hair that slanted like lashes of ink across his forehead, the sharp line of his jaw, his height and powerful build. But his full lips had a twist of cruelty, an aspect that was hard and faintly mocking, confirming my earlier suspicion. His black eyes were framed by thick brows, which were now drawn together in thought and mild annoyance. While his armor was impressive, my gaze was drawn to his boots—faded leather stained an unmistakable reddish brown.

I stared. At some point in recent days, this man had walked through blood—and not a small quantity of it.

"We come from the village of Azmiri," Lusha said, her face impassive beneath the heavy weight of Jinsang's gaze. "We seek a private audience with the emperor."

The soldiers began to mutter. The captain fixed Lusha with a look of blank astonishment.

"The emperor does not give audiences to witches," the general said. "You will answer my questions, and then I will determine your fate."

I tried desperately to catch Lusha's eye. We had to tell the general everything—River's expedition, our journey to the Ashes. Perhaps if we showed the general the star, she would believe us.

But Lusha, sensing my gaze, shook her head once, almost imperceptibly.

"We answer questions from the emperor alone," she said.

It was madness. The general would not haul a group of suspected witches before the emperor. Again I tried to catch Lusha's eye, and again I was ignored.

The general silenced the soldiers' muttering with a flick of her hand. She turned back to Lusha, perplexity lessening the steel in her gaze. "What message would a witch have for the emperor?"

"We are not witches." Lusha's voice was like a lash.

"Yet you travel in the company of one." She made a dismissive gesture. "Have it your way. You will come with us." A soldier brought forward two mares, which huffed and stamped at the ground. They were still uneasy after the shadow-magic they had witnessed.

"Where?" Lusha demanded.

"The boy must be taken to the prison on the outskirts of the Three Cities for interrogation and execution," Jinsang said, each word sending a shaft of ice through my heart. "The rest of you may meet the same fate, or you may not, depending on your answers." The general turned and began snapping orders.

Prison. Execution. *Tem.* "Lusha—" I whispered.

"Be quiet, Kamzin," she snapped. "I'm trying to keep us alive."

Realization came in a blinding flash—Lusha didn't answer the general's questions because she knew doing so would be pointless. The general would take one look at the "star" she carried, and hear her allegations against the famed River Shara, and accuse her of lying and slander—perhaps even kill her then and there for wasting the army's time. Our story was simply too strange to be accepted readily, and Lusha had sized up the cold, mercenary general and determined that our safest course was to stay silent. I recalled how her hand had trembled against my shoulder as she returned the general's gaze. At least this way, we were still alive. For now.

"What have you gotten us into, Kamzin?" Lusha muttered.

I couldn't reply. All I could think about was Tem.

What were we going to do?

I felt the captain's attention on us, though he was busying himself with his horse's saddle. For a moment, I thought I would pass out again. The lingering sensation of Azar-at's spell was disorienting. I pressed my hand to my chest. Though the pain had gone, the memory hadn't—it lingered like cold sweat.

If I used the fire demon's magic again, would it help us? Or would it only throw us into a different peril? I knew even as the thought occurred to me that it didn't matter.

I couldn't use Azar-at's magic again. I couldn't trust it. And I couldn't trust myself.

Lusha's hand tightened on my arm. But then one of the soldiers brusquely helped me to my feet and indicated that I should follow her.

TWENTY

NIGHT FELL BEFORE we stopped. We were close to the main trade road from the east, and the trees were thin, so the soldiers led us into a sheltered ravine to make camp.

I sank to my knees before the shallow stream that trickled down the hillside. It was choked with leaves, but I was too thirsty to care. I drank deeply, then cupped the cool water between my palms and splashed it over my face and neck. The warmth of the air was strange—I had grown used to the bone-deep cold of the north. The breeze played with the thin sleeves of my tunic.

My reflection gazed back at me, drawn and ragged. Tem's absence was like a missing limb. We had been separated before, but not like this—not with a wall of swords and grim faces between us. Had they injured him? I had caught only an occasional glimpse of him all day—his head had been bent, and the soldiers had stripped him of his *chuba* and, undoubtedly, his talismans. His guards had hung back from the main troupe, no doubt to prevent us from communicating.

I pressed my face into my hands. I was tired and hungry, and I couldn't *think*. My mind circled endlessly back to the Ashes, and to River. For some reason, my palm still tingled, off and on, from the memory of River's magic. I had hoped to ignore the pain, to bury it deep and deal with it when I had space to sort out my feelings. But it had only worsened.

Lusha settled on a rock nearby. As usual, she seemed mostly unaffected by the day's rough hiking, her hair sleek again, her *chuba* casually threaded through the straps of her pack. She calmly brushed a leaf from her boot.

Captain Elin's manner throughout the day had been strange. He'd alternated between ignoring us entirely, striding along with his cool gaze turned inward, and attempting—with little success—to engage Lusha in casual conversation. After she had refused his offer of a horse, he seemed to have decided to travel on foot as well, often positioning himself at Lusha's side. She paid little more attention to him than she did to the trees we passed—which, unfortunately, he seemed to take not as a rejection but a challenge. My face almost hurt from the effort of preventing myself from rolling my eyes. The captain was certainly harder to put off than most of Lusha's suitors, but I had no doubt that his interest would wane after a few more icy comments. Or, I mused, with a sense of despair that grew ever nearer to hysteria, once we were all publicly executed.

"What I don't understand," the captain said now, kneeling on the other side of the stream, the moonlight sharpening the already sharp line of his cheekbone, "is how the boy was able to attack us. The witches' powers have been bound for centuries, though there have recently been rumors to the contrary. How do you explain it?"

I stiffened, disliking the captain's proximity. There was a stillness about him, present even when he was in motion, that I mistrusted, for it put me in mind of a stalking hunter. The dark circles under his eyes lent his handsome face a weary elegance, but what was he wearied from? The soldiers of the Fifth were professional killers, and I had no doubt, returning that cool gaze, that this man had seen death many times over. It was a gaze that was too knowing for his young face. Part of me wished we were still dealing with Jinsang, but the general had already departed, taking two men and heading back to the main force of her army. We would be escorted to the prison by Captain Elin and a group of about a dozen soldiers.

Lusha studied him. "You expect a witch to answer that? You're either very stupid, or you doubt your general's conclusions—in which case, you are a callous monster for handing us to the warden for execution. Which is it?"

The captain smiled, as if appreciating this speech. "You showed more courage before the general than I've seen from grown soldiers. You turn aside my questions as if your survival didn't hinge on my opinion of you. Are you truly as fearless as you appear?"

"Perhaps I just don't find you very frightening." Lusha stood as she said it, dabbing her hands dry with her *chuba*. "I don't much care for the opinions of men who threaten unarmed captives."

"It wasn't a threat," he said, seeming to take pleasure in throwing Lusha's words back at her. "Merely a statement of facts. I still haven't decided whether or not you're witches."

"Do we look like witches?"

"A meaningless question, given that they are masters of disguise."

"Captain Elin," one of the soldiers said. "We've set up the night watch. Standard rotations."

"Thank you," the captain replied calmly. The soldier bowed and departed. I hoped the captain would follow, but he stayed where he was.

"Elin is an unusual name," I said, to prevent his gaze from wandering to Lusha again. "It's the word for 'poppy' in the shamanic language."

"A nickname," he said. "Most of us don't use our real names when out on patrol. These woods are full of bandits—if they heard a nobleman's name spoken aloud, it would create a target for ransom."

"You're a nobleman?" Lusha said. Her tone was as cool as his. It was impossible to tell if this information impressed or bored her.

The captain smiled. He moved closer, until there were only inches between them, and placed his hand on the tree behind her. "I am, firefly. My family has enough wealth to plate your little village with gold. There, I can see I've caught your interest at last. You're impressed."

"I'm impressed that a brute like you convinced someone to make him a captain," she said in a calm voice. She could have been remarking on the make of his *chuba*.

Surprise and a sudden, hot anger filled his face. Then, to my astonishment, he smiled. The anger vanished, but the surprise remained. "You have a sting, don't you? No matter. We'll have all day tomorrow to become acquainted. I'll find a way to impress you." When he smiled, some of the tension in his face lightened, and he looked like what he was—a young man. Then he moved away, returning to his former self—cool, commanding, predatory. I didn't trust a single inch of him.

"You shouldn't bait him," I said, once he was out of earshot. "He's captain of the *Fifth Army*."

"I know what I'm doing," Lusha snapped. To my surprise, her cheeks were faintly flushed.

"Like you knew what you were doing when we were searching for the star?"

Lusha shushed me violently. I didn't see what the problem was—the soldiers had no idea what she carried. They had searched us, of course, but they'd been perplexed by the gray rock they found inside Lusha's pack. The captain had narrowed his eyes, taking it into a patch of sunlight for examination. He glanced at us and shrugged.

"The heart of one of your admirers, I presume?" was all he had said before returning it to Lusha.

Branches rustled above us. I turned my head, but saw nothing. Somewhere, a raven croaked.

A soldier bound Lusha and me for the night, lashing our hands with rope that was then secured to the trunk of a tree. Two soldiers stood guard, while the rest retreated to another campsite that I glimpsed through the trees. I could just make out the back of Tem's head.

After securing us to their satisfaction, the soldiers barely moved. Both kept their eyes fixed on nothing in particular, as if Lusha and I were not the sole reason they were standing there like incongruous statues. Their gazes only flicked to us if we made a sudden movement. One of the soldiers, I noted with disgust, was wearing the *kinnika* around his neck.

In a voice barely above a whisper, I said, "We have to get away."

Lusha shot me an exasperated look. "Really?"

I narrowed my eyes. "I don't see you making much of an effort."

"You haven't been paying attention."

"Then what's the plan? And please don't say it's flirting with the captain. I don't want to lose what little food I have in my stomach."

"No."

"Then what?" I swallowed. "Lusha, you know I can't use Azarat's magic again."

"Not Azar-at." Lusha's voice was so sharp that one of the soldiers glanced her way. She leaned back against the tree. "Wait until dark."

Of course she wasn't going to tell me. I swallowed a retort. In spite of myself, though, I felt a shiver of hope. I knew from experience that when Lusha came up with a plan, it was never halfhearted.

I examined my binds. They were tight enough, but not painfully so, and I thought I could probably wriggle out of them if given time. Whenever I strained, though, one of the soldiers lifted his bow.

Lusha, beside me, hadn't moved. I could just make out the line of her implacable profile. Something fluttered overhead, and the soldier started, scanning the darkness. But the bird was already gone.

Time passed. The clouds split apart, and I caught glimpses of stars between the branches, tiny pearls snared in a net. Trees were scarce in Azmiri, and mostly of the skinny, sharp-needled variety. It was strange to view the sky through leafy boughs.

I shivered. I was a long way from home. Was Azmiri all right? Losing the star wouldn't prevent Esha from continuing his attacks.

The constellation Damaya's Drum disappeared slowly behind the leaves, replaced by the Great Boar. I was tired, so tired. Occasionally, the breeze brought us a murmur of conversation from Elin's camp. But for the most part, the night was quiet, the trees becalmed. I closed my eyes, intending to rest only briefly.

A twig snapped, jolting me awake. I felt someone's breath on my cheek, warm and soft. I opened my eyes and choked on a scream.

A girl leaned over me, her face only inches from mine. It was the girl I had seen before, in the tent back in the Ashes—the one with my face. But not just my face—she had my long hair, my height, my clothes. For a moment I could only stare, transfixed. It was like looking into a mirror.

But the girl didn't start when I did. She leaned back slightly when she realized I was awake, her mouth half-open as if about to speak. She seemed equally fascinated by me. Her hair was a mess—a snarl of leaves and tangles, and there was a scratch across her cheek.

I raised a hand to my own cheek, where a branch had grazed it. The girl reached out and removed a twig from my hair.

"Lusha." I grabbed her arm. She leaned against the other side of the tree, gazing into the forest.

She turned. "What?"

I expected her to jump at the sight of the girl, but she showed no sign of surprise. I whirled back around.

The girl was gone.

One of the soldiers was gazing at me strangely. Had he been watching me this entire time? If so, how had he failed to notice my double crouching over my sleeping body? I began to shake.

I was going mad.

"Kamzin, what's wrong?"

"Nothing." I turned away. "Thought I saw something."

I folded my arms over my knees, trying to still the shaking. But it emanated from some fundamental part of me, and wouldn't stop.

I knew what happened to shamans who borrowed magic from fire demons. I had recounted one such story to River, of a woman who went mad and began murdering her neighbors. Was that what was happening to me? Was this how the madness began? The girl had seemed as vivid as Lusha, or the soldiers.

I bit down on my lip so hard I tasted blood.

A raven landed on a rock in the stream, settling its wings against its back. The bird cocked its head at the closest soldier, as if sizing him up. The man made a threatening gesture. The bird didn't flinch.

Biter. I recognized that long, curved beak. What was he doing?

I started as another raven landed by my side. The soldier behind me stamped his foot, and the bird leaped to a perch a few feet away.

"Jumpy?" Lusha said.

The soldier flushed at her scornful tone, and tried to assume a semblance of his former stoicism. Biter continued to stare from the rock.

A whisper of motion overhead. I glanced up and found several pairs of beady eyes gazing down at me.

The soldier let out a muffled curse. He had seen them too. But before he could do anything, the birds floated to the ground, forming a rough semicircle around him.

"What is this?" the man said, shifting his bow from one raven to another. They kept moving, darting from tree to ground and back again, croaking eerily. One soared so close to the man's head that he loosed the arrow by accident—it thunked harmlessly into a tree.

The other soldier seemed to be having similar difficulties. After loosing his own arrow, unsuccessfully, he had tossed his bow aside and drawn his sword. He swiped first at one raven, then another, the creatures nimbly dodging the blows. It was like battling the wind.

Someone seized my wrist, and I started. Lusha had freed herself and held a knife—had the ravens brought it? Within seconds, she had sliced through my ropes.

The soldier closest to us seemed half out of his mind. More ravens had settled in the nearby trees—the man loosed arrow after arrow until his quiver was empty, then began slicing at the air with his sword, each time missing the mark.

"Send for the captain," he said to the other soldier, who barely seemed to hear him.

Shouts rang out from the other camp. To my astonishment, the soldiers there seemed to be engaged in a flailing battle with an invisible enemy. Then I saw a flash of feathers as a raven swooped past their campfire.

I had enough time to marvel at the sight of the fearsome soldiers of the Fifth Army locked in battle with a flock of birds before Lusha crept up behind one of our guards and struck him on the head with a rock.

I surged to my feet. The second soldier didn't even notice—ravens skimmed his scalp with their claws. Following Lusha's lead, I hefted a rock, and slammed it against his skull.

The man dropped like a dead branch. I poked him with my foot, but he merely let out a low groan.

I snatched the *kinnika* from around his neck. Then Lusha and I ran toward the chaos of the larger camp, ravens trailing like the train of a dark dress.

"Tem!" I yelled.

He looked up, his eyes widening. He was restrained by two

soldiers, though he didn't appear to be struggling. They must have assumed he was the cause of this—and why wouldn't they? The ravens who had accompanied us joined the others attacking the soldiers.

I tossed Tem the *kinnika*. He caught them one-handed, already mouthing an incantation. The bells sang out, and the soldiers restraining him staggered back as if propelled by an invisible force.

I was at Tem's side in a heartbeat, my arm around his shoulders. "Can you run?"

One side of his face was bruised, and he held himself stiffly, but he nodded.

Lusha reappeared, holding her pack. Motioning, she dashed into the trees, and Tem and I followed. Behind us, the soldiers were still fighting their impossible battle. Ravens lay dead on the forest floor, but it made little difference. Each time they killed one, another took its place.

We plowed through the forest at a stumbling run. Several ravens came along, flitting ahead of us like sentinels. Tem tripped over a root.

"Lusha," I called, "slow down. Tem can't—"

"And where, pray tell, are you going?"

Lusha stumbled to a halt so abruptly that I collided with her. The captain stepped out of the trees, bow drawn, arrow nocked, his expression savage.

"I presume these creatures are yours?" He neither flinched nor shifted his gaze as a raven fluttered past his head. He stopped before Lusha, the arrow mere inches from her throat. "And that they would mourn if I loosed this arrow?"

Lusha held up a hand, and the ravens stopped swooping. They clustered in the branches like deathly spectators in an arena, their black gazes fixed on Elin.

Lusha didn't look at the arrow. She only looked at the captain. "You won't kill me."

"No? You seemed so certain of my malicious intentions earlier. And that was before you threw my army into chaos."

Lusha moved forward so that the tip of the arrow brushed her skin. "If you were going to kill me, you would have already done it. For some reason, you're holding back."

"Do you truly not know the reason?" His voice was low. His fingers gripping the bowstring were white. "What are you? Tell me the truth."

"I have. We are not witches. We mean no harm to anyone."

"Says the girl who can command a flock of ravens with a gesture, and a man's heart with a glance."

I expected Lusha to fix him with that cool look she gave all men who were too familiar, no matter how handsome they were, or give him a sharp retort—but to my astonishment, she did neither. Her lips parted, as if she was uncertain how to respond.

The captain seemed to sense this. His bow lowered slightly, his chin only inches from her forehead. Lusha made no move to step back, merely gazed up at him. Elin's hair tumbled forward, obscuring one eye.

Then Lusha's arm shot up, so quickly I saw only a flash as her knife sliced through the captain's bowstring.

"Kamzin, run!"

Tem and I fell back as the ravens descended in a swarm. The captain gave a shout, stumbling as the creatures converged on him, pecking at his cloak and any exposed inch of flesh they could find. He appeared, for a terrible moment, to be shrouded in a plume of darkness, a darkness with talons and sharp beaks. Then Lusha shoved me ahead of her, and we stumbled into the forest.

TWENTY-ONE

River

FOR THE FIRST time in his life, he was cold.

Light flickered through his eyelids. He coughed and inhaled a mouthful of snow. He shoved himself upright, though the world spun, desperate to be free of the snow that covered him like a smothering layer of blankets.

River blinked, scattering the snowflakes that clung to his lashes. For a moment, he didn't remember where he was. He had been on an expedition, but where? Where was Norbu, and Mara? Had the barbarians captured him? His hands shook as he brushed snow from his arms and shoulders. The snow was pink.

He looked down at his hands, covered in blood, and remembered.

He surged to his feet. His side gave a vicious throb, but he ignored it.

Esha.

He would kill his brother. He thought it calmly, though he was filled with a black fury he hadn't felt since Thorn had sent him word of Sky's death. Esha had killed Sky, the only thing in River's life that had mattered. River would kill him. It was as simple as that.

With shaking hands, he examined his wounds, peeling back the torn, frozen layers of his *chuba*. His shoulder was completely healed—ordinary knives were largely useless against witches. The two wounds in his side were ugly and dark. Yet they seemed to have stopped bleeding.

He should not be alive. Esha had used an obsidian dagger. Yet apart from the chill that nestled under his skin, and the pain—both of which were bearable—he felt almost normal. He considered the mystery for a moment, then discarded it. There were more important things.

The wind howled; the clouds churned. His *chuba* billowed around him, his hair tossing in his eyes. Since he had fallen unconscious, a ferocious storm had covered the mountain—he guessed it was morning, but it was impossible to be certain. He paid the elements no attention. He pressed his face into his hands and was surprised to find his cheeks wet.

He didn't know how long he stood there, leaned against the mountain, as the wind moaned and the snow raged. He could only think of Sky—alone, vulnerable. River had left his eldest brother, who had always protected him, not realizing that he might need protection himself.

He didn't move until what he felt crystallized into something hard, sharp, deadly. He wiped his face. Grimacing against the pain he anticipated, he shifted into a hawk.

Agony. He hadn't lied to Kamzin—changing shape when injured was something to be endured as a last resort. He crouched for a moment, the wind tugging at his feathers, as waves of pain crashed and receded. Then he launched himself into the air.

The wind whipped him toward the mountainside, but he fought it, before letting a gust sweep him into a valley. He saw no sign of Esha or any of the others.

He folded his wings and plummeted toward the ground. Hail tore at his feathers, sharp as nails, and he was tossed around like a doll. He fell for some time—it had been high in the mountains, where he had confronted Kamzin—before opening his wings and settling on solid ground.

Esha was gone. He forced himself to swallow his fury and view the problem rationally. Even if he found Esha, what could he do? His elder brother might not have the Crown, but neither did River, whatever Esha thought. Esha had allies—he had every witch in the Nightwood. River couldn't stop him alone.

And he had to stop him. He wouldn't give up his search for the star—River knew him too well. Once his brother decided on a course of action, nothing would turn him from it. And what he planned to do with the star was so terrible that River could barely bring himself to consider it. He had to move fast.

There was only one person with the power to stop Esha. It wasn't an appealing prospect, but River had few options.

River hadn't been there to protect Sky, but he would be there now. He would stop Esha from turning Sky into something twisted and wrong. Sky would rest in peace, as he deserved. It was as much as River could give him.

The shadows stirred, and River was airborne again, leaving behind only faint marks in the snow, which the wind soon erased.

TWENTY-TWO

WE RAN—FOR HOW long, I couldn't say. Until the trees grew too thick and tangled for speed, and the sound of the stream faded to nothing. Hills rose up on all sides, partly obscuring the sky.

"Lusha," I gasped. "I can't—my shoulder—"

She finally stopped, and I collapsed in a half sprawl on the forest floor. Each deep, gasping breath seemed to send another arrow into my shoulder. I was certain I would faint again. Lusha collapsed beside me, lowering her head between her knees. The bead of sweat trickling down her cheek caught the moonlight as she turned her head.

"Well, if the captain wasn't already convinced we were the enemy, he is now," I said, once I was able to speak.

"They'll follow us," Lusha said. Biter settled on the leafy ground beside her and let out a low croak. "We have to keep moving."

I touched Tem's arm. He was hunched forward, his face reddened. Beneath that, though, there was a grayish tinge to his skin.

"Did they hurt you?"

He shook his head slightly. "It's not that."

I wrapped my arm around his shoulders, and he leaned his head against mine. Lusha, to her credit, didn't speak, though I could sense the urgency radiating from her.

"The strangest part is," he murmured, "I'm not that surprised." He drew back. He was smiling, but it was a sad thing, as gray as the rest of him.

I didn't have to ask what he meant. Tem had never *fit*. Overlooked and ignored by the villagers, including his own father, he had never seemed part of Azmiri, despite rarely setting foot outside the village boundaries.

"I don't want to be like them," he said.

"You're not." My voice was fierce. "You're *nothing* like them. Just because you share their magic—that doesn't mean anything."

"The magic—" Tem faltered. "I don't know how I did that."

"Your powers must have been bound by the emperor's spell, just like River's were. At least partly."

Tem swallowed. "What I did felt—wrong. Is that how Azar-at's magic feels? Wrong?"

"It's not the same," I said. "Your magic isn't wrong. It's part of you, and I refuse to believe that any part of you is wrong."

His expression lightened a shade. "Including my two left feet?"

"*Besides* that."

He was quiet for a long moment, his gaze distant.

"I've always wondered who my mother was," he said. "Was she one of the witches who attacked those soldiers in the Amarin Valley last year? Or set Jangsa on fire? All those people . . ."

There was nothing I could say to that. I just kept my arm around him until he drew a long breath.

"All right," he said. "I can keep going. But *where* are we going?"

"The Three Cities," Lusha said without hesitating. "Kamzin's original plan is the best we have. We take the star to the emperor. We tell him everything we know about River, about their plans, everything. Hopefully his shamans can use the star to recast the binding spell before the witches attack the Three Cities."

"But how will we get an audience with him?" Tem said. "I doubt his guards will be eager to listen to us." It was an understatement. In our torn and dirty clothing, our haggard appearance, we could pass for beggars. My face was chapped and sunburned and frostbitten. My tangles had tangles. We had no fresh clothes, no money. The emperor's guards wouldn't let us near the palace.

"I'll figure something out," Lusha said. Biter croaked, as if in agreement. Several ravens had settled in the trees around us, perhaps having tired of pecking and clawing at the soldiers. A shiver crawled down my back as I felt their eyes on me.

"Lusha," I said, "where did you learn that trick with the ravens?"

She blinked at me. "I didn't. It was Biter."

"Biter." The raven croaked again at the sound of his name. He hopped onto Lusha's shoulder and plucked a twig from her hair. The intelligence in his gaze was eerie—was this the first time I had noticed it? Biter was Lusha's lifelong familiar, as Ragtooth was mine, his presence as mundane and unquestioned as an old footpath. But what did we really know about familiars and their powers? Very little—Biter had shown that tonight. The myriad dangers we had faced since leaving Azmiri had brought to light more than just Tem's abilities.

Distant shouts reached my ears. The soldiers had found our trail. Lusha made an impatient gesture, and we ran on.

TWENTY-THREE

WE ENTERED THE Three Cities under cover of darkness.

The roads climbed and descended, twisted and turned over the hilly ground, nearly causing me to lose my normally unfailing sense of direction. There was only the glow of a passing traveler's lantern—or dragon, if they could afford one—to illuminate our way, that and the patches of light spilling from mansions and well-kept shops.

We were exhausted. In the two days since we had escaped the Fifth Army, we had barely rested, stopping only occasionally to snatch our sleep in shifts. On the second day, Tem, who looked like a wisp of his former self, had begun to stumble—eventually I had taken his arm in mine and steered him through the forest while he leaned his weight on me.

As Lusha was the only one of us who had visited the Three Cities, she led the way through the winding, hilly streets. I was only too happy to let her—I felt more intimidated by the city than I ever had by the height of a mountain, or the darkest depths of a forest. Every dwelling loomed large, swollen with impossible luxury.

The Three Cities were no longer three—they had, at one time, been separate, gleaming entities, with their tiered temples and palaces of whitewashed stone, nestled among the low hills that surrounded Dawa Lake. Over the centuries, though, the cities had overflowed, with buildings established outside their walls, lining new roads cut into the fertile soil of the hills. As the Empire's prosperity grew, even the wealthiest nobles built their palaces here, as the old walls no longer seemed like a necessary protection against anything. What did the Three Cities have to fear? The witches had been defeated, and the emperor's mighty armies were more than a match for any barbarian tribe. The walls remained, but sections were torn down to make way for new thoroughfares. Though they were still manned by soldiers, the gates were now little more than decorative relics. The Empire's strength was no longer expressed by its walls, but by its armies and shamans.

As we drew deeper into the city's heart, more guards appeared, posted at corners and in squares. We slowed when we approached them, but they stared at us anyway. It was the middle of the night, and there weren't enough people around to make our presence inconspicuous. Surely that was all it was. I met the gaze of a burly guard, who narrowed his eyes at the three of us.

When we rounded a corner, and the palace came into view, I wasn't ready for it.

The emperor's seat was perched on the tallest hill in the Three Cities, nestled against the peak with the earth pressing into its back. It was whiter than bone, its star-silvered windows and splashes of green or blue dragonlight the only contrasts to the purity of the façade. A series of staircases zigzagged their way up the hill on three sides, also made of whitewashed stone, and patrolled by guards visible only by the dragons that strolled at their sides. Yet they seemed tiny—insect-like specks against the enormity of the gleaming palace complex.

River would have climbed those stairs countless times. I swallowed. I had been trying not to think of River. I shouldn't be haunted by the memory of him hunched over the snow, given all that he had done. But the grief wouldn't lift. I would never have the chance to reconcile the River I had glimpsed in my visions—the boy desperate for his brother's approval, the teenager willing to sacrifice his soul to lift the curse on his family—with the witch who had left me on Raksha's summit.

"How are we going to get inside?" Tem said.

Lusha was frowning. "We should find somewhere to stay for the night. In the morning, we'll send word to Amvar, one of the emperor's seers. He should be able to get us an audience with the emperor. I met him during my visit with Father—I think he'll remember me."

"You think?" I repeated. "Lusha, we have to take the star to the emperor now. He has to recast the binding spell—"

"We can't just stroll into the palace." Lusha glowered at me. "The guards won't let us near the emperor. To them, we're no one. Do you have a better plan?"

I didn't. Lusha turned right at the next square. We paused outside an inn lit by so many lanterns it illuminated the entire street. I thought yearningly of the baths and hearty meals within those walls that awaited travelers with sufficient coin.

"So many guards," Lusha muttered. "There weren't nearly this many when I came here with Father."

This struck me as ominous. "With all the attacks on the villages, the emperor must have put the city on alert."

And indeed, when I thought about it, the city did seem on edge. The few residents we passed eyed us furtively, as if suspicious of our presence but not wanting us to know it. Many of the shops boasted gates wrought of iron that gleamed with newness.

Tem touched my arm. "Kamzin."

I turned. Two men were coming toward us. I recognized one as the burly guard I had briefly locked eyes with. That had been blocks ago. His companion had his sword unsheathed.

I felt a chill. What was going on? We had done nothing but walk through the city.

"This way," Lusha said, motioning us down a narrow lane. Once we were out of sight of the guards, we broke into a run.

"I don't understand," Tem said. "They followed us—why?"

Lusha shook her head once, sharply. The guards had rounded the corner behind us—and now they were running too.

Lusha turned down another street. I wasn't sure how much

longer I could keep going on so little food and sleep. But she led us to the first doors that presented themselves, framed with a golden awning. The enormous handles were hung with long, beaded tassels.

"Lusha, this is—"

"Open them," she said to Tem.

Tem was so exhausted it seemed to take his eyes a moment to focus. He lifted one of the *kinnika*, pressing his hand against the wood.

The door cracked in half.

"Tem!" I cried.

"I don't know how to unlock doors, Kamzin," he said wearily.

"Never mind that." Lusha pressed against one half of the broken door until it opened wide enough to squeeze through. She shoved the two of us through, then followed quickly after, pressing the door shut.

Inside, it was dark and perfectly silent. The smell of juniper incense was overwhelming—I had to suppress a sneeze. Thick wooden pillars supported a shadowy ceiling painted in vivid, geometric patterns. At the far end of the long room was a shrine, empty now, on which could be placed statues of different spirits. The walls were hung with tapestries depicting ancient heroes and emperors, who could also be prayed to by visitors kneeling on the stone floor. The only illumination came from a few candles burning on low tables along the walls.

We had just broken into a temple.

"Now what?" My voice echoed through the large, empty space.

"Not only do we have no way into the palace, but the emperor's guards seem to think we're criminals."

Lusha's hand went to her pack, where the star nestled inside a spare tunic. "We'll make for Amvar's house."

Tem coughed. Lusha put her finger to her lips, but he didn't seem able to stop—the incense was too much for him. Lusha beckoned, and we hurried after her. I shivered as we passed beneath a lurid tapestry depicting a hero with a hideous scowl—her eyes seemed to follow us, as if her spirit inhabited the woven threads.

We came to a small room with tables laden with food offerings—a pitcher of souring milk; khir; spiced lamb; a bowl of soft cheese. I knew that in large temples like this, food was often left out for the spirits at all times—though from the smell, these offerings hadn't been freshened lately. A small door led off the room.

Lusha hurried forward, her hand going to the handle, when suddenly it opened, swinging inward. She started back, knocking me against the table of offerings. The milk overturned, spattering all three of us, and my elbow landed in a bowl of rice.

The young man who had entered seemed equally startled, staring at us with round eyes. He was clad in the black robes of a temple attendant. We stared at each other for a heartbeat, and then the man's eyes narrowed. He turned his head as if to call to someone.

"Go," Lusha said. Tem and I were already moving—back through the temple, past the enraged hero. We reached the doors, and I thoughtlessly wrenched the handle on the broken side.

"Watch out!" Lusha shouted as the heavy block of wood fell backward with a creak. Tem yanked me out of the way, and the door slammed into the stone floor, the sound reverberating.

I groaned. Any spirits that may have been slumbering in the temple—along with any living neighbors—were not likely to be asleep anymore.

We darted back onto the street. Fortunately, there was no sign of the guards.

"Do you actually know where you're going?" I asked Lusha.

As if in response, she stopped short. She had seen something around the corner of the next street.

"Guards," she said, stepping back. "Headed this way. They must be sweeping the neighborhood."

There was no time to run. Lusha motioned to a wall over which the boughs of fragrant fruit trees leaned—a garden. Tem gave Lusha a boost while I easily hauled myself up. Then the two of us helped Tem scale the wall—he was so exhausted his feet kept slipping. The three of us landed atop a prickly bush just as the sound of pounding feet reached us. The guards continued past the garden at a rapid pace. We lay unmoving until the sound faded.

"Where are we?" Tem said.

"The merchants' quarter," Lusha replied. She glanced around us. "In someone's goji patch, by the looks of it."

I extricated myself from the vines, cursing as they caught at my *chuba*. The reddish stains from the crushed berries did not exactly enhance my bedraggled appearance—nor did the sweet rice tangled in my hair. Dragonlight flickered through one of the shuttered windows of the house looming over the garden, and I fell silent.

"We can't stay here," Tem said.

"We're safer here than on the streets." Lusha rubbed her brow. "I don't understand how he sent word so quickly."

It took me a moment to grasp what she meant. Dread settled in my chest.

"Elin," I murmured.

Lusha nodded. "Three witches escaping the Fifth Army is not exactly a common occurrence. He must have sent a messenger to the Three Cities with our description, and a warning that we were at large."

We froze as another set of footfalls stampeded along the lane. But they too continued past the garden without pause.

"What are we going to do?" I whispered.

Lusha made no reply. For the first time I could remember, she seemed defeated. She slumped against the wall, her *chuba* slipping off one shoulder.

I felt that now-familiar tug—the urge to use Azar-at's magic. But where before I had seen it as a harmless thing, now it frightened me. The fire demon would be near, crouched somewhere out of sight. Naturally, the harder I pushed away my thoughts of magic, the more they filled my mind.

I thought of the girl with my face, staring at me from the darkness. I shuddered. If those hallucinations were connected to Azar-at—the beginnings of the madness that afflicted all shamans who used a fire demon's power—they would only worsen if I cast another spell.

An hour crept by. Tem's head slumped forward, and he barely murmured when I shook him. In the end, I let him sleep. Biter alighted briefly in the fragrant pear tree, then flew off, disappearing into the night on quiet wings. I felt a twinge of envy.

I started awake at the feeling of someone tugging at my hair. At some point, I had nodded off, my head falling onto Lusha's shoulder. She was removing leaves from my hair with gentle fingers.

"This is familiar," she said. "How many times did Father scold you for coming home with leaves and pinecones tangled in your hair?"

"Not since I was twelve," I replied in a dignified voice. But I let her pluck the foliage, feeling surprisingly soothed.

"'You can't just wander in to dinner looking like some forest beast,'" Lusha said, mimicking Father's tone precisely.

I laughed. She tugged at another tangle, her expression growing thoughtful. "We should split up. They're looking for three travelers—we're too easy to pick out."

This struck me as a bad—even ominous—idea. "The guards have seen us. Splitting up won't change that. We should stick together and make for the seer's house as quickly as possible."

Lusha was already shaking her head. "His house is in the next quarter—there are too many guards between here and there."

Her tone carried a familiar note of finality that never failed to annoy me. I opened my mouth to argue, and then, slowly, closed it. I felt almost disappointed—after everything Lusha and I had been through, we were still arguing?

I let out my breath. Lusha would never stop infuriating me—expecting otherwise was unrealistic. We were flint and steel—we would always spark when we were together. It didn't mean anything. I would still lay down my life for her, or follow her to the edge of the world, even if we spent the entire journey arguing.

"All right," I said. "You go with Tem, and I'll follow."

Lusha blinked. Her eyes narrowed in suspicion, and I returned her gaze blandly. I felt lofty and high-minded for letting go of the argument, though there was a part of me that also enjoyed Lusha's confusion.

"Right," she said, regaining her authoritative composure, "we'll wait to see if they come this way again. Then we run."

I nodded. "I'll go first."

"You're not going by yourself." It was Tem—I hadn't realized he was awake. "If anything, it should be you and Lusha. I have the *kinnika*—I can protect myself."

Tem, to my eyes, didn't seem to be in a state to protect anyone. The bruise from the blow the soldiers had dealt him had darkened, and his face was lined with fatigue.

"Tem—"

"I don't want you to go off alone again, Kamzin. It was hard enough last time, when you went after him." There was a pleading note in Tem's voice. It took me a moment to realize that he was talking about Raksha, when I had left Tem and Lusha in the cave to chase River to the summit. Tem had been asleep when I left. It had been cruel not to say good-bye, given that I had been facing almost certain death, but I had known he would only plead with me to stay.

I pressed his hand and gave a short nod. Lusha and I clambered back over the wall, leaving Tem to follow.

"I don't like this," I said. Lusha's jaw tightened, but she said nothing. Fortunately, the stars were fading, and more people were about—people with carts and yaks and horses. Despite myself, I began to relax. It was true that no one looked as disheveled as us—our appearance drew stares from several passersby—but we would be more difficult to find in a crowd.

"Almost there," she murmured as we turned a corner. From one of the rooftops, a raven gave a cry.

I didn't have time to react. I was wrenched from behind, Lusha's arm torn from mine. She yelled, and the raven seemed to echo her, a mournful sound. I struggled instinctively, but two guards had me in a grip like stone. Lusha was also held by two captors, and before us stood a man with his sword out.

His sword—not the obsidian dagger that dangled from his belt. Yet I didn't have time to fully process this—one of the men was speaking.

"This is them?" he said.

The man regarding us nodded. With a start, I recognized him as the burly guard who had initially spotted us. "Where's the boy?"

"Got away from us. We'll find him."

"You're making a mistake," Lusha interjected. "We're not witches."

"Witches?" The burly man's brow furrowed. He glanced at the others, as if for an explanation. "What's this?"

"Search me," said one of the guards holding Lusha. He was middle-aged with a vague sort of frown that put me in mind of Norbu. His hair, like many of those we had passed in the streets, was dyed the color of blueberries in deference to the latest style. "We have our orders. He doesn't want to be kept waiting."

"No." A look of trepidation passed over the burly man's face. As if to conceal it from the others, he added in a light voice, "That's the nobility for you."

"Where are you taking us?" I demanded. The men were half marching, half dragging us down the still-shadowed street. The man with the sword followed, but he held it almost lazily.

"Sorry about this," he said, when I glanced over my shoulder. "But you did run off before."

"Isn't that what most people do when they're being followed by armed guards?" I snapped.

The man frowned. "Only if they've got something to hide, in my experience."

I felt a wave of desperation. No doubt we were being taken to some dank prison to be held for interrogation, just as the general had threatened. Obtaining an audience with the emperor would now be impossible. And Tem—where was Tem? I sent out a silent prayer to the spirits that he had escaped, though I doubted they would be in the mood to heed me after tonight.

The soldiers led us through narrow lanes and alleys, seeming to wish to avoid attention. Being unfamiliar with the city, I was startled when the road opened, revealing the palace hill. Were the guards taking us to the emperor's dungeons?

I swallowed a hysterical laugh. Well, at least we would succeed in gaining entrance to the palace.

Even as the palace loomed larger, it was impossible to believe it was our destination. Grand white staircases led up to tiered walls of apartments, courtyards, storehouses, and who knew what else—the palace had the appearance of multiple grand mansions stuck together, but the effect was not haphazard. It was of overwhelming luxury. We moved past homes of increasingly stately mien, and then we were ascending.

The guards led us up a smaller stair, from which fewer lights gleamed. Behind us, the Three Cities lay scattered over the hills like a child's discarded toys, and beyond the towers were glimpses of the lake, starlight glancing off its smooth surface. My breath caught at the sight of that endless stretch of water. The guards chatted among themselves, and I found myself wondering at their ease—was this how they behaved around all captured witches? Or had Elin left that detail out? My stomach felt twisted and strange. The palace was all blunt, towering opulence. Gazing at it, I found myself wondering how I had thought the Three Cities could be overthrown, or even threatened. Then I recalled everything I had seen of the witches' powers. I thought of an army with those same powers, and of mighty walls incapable of holding out the darkness.

The door at the top of the staircase was manned by palace guards, recognizable by the emperor's symbol, the mountain poppy, emblazoned across their armor. They swung the doors open for us without question, as if we had been expected. One tossed a ribald remark at the burly man, who replied with good-humored dismissiveness.

Our captors led us through what appeared to be servants' passages, narrow with low ceilings, though still adorned with evidence of wealth—a richly woven tapestry here, a well-fed palace dragon there, scampering through an open doorway. At this early hour, the place was quiet—the few servants we passed mostly ignored us. And then, before I even had time to take in my surroundings, or the fact that I had passed unchallenged into the emperor's palace, the guards were ushering us along a loftier series of window-lined corridors, through enormous doors of carved oak inlaid with jade, and into an apartment of impossible luxury lit by several of the fattest dragons I had ever seen.

The room was expansive and high-ceilinged, the far wall lined with glass windows, the floor scattered with costly wool rugs. Another intricately carved door, slightly ajar, led perhaps to private chambers, or perhaps a series of beautiful receiving rooms like this one. I blinked, not quite taking it in, as I turned my gaze to the exquisitely dressed nobleman who stood before us.

"Hello, Kamzin," River said. "What kept you?"

TWENTY-FOUR

"THANK YOU, DAREN—I'M sorry my friends gave you so much trouble," River said.

"No matter, *dyonpo*," the man replied. "We don't have much opportunity for exercise in the Three Cities."

The other guards smiled, though they seemed less at ease in River's presence, their posture stiff and their eyes lowered respectfully.

"Why would you?" River said. "There's no safer place than the heart of the Empire. Send word when you find the boy."

The guard nodded, and they bowed themselves out, leaving us alone with River.

I felt as if I were falling. For a long moment, we simply stared at each other. Was I dreaming? I saw River in the Ashes, covered in blood—dying. Yet here he was, looking handsome, clean, and polished, dressed in an expensive silk tunic of dark crimson. His boots were glossy and of the paper-thin style favored in the Three Cities. He was the very image of the young nobleman I had met at the banquet in Azmiri, though he had not bothered to turn his hair blue again. Then the shadows at his feet stirred, and it was as if I were seeing two versions of him, one overlaying the other.

He wore a slight smile, his hands in his pockets. Absurdly, I remembered that I had rice in my hair.

My heart was pounding, and I was filled with a strange, painful relief that twisted in my chest. I had taken an involuntary step forward, and I forced myself back. A thousand questions sprung to my lips. Instead, I found myself saying, "I thought you were dead."

His gaze turned inward. "So did Esha. He never would have left me on that mountain, otherwise."

"But the dagger was obsidian," I said. "The stories say that even a scratch will kill a witch. But you're here."

"I'm here," he said. "If you're asking for an explanation, I'm afraid I don't have one."

"Those guards were yours," I breathed. "You had them watching for us. Why—how did you know—"

"You told me where you were going," he said. "You do know that Azar-at can read your thoughts? You don't need to announce every spell you cast—though I suppose it's like you to do everything as dramatically as possible."

I couldn't focus. River was here. River was alive. It was too much.

"You want the star," Lusha said. Her expression was unreadable. She hadn't drawn her dagger, but her posture was wary, ready to fight or flee. "That's why you followed us. That's why you posted guards to watch for us."

"I want to keep the star from Esha," River said. "That's the beginning and end of my interest in it."

"You expect us to believe that?"

River let out an exasperated breath. "The star was Esha's plan. I'm not following his plan anymore. I have my own."

"He's your brother," Lusha said. "How can we—"

"He will try to kill me," River said, "the first chance he gets. He almost succeeded in the Ashes. He believes I have a power that I don't, and he'll stop at nothing to take it from me. He killed my brother. And you believe I'm still on his side?"

River's voice was cold. Lusha didn't flinch, but some of the wariness left her face.

"I don't know what I believe," she said. "But I know you saved Kamzin's life. For that, I thank you."

Now it was River's turn to gaze at Lusha in disbelief.

"You don't need to thank me," he said finally. "We're not all like Esha."

"I'm not convinced of that." Lusha folded her arms. Her gaze, as she regarded him, was cold—but not fearful. With her imperious posture and disapproving frown, she didn't seem out of place surrounded by such luxury, despite the fact that her *chuba* was torn, her boots muddied, and her hair disheveled. "I'm thanking you for what you did in the Ashes—no more, and no less."

He turned to me. "I take it from your surprise at my survival that you haven't had any more . . . visions."

"No." I felt that uncomfortable sense of displacement. "Have you?"

He smiled. I didn't think I would ever get used to how quickly his moods shifted. "No. I'm glad it worked."

"What?"

"Once I realized Azar-at was the cause of all this, I focused on closing my mind. I've done it before, when I didn't wish to communicate with him. I wasn't certain it would be effective for this."

"That sounds useful." How many times had I wished I could block the creature's voice from my thoughts?

"I don't think it severs our connection," he said, glancing away from me. "I don't know how to do that."

I flushed, wondering again what he had seen when he had shared my thoughts. "Why are you here?"

"It's simple. I can't defeat Esha alone. So I will help the emperor do it. I know how Esha thinks, and I know what he's capable of. The emperor sees me as his friend, and will listen to my advice. So for now, I'm here."

"For now," I repeated. "And that's supposed to convince us to trust you?"

He shook his head slightly. "You use that word often. I've never asked you to trust me. But you can trust that I want Esha dead. He thinks himself a leader, but he destroys everything he touches. He'll destroy his own people eventually, if he isn't stopped." His voice was eerily flat.

Lusha's hand went to her pocket, where she had carried the star since our escape from the soldiers. "Then he still plans to attack the Three Cities."

"I'm sure of it," River said. "Nothing will dissuade him, especially now that the star is here."

Lusha set her jaw. "We're not giving you the star."

River gazed at her. She glared back, wan but determined. Lusha knew as well as I did that if River wanted to take the star, he could. I remembered how easily he had overcome us in the Ashes.

"Fine," he said. "You can hold on to it. There's little danger that Esha will attack soon. I suspect they're regrouping—the attacks on the villages have stopped."

"Stopped?" I was weak with relief. Did that mean Azmiri was safe?

"The nearest villages have been sending daily reports," River said. "Suddenly, it's quiet—losing the star was a blow. Esha was already struggling. Some witches have fled rather than answer to him, and more will follow, if they decide that their emperor is weak. I know Esha—he'll need time to come up with a new plot."

River turned to me. "Where were you, anyway? I've had the guards on the lookout since my return yesterday. I was starting to worry that Esha had found you."

I opened my mouth to reply—to tell River about Azar-at's trickery, and our capture by the Fifth Army. Then I stopped, confused. After all that had happened, it was alarming how easily I found myself falling back into trusting him, into accepting the *rightness* of his presence. Yet we couldn't trust River—could we?

I thought of the guards River had posted to watch for us and bring us safely to the palace. I thought of him saving my life in the Ashes, the odd expression he had worn when he had laid eyes on me again—as if he couldn't quite believe I was real, but wanted to. His expression was similar now, his familiar, mismatched eyes holding nothing more sinister than curiosity.

Did trust have to be complete to be real? Was it possible to feel for someone only a glimmer of trust, an ember rather than a flame? I looked at Lusha. She shook her head slightly, raising her eyebrows in an expression that was a perfect mirror of what I felt. My palm tingled, a memory of the power that had briefly surged through his—my—hand. For a moment, I felt a strange sense of loss—I would never see the world through River's eyes again.

Hesitantly, I described our journey from the forest, including our capture by the Fifth Army. River showed no reaction when I described the powers Tem had revealed. As I spoke, there came a slight sound. River's gaze fixed on something behind me, and I realized the door had opened.

"Here he is," said the guard. His hand rested firmly on Tem's shoulder.

"Tem!" I surged forward, wrapping him in a hug. Distantly, I heard River dismiss the guard, the door closing. Tem seemed dazed.

"Are you all right?" I said. I placed a hand on either side of his face, searching his eyes.

He brushed me away. "Fine. But I don't—" His gaze fell on River.

"There," River said with a dismissive gesture. "I've found your shaman, Kamzin. I only hope he was more successful at hiding his identity from the guards than he was from the Fifth—"

That was all he got out before suddenly, he was flying through the air.

Flying backward, hitting one of the windows so hard it cracked, and falling to the ground. The dragons snorted with alarm and sailed through the half-open inner door.

"Tem, stop," I shouted, lunging forward and grabbing his arm. He was holding the *kinnika*, his hand already going for the witch bell.

"Is that it?" River was behind us suddenly, brushing shards of glass from his sleeves. His eyes shifted from Tem to the witch bell. "I wouldn't recommend that one, personally. You might only be a half blood, Tem, but you'll still end up with a nasty headache. You've felt it, I'm sure. Did you still refuse to accept the truth, afterward?"

At that, Tem's face grew darker than I'd ever seen it. Tossing the *kinnika* aside, he lifted his hand, and the floor split apart.

I stumbled and fell as roots—*roots*—tore through the stone floor. Lusha staggered back and tripped over a chair. A window shattered, and I threw up my arms instinctively. The roots swarmed toward River, who made a sound that was somewhere between dismay and annoyance. He shook a few roots from his ankles, then turned with an exasperated curse and simply *walked up* the wall behind him, casting aside a basic law of nature like an overwarm cloak.

Tem faltered briefly before throwing his hand up again. A vicious wind cascaded through the broken window, sweeping me off my feet. I ducked as a table soared past my head—it struck the wall with an earsplitting *crash*. But River was already gone, changing into an owl and soaring through the air. He settled calmly on one of the dragon perches and gazed at Tem as if to say, *Well?*

"Tem," I said, coughing. The air was choked with dust. "River isn't—"

But Tem gave no sign of hearing me. He gave no sign of being aware of anything, apart from River. Slowly, he lifted his hand again.

The perch burst into flame.

Hungry fire spread down the stone wall as if it were made of paper. It was witch fire, dark and wrong, barely warm against my skin despite its ferocity. River made a sharp sound, not exasperated anymore, and vanished. A few feathers floated to the ground. As I watched in horror, the fire spread to a chair—and then the rug I was crouched on.

"Stop," I shouted. I was on my feet again, sidestepping broken boards and lifeless roots. I snatched up the fallen *kinnika* and sounded the scorched bell as hard as I could.

Tem stumbled, his hands lifting to his ears. In that moment of hesitation, I grabbed him and pulled him to the ground. His head struck a root with a force that I felt through my hands, but I made no move to loosen my grip.

His eyes opened again and seemed, finally, to focus on me. "Kamzin—"

"Put it out." The flames surged closer, and the air was thick with smoke. Lusha had taken up the *kinnika* and was muttering an incantation, which seemed to be having no effect. "Now, Tem."

He raised himself onto his hands, blinking hard. He took in the flames as if dazed. "I—I don't know how."

"You don't know how? Do what you just did, but the opposite!"

"It's not that easy. I—" He stopped, and a wave of weariness passed over his face. His eyes drifted briefly shut before snapping open again.

Lusha screamed. A tongue of flame surged toward her. But suddenly, River was there, dragging her out of the way. He dropped her unceremoniously on the ground. He made a gesture, and the towering flames consuming the furniture went out like snuffed candles. Plumes of smoke leaped hissing into the air, and the wall hangings cracked and fell in a shower of sparks.

I collapsed onto my side, choking on the smoke that flooded the room. River grabbed Tem by the shoulders and shoved him onto a chair. A shadow uncurled like a snake, sliding up the back and wrapping itself around Tem's arms and chest. Tem sagged forward, but the shadow caught him before he fell, and held him there.

"Here," River murmured in my ear. He had found a flask and was pressing it into my hand. I drank too fast, spilling water down my chin, desperate to clear the smoke from my throat. I leaned into River, my hand reaching out instinctively to grip the edge of his tunic. The faint smell of wildflowers tickled my nose.

When finally I stopped coughing, River helped me to my feet.

Lusha was throwing open the remaining windows, flooding the room with fresh, clean air.

"You can let him go," I said.

"Can I?" River gave Tem a cool look.

Tem was quiet, fixing River with a gaze that still held an echo of his former fury. He glanced at me, then nodded once.

The shadow uncoiled, and Tem fell forward. I was at his side in an instant.

"I'm sorry," he murmured. His face was drained of color.

"It's all right." I wrapped my arms around him. "We're all right." My own exhaustion, held back until now by nervous energy, swelled. Tem was here, none of us were about to be flung in a dungeon, and if River was right, we were safe from Esha—at least for now.

Someone was pounding on the door. "Wonderful," River muttered, moving to answer it. Several raised voices emanated from the corridor. River gave a curt response, then slammed the door shut. There was a moment of startled silence, and then came another knock, more timid this time.

"They'll go away," River said. "Most of the palace staff thinks I'm half-mad." He surveyed the wreckage of the room. "Still, I'm not sure that will pass as an explanation for this."

Tem's head nodded forward. Against his ashen skin, the bruise was even darker.

"What's that?" River wasn't looking at Tem—he was looking at me. He touched my shoulder, thumb brushing my neck. I flushed, and remembered that my *chuba* was stained with old blood.

"Oh—nothing," I said. "Ended up on the wrong end of the arrow."

"Nothing." River gave his head a rueful shake. "The three of you need rest."

"No," I said, even as weariness surged again. I still had a hundred questions for him. And we had to figure out what to do next. I opened my mouth, but Lusha intervened.

"We can rest after we've spoken to the emperor," she said.

"The emperor is away from court," River said. "He won't return until tomorrow. In any case, I've already warned the General of the Second Army that the witches are preparing an attack. He's agreed to deploy soldiers throughout the Three Cities, though he won't take additional action without the emperor's approval."

He didn't understand. "We have to give the emperor the star now. River, we don't know when—"

I was prevented from continuing by Lusha, who, shifting position, lowered her knee onto my hand. I yelped.

"Sorry," Lusha murmured, shaking her head at her awkwardness. Lusha was never awkward. She turned her face toward mine, and I saw the warning written clearly in her eyes.

"The star is safe here," River said. "And the emperor has no need for a resurrection spell."

"But—" I began. There came another, more determined knock at the door, and River moved to answer it with an exasperated sigh.

Lusha was looking at me, her expression ferocious. "Kamzin."

I understood.

River didn't know what the star was for. I searched through my visions of him, and saw my guess confirmed. He knew that it was a source of power, and he knew now that it could raise the dead. But he didn't know that the emperor had used a fallen star to bind the witches' powers.

I sat back, stunned. Little was known about the binding spell—not even Chirri knew how the emperor had cast it. River, clearly, couldn't learn the truth about the star. As much as he hated Esha, I didn't think for a moment that he would allow the emperor to recast the spell.

Lusha was still watching me, a wariness in her expression. I had, for a brief moment, forgotten that River wasn't one of us. Lusha hadn't. Did she think I would hesitate now, out of loyalty to River, or reveal the star's true power?

I thought of how River had saved me in the Ashes. I also thought of how he had lied to me, used me to get what he wanted, and abandoned me on Raksha.

I swallowed. I met Lusha's gaze and nodded once.

"The servants are preparing your rooms," River said, returning.

I didn't meet his eyes. Lusha said, into the silence, "Tem will need a healer."

"I'll see to it."

Moments later, we were being escorted down the corridor by palace servants. After strolling for what felt like an hour, they stopped outside a set of enormous doors more simply carved than River's, but still imposing. One of the servants, a young woman, motioned for Tem to enter.

"I'll stay with him," I said, taking his arm. The girl raised an eyebrow at me, and I flushed. "I don't mean—"

"Kamzin." Tem gave me a weary smile. "I'll be fine. And you need to rest too."

I stepped back and watched him disappear through the doors. Lusha's room was next to Tem's, while mine was on the other side of the corridor. When the door swung open, I drew in my breath.

The room was high-ceilinged, the walls hung with woven tapestries in bright patterns. All the windows were shuttered save one, which overlooked a courtyard crowded with vines and a fountain, its water catching the dawn light like jewels. The bed towered over the room, draped with so many blankets and hangings it was difficult to see how I would even climb in. In the end, I merely pulled off my boots and soiled *chuba* and fell on top of it.

It wouldn't work, though. There was no chance I would be able to sleep, not with Esha lurking and my thoughts of River and the star and the binding spell making my head whirl. We'd made it to the Three Cities, but what were we going to do next? I thought about rising again, to go to Lusha's room and work out a plan. But my face seemed to be glued to the pillow. I had barely a second to note how long it had been since I'd lain in a proper bed before sleep took me.

TWENTY-FIVE

WHEN I AWOKE, it was early twilight, and the room was swathed in pale shadow. For a moment, I didn't know where I was. I lifted my head, blinking, as the memories came trickling back. The bed smelled of lilies. A lock of hair fell across my face, and I grimaced. I didn't smell anywhere near as pleasant as the bed.

A fragment of a dream lingered. I had been soaring above a moonlit mountain range, held aloft by vast, silver wings. Only geese could fly that high, but in my dream I was not a goose, nor was I myself. Ahead of me rose towering plumes of white cloud, and I dove inside them, reveling in the sensation, like the brush of cool silk. Everything was white and ethereal, apart from glimpses of blue sky where the clouds tore.

I shivered. The dream had been unusually vivid. I couldn't recall ever having one like it, and that made me uneasy.

I put the dream out my mind. I was starving, but I had no idea how one went about requesting food in the emperor's palace. Someone—a servant, I assumed—had visited the room since I'd fallen asleep, for my boots and *chuba* were gone, and clean clothing had been placed across the back of a chair. There was also a decanter of water on a table.

I rose, stretching. My body ached in a way it hadn't before. More likely, I had simply failed to notice it.

When had I last rested? Truly rested, not snatched a few hours of sleep in a tent battered by wind or snow? I couldn't remember.

Ragtooth slept at the foot of my bed, perfectly round, his tail a blanket for his face. When had he appeared? I hadn't seen him since we'd left Sasani Forest. He didn't stir when I sat up.

Something nagged at me—a feeling of being watched. "Azar-at?"

Yes, Kamzin.

The fire demon emerged from beneath the bed. The sense of calm evaporated.

Do you need something?

"No," I said quickly. "I just . . . wanted to see if you were there."

I am always here.

"Right." The creature was incongruous against the palace luxury, its smoke-fur brushing the silky blankets, its large paws resting on jade-studded tiles. "Has anyone come to check on me?"

River. Tem. Lusha. Servants.

"River was here?"

Yes. The fire demon's tail wagged. *Then he left.*

I had the impression that this fact disappointed Azar-at, but, as usual, it was impossible to be certain if I was imagining it. I said, "Stay here. I'm going to have a bath."

Yes, Kamzin.

The bathing room was, as I had guessed, behind the door across from the bed. It was an expansive space. Towels and soaps waited on a table beside an enormous bath cut into the stone floor. The water flowed from golden taps, and it was *hot*, filling the room with steam. I tried not to linger, being eager to return to Tem and Lusha, but I couldn't resist. I scrubbed myself from head to toe and carefully removed the bandage on my shoulder. The wound was crusted with dried blood, but it didn't appear infected. Someone had left clean bandages by the edge of the bath, and I applied them carefully, wincing.

Ragtooth padded into the room. He lowered his head over the bath to drink, encountered bubbles, and sneezed.

I eyed the fox. "How did you get into the palace? Climb in through the window?"

Ragtooth occupied himself with washing his nose. Against the finery of the bathing room, it struck me how much mangier he had become since leaving Azmiri. But, I told myself, that was to be expected—the journey had taken a toll on all of us.

"You clearly need this as much as I do." Before he could flee, I seized the fox around his belly and dunked him in the water.

Several bite marks later, I placed Ragtooth, thoroughly scrubbed and dripping, back on the edge of the bath. Sodden, he appeared barely a quarter of his original size. He fixed me with a baleful look, clearly plotting revenge.

"You're welcome," I said. Unable to resist, because he looked so small and mournful, I tickled his belly, drawing my hand back just in time to avoid his teeth.

Once I was clean, I wrapped myself in a towel and wandered back to my room.

To my astonishment, two servants were waiting for me. One held a tray containing a comb and several vials of what looked like oil.

"We've been asked to attend you, *dyonpa*," the closest servant said. She was perhaps a year or two older than me, with a gap-toothed smile and round cheeks.

Dyonpa. It was a word used only for the nobility. I looked longingly at the scented oils, but I didn't have time to be pampered by servants—I needed to find Lusha, to work out what we were going to do next. I had already slept too long. "I—thank you, but I—"

"Sit," the second girl said, somehow turning the command into the gentlest request. I sat on the edge of the bed, which had been made in my absence. They patiently combed the snarls from my hair, applying oil to soften it. They *tsk*ed over my bruises and blisters, my broken and missing toenails. Then they helped me into my clothes—a dress of deep blue brocade that fell to the floor and belted at the waist. It was so soft and so warm I felt as if I were wrapped in a blanket. The gap-toothed girl motioned for me to sit again, and began to massage my feet with a different oil.

"No, that's all right." I pulled my feet out of her grasp. They were so unsightly I felt guilty even displaying them to these pampered attendants. "Thank you."

"As you wish, *dyonpa*." The girl gave me a quick, sly smile. "We've seen worse, you know."

I almost laughed. "Have you?"

"Explorers," the girl said, as if it explained everything. They rose, bowing themselves out. With a sigh of relief, I turned to the tray of food they had left. It was piled high with sweet bean cakes, roasted apples, clear green tea, and several spice-studded dishes of noodles with strangely shaped vegetables that I didn't recognize, but that tasted heavenly after weeks of stale rations. As I ate, I became aware that the room had brightened. I rose, opening the shutter that the servants had closed.

Warm sunlight spilled over me. In the courtyard below, two men in seers' robes stood by the fountain, heads bowed in conversation. Birds sang among the leafy paths.

It was morning, not twilight. I had slept an entire day.

Panic filled me, and the food somersaulted in my stomach. What had happened, while I slept? Had there been more attacks?

Behind me, the door opened. I whirled.

"Calm down," Lusha said by way of greeting. "It's just me."

I surged forward. "The star— Is Esha—"

"The star is safe," Lusha said, patting the pocket of her *chuba*, which, while plain, was woven from expensive silks. "It's as River said—the villages are quiet, according to the messengers. The witches seem to have retreated."

I absorbed this dubiously. Esha hadn't struck me as someone who gave up easily.

"I agree," Lusha said, noting my expression. "Sit down, Kamzin. Eat. The Empire won't fall while you finish your *laping*."

I sat, irritably, but didn't touch my breakfast. "So you think your pocket meets the definition of 'safe'?"

"I can't trust it with anyone else." She sat beside me, absently helping herself to an uneaten cake. Her eyes were shadowed, her face pale, and I wondered how much she had rested. "That's what I came here to tell you. The emperor returns to court today—I have to convince him to meet with me, so I can give him the star. He needs to recast the binding spell."

I frowned. "Can't you give it to one of the royal shamans?"

Lusha gave me a look. "You know as well as I do what Three Cities shamans are like. I spoke with several of them yesterday— without revealing anything about our expedition, of course—and they're hopeless. All they know of fallen stars is rumor and legend. Besides, I can't say too much—what if River finds out what the star can be used for?"

I rubbed my head, which was beginning to ache from the weight of dealings and double-dealings. "I wish we could—"

"We can't." Lusha didn't speak again until I met her eyes. "If River finds out the star can take his powers again, what do you think he'll do? Shrug and make a joke about shamanic magic?"

My mouth was suddenly very dry. I pictured River on the summit of Raksha, the expression he had worn after I tried to stop him from lifting the binding spell. "No."

"The binding spell was cast two centuries ago," Lusha said. "The only person who certainly knows how is the emperor himself, because he was there."

I shivered at the reminder of Emperor Lozong's unnatural life span. It was said that he had ruled for over two centuries, kept alive by some strange shamanic spell. Most outside the Three Cities believed it a tale invented by the first Lozong's descendants to intimidate his enemies. Lusha rose and moved back to the door.

"Where are you going?" I demanded, following.

"I told you." Lusha's hand was already on the door. "I'm going to speak to the emperor's advisors to request a private audience."

"What should I do?" I said.

"You don't have to do anything," she replied. "Stay here, and wait for me to return. Don't speak to anyone—especially not River."

And with that, she was gone.

I stared at the door for a moment, angry and uncertain. I was reminded of all the times Lusha had challenged me in the Ashes—she had thought herself in charge then, and she still did here, hundreds of miles away. She had formed her own plan, and then she had rushed off without allowing me a word in edgewise.

And was it the right plan? Was it wise to wait for the emperor, rather than entrusting the star to his shamans, hapless as some of them might be? Muttering to myself, I stood. I didn't know where I was going, and I didn't care. I was most certainly not going to stay where I was and wait for Lusha.

I slipped on the shoes the servants had left me—they were as flimsy as slippers and instantly made me ill at ease. I couldn't run in these, or climb, or do anything useful. I reminded myself that I was in the palace, and was unlikely to be called upon to do more than walk down polished corridors, but the disquiet remained. I missed my boots.

I slipped out the door. Tem's room, to my disappointment, was empty—the corridor was empty too, apart from a bored-looking guard stationed at either end.

I strode down the corridor, trying to look as if I had come this way a hundred times. The guard didn't even look up. He seemed to be cleaning his nails.

The guards of the Three Cities, on the whole, seemed to be a complacent sort.

I froze. A door had appeared on my right that I didn't recall passing before. It was tall and forbidding, made of a strange black wood that set it apart from the other doors in the corridor. Something about it was familiar.

I reached out, but the door shattered beneath my fingers as if it were made of fog. I leaped back. Behind the door was another narrow, ordinary corridor leading to a flight of stairs.

Was it some form of shamanic magic? If so, what purpose did it serve? I glanced down the corridor at the guard, to see if he had noticed, but he wasn't looking at me.

Uneasy, I continued on my way, pausing outside the ornate doors that led to River's rooms. I wondered if he had sealed them, to prevent anyone seeing the damage from Tem's magic, then I remembered what he had said about the palace staff being afraid of him. I pushed on the door. Sure enough, it opened.

The room was in slightly less disarray than when I had last seen it. The roots had burrowed back through the palace foundations into the hillside. The broken windows had been shuttered, the burned furniture removed, and several new rugs had appeared, but these were inadequate to cover the enormous crack in the floor or the scorch marks everywhere. One of the dragons had returned—it lay on its back on one of the perches, tail dangling over the side.

I gazed around the room. It had been sparsely furnished before, and while clearly intended for nobility, had an unlived-in feel. I tried to imagine River spending any amount of time in this place, and couldn't. But then, River had always seemed more at home in the wilderness than anywhere constrained by walls.

Behind the door at the far end of the receiving room was a dark hall lined with tapestries, and several more doors. My curiosity flared. River's life as a courtier was unfathomable.

I paused, listening guiltily for sounds of approaching footsteps. I would only take a quick look around, I told myself.

Each of the doors opened onto a different, empty room, clean in a neglected sort of way, as if the only activity the room saw was when someone visited to sweep out the dust. Except the one at the end.

That door opened onto a room much larger than the others, which was furnished simply with a bed, a painted cabinet, and a small shrine that was empty of the usual spirit statues. River seemed to have very few possessions. The bed was piled with woven blankets and seemed freshly made. I wondered if the servants changed it every day, even when River wasn't there, in case he returned unexpectedly.

It was almost disappointingly ordinary. I didn't know what I had been anticipating—I knew River slept, after all, and it wasn't as if he'd decorate the place with spiders and human bones. The room had a familiar scent, faint but unmistakable—smoke and wildflowers. I hesitated, considering turning back, but something made me wander past the threshold.

I went to the window. The view of the Three Cities was breathtaking, almost too much to comprehend. The place was alive, streets filled with the bustle of figures too small to discern. The lake was a distant pool of silver that seemed to melt into the clouded sky.

"Beautiful, isn't it?"

I jumped. River was leaning against the doorway, an unreadable expression on his face.

"I'm sorry," I said. "This is your—I didn't—"

"It's all right." A smile flickered. "This isn't really mine. At least, I never thought so."

I swallowed, regretting the whim that had driven me to explore River's rooms. He seemed at ease with my presence, however, strolling over to the cabinet and opening a drawer, as if having girls simply wander into his bedroom was a commonplace occurrence.

I flushed, wishing I hadn't had *that* thought.

"The emperor wants to meet you," River said, his back turned.

"He's holding a banquet this evening."

"A banquet?" I felt a moment of panic. "I'm not attending a royal banquet."

"It's not exactly optional," River said apologetically. "The emperor has extended you an invitation. He will be . . . upset if you refuse."

This didn't help matters. "Why is the emperor holding a banquet when the Empire is under attack?"

"He's been absent from court for over a fortnight. That always puts him in a terrible mood. None of his advisors will have his ear until he's had some wine, listened to a few songs, and flirted with a courtier or two."

I made a scornful sound. "Is he the emperor or a child?"

River glanced at me. "He is ancient."

I swallowed. "What do you plan to do?" I said, because I was genuinely curious. River had, after all, risked his life in returning to the emperor's court. And he wasn't here out of concern for the Empire's safety.

"I meet with Lozong's generals tomorrow," River said, his voice muffled as he leaned over a drawer. "I'll tell them everything I know about Esha's plans. Then I'll help them hunt him down."

"What will you tell them?"

"That after the binding spell broke, I spied on the witches in the Nightwood." He flashed me a smile. "The best lies double as truths."

I felt cold. If River could lie so easily to the emperor, then I should have no problem lying to him. I gazed at the back of his tousled head. Once the emperor recast the binding spell, we would go back to being enemies.

I felt a tiny flicker of triumph at the thought of River realizing that I had deceived him. It surprised me. My anger was still there, and part of me wanted to hurt him as he had hurt me.

Yet I knew what the emperor's spell had done to River and the others. It hadn't destroyed them, but it had taken away what they were. *Living death*, Lusha had said.

A little shiver ran down my spine. "What do you want me to say?"

"You don't have to say anything," River said. "The emperor wants to meet the girl who guided my expedition to Raksha, but he's unlikely to question you. You don't have to be part of this anymore, Kamzin. I should think you'd be happy about that."

My heart was beating too quickly, and I felt an echo of my irritation with Lusha. *You don't have to do anything.* Here was River, saying the same thing—telling me to sit back, to let others worry about the fate of the Empire. As if Azmiri's safety didn't concern me.

I glared at the back of his head. They were both insufferable.

"Here." River came to my side, pressing something into my hand. The blue of his tunic deepened the gold of his left eye—it seemed to glow like a cat's. I glanced down—he had given me a dagger, the hilt elegantly carved, the blade black and glossy. Obsidian.

"This is yours?"

He smiled. "It's no danger to me unless I fall on it. I've been hearing strange rumors from some of the servants—you should keep this close to you."

I looked at it glumly. I doubted I would be any more skilled with a dagger than I was with a bow. It would be better for River to give it to Lusha.

As if reading my thoughts in my eyes, River closed his hand over mine. He guided the dagger toward himself, allowing the tip to rest against the fabric of his tunic, just below his ribs.

"Here," he said quietly. "Like this. Or here." He lifted the dagger to his throat, pressing it against the hollow between his collarbones.

My hand, covered by his, felt very hot. My fingers were only inches from the curve of his jaw. When he released my hand, I let it drift down, the point of the dagger skimming his tunic. He held my gaze, his lips parted slightly, as if about to speak, but no words came. I could count every freckle on his nose, and every black eyelash.

I had a sudden thought, which surfaced like something rising through fog. "What strange rumors?"

He blinked. "There have been sightings throughout the palace, and elsewhere in the Three Cities. Illusions of shadow."

I felt a chill. "What sort of illusions?"

"Doors opening onto unfamiliar passages. Dark towers that disappear when the dawn touches them. Walls of shadow where no walls existed before."

"Dark towers," I murmured. It didn't make any sense. Yet the description was familiar—it was what we had found on the summit of Raksha. The witches' ancient, abandoned city—strange ruins made of shadow tucked into that wind-blasted peak.

"I saw something like that in the corridor," I said. "It was like the sky city."

"Not 'like,'" River said thoughtfully. "I think it *is* the sky city. Traces of it, anyway."

I stared at him, uncomprehending. "Is Esha doing this?"

"No. The sky city isn't really a city. It's . . . alive. Sentient. And it can move from place to place. According to the stories, it wasn't always on Raksha. It was somewhere else, somewhere far away."

"But—" I still didn't understand. "Are you saying it's starting to move here? To the Three Cities? Why?"

"I don't know. Perhaps it believes the Empire is falling."

Suddenly, I felt very small. I realized, perhaps for the first time, how ancient this conflict was, how much stranger than I had imagined. "Can we stop it?"

"I don't know." River rubbed his head. To my surprise, he looked as if he shared my thoughts. "The apparitions began appearing the day the binding spell shattered. But if Esha is defeated, if this goes no further—perhaps. Esha will strike the Three Cities eventually, even though they're outnumbered. He's foolish enough for that. It's just a matter of when."

I noticed his use of the word "they," and wondered if he was aware of how he switched back and forth. "You wish I hadn't come here, don't you?"

He looked surprised. "I wish neither of us had." His voice was quiet and honest. "I wish we were both far away, beside a campfire under the stars. But there's nothing to be gained from wishing."

I was taken aback. How many times had I thought the same thing, even after learning what River was? His words painted a picture that made me ache.

"I don't know about that," I said. "I used to wish for a way to escape Azmiri. I used to lie awake at night, imagining what it could be like."

He smiled at that. "And is this what you imagined?"

I laughed, surprising myself. "Not exactly."

River's hand moved. For one dizzying moment, I thought he was about to brush the hair from my face. But then he seemed to catch himself, the hand drifting to rest on the windowsill. I had gone still, my eyes resting on his. It was impossible not to recall that we had shared the same thoughts.

I took a step back. "I should find Tem."

River nodded. He searched my face, his brow furrowed, and then he turned away. "He's probably in the libraries. He spent all of yesterday evening there."

I groaned. Tem would be beside himself over a library so large it was spoken of in the plural.

"I can take you there," River said, his expression brightening.

I nodded, though part of me regretted my suggestion. I wondered if being around River would ever be straightforward, or if it would always feel like navigating a labyrinth.

River led me out of his rooms and down a staircase that led to a grand, colonnaded walkway. The city lay to our right, shimmering with a fine mist.

We were not stopped once. River called out greetings to each armoured guard we passed, and they answered easily, often with smiles or jokes. He must have trod these corridors dozens of times, and while it was clear his presence was unanticipated, the guards didn't seemed surprised by it. The Royal Explorer, I recognized, was accustomed to coming and going as he pleased, and the guards were used to his returning unannounced from some treacherous expedition or other. More than one called out a question about his mission, which River smoothly evaded. He was good at lying, and even better at sidestepping.

"I'm beginning to understand how you fooled the emperor for so long," I muttered, after leaving behind a guard who had gone so far as to clap River on the shoulder.

He flashed me a smile. He was enjoying himself as usual, as if this was all a game. "Would you prefer it if they attacked us?"

I gave him a look. To my eyes, River, radiating magic as he was, could not look more like a witch. And yet—I squinted. If you didn't look too closely, if you ignored the way the shadows at his feet moved, as if of their own volition, if you looked at him without expecting to see anything otherworldly . . . perhaps most people wouldn't notice. The guards certainly didn't, and none of the courtiers we passed did more than bow respectfully.

"How does that feel?" I said.

He glanced at me. "I've been the Royal Explorer for over three years. I'm quite used to people bowing to me."

"Even people you tried to destroy?" I said evenly.

River gave me a vaguely puzzled look. "I had no particular

wish to destroy them. All I wanted was to break the binding spell."

I was exasperated. "And you didn't think beyond that?"

"Not really." A defensive note entered his voice. "Why should I? Do I owe something to the Empire? To the emperor who stole our magic?"

"No." I thought of what Mingma had said about witches valuing fairness. "But you owe something to me. Is that why you saved my life?"

"I'm not sure I owe you anything. You may have helped me reach the summit of Raksha, but you also tried to kill me there. Have you forgotten that part? I haven't."

"Given the circumstances, I don't think you can blame me," I muttered. "But it's good to know you don't regret anything."

"I don't."

"Fine."

We walked on in stormy silence.

"I suppose I should have told you what I was planning," he said, in an odd tone that was half-exasperated and half-rueful. "That wasn't—I didn't enjoy lying to you."

I stared at him. It wasn't an apology, but it was the closest I'd ever heard him come to one.

"If you had told me, I would have tried to stop you," I said slowly.

"I know."

Another silence. "It wasn't just me you lied to," I said. "What about Mara? Norbu? I'm sure there are dozens more."

"They don't matter," he said, again in that vaguely puzzled

tone, as if it was so obvious he didn't know why I was asking.

I couldn't think of anything to say to that.

After a moment, River said, "Tem seemed surprised by his new abilities. Though he didn't seem particularly inclined to thank me."

"I think Tem was happy the way he was."

River's gaze was thoughtful. "He's unusual. Witches can't use shamanic talismans. Most talismans are imbued with our own magic, and the binding spell prevented us from using our powers in any form. I always thought it was strange, but it must be his human blood. He has a foot in both worlds."

I stopped midstep. River turned to look at me.

"You knew," I breathed. "You knew all along about Tem."

The amusement returned to his eyes. "I wasn't certain until our encounter with the *fiangul*. I know many revered shamans, and not one of them could do what he did in that pass. That sort of affinity with magic is not a human trait." Then, he mused, "I wonder who his mother was."

The world's strange new pattern seemed to come into clearer focus. I thought of all the things Tem was capable of—how he could master a spell as easily as breathing, as easily as Chirri, if not more.

We had come to a stop in a space that was neither inside nor outside, a turn in the wide hallway that was open to the gray sky and the green slope of the palace hill. Grasses stirred in the wind beyond a little balcony, and I could make out the marks of a trail disappearing over the brow of the land. The sun broke through the clouds, and its light fell on us.

"It used to be more common," River said. "Centuries ago, there were many humans with witch ancestry. It's still true that the stronger shamans have some connection to us."

The sunlight was on River's face, illuminating the strands of copper in his hair. For the first time, I noticed a subtle similarity between him and Tem—it was not their appearance, but something in the way they held themselves, a lightness or unconscious poise. "Will he be all right?" I said.

"I would think so. If he can work out where he fits."

I gazed at him. Someone was approaching from the other end of the hall with a purposeful stride, but I didn't look up. The man was making an unnecessary amount of noise, his arms slicing back and forth so that the fabric of his *chuba* made an aggressive rustling sound, his boots thudding against the tiled floor. River seemed about to speak again, and was waiting until the passerby was out of earshot. But instead of turning the corner and continuing on his way, the man came to a stop when he reached us.

"Kamzin," he said, looming beyond River's shoulder, "what in the name of the spirits are you doing here?"

It was Mara.

TWENTY-SIX

MARA WAS WORN and travel-stained, his face shadowed by an unkempt beard. He had, evidently, only just arrived in the Three Cities, not even pausing to change out of his traveling clothes. He didn't glance at River, whose back was to him, but stared at me as if he'd seen a ghost.

"Where's Lusha?" he demanded. "I came with utmost haste through the Aryas to warn the emperor of the witches' plot, assuming all the while that you were still in the north, searching for the star. How is it that you came to be here?"

"It's a long story," I said hesitantly. River had taken a step back and leaned casually against the wall, a glint of amusement in his eye that I didn't trust.

"Is Lusha all right?" Mara pressed.

"She's fine." And, though he hadn't asked, "Tem too."

Mara ran a hand over his face. "And the star?"

"Oh, you're not going to ask about me?" River said. "After all our years together."

Mara glanced at him for the first time, then did a double take so violent it seemed to involve his entire body.

"You—" He grabbed my arm, yanking me backward so hard that I briefly levitated. "Kamzin, stay back."

I shook him off. "Mara, you don't—"

"Have you enspelled her?" Mara's face was white as he glanced from River to me. He had drawn an obsidian dagger from his *chuba*, and his hand, as he gripped it, shook violently. I didn't think I'd ever seen Mara so rattled, even when we'd faced the *fiangul*. "Is that what this is? Did you take her memories?"

"Her memories of what?" River said.

Mara made a move toward him, and I leaped between them. "Mara, stop. He doesn't mean that—River's helping us."

"And I've already warned the generals of Esha's plot," River said. "I'm afraid you're superfluous, Mara. No doubt the feeling's familiar by now."

"Oh, you've warned them." Mara let out a humorless laugh. He didn't lower the dagger. "I'm sure you did. You've no doubt convinced them to adopt whatever course suits your ends. Kamzin, if you've placed even a shred of trust in anything he says, you're a fool. He's capable of nothing but guile."

"Was it guile that rescued you in the Amarin Valley?" River said. "Or pulled you out of the Iriad Rapids? Saving your life was

322

certainly ill-advised, but I don't recall guile being part of it."

I shot him a glare. "You're not helping."

He rolled his eyes and pushed off the wall. "What can I say? Mara, I have no intention of harming you—or anyone else, at the moment, apart from my brother."

Mara's grip tightened on the dagger. "Do you think your lies will sway me? I am not as easily taken in as a naïve village girl."

Anger flickered in River's eyes, and he turned to me. "You see? I tried."

"Mara, put the dagger away," I said.

"Yes, do," River said. "I've been stabbed quite enough recently."

"I saw what you did to Jangsa." Mara's voice was hoarse. "I was there."

"Jangsa." I thought of the plumes of black smoke. "Did the villagers survive? What did you see?"

"Death," he said quietly. "Death and devastation. Like nothing I've ever witnessed."

I closed my eyes. River showed no reaction whatsoever. Then he asked, unexpectedly, "Does the elder live?"

Mara gave him a look of pure venom. "Yes. By some miracle of the spirits."

River nodded. "That's good. I liked him."

He looked so unaffected that I had to suppress my own urge to leap at him. But being angry at River for lacking customary human feelings was, I was beginning to realize, like being angry at the wind for rustling the leaves.

I turned to Mara. "Speak to Lusha. She can explain everything." And then, because I couldn't resist, "No doubt better than a naïve village girl like me."

Mara, having noticed no sarcasm in my words, gave River a ferocious look. "I won't leave you alone with him."

"Mara," River said, "you're interrupting us. You can leave by choice, or we can come to some other arrangement." He had looked more ruffled by Mara's characterization of me than his account of Jangsa's destruction.

"Lusha will want to see you," I said quickly, as Mara's expression grew ugly. "She kept wondering when you would arrive. She was worried."

Mara blinked. "She was?"

I nodded, wondering what Lusha would do to make me pay for this later. "She thought the *fiangul* might have attacked you in the pass. I told her that if anyone could make it back to the Three Cities in one piece, it was you, but I don't think it helped."

Mara seemed to draw himself up straighter. "I kept a careful eye on the weather. I always do."

"She's probably in the observatory," River interjected, for Mara's tone implied he was about to elaborate. "I'd check there."

Mara gave him a long, cold look. "If I find you've tampered with her mind or harmed her in any way—"

"I doubt Lusha's mind is as easily tampered with as some," River said. "In any case, I don't have that power anymore."

"I'll have my account from her." Mara turned, his concern over my safety evidently dissipated. Midstep, his brow furrowed and he

324

paused, drawing something from his *chuba*.

"Here," he said, holding out a small item wrapped in oilcloth. "From the Elder of Jangsa."

I took it, surprised. "For me?"

"For Tem." With one last, dark look at River, Mara swept away.

River let out a long breath as Mara's footsteps faded. "Good thinking. I thought he'd never leave."

"Lusha won't thank me." I unwrapped the parcel. "What is—?"

I fell silent as a small, crudely carved bell tumbled into my hand.

"This looks like one of the *kinnika*," I murmured. I rang it, and it made a sound so high it was almost inaudible. I examined the bell for images or characters, but there was nothing, only a faint crosshatching along the rim.

I held it out to River, but after grasping it he quickly dropped it back into my palm, as if singed.

"What is it?"

"It's like ice." His brow furrowed. "You don't feel it?"

"No." The bell was cool, but warmed against my skin, no different from ordinary metal. "Does the sound hurt you?"

River shook his head. I rewrapped the *kinnika* carefully. The elder had sent it to us—no doubt it was important. "Tem will know what it's for."

River led me down the corridor to where it opened onto another hall as wide as a room. He stopped in front of a mighty set of oak doors, which stretched all the way to the ceiling. They were carved with dozens, if not hundreds, of tiny wizened figures, each holding a brush and a scroll. A guard stood on either side, both looking as bored as the others I'd seen, though they drew themselves to attention when they recognized River.

"What's this?" I said, certain some fearsome sight awaited me on the other side of the doors—the emperor's personal receiving room, perhaps, or the royal shamans' training arena.

"The libraries," River said.

We stepped through, pushing against doors as heavy as boulders.

I drew in a breath. I had never seen a room so large. At least a dozen stories spiraled up from the cavernous atrium, all lined with shelves upon shelves of scrolls. The polished stone floor was crowded with desks occupied by scholars and shamans, some murmuring quietly together, others sitting in silence, heads bent over tiny writing. The Elder's library in Azmiri, which Father often boasted was the largest in the Northern Aryas, could fit inside this place hundreds of times. Dragons—wisely, I supposed—seemed to be banned. Lanterns dangled from railings and cast their soft glow across desks—a necessity, for there were few windows, and the place was all golden shadow.

I turned to River, but he was gone. The enormous doors folded shut with barely a whisper.

I squared my shoulders, turning back to the room. Given my history with Chirri and her incomprehensible research assignments, libraries were far from my favorite place. Fortunately, I spotted Tem almost immediately, ensconced at a desk against the wall, his nose so close to the scroll he was examining I suspected it would be stained with ink. His hair was uncharacteristically tucked behind his ears, and the lantern light glanced off the sharp planes of his face.

When I tapped him on the shoulder, he leaped in the air.

"Did you sleep at all, Tem? Or have you been here since yesterday?"

He gave me a rueful smile. He was dressed in a dark, knitted tunic and trousers of a finer material than I had ever seen him wear. The bruise on his cheek seemed to be fading, and while still drawn and thin, he looked rested for the first time in weeks. "Not quite. But after what I discovered yesterday, I couldn't stay away." He paused, blinking at me. "You look—"

"Terrible. I know."

"No. Kamzin, you look better." He stared in astonishment. "I'm covered in bruises, and when I stand up, I feel as if I'll faint. You look as if you never left Azmiri."

I took stock of myself. I was still tired, perhaps, and though my muscles had been soothed by the hot bath, my legs ached slightly. But overall, Tem was right—I felt almost like my old self.

"Only you could climb the highest mountain in the Empire, hunt down a fallen star, and escape the Fifth Army without a scrape," Tem said, shaking his head.

"None you can see," I said lightly. "Where's Lusha?"

"I'm not sure—she was here a while ago. She's been trying to get an audience with the emperor without River finding out, but apparently he won't be returning before the banquet."

Something stirred in my memory. "Tem, River said that he

closed his mind to Azar-at. Do you know what he meant?"

Tem gave me a sharp look. "Why do you ask?"

"I had a dream last night. It was—well, unusual. It reminded me of the visions I had. I'm sure it was only a dream," I hastened to add. "But I just wondered."

Tem looked thoughtful. "There is a technique used by shamans to block spells of the mind—memory spells, spells to induce madness or love. I don't know how it's done—I believe training involves meditation. You have to have a very focused mind. But this isn't a spell—I'm not sure you can compare it."

"Focused," I repeated. "So, this technique might not work if you were distracted. Or asleep?"

He nodded slowly. "That would make sense."

I swallowed. If I had shared River's dreams, it meant he had been right—we were still connected.

"If I end my contract with Azar-at," I said, "does that mean the visions will stop?"

"I don't know." Tem's voice was quiet. "River experiences them, though he isn't bound to Azar-at anymore."

I glanced down at the scrolls on the desk. Suddenly, I wanted to change the subject. "What did you discover?"

"A few things." An oddly nervous look passed over Tem's face. "Where's Ragtooth?"

"Ragtooth?" The question brought me up short. "Asleep on my bed. Why?"

Tem was already nodding. "Of course. He always turns up."

I blinked. "Why are we talking about Ragtooth? Did you come

here to research familiars, or the star?"

"The star, obviously. But then River told me about Ragtooth, and so . . ." He made an overwhelmed gesture at the scrolls piled before him.

For a moment, I was so surprised that Tem and River had spoken without killing each other that I didn't take in what he had said. "He told you—"

"He's seen Ragtooth a lot over the last few days," Tem said. "Always when Ragtooth should have been miles away, with us."

"How is that possible?"

"It isn't," Tem said. "Not even the most powerful shamans have the ability to travel from place to place like that." He paused. "Fire demons do—Azar-at brought us here."

I shook my head. "This is ridiculous. River must have imagined what he saw. You know as well as I do that Ragtooth's sole power is stealing food."

Tem gave me a long look. "Kamzin. You've never been reasonable when it comes to Ragtooth. You see what you want to see, and you push aside any questions about what he is."

I was taken aback. Something about the conversation felt wrong, somehow. "He's mine. He's always been mine. Why would I question that?"

Tem riffled through the papers on the desk. His expression was animated, though what was exciting about a pile of yellowed scrolls eluded me. He had looked the same whenever he solved one of Chirri's impossible assignments. "Did you read the scrolls about familiars in your father's library?"

"I thought you wrote that essay."

Tem gave me a long-suffering look. "I did. Azmiri doesn't have much information—old stories, mostly, about ancient heroes whose familiars are mentioned only in passing. They always choose heroes—that much is clear."

"They?" I repeated.

"Wind demons," Tem said. He unearthed a smaller scroll, and handed it to me. "Beings like the fire demons, but of a different race, you could say. Elemental spirits drawn to mountaintops and wild places, and the sorts of people who roam them. As I said—heroes."

I gazed at the scroll without seeing it. "Tem . . ."

"I know it's hard for you to accept," he said quickly. "But it all fits. The ancient scholars use the words 'familiar' and 'wind demon' interchangeably. They can take on any form. Like fire demons—like witches, to a certain extent, though witches have a unique lineage. But they usually choose the form that best suits their master. Some can appear and disappear at will, but no matter what, they always return to the person they have chosen to serve."

This was mad. The idea that Ragtooth was anything other than the spoiled, cantankerous fox who had been at my side since I was a baby was impossible to process. "So you're saying Ragtooth has his own magic? Like Azar-at?"

"Not quite like Azar-at," Tem said. "Like fire, Azar-at's magic devours. It requires sustenance to exist—that is its defining characteristic. I don't know precisely what powers the wind demons have, but it seems they're a kind of protector spirit."

I thought back to Raksha. "Ragtooth was hurt. He nearly died."

"They're not invulnerable," Tem said. "Neither are fire demons. They can be hurt. Even killed."

I bit my lip. The scroll Tem had handed me showed an ink sketch of a man with long hair and a fierce expression, holding a bow. At his side was a small creature that resembled a fox. The way its head was tilted—

I put the scroll aside. "Tem, Ragtooth is *Ragtooth*. If he had any special powers, don't you think I would know?"

"All right." Tem held up his hands in a gesture of resignation. "I won't say any more—for now. But just think about it, Kamzin. The signs are there, if you'd only notice them."

I frowned. I wasn't sure why I was reacting this way. I should have been laughing at Tem's suggestion that Ragtooth was some sort of mythical beast. Yet the notion bothered me on some fundamental level. It made me feel off balance—I didn't even want to consider it. I wished Ragtooth were here now, so I could gather his warm, familiar weight into my arms.

"I did come here to investigate the star," Tem said. "It sounds like they were widely sought after in ancient times—before the Empire, when this region was just a collection of warring villages. Shamans managed to catch several of them."

"Really?" I pictured Norbu trying to track down a star, waving his useless talismans about. Tem heard the skepticism in my voice.

"The shamans that lived centuries ago weren't like the shamans of today," he said. "They were stronger. Not as strong as the witches, it's true, but they had their own magic."

"What happened?" I asked.

"The conflict with the witches," Tem said. "I read in the scrolls that the strongest shamans had witch blood—but as the Empire formed, and the emperors increasingly treated witches as the enemy, our bloodlines no longer mingled. Most shamans now have no witch blood at all, or if they do, it's very distant."

"That makes sense," I said carefully. Tem spoke in an even tone, but there was a tension in his body. "River said something similar. And if witches carry magic in their blood, any shaman related to them would have an advantage."

There was a small silence. Tem said, his voice distant, "It's strange. The Empire has nearly hunted them to extinction. The binding spell was a part of that. No doubt the emperor thought it would make us stronger—but in a way, it's also made us weak."

I frowned. "What are you saying—that the spell shouldn't be recast? That the emperor shouldn't have cast it in the first place?"

"No." Tem shook himself. "I guess I'm saying it would have been better if he'd never had to."

I thought about it. Until recently, I would have argued with him—like every other child in the Empire, I had been raised with fireside stories of witches lurking in the shadows, monsters ready to burn our village to the ground or devour children. But now?

I thought of River, who had betrayed me thoughtlessly, but who had also saved my life more than once. I looked at Tem and felt something inside me soften. Tem wasn't a monster. And yet he was one of them—his powers proved it.

I shook my head. The fireside stories didn't make sense anymore.

"Here," Tem said. "This account isn't entirely about fallen stars—but it does reference spells of resurrection."

Dubiously, I took up the papers Tem pressed into my hands. He rose to hunt down yet more scrolls, though the pile of papers on his desk was already teetering. We remained there for what might have been an hour, but which felt like much longer. As Tem handed me yet another scroll, murmuring excitedly over the notes he was accumulating, I thought back to all the time we had spent together in Father's library, poring over Chirri's assignments. The more abstruse the topic, the more delighted Tem became, and it was no different now. Most of the lore about fallen stars was written by seers, and thus tangled up in prevarications and theories so vague and meandering you became lost in them. For my part, I was beginning to wish I had never left the comforts of my rooms when a man approached us.

"The Royal Explorer has sent for you," the man said. His voice, though pitched at an ordinary volume, caused several nearby scholars to shoot him poisonous glares. "He says it's urgent."

"What's happened?" I demanded. Had the emperor returned? Had someone discovered River's identity?

The man only shook his head. "Please come with me."

"Urgent," Tem muttered. He didn't appear pleased at the

prospect of being dragged away from his scrolls at River's behest. I wondered again what they had spoken of when I was asleep.

I gave him a warning look—it wouldn't do to disrespect the second most powerful man in the Empire, a man who, while he might intimidate the palace guards, clearly also had their respect. Tem caught my look and squelched any protest he had been considering. Setting aside our scrolls, we rose and followed the man outside.

TWENTY-SEVEN

I DIDN'T KNOW what to expect from a royal banquet. I had pictured layers of luxury, tables piled high with wine and delicacies, dragons lounging everywhere in a spectacular display of wealth, courtiers in exquisite dress.

What I found surpassed anything I could imagine.

The banquet hall was enormous—it could have spanned the entire length of Azmiri. Its ceiling was held aloft by square pillars painted in intricate patterns of alternating colors, often woven with yellow poppies. It opened onto grand balconies on two sides, admitting the night air and glimpses of the gleaming city below. Fires roared in massive, gilded fireplaces. Hundreds of palace dragons crouched on brackets in the pillars, or fluttered to and from perches that hung from the lofty ceiling. Their lights were not only the expected blue and green—some glowed a deep violet or crimson I had never seen in a dragon before. I wondered if they had been bred that way, or if their color was the result of a spell. If so, it seemed a wasteful sort of magic. The light flickered and changed continually, throwing strange shadows in every direction.

Every noble in the Three Cities, it seemed, had showed up to welcome the emperor home. Some wore long, close-fitting *chubas* sequined with jewels across the shoulders and back, paired with the same ridiculously thin boots River had worn. The women wore dresses woven from silk so vibrantly colored I was tempted to squint, their ears weighted with enormous jeweled earrings, their shoulders and throats draped with necklaces. Gloves were clearly in fashion—almost everyone wore them, men and women, gloves of a glistening silk dyed in a variety of colors, the most common of which seemed to be a pure white that struck me as a strange choice for a dinner. The common trait of all Three Cities dress, I thought with some disdain, seemed to be its unsuitability for anything beyond lounging about indoors.

At my side, Tem was silent. He gazed around the hall with an expression that was more blank than amazed, as if he was not even certain where to look first.

I took his arm as two women passed, their gazes sliding over him. Tem looked startlingly handsome, the image of a young nobleman at his first royal party. His *chuba* was the deep blue of twilight, cut in a way that emphasized his height and broad shoulders. His hair, which normally curtained his face, was swept back, highlighting the sharp lines of his brow and jaw. River's tailors had certainly done their job, I thought, as I noticed my own gaze being drawn to Tem more frequently than usual. I turned back to adjusting my dress. A dragon scurried over my feet, making me start. Clearly, dragons were indulged here in a way they never were in Azmiri.

"You look . . ." Tem blushed.

I rolled my eyes. "I look like I'm wearing a costume."

"No, it's— I've never seen you like this."

I made a dismissive gesture. To my annoyance, it had turned out that the supposedly "urgent" business River had needed to attend to that morning had involved hiring the most overpaid tailors to array us in the most overpriced garments. The silk that swathed me was a vivid red with a white band at the top of my waist. The servants had pinned my hair up and woven it with gold chains, though I had refused any other adornment, as well as the silk gloves they had offered me. Whenever I moved, the gold tinkled softly. In spite of the fine clothes, I knew I gave the other guests little reason to turn their heads. While the dress emphasized my curves, it also emphasized my stoutness, and I had seen in the mirror how ruddy my face was from days spent battling the harsh elements.

It didn't matter. I didn't care what I looked like. I had allowed the tailors to make me look like a courtier, knowing that I couldn't very well appear before the emperor in my filthy *chuba* and worn boots. Where was he? When would he return? River had vanished that afternoon to learn what he could, and to investigate the stories he had heard from the servants. I didn't like him going off on his own. The more people he talked to, the greater the risk that someone would notice the change and realize what he was.

Lusha had vanished into the crowd almost as soon as we were admitted to the hall. Not out of any eagerness to join the party, I guessed, but as a result of frustration and nervous energy. Lusha didn't like waiting, though she had tamped down her feelings, allowing the tailors to fit her into a dress of golden yellow, weave her hair with jewels, and thread her ears with long strings of colorful beads. The result was that she could have passed for an empress, even in comparison to other courtiers in equally rich dress. I glimpsed her now, a ray of gold, standing by one of the balconies with her arms folded, pointedly ignoring the young man attempting to speak with her as she scanned the crowd, and giving off the powerful impression that this was her hundredth royal banquet.

The star, absurdly, was nestled in the pocket of Lusha's dress. When I had suggested leaving it in her room under guard, I had been treated to a look so icy it froze my tongue.

A murmur swept through the crowd, and I felt Tem stiffen beside me. I turned in time to see River parting the courtiers. A small number called out his name, and he stopped to exchange a few words. I saw smiles, welcoming shoulder claps. Occasionally, the sound of laughter drifted toward us. River looked perfectly at ease. There was something almost mesmerizing about it—the heads turning in succession, the swirl of brightly clad movement his arrival caused, like autumn leaves stirred by a wind.

"Beautiful," he said, once he reached us. For a moment, I wasn't certain what he meant—but he was staring at me.

I stared right back at him. In contrast to the courtiers, arrayed in colors so bright I suspected one-upmanship on the part of the Three Cities' dyers, River was all in black from his boots to his *chuba*, which was thin, close-fitting, and obviously beyond expensive. It would have looked impractical on anyone else, but I knew that River bore the cold as lightly as a fish in an icy stream. Absurdly, in place of jewels, his *chuba* was studded with what appeared to be obsidian beading. Even the gloves were black, a silk so fine it gleamed like glass. River, with his beautiful face and strange eyes, and the invisible pull of his presence, would stand out in farmers' clothes. Dressed as he was, it seemed as if every eye in the vicinity was on him. It was the opposite of a disguise.

And yet, I thought, perhaps that had been the point. The clothes were as striking as everything else about him, but they also elided other evidence of difference, offering a harmless reason for an observer's attention to linger. Perhaps it was a more effective disguise than any attempt at ordinary dress, which would have only created a contrast.

"The emperor will arrive soon," he said, taking no notice of my silence, or the fact of the crowd's parting around where we stood. "He's only just returned to court. In a foul mood, by all accounts."

"I see." My stomach, already in knots, did a somersault at this news.

River was staring at me again, after allowing his gaze to drift over the courtiers. I narrowed my eyes. I was growing tired of being regarded like some sort of exotic animal—first by Tem, now him. River seemed to notice my reaction, and smiled apologetically. Music flared somewhere on the balconies—several lutes and hand drums. River seemed about to speak. But then one of the courtiers appeared to work up the courage to cross the moat that had opened between us and them. She placed a hand on his arm, and River, appearing to recognize her, allowed her to lead him away.

"Where are you going?" I said in disbelief. He couldn't just abandon us here. I would rather be abandoned outside a den of red-toothed bears.

River merely cast a smile over his shoulder and was soon swallowed up by the crowd. To my dismay, the courtiers began dividing into twos, and music swelled through the hall as other instruments joined the first.

Tem, thank the spirits, didn't take my hand. He was eyeing the swirl of courtiers with something resembling panic.

"I think I'll visit the libraries," he said.

"You were there all day!"

"The emperor isn't here yet," Tem pointed out. "And when he arrives, I doubt he'll be interested in speaking to me."

"I don't think we should split up."

Tem gave me a look. "Would you rather I asked you to dance?"

I took a step back, bumping into one of the courtiers in my haste. "Enjoy yourself, Tem."

"Thank you, I will." He walked away, a lightness in his step that I hadn't seen since we left Azmiri.

Keeping an eye on Lusha, who was busy ignoring a different suitor, I wandered to the opposite end of the hall, where there were tables piled with delicacies. Courtiers ate with their hands, for the most part, as they stood and talked, or lounged on plush rugs. Servants brought bowls of scented water for hand washing, which were constantly replenished. I couldn't help staring. This method of dining was luxury so impractical that I found it difficult to comprehend.

I had only eaten a few bites when someone tapped me on the shoulder. I turned and found a young man, bony but handsome in his courtier's clothes.

"May I?" He extended his hand.

It took me a moment to realize that he was asking me to dance. "I don't—"

"I don't either," he said, with a sheepish smile. "But you are so lovely that I thought I might make an attempt."

I hesitated. I was about to make some excuse and turn away, but then my thoughts flashed to River's retreating back, and something made me give the young man a smile. Everything about the emperor's court made me uncomfortable, from the richly clad courtiers—more people than I had ever encountered in one place—to the din of music and conversation. It was a feeling I hated, and I was going to fight it, and win.

I splashed my fingers in the bowl offered to me by a servant. Then I took the man's hand and let him lead me into the crowd. As I did, one of the dragons nipped at my heel. I started.

"They're not very well trained, are they?" I said.

The courtier, who hadn't seen, gave me a puzzled look. We stepped onto the balcony, and I grew cold in my silk dress. I didn't shiver for long, however, for the young man immediately pulled me into the whirl of dancers, and it was all I could do to keep my breath.

Below the palace, the city lights shone like fireflies. Surely they could hear the music down there, see the palace on the hilltop glittering with torches and dragonlight. It would look like a beacon hovering in the sky. I gazed out over the shadowy landscape and shivered.

"Everything all right?" the courtier said. He drew back to look at me. He really *was* handsome, his slenderness emphasizing the sharp lines of his cheekbones. I forced a smile, which grew into a real one as he spun me in a circle.

"Do you live in the Three Cities?" I asked.

"Yes," he responded with a question in his voice, as if uncertain where else someone could live.

"It's lovely here," I murmured. For a moment, I seemed to step outside my body, to watch myself dancing in the arms of a wealthy courtier on the balcony of the emperor's palace. There came a familiar stirring in my chest, as I had felt setting out from Azmiri, and gazing up at the peak of Raksha. I was standing where no one in Azmiri had stood, except perhaps my father, who made rare visits to the Three Cities to pay his respects to the emperor. In spite of everything, my heart sped up, and excitement kindled inside me. My grip on the courtier's arm tightened.

342

He caught my changed expression and smiled. "You've never been to the palace before, have you? Where are you from?"

An image of Azmiri, which would now be quiet and slumberous, tucked into the mountainside below the stars, floated through my mind. Like Tem, I had never belonged there. If I didn't belong in the place where I had spent my life, where did I belong?

"It doesn't matter," I said, turning my face away. "Nowhere."

He smiled again. "Well, *nowhere* has some charming inhabitants, I must say."

I smiled back, and he spun me. As he did, something caught my eye. It was River, the obsidian beads glittering on his black *chuba*. I couldn't *not* stare—everyone else was. Couples stood back when River and his partner, who wore a dress of shimmering azure, drew near. She was beautiful, of course, with generous curves and the sort of features artists gave to long-dead empresses in paintings. I felt a stab of something that was not quite annoyance, but closer to mischievousness. I recalled the dance in Jangsa—that had been wilder, less formal, but River had moved just as gracefully as he did now. His expression was animated as he talked to his partner, who seemed to be laughing, her kohled eyes bright. I maneuvered myself and the courtier close to them.

The dance required partners to swap briefly before returning to each other. As River's hands left the girl's, I drew the courtier into the path of another couple. His hands lifted to those of the girl in the blue dress, and I stepped neatly into River's arms.

He started, and I grinned at the rare look of surprise that flitted across his face.

"Where did you come from?" He began to smile.

"I thought you could use a break from being fawned over," I said.

He laughed at that, and spun me away from the main crowd. The music faded farther along the balcony, where there were only a few dancing couples, and several more seated close together on low benches. There were fewer dragons here too, and the shadows deepened.

"I don't think I ever asked how you like the palace," River said into my ear. I couldn't see his face.

"It's . . . a nice place to visit," I said.

"No, it isn't."

"You seemed to be enjoying yourself."

"It was the company I was enjoying—that's all, I promise you."

"Would you rather be in the Nightwood?" I pulled back far enough to see his face. "What's so terrible about banquets and gilded fireplaces, and pretty courtiers hanging on your every word?"

"You tell me." He motioned with his chin toward the crowd we'd left behind. "You may have broken that boy's heart."

I made a dismissive noise. My heart was pounding. I could feel the warmth of his hands, gloved in the softest silk, against my bare skin. "Don't change the subject."

"I wouldn't rather be in the Nightwood."

His eyes held mine, and my stomach turned over. Something made me think of my dream, the crane soaring through clouds. "But you'd rather be out there. Not here."

He paused. "Yes. Wouldn't you?"

I ignored the question. "How many animals can you turn into, anyway?"

"I don't know. I haven't tried them all." He said it in an off-hand way, as if it was a matter so abstract as to be unimportant.

"Isn't that unusual? I thought witches could only take the shape of a single animal."

"I think that's true, for most."

"Not for you, though."

"No."

I thought about what Esha had said about River's powers being greater than his, and his reference to the Crown. But before I could ask about it, the music died, and the chatter quieted. River pulled away, his attention on the raised dais just visible at the far end of the hall. He drew me inside, toward the edge of the crowd. Their faces were all turned in the same direction.

"The emperor," he said.

I craned my neck, silently cursing my shortness. River, after a glance at me, took my hand and led me into the crowd, which parted before him. With fewer heads blocking my view, I could see the dais clearly, and also the three figures moving toward it. They didn't clear the way as River did—it was already cleared for them, courtiers stepping back to form a passage, heads bowing like sheaves of grain.

One of the figures, the most elaborately dressed of the three, to whom my eyes went instinctively, was white-haired, though his shoulders were thrust back and his spine unbent. I couldn't see his face, but I could see the faces of the two people at his side—a woman in her thirties, her *chuba* worn over a dress of rose-colored silk. And the other was Captain Elin.

My mouth fell open. Captain Elin was here, and he was talking to the emperor. There was a powerful incongruity about it—when I had last seen him, he had been menacing and battle-worn, dressed in bloodstained armor with a sword at his side. Now he stood here at a gilded banquet, dressed in a cloak of pure white that swept the floor behind him. The stubble on his face was gone, and his hair was clean and brushed, though several wayward strands still fell across his forehead, partly obscuring one eye. He stood several inches above most other men in the hall, and while he wore no sword or armour, something in his bearing—the soldier's walk, perhaps—kept alive the undercurrent of menace that I remembered.

I forced my attention away from Elin to the white-haired man. "That's the emperor? You said he looked young."

"I think your attention is in the wrong place," River said. He seemed half lost in thought, his eyes on the three figures.

I looked back at the emperor, not understanding. Even as the woman in the rose dress bowed to Captain Elin, I still didn't understand. The white-haired man bowed also, and stepped back to join the crowd, who watched the captain expectantly as he stepped onto the dais and seated himself on the elaborately carved throne.

The scene before me seemed to freeze, as if rendered in ink on a canvas. For a moment, it was all I could do to breathe.

It can't be.

"River," I said, my voice very low, "who is that man on the throne?"

River gave me a puzzled look. "Who do you think?"

My entire body was numb. "That. Is. The emperor?"

I saw Captain Elin gazing at Tem with murder in his eyes. Saw him binding us, saw his arrow pointed at Lusha's throat. I saw the ravens attacking him as we fled into the forest.

River was watching me. His hand was still in mine, and he brushed his thumb against my knuckles. "What? Tell me."

A booming voice rang out. It was the woman who had accompanied Elin to the throne—she stood below the dais upon which the captain lounged, looking simultaneously tense and bored, his eyes scanning the crowd as he sat with one ankle propped on his knee.

"The emperor welcomes River Shara, Royal Explorer of the Three Cities and the Empire," the woman announced.

As the captain's eyes turned toward the place where we stood, I stepped behind a taller courtier. River was still looking at me, nonplussed, even as before him another corridor was opening. He turned his face back to the dais. He couldn't very well delay, with all eyes upon him. I wanted to grab at him, to tell him we needed to leave *now*, but I stood frozen, unable to look away.

Calmly, River strode forward, the hem of his black *chuba* stirring with each step. It was enough, if you didn't look closely, to disguise the way the shadows at his feet shifted strangely, as if they were drawn to him. Once again, I was reminded of the effectiveness of River's nondisguise.

He stopped at the edge of the dais and gave a short bow. Beneath my fear, it struck me how strange it looked for River to bow to anyone, but the emperor didn't seem to notice, or perhaps he had simply grown used to it. He leaned back in his throne, a surprisingly genuine smile on his face. He gazed at River as one would an old friend, and I recalled that River was one of the emperor's closest advisors. And of course he was—though the generals had more actual power, the Royal Explorer's rank was above theirs. The emperor couldn't very well give the honor to someone he didn't trust.

"Welcome home, River," Captain Elin said. "I trust you had an uneventful journey?"

A ripple of laughter went through the crowd. There was something familiar in it, the recognition of an old joke. River smiled.

"It was productive, Your Highness," he replied. His voice was clear enough to carry across the crowd. "Shall I bore you with the details?"

The captain's gaze held a hint of affection that looked strange in a face like his. The courtiers laughed again. "Later. I'll permit no serious talk now. You've returned safely, and that warrants celebrating."

River lowered his head. The captain turned toward the woman at his side. As he did, his gaze fell on me.

Shock spread across his face. I ducked behind the tall courtier again, having forgotten myself for a moment. But unfortunately, every eye that had been trained on the emperor had noticed his reaction and followed his gaze to where I stood.

"There, that—that girl." The captain seemed to falter, but when he continued, his voice was steady again. "Bring her to me."

I tried to run, but there were too many people in the way, and the crowd was parting again, people stepping back to witness the source of the confusion. A guard appeared out of nowhere and seized my arm. He half dragged, half led me to the dais, sending dragons darting this way and that. The captain leaned forward now, both hands gripping the arms of his throne.

River watched as the guard led me to his side. He was good at concealing his shock—I had only caught a flash of it, now buried under an opaque expression.

"Your Highness," River began, "what—"

"This girl is a witch," Elin announced. The crowd gasped in near-perfect unison, which I might have found comical under different circumstances. As it was, there was nothing amusing about the expression in Elin's eyes.

The emperor's eyes.

River's composure had slipped a hair. "There must be some mistake."

"Don't be fooled by her appearance." The emperor stood and came toward me. I shrank back instinctively—I had thought him equally fearsome in his royal garb as he had been in his blood-stained armor. In truth, he was far more terrifying now, his roughness subsumed by royal manners, his sword traded for the might of an Empire. He moved and spoke with the confidence of a man who could end lives with the flick of a finger.

"I came upon her and her companions on patrol with the Fifth Army," he said, his gaze never wavering from my face, as if he thought I might disappear. "But they slipped from my grasp."

Understanding dawned in River's gaze. I could see him take in the situation and turn his thoughts to dealing with it.

"We had no idea who you were," I snapped, which was nonsensical, but I couldn't help myself. Captain Elin was the emperor.

And then, immediately after that thought, *Lusha attacked the emperor.*

Emperor Lozong stopped in front of me. Even if he hadn't been on a dais, I would have had to look up at him—as it was, the distance between us made my neck ache.

"I always travel under an alias when I inspect my armies in the field," he said. "So as to hide my identity from bandits and assassins. Little did I know I would be concealing myself from a group of witches. And are your companions here as well?"

"I am," said a voice from the crowd. To my dismay, Lusha stepped forward, all glittering jewels and flashing eyes. The emperor stared. He could have given the command to have Lusha seized too, but he seemed to be momentarily struck dumb. Lusha came forward as calmly as River had, bowing as if she were just another courtier paying her respects. Standing next to her, though, I could see the pulse racing in her throat.

"You called yourself a captain," she said. "Yet, as it turns out, you were not what you appeared to be. Is it so difficult for you to imagine that the same is true for us?"

The emperor blinked. He seemed to be recovering from his shock, and some of the venom was returning to his expression. "Explain."

"We are not witches." Lusha didn't flinch beneath his gaze, though he could have at any moment chosen to nod to a soldier and have her slain at his feet, which something in his eyes suggested he was considering. "Nor are we in league with them. We are travelers from the village of Azmiri. We accompanied the Royal Explorer to Mount Raksha."

River was gazing at Lusha as if she were a particularly complex chess board. Seeming to come to a decision, he said, "It's true, Your Highness. These two are no more witches than I am. In fact, I couldn't have completed my mission without their help."

The emperor stared at River. He could not have looked more shocked if River had burst into flames.

"How can this be?" he said after a long, deadly silence, during which I could hear every breath drawn by the silent courtiers. "Someone is playing me false."

River gave him a calm look. "Do you trust me?"

His expression was composed, his tone even but for the vaguest hint of a reproach. The performance was so note-perfect that I shivered.

"Please." Lusha stepped forward again, and the emperor's gaze drifted to hers as if against his will. "Please, Your Highness. I can explain everything, if you'd allow me. Not only that"—her cool gaze shifted to River—"I can tell the story of how the Royal Explorer brought you a fallen star."

"Lusha," I said, but my protest was swallowed by the murmuring that swelled through the hall. I hadn't expected her to do this now.

The emperor's gaze moved from Lusha to River, who showed no reaction. Yet I could feel him tense as he repressed his surprise.

"Is this true, River?" Emperor Lozong's expression held a hunger that struck me as eerie. For a brief moment, I saw his age in his eyes.

River was quiet for a moment. "I had planned to share the good news with you in private, Your Highness."

The emperor let out a low laugh. Something in him seemed to shift as he gazed at Lusha, and it struck me, suddenly, that he *wanted* to believe River. She returned his gaze, her expression cool except for the faint flush on her cheeks.

"Your word means more to me, River," the emperor said finally, "than that of any other. And so I consent—I will listen, and then I will judge these two, though they have given me little reason to trust them."

Lusha said, "If we could speak privately—"

"It seems a shame," the emperor interrupted, an odd smile tugging at his mouth, "to waste a dress like that, Lusha. And I enjoy conversation while I dance."

He made a gesture, and one of the musicians started to play. The sound of the bone flute was soon joined by other instruments—drums and cymbals and bells—until the hall was filled with music twisting through that echoing space. The buzz of conversation resumed as the courtiers' attention was drawn from the dais. Some drifted away, while others paired off and began to dance.

"Keep that one under guard," the emperor said, stepping off the dais with a gesture in my direction.

I opened my mouth, outraged, but River said, "I'll stay with her."

The emperor gave a shrug. As the music soared through the hall, he took Lusha's hand. A space opened for them among the swirl of couples, and the emperor took her in his arms, holding her perhaps a little more tightly than was customary. Lusha looked supremely unconcerned, returning his grip without flinching. He spoke in her ear, and she drew back to reply, her face still flushed. Then they disappeared into the throng of dancers.

The courtiers in the vicinity were still staring at me, while the guards, not explicitly dismissed, hovered nearby. Before I even had time to think, River was taking my arm and pulling me through the crowd almost as roughly as the guard had. One took a step toward us, but River simply glanced his way, and the man fell back.

"Tem," I managed to get out, once my brain was working again, "we have to find him—the emperor knows—"

"Yes, the emperor knows a good deal more than I thought," River said, his voice low. We were on the balcony, the air cold against my flushed skin. River ignored the comments tossed his way and drew me into a sheltered nook against a stone pillar. Then the world went dark.

I gasped. River had drawn the shadows over us like a blanket, through which the flickering lights of the fires and dragons were visible only dimly. The night was just as chilly, the breeze fluttering through the veil unimpeded. It was such a strange sensation that I could only stare at him as he pressed me against the stone, his face inches from mine.

"You met the emperor," he said. "He held you captive for hours. How could you not have known who he was?"

I shoved at him ineffectually. "Is it my fault that everyone in the Three Cities has a secret identity? I suppose the tailor who attended us is also General of the First Army?"

River scrubbed the side of his head, mussing his hair further. "This isn't a joke. Do you have any idea how much danger you're in? The emperor thinks you're a witch."

"Yes, we've established that the emperor is terrible at spotting witches. I don't see how that's my fault."

"Why did Lusha tell him about the star?" River's voice held a dangerous note now. "She's up to something, isn't she? I saw it in her face. What is it?"

All my anger flooded back, everything I had been carrying since Raksha, intensified. "The star is capable of more than you realize. Lozong used a fallen star to cast the binding spell."

River blinked. He seemed, for a moment, too shocked to speak.

Then his expression darkened.

"Did he?" His voice was eerily calm, and for the first time I saw an echo of his terrifying brother. "And you weren't thinking of sharing that detail?"

"No. Because this isn't about you. This is about my village. My family."

"I believe I said something similar when we stood on the summit of Raksha. I seem to recall you sending me over a cliff afterward."

His words brought me back to Raksha, and for a moment I felt as if we stood again on that windswept summit, facing each other. "You won't do anything to me."

"You're right. I won't do anything to you. But I will find Lusha and take the star from her before the emperor can use it."

My anger boiled. "So you can use it against us?"

"So I can destroy it, if I can. I've had enough of this. No one should have the kind of power you speak of. Not the emperor, not Esha. Not you. If you don't see that, you're no better than him."

I reeled. "I—"

"You have to leave." River seemed to speak half to himself, his attention on some point beyond my shoulder. "The emperor doesn't trust you. He'll trust you even less after the star disappears. Your life is in danger."

I let out a disbelieving laugh. "My life is in danger? Is that supposed to be news? I'm not going anywhere. I'm staying here."

His gaze returned to mine, sharpening. "You have no idea what—"

"You're in greater danger than I am." I glared at him, suddenly furious. The tumult inside me, the fear and anger and shock—the captain's true identity, the overwhelming majesty of the palace, the looming attack—all were overtaken by a single resolution: River was not going to leave me again, and I was not going to leave him. "Any moment, someone could guess what you are. Every guard carries an obsidian dagger next to their sword. You need someone to watch out for you—why is that so hard to accept? I saved your life. You said it yourself."

He stared at me. I knew, somehow, that we were both seeing the same thing—him clinging to the ice after falling from the Ngadi face, closer to death than he had come at any point during his career as Royal Explorer. At some point, we had moved even closer together. He was still gripping my arm. I heard courtiers' voices, very close—people were walking past us, unseeing, as if we were caught in a separate world.

"You're impossible." His voice was low, and the statement had a strange resonance, as if he was voicing a long-held belief. "Do you care so little about your own life?"

It was as much a statement as it was a question. River's expression was a tumult—exasperation warring with anger and concern. I was tired of it, suddenly. Tired of arguments and half-truths. So I grabbed the back of his neck and kissed him.

I half expected him to freeze in surprise, but he reacted almost instantly, as if I had anticipated what he had been about to do himself. He placed his hand against my face, pressing me harder into the stone column as he kissed me back. The shadows around us seemed to ripple as I wrapped my arms around his neck and drew him closer.

TWENTY-EIGHT

THE SOUND OF shouting broke us apart.

I would have ignored it—I would have ignored anything, in that moment—but River made a sound of surprise and drew back. That was when I realized that, in addition to the shouting, there was the smell of burning.

The shadows River had summoned dispersed, and he stepped away from the pillar. I followed somewhat unsteadily. River was holding my arm. I could still feel his hand sliding up the back of my neck and into my hair, where it had tangled. My heart hammered and my face was too hot, but slowly, my senses were returning.

I had kissed River.

I felt faint, but not from the kiss. What was wrong with me? River was my enemy. We had spent days fighting for control of the star. He had betrayed me on Raksha, while I had left him to die in the Ash Mountains. Yet I had kissed him. And I wanted to kiss him again.

I forced my attention back to the hall. The courtiers near us on the balcony had frozen, craning their necks—it was clear that something was happening inside the hall, but what? The dragons' lights darted chaotically.

"Kamzin." River's hand tightened on my arm.

I turned, following his gaze. The lights of the Three Cities flickered below us—but some lights burned too brightly under the starry sky. I caught another whiff of smoke, and froze.

"The city is burning," River murmured.

It was true. As I watched, a temple began to glow, flames licking at the night. At least a dozen buildings were alight in as many quarters.

But that wasn't what made me freeze. It was the shade of the fire, darker than ordinary flame, as if leeched of heat. And yet it devoured buildings hungrily, burning stone and wood alike.

Witch fire.

Several courtiers joined us at the railing, their faces gray with shock. People small as insects gathered in the streets below, gesturing and shouting. Soldiers, recognizable by the armor that flashed in the firelight, seemed to be herding them away from the burning buildings. The scene was chaotic, especially in contrast to the placid bustle that had filled the streets earlier that day.

"The soldiers are evacuating the city," River murmured, his sharp eyes distinguishing what I could not.

The shouts inside the hall took on a darker quality. "Lusha," I breathed. Lusha was still in there, dancing with the man the witches had come to the Three Cities to kill. The realization drove every other thought from my mind. "We have to find her."

River held out his hand.

I looked at him. There was no anger in his face, or deception. He looked serious and oddly uncertain as he waited for my response, his hair in disarray and his familiar eyes searching mine. The last of my misgivings flickered and died. I took his hand, and we dove into the chaos.

For chaos it was. The musicians had fallen silent, their songs replaced by an alarmed babble that echoed throughout the cavernous hall. Near the balconies, nothing seemed to be happening—some courtiers stood motionless, looking about uncertainly, while others pushed toward the arched doors at either end of the hall. Someone screamed, and more joined the pushing.

My breath faltered as I realized why.

The hall wasn't on fire, as I had first feared. Strange apparitions had flickered into existence. Pillars of shadow like dark twins of the columns that supported the roof. At first, I thought that was all they were—ordinary shadows thrown by the dancing firelight. But nothing could be casting them; they stood alone, hovering like black fog.

I cried out as shadow-pillar reared up not a yard away, opaque and featureless. A frightened dragon darted past, and the pillar seemed to shatter where the beast's blue light touched it. It drew together briefly, then dissolved.

Unconsciously, I stepped forward, reaching out to the strands of shadow. I felt nothing but air.

Another scream. I whirled. Against the wall, a towering staircase had appeared, leading to a broken wall—but it too was shadow, darkness without substance. Courtiers were fleeing en masse now, identical looks of horror on their faces. The hall was emptying.

It was all terrifyingly familiar.

"It's the sky city," I murmured. River gazed at the apparitions with narrowed eyes. His expression was distant, as if he was sensing something I was not.

I wrenched him around. "What's happening?"

"I don't know." River's expression was grim. "But it sounds like Esha's decided to pay a visit."

Esha. Terror overwhelmed me. "River, Lusha has the star."

River took my hand again, and we pressed toward the emperor's dais, which seemed to be at the heart of the disturbance. Hands grasped at River's arm, and fleeing courtiers called to him to stop. River ignored them.

Someone plowed into us—one of the guards, empty-handed, covered in blood. I recoiled, but River merely shoved the man aside. Ahead of us, through the kaleidoscope of fleeing courtiers in their colorful costumes, I could make out a knot of guards in a semicircle around a hunched figure. Emperor Lozong. And between us and them, battling a dozen guards, was Esha.

It was as if the hall had been upended. Esha was here, tall and skeletal and menacing, a monster from a nightmare. I had last seen him on a snowy mountain crag, and before that—through River's eyes—in the dark wilds of the Nightwood. Now he was surrounded by the finery of the Three Cities. Two worlds seemed to crash together in a violent swirl.

Esha dodged an obsidian-tipped arrow fired by a guard, then lifted a hand, summoning a wind that lifted the guard off her feet and slammed her into a column. She fell to the floor and was still.

I had thought it a battle, at first glance. But it wasn't. No guard or shaman could be more than a minor obstacle to a witch as powerful as Esha. They were moments separating him from the emperor. It was a slaughter.

Between Esha and the emperor—wounded, from his posture— were perhaps fifteen guards. Esha had three witches with him— three that I could see. Though the hall was mostly empty now, some people were running toward their emperor, weapons in their hands. A man dressed in shaman's robes raced past me, brandishing a fistful of glittering talismans. I thought of Norbu and felt a stab of fear. One of the dragons that scampered over the floor transformed into a lean, long-haired witch who dragged the shaman to the ground.

The dragons.

My mind balked, even as I watched another dragon transform into a witch with gleaming eyes. There were dragons at every feast, every gathering throughout the Empire. They were shepherded from place to place by everyone wealthy enough to afford them, as omnipresent as purses or talismans, and as unremarkable.

They were the perfect disguise.

"River," I breathed, "the witches are—"

"I know." His voice was dark. "Esha must have gathered all those able to assume the shape of a dragon and snuck them into the palace, disguising them among the royal dragons. It's . . . well, it's just the kind of thing he'd come up with."

"You didn't think he would attack now," I said, fury rising again. "You said—"

"I was wrong. I didn't think he would be this reckless."

Esha killed another guard, swathing his face in shadow and then running him through with his own sword.

"Hello, Esha," River said.

He barely raised his voice, despite the chaos of the scene. Yet Esha's shoulders tensed.

When he met River's gaze, a smile flickered on his face. It was not a happy expression, but one of dark satisfaction. He held up a hand.

The witches stopped fighting. Shadows writhed and spun, and witches emerged from them. The nearest witch was no more than five paces from the guards' shields. For a moment, neither side moved. There were perhaps two dozen guards in total—not including those who lay motionless on the marble floor—and as many witches.

River's gaze held his brother's. "I didn't think banquets were to your taste."

The guards gazed at River in astonishment. One seemed to be motioning him back—he was young, with a boyish face. I recognized him as one of those who had greeted River that morning.

Scanning the hall, I reached into the pocket of my dress and withdrew the obsidian dagger River had given me. Where was Lusha?

Esha was smiling—or, rather, he was holding his mouth in a way that might have been a smile, on someone else's face. "I was hoping we would find you here. Thorn discovered that your body was missing when he returned to the mountain to check. Now we won't have to hunt you down—it makes things easier."

"Oh, I'm afraid it doesn't," River said.

"It's interesting, isn't it?" Esha's voice was strangely calm, given the blood spattering his face. "Obsidian doesn't seem to have the same effect on you as it does the rest of us."

"Would you care to test that theory yourself? I'd be happy to lend a hand." River's eyes drifted over the other witches, to a shadowy rampart suspended in midair. "What have you done, Esha?"

"I've done nothing," Esha said. "You did."

River gazed at him blankly. In the distance there were shouts and cries, the sound of glass breaking. But here, at the center of it all, nobody spoke. The air sang with tension. I could just make out a sliver of the emperor's face through the ranks of his guards, contorted with fury and pain. The guards' eyes flicked warily between Esha and River. The young guard watched him almost beseechingly. My grip on River's arm tightened.

"Our ancestral home," Esha murmured. "It's beautiful, isn't it? It will be even more beautiful after we raze this palace to the ground. Can't you see it? A city of darkness, perched in the Empire's ruins."

"I don't see how I—" River began.

"You woke it," Esha said. "Unintentionally, I'm sure. Our city isn't a pile of stones and useless finery, like this place. It sensed the Empire was falling, and a new one rising to take its place. But it couldn't truly reawaken on its own. Nor could those who once lived there, so many centuries ago, walk again. But with the star's power . . ."

I shuddered as Esha's words sunk in. I looked at the emperor. He gripped his side, blood spilling through his fingers. It didn't look like a sword wound. His arm had been clawed too—one of the witches had attacked him in animal form.

River's gaze had found the emperor too, and his expression was grim. Esha's lip curled. "Do you truly care about the life of the man who sentenced us to exile and torment?" he said. "I was right about you—you are a traitor. Sky would be ashamed."

At the mention of Sky, River's expression grew so cold that I took a step back. The faces of the courtiers and guards, as their eyes moved from River to Esha, were uncomprehending.

"Ah, but I forgot," Esha said, "you're a traitor here too." He gestured. "Bring her to me."

A witch with long, lank hair came forward, a captive in tow. My heart stopped.

Lusha.

She didn't struggle against the witch, though he dragged her roughly. Her golden dress rippled like fire. When the witch tossed her into Esha's grasp, she barely stumbled, and gave the first witch a glare so fierce he actually flinched.

Esha took Lusha's hand, as if he was going to escort her

somewhere. As he looked her up and down, there was a quality in his gaze that disgusted me. "This is one of the shamans you helped in the Ashes, isn't it? You allowed her to escape, to bring the star to the emperor, which no doubt was your plan all along." His filthy nails dug into Lusha's skin, hard enough to raise droplets of blood. Lusha didn't flinch, merely stood there as Esha drew something from a fold in his ragged cloak—

The star. It was as lifeless as ever—a fragment of stone, gray and unremarkable.

"Doesn't look like much, does it?" Esha said. "Shall we test its power?"

The star began to glow against his palm, burning with the dark orange hue of witch fire. Then—

Light flooded the hall. I forced myself not to look away, but to squint through the brightness. Esha drew a shadow over the star, muting but not extinguishing its glow.

A murmur rose through the hall. The guards stared at each other. Shadowy figures wove their way between them, while a dark wall reared up out of nothingness, momentarily separating us from the emperor. One of the figures flitted into the shadow-tower that leaned at the edge of the hall, which seemed to be growing more solid by the minute.

"Esha—" River began.

"The Three Cities will burn." Esha smiled. "And a new city will rise from the ashes. The sky city is coming back to life. And so are the people who lived there."

I stared at the shadow-figures in horror. It was difficult to guess their number; they flickered in and out of existence like the towers and doors of the sky city. But more kept appearing as the star pulsed in Esha's hand.

One of the shadows paused at Esha's side. It had solidified enough for me to tell that it was a woman, her hair undulating around her face. But the way she stood was strange, puppet-like, and her proportions were all wrong. How long had she been dead? I felt a wave of nausea.

Esha's mouth curved. "Let's see what they can do."

The shadow surged forward, moving with a jerky, insect-like grace. I leaped back instinctively, but another witch was there. He shoved me forward, laughing, but River caught me in his arms before I fell.

I screamed as darkness engulfed us, darkness that warped and stretched, forming a curving wall with the texture of stone. We were trapped within a round tower that had simply appeared in the banquet hall, as suddenly as the other apparitions. Terrified, I pounded my fists against the shadow-wall, but it barely wavered. Lusha was on the other side of that wall.

River cursed. He was looking up, having heard something I had not. I followed his gaze—two more dead were thundering down shadow-steps that wound up the tower. They made a noise that was like boots against stone, and yet oddly echoing, as if the sound were carried across a distance that did not exist.

"Go!" River shouted.

"Go?" Where could I go? There was solid shadow all around us. And yet, as I watched, the marble floor of the banquet hall seemed to shimmer like heat haze. More steps appeared, descending through the floor itself, coiling into what I assumed was the hillside below the palace. I stared, unable to comprehend it.

River had no such hesitation. He leaped past me, *through the floor*, which was suddenly as immaterial as cloud, dragging me behind him. The shadow-steps bore our weight, though I had the sense that they were resisting me. They felt sticky, somehow, as if reluctant to allow me passage.

I let River drag me to the bottom of the mad staircase. There we reached a long, low corridor—such as none that I had seen in the palace. It was shadow; everything was shadow, featureless and undulating.

"Where are we?" I yelled, shaking off River's hand.

"Somewhere that shouldn't exist," River said. "The sky city is taking over the palace." River, infuriating River, wasn't panicking at all. He gazed around as if we had just stepped into a gallery lined with unusual paintings.

My head spun. I thought of Lusha, standing at Esha's side, and Tem, who had been in the libraries when the witches attacked, and could be in as much danger. "How do we get out?" I was still yelling. And shaking. I had just descended a staircase made of shadow, in a tower that had formed out of thin air.

River placed his hand over my mouth and shoved me into a bracket in the wall.

I was so angry I contemplated biting him, but at that moment, the dead creatures reached the base of the staircase and thundered past us. River waited until they were gone—to my eyes, they were simply swallowed by the darkness—then he grabbed my hand again. When he pulled, however, I didn't move.

I cried out. I was stuck—the shadow-wall clung to me, drawing me back into itself.

"Kamzin!" River looked alarmed at last. He wrapped his arms around me and pulled me free. The shadows fell back like obedient dogs, but River didn't let me go. He took my face in his hands and kissed me.

I drew back, my heart pounding. "I don't think that's helpful right now!"

"Oh," he said, as if this was actually news to him. "Sorry. Are you all right?"

"Of course I'm not all right! I didn't particularly like your ancestral home the last time I visited. It isn't growing on me."

He gripped my hand. "Stay close."

We were running again, into pitch darkness. I couldn't see a thing. River, though, pulled me along without pausing—clearly, I was supposed to trust that he wouldn't slam us into a wall. I was beginning to feel like a doll dragged along by an absentminded child.

"River," I gasped as I stumbled over my own feet again. Light flickered—River cupped a small, dusky flame in his palm, not as bright as ordinary fire, but enough to illuminate my way. We came to the bottom of another tower that curved upward into gray light. The banquet hall? Did it even exist anymore, or had the shadow city replaced it? This tower had no stairs, unlike the first—there was no way up.

I brushed the wall. It seemed more solid now, clearly stone, though it was a strange, black stone like nothing I'd ever seen. It reminded me of witch fire, which was both like and unlike ordinary flame, a thing of nature subtly twisted, wrong.

"I hear fighting," River said, gazing up at the light. "The emperor's reinforcements must have arrived." He turned to me. "I can—"

He got no further, as one of the dead witches lunged out of the wall.

TWENTY-NINE

I SCREAMED. THE witch was part darkness, like the dead who had chased us, but more defined—were the creatures gaining substance? Her hair floated, as if she stood underwater, and her feet didn't quite touch the ground. I couldn't make out any features in her face, apart from the hint of a mouth, stretched in a grimace or scream.

She went straight for me, but River raised a hand and blasted her back.

Other figures leaped out of the darkness, faster than River could react. One grabbed at my hair and wrenched me so hard I fell to the floor with a cry of pain. Another was on me in a heartbeat, grasping at my neck. Its hands were the texture of dried flowers, light and brittle.

"Kamzin!" Out of the corner of my eye, I saw River make a

sweeping gesture. The shadow-figures began to whirl and spin together, as if caught in a fierce wind. They tried to struggle, but it was no use. River sent them soaring back down the passage, where they were swallowed by the darkness.

I stood up, rubbing my head. Apart from a scratch on my neck from the shadow-creatures' hands, I wasn't hurt. River, though, was leaning back against the wall, breathing hard.

"Are you all right?" I asked nervously. The last time I had seen River look like this, it had been in the Aryas, after he had used Azar-at to cast the spell that rescued us from the avalanche.

River gazed down at his hands. He let out an incredulous laugh.

"I think Esha was right," he said.

"That is the least comforting thing you could say right now," I said. "Right about what?"

"The Crown."

"What's that?" I said. "You mentioned it before. Or Esha did, in the Ashes." I couldn't remember, precisely, how I had learned of the Crown. A thread of memory stirred from the moments I had spent in River's mind. He had thought about it, at least briefly. "It's not an actual crown, is it?"

"No. It's a sort of magical gift. Passed down from one ruler to the next." He brushed his hand against the black stone. "I wonder . . ."

"Ruler?" I froze. I yanked him around to face me. "Ruler. You? Are you—are you the shadow emperor?"

"Esha thought that the Crown had passed to me. It's why he wanted me dead." He seemed to think. "I should have died in the

Ashes. The dagger was obsidian. But somehow . . ."

"So what does this mean?" I felt cold. River's mother was a monstrous figure from dark stories that had terrified me as a child. It should have made me want to draw away from River—instead, I drew closer, more frightened of the spectral figure of my imaginings, which my mind couldn't match up with him.

"I don't know." River smiled, an unexpected flash in the darkness. "But I know Esha will be furious."

"Can you order him to stop?" I said. "Or, I don't know, stand in front of an obsidian arrow?"

"I can't order anyone to do anything. That's not how the Crown works. You can't compel a witch—it goes against our nature."

"Well, what's the point of it, then?" I felt increasingly desperate. Lusha was in danger, and I was trapped down here in some impossible shadow dungeon, unable to reach her.

"I suppose we'll see." River drew me forward, and then we were rising—a cloud of shadow formed beneath our feet, lifting us. I gripped River's hand so tightly it turned white. I didn't trust the shadows of the sky city, which clung to me like spiderwebs. But the shadows River had summoned didn't seem inclined to ensnare me—they were as soft as spring grass, and cool against my bare calves.

We rose higher. If we were still somehow beneath the palace, we should have struck the floor. But the floor was gone, and we rose through the shadow tower until the light of the banquet hall flickered through its walls. River placed a hand on one of the shadowy stones, murmuring something, and they parted, forming an uneven doorway. I stepped through onto the polished marble of the emperor's palace, my legs trembling.

There was no one near. We were at the far end of the banquet hall, close to the corridor that led to the libraries. My thoughts flashed to Tem.

"Kamzin." River's voice was low. I turned.

Shadow staircases hung suspended in midair. A pagoda of darkness reared up before us, its door half-buried in the marble floor, as if the palace were a tide in which it was sinking. There was also the edge of what looked like a wall, tall and crenellated, jutting at a haphazard angle from the outer wall of the palace. It seemed to continue on the other side.

A scream rang out, and I was running. I didn't know who had screamed—it didn't matter. I dodged an empty door frame that hovered at head level and seemed to lead to nothing but more shadow and the hint of something vast, a room larger than the banquet hall.

"Lusha!" I yelled. I circled around a strange half tower, and suddenly there was a knot of a dozen soldiers firing arrows into a sea of armor and shadow.

It was chaos. I couldn't make out the emperor—perhaps his guards had managed to ferry him from the hall. I couldn't see Lusha or Esha. Scarcely a yard from where I stood, a witch fell writhing to the floor, an arrow in her back.

"What are you doing?" A guard seized my arm, and I recognized River's friend. "I thought you left with the emperor. Get back!"

He would have dragged me bodily from the hall, but River had caught up to us. The young man dropped my arm. "*Dyonpo Shara*, I meant no—"

"Where is the emperor?" River interrupted.

"He's been escorted to safety while we deal with these creatures."

My gaze swept the hall. It was clear that the soldiers were not "dealing" with anyone—their numbers had swelled, but so had their dead. And more shadow-figures had joined the witches.

River seemed to be eyeing a tower that loomed over the rest—it went right through the ceiling of the hall. I wondered briefly what the palace must look like from outside, with strange shadowy architecture jutting out like appendages.

River raised his hand. There was a sound like the crack of thunder, and the tower split in two. The upper half toppled toward the crowd of witches and guards, who scattered, shouting. When the tower struck the floor, it exploded into tiny shadows like shards of glass, which then dissolved into nothing.

There was an eerie silence.

Everyone was staring at River now. The guards, including his friend, had fallen back, an uncomfortable echo of his earlier reception at the banquet. But it wasn't respect in their faces now. It was fear. River didn't look any different—not to my eyes, at least. But it was clear, from the expressions on the guards' faces, that they were no longer oblivious to the magic radiating from him.

Esha stepped out of the crowd. In one hand, he held the star, and with the other, he held on to Lusha, who, to my infinite relief, seemed unharmed. Her eyes fixed on mine, and I saw my own relief reflected there.

Lusha gave Esha's hand a gentle tug. He glanced at her, triumph still glowing in his red-rimmed eyes. She gave him a steady look, then swung one of the guards' obsidian daggers toward his heart.

Her aim was good, but Lusha was not left-handed, and when Esha dodged with a hiss she couldn't recover quickly enough. She fell back, dagger raised.

"Kamzin," she said, her voice clear and carrying, "command it to stop."

I could only stare. "What?"

"The star. It will listen to you. You found it, and that's—"

Esha struck her so hard it sent her reeling to the ground, where she lay unmoving.

Fury erupted inside me, and I surged forward. The star's light seemed to waver slightly. It tore itself from Esha's grasp and hovered in the air. How was I supposed to order it to do anything?

"Stop," I said weakly. I felt foolish, speaking to a glowing rock, but I pressed on. "Undo it. Please."

Nothing. Except, perhaps, the smallest flicker in the star's light, so small I may have imagined it.

"Please," I said again. "Don't do what he wants."

To my amazement, the star dimmed. The shadowy figures wavered like mist.

Esha's expression was a storm of rage. He had barely glanced at me this entire time, and I found myself grateful that I had been spared, until now, the full horror of his attention.

With difficulty, I tore my gaze away and focused on the star. It was glowing painfully now.

"Send them back," I said.

The star rose higher. Esha made a grab for it, but the star darted away. Guards and witches alike cowered, pressing their hands against their eyes. Tears streamed down my face, but I forced myself to stay focused on the star. I held out my hand, but the star bobbed once and darted between the columns and over the balconies, disappearing into the night.

It seemed as if everyone was staring at me, including River, blinking the light from his eyes. The shadow-figures were gone, though not the towers and ramparts, the doors that hovered like holes in the air.

Esha raised his hands, and shadows rolled toward me like vines.

I cried out as they encircled me. River wrapped me in his arms, and they surrounded him too. Rather than forcing the shadows back, he pulled them toward us, calling others with them so that we were briefly wrapped in a churning cloud of darkness. I clung to River, my hair whipping around my face. Through the swirl of shadow, I watched as the hall grew painfully bright and stark. River was summoning all the shadows in the vicinity toward himself, as I had seen him do in the Ashes.

The other witches cried out as the shadows surrounding them were torn away. River shaped the shadows into a net and flung it over Esha.

The shadows enveloped Esha like an enormous wave, thick and

heavy. His hand briefly surfaced, grasping for something, before it vanished.

"The palace is lost." River grabbed one of the guards by the shoulder and shoved him. "Get everyone out!"

The guards stood gazing at him with dumbfounded expressions. The witches seemed to be having a similar reaction—they stood blinking and disoriented in the unnatural bright of the hall. Their power was tied to the darkness, and without it, they were weakened. Clumsily, the guards began to retreat. One of them pulled Lusha to her feet and dragged her away.

"Kamzin, go," River said, his voice strained.

I stared at him. "I can't. Lusha—"

"I can hold them off for now. You have to go after the star. Esha will try to recover it."

I looked from him to the guards, to Esha, pinned beneath a net of shadow. River's jaw was set, his face pale. He was struggling to hold Esha, and the witches were regrouping.

"River—"

He shoved me roughly toward the balcony. *"Go."*

I gave him one last look. Then I ran.

THIRTY

SOMETHING LUNGED AT me as I darted through the balcony door—a shape that was half bird, half shadow. I swung my fist and felt it collide satisfyingly with something warm and feathered. The witch fell back, and I didn't pause long enough to see if she would follow. My skirts flapped around my legs, and my bare arms and throat tingled in the cold air. I wasn't cold, though—I was hot.

I had run the length of the balcony that framed the hall, past a few startled courtiers who had been too far away to hear what had happened, and now stood clustered together, uncertain. It had all happened so fast. The emperor. The attack. The star.

Something flickered above me—the star was still there, hovering over the roof of the palace observatory. Was it trying to launch itself back into the sky?

I jumped off the edge of the balcony, dropping several feet to the hillside below. The shadows were thick, and I shuddered, picturing Esha's skeletal hand reaching out from the darkness. Could River hold him back alone? It seemed impossible that anyone could, and yet it was clear that River was stronger than Esha. I recalled the way he had drawn the shadows toward us—they had responded almost eagerly.

I thought of Lusha, dragged away from the banquet hall by the emperor's guards, and felt a stab of fear. River had said he would protect her. But could he?

I sprinted up the grand stone staircase, past a pair of royal shamans clothed in their traditional red *chubas*. One called after me, no doubt startled by my wild appearance, but I ignored her.

Above the main floor of the royal observatory, which was already higher than much of the rest of the palace, were several tiered floors ringed by balconies. Instead of going inside, I leaped to grasp the edge of the sloping roof and hauled myself up, first slinging an elbow over the edge, then a knee, until I was able to roll my body onto the roof. My skirt caught on a nail and tore. The curved tiles were slippery, but I had clung to ice sheerer than this, and clambered up them with little difficulty. I repeated the same process to reach the third-story balcony, and the one above. There I paused, glancing into the observatory's inner sanctum. It had no windows or walls, its structure supported by pillars of whitewashed stone. A young man sat on the floor next to a telescope, head bent over a scroll. Incredibly, the man seemed to have no idea what was happening to his city. But, I realized, it hadn't been fifteen minutes since the witches attacked the palace, though it felt much longer. And this high in the observatory, you were cut off from the world below.

I felt a pang. There was something in the young man's attitude of absorbed attention, the fall of hair across his face, that reminded me of Tem. Where was he now?

I reached the observatory's roof in less than a minute. I leaned forward on my hands, which trembled slightly from gripping the sloped tiles, breathing hard. The breeze lifted the hair off my neck and stirred my dress. I had almost forgotten I was wearing it. The fine fabric was stained now with smudges of roof dirt, and the hem was torn where it had caught on a tile.

Smoke wafted past, and I turned. The fires dotting the city were more numerous now, though they hadn't consumed more than a handful of buildings—but they would, if left unchecked. I swallowed, thinking of the ruins that stood on the outskirts of Azmiri, the stone still warm to the touch after years of snow and rain.

Something sparked at the edge of my vision, colder and brighter than fire. I turned and found myself face-to-face with a girl.

A girl with my face.

I shrieked and nearly tumbled backward off the roof. The girl grabbed me by the arm, pulling me back to equilibrium.

"I've seen you before," I whispered.

The girl only looked at me. She was wearing a red dress now—identical to mine—but before, she had worn a *chuba*. My *chuba*. I pictured her bending over me in the tent in the Ash Mountains, and then in the forest, her eyes luminous in the dark.

I had thought I was going mad. Yet she stood before me now, flesh and blood, with identical smudges on the front of her dress, as if she were my mirror image.

"What are you?" I said.

She smiled faintly at that, and held out her hand. Hesitating, I took it.

Light flared, spilling out from our joined hands. I jerked back in shock, and it flickered and died.

"You're—" I took a step back, realized I was balanced on a precarious, slick roof, and stopped. "How is this possible?"

"I came up here to see if they would take me back." The girl was gazing up at the stars. Her voice was like mine, but fragmented, strangely wavering. "But they can't hear me, and I don't have the strength to make the trip."

I forced myself to speak through my shock. "I found you. Is that why—is that why you look like me?"

"I suppose so." The girl was still staring at the sky. "I don't remember what I used to look like. The first person I saw after I fell was you. So that was the form I took, whenever I felt like seeing the world through human eyes again."

"You vanished," I said. "When I saw you before, you vanished."

"I was frightened," she said. "I didn't understand what had happened to me. I'm sorry."

She seemed so downcast that I said, "It's all right. No one could blame you for being afraid."

"I never used to be afraid," she said sadly. "Please don't let that red-eyed man use my power again."

I swallowed. My thoughts whirled. I wished more than anything that Lusha was here—calm, self-assured Lusha, who would certainly have some logical explanation for this. "What's your name?"

Her brow furrowed. "I don't know. That was . . . a long time ago."

She sounded so forlorn that I reached out and touched her hand. Her skin was as cool as the night air, but she was solid, substantial. Not a ghost.

Light flared again when I touched her, but after a few seconds, it faded to a soft glow.

"That's better." She sounded relieved. "I feel stronger when you touch me. Almost as if I could make it back."

"No, you—" I paused, drawing my hand back. The girl watched me. "You can't. Not yet. Please—we need your help."

She shrugged. "It's your decision."

"Is it?"

"You seem to be able to command me," she said. "Even now, when I tried to escape, I could only get so far."

"I'm sorry," I said. "But I promise, if you help us, I'll help you. I'll do whatever I can. If I need to take you back to the Ashes, I will."

"Thank you, but I don't think that will be necessary." The girl gave me a thoughtful look. "You're a strange sort of person. I just told you that you can command me as you like. Yet you're still asking for my help."

"Of course." I thought of the witches setting fire to the city, and River, his face strained as he held Esha back. Even still, I couldn't order the star to help us. I wasn't like Lusha, who could coolly discard moral qualms if she felt a situation required it.

"You're better than he is," the girl said.

"Who?"

"That man. The one your sister danced with. He killed the star he caught. I could sense it on him—he spent and spent its power until nothing remained."

I didn't know what to say. "I'm sorry."

She shrugged. "It doesn't matter. I will help you willingly. And then—you will help me get home?"

"However I can," I promised.

She smiled, making the light flicker again. "I believe you."

She held out her hands. Hesitantly, I took them, squinting against the explosion of light. It came, but even brighter than I expected. And then—

The star stepped *into* me.

I staggered back. It was like being doused in ice water, followed by a brief flare of heat. When the sensation settled, I looked down at my hands, and found that they were glowing.

I sat down hard on the roof, my legs weak with shock and the strangeness of what I felt. I focused my attention on the glow that enveloped me, imagining that I was pressing it down, forcing it deeper inside me. I had no idea what I was doing, but I thought the star responded. After a few deep breaths, I looked back at my hands. The glow was gone, but my skin had the slightest glimmer to it, as if I had been dusted with ice crystals.

"Thank you," I whispered.

Setting my jaw, I lowered myself over the edge of the roof and made my way back to the palace.

THIRTY-ONE

I SWUNG MYSELF down from the roof, landing with bent knees on the pavement. Absently brushing at my dress, which was even more of a mess now, I turned.

And walked straight into Lusha.

I shrieked. Lusha grasped my shoulders, pushing me to a safe distance. "It's just me. Calm down."

I stared. When I had last seen Lusha, the emperor's guards had been dragging her from the hall, unconscious. "Are you all right?"

"Fine." She tucked her hair behind her ears. At her temple was a darkening bruise. "I woke just before one of the men slung me over his shoulder. I think they thought I was—" She stopped. "I saw you leaving the hall, so I followed."

Though her voice was steady, her hand trembled, and I knew

that she was more shaken than she let on. I brushed her hair aside to examine the bruise. "Lusha—"

"We don't have time," she said, pushing me away. "Did you get the star?"

Of course her first question would be about the star. "I'm fine too, thank you."

"I can see that." She gave me a *stop wasting time* look. "Where is it?"

"Can't you tell?" I stepped back and spread my arms. I expected—and was looking forward to—the look of astonishment on her face, but to my surprise, she only nodded.

"Good. Let's go." And she turned and walked away, leaving me reeling. I had to run to catch up.

"Wait—how did you know?"

"I thought I would be the one the star chose," she said. "I did find it, after all—"

"*You* found it?"

"—but after discussing it with Lozong, I realized that the star always obeys the person who first touches it."

"He would know," I said darkly. "What did you tell him?"

"Everything, of course."

"'Everything'? You mean you told him about River?"

"That his closest advisor has been plotting against him from the beginning? Against the Empire? Of course I did."

I stared at her. "River was *helping* us."

"Was he?" Lusha gave me a sharp look. "I think he was helping himself. I have no intention of playing guessing games about River's motives. The Empire is at stake, and River has never been on the side of the Empire."

"And you think it's that simple?" I was furious. Lusha had made this decision without even thinking of consulting me. "What about the emperor? Do you really think he's blameless in all this? Do you trust him?"

"He did what he thought was right. Besides, he is the *emperor*. We owe him our loyalty. We owe River nothing." She noticed my expression and made a frustrated sound. "What does it matter? I saw River use his powers in the banquet hall, and so did a dozen guards. They know what he is now."

It came to me, in a blinding flash, that Lusha really *did* think it was simple—all of it. She had always seen the world in absolutes. There was always a right course, in Lusha's mind, and a wrong one. It was, in part, why she was such an effective leader: she fixed her mind on a goal with single-minded purpose, rarely doubting her choice. It was an efficient way to view the world. But it was also, I had come to realize, dangerously shortsighted. I thought of River's mother, driven mad by the binding spell. I thought of all the witches who had grown up hating the Empire with an all-consuming intensity. Now the Three Cities were burning, and where did the fault lie? I wasn't sure the question had an easy answer.

"You and the emperor covered a lot in one dance," I said, my voice cold.

"He's . . . very easy to talk to." She wasn't looking at me, and

I noticed that her face had more color than it had a moment ago. "Once you get to know him."

"Once he stops lying about who he is, you mean."

"He apologized for that. He couldn't very well reveal himself when he thought us all witches. Are you really going to lecture me about trusting people who hide their identities?"

"Wait." My head was spinning. We weren't heading back to the palace—Lusha steered me to one of the grand staircases that led down to the Three Cities. "Where are we going?"

"The shamans' residences. The head of the Royal Guard felt it wasn't safe for the emperor to remain in the palace. He's being taken there by stealth, with only a handful of guards. Several hundred shamans live there. It's the safest place in the Three Cities."

"What about River?"

"I don't know." Lusha finally stopped her headlong pace and turned to face me. "They pulled me out of the hall. The last I saw, Esha had broken free of River's spell."

"What?" It was almost a shout. I turned, and would have run back to the palace if Lusha hadn't grabbed my arm.

She pulled me to face her again. "Kamzin, he can't help us now."

"I don't care if he can *help us.*" I wrenched away from her. "I care if he's all right."

"The Three Cities are burning." She enunciated each syllable. "If the emperor's shamans can't stop the fire, it will devour everything in its path. If the emperor can't stop the witches' invasion, the Empire will fall. Right now, we have to focus."

I felt, suddenly, very small. I could see the halo of light behind Lusha cast by the witch fire. "Focus on what?" I asked.

"The only army left in the city is the Second," she said, pulling me down the stairs. "The soldiers are arming themselves with every obsidian blade and arrow they can find, and they're going to sweep the city. We're to bring the emperor the star."

"You mean me," I said. I looked back up the stairs. I didn't want to leave River.

"You may be the only one who can stop this." Lusha's voice held no resentment. Her focus, as it always was during a crisis, big or small, was on the goal, not her own feelings. "I promised the emperor I'd find the star and bring it back to him."

Dazed, I allowed Lusha to pull me forward. We reached the bottom of the stairs and sprinted into a swirl of light and darkness.

The fire was no longer confined to a few scattered buildings—entire streets were ablaze, separated by eerily dark, pensive blocks. Across from the palace, a mansion tucked into a smaller hill was engulfed, painting the street below with contorted shadows. A row of shops went up a block away. I choked and gasped from the smoke that filled the air.

Steadily, the fires were spreading.

As we moved deeper into the city, we passed men and women fleeing in various states of undress. One man appeared to be wearing a nightgown and was towing a heavily burdened yak behind him. Two shoeless women ran by, one almost colliding with Lusha. Dragons flapped around them in a chittering whirl of alarm.

"Where are the soldiers?" I said, between coughs. The smoke

was strangely sharp—it stuck in my throat like brambles. Just as I spoke, though, I saw them: three soldiers in an empty square who seemed to be fighting the darkness. As Lusha and I watched, a witch swirled out of the shadow and wrapped his arms around the closest soldier's throat. Another fired an arrow that struck the witch in the side, and he fell to the ground, writhing. But another witch appeared and, with a gesture, summoned a gust of wind that slammed the soldier into a wall. He slid to the ground and lay unmoving.

Lusha pulled me down an alley before the witches saw us. We emerged across from what was clearly a tavern frequented by traveling merchants. Several abandoned yaks stood tethered outside, grunting and straining at their ties.

Pausing, I drew the obsidian dagger from my pocket and slashed it through the yaks' tethers. The beasts huffed, startled, and then they turned and thundered down the street.

"We don't have time," Lusha snapped, grabbing my arm again. "Come *on*."

But before I could move, the tavern burst into flame.

I didn't see the witch who lit it. There was only a stirring in the darkness, and then the creature was gone, off to wreak havoc somewhere else. Embers leaped into the street, singeing my *chuba*. One landed just below my eye, and I gasped. The searing pain didn't fade even after I brushed the ember away with my sleeve.

The house behind us went up, screams echoing within. Lusha stood frozen, stunned, as plumes of fire rained down. I grabbed her and hauled her out of the way as the gate plunged toward us, the iron burning as easily as kindling.

"Kamzin!"

I whirled. A small group ran toward us, dressed in shamans' robes. Except for one, a tall, lean figure in the *chuba* of a nobleman.

It was Tem.

He rang one of the *kinnika*—it sang out with a cold, high tone. He shouted an incantation, and the house went out as suddenly as it had ignited.

Tem gripped my arms. He had the bell that Mara had given us, which he had attached to the string of *kinnika* around his neck. His face was pale, but he was *alive* and unhurt. Two of the shamans he was with paused before the tavern and began chanting an incantation. The flames sputtered but did not die.

"Are you hurt?" Tem demanded. "I heard about what happened in the hall—at least, parts of it. No one is certain what's going on—except for the obvious, of course. The witches want to burn the city to the ground."

I shook my head, stunned. Tem stepped back and rang the *kinnika* again. His tall frame was briefly silhouetted against the shadowed orange glow—he seemed, to my eyes, to have grown a foot, and his *chuba* whipped about him in the wind, churned up by the hungry flames. The tavern was extinguished—all of it, down to the last ember. It smoked lightly, as if the flames had been extinguished hours ago.

I stared at him. Tem turned back to me.

"My theory was correct," he said in his thoughtful, familiar voice. "When paired with a fire incantation, the bell has the power to counteract the witches' fire, including some of its aftereffects—"

I grabbed him and pulled him close. His arms wrapped around me as if instinctively. I noticed, not for the first time, how good it felt to be in Tem's arms.

He pulled back, touching my face where the ember had burned me. "You *are* hurt." It was almost accusing.

"I'm fine," I said, but Tem was already reaching for one of the bone *kinnika* and murmuring a healing incantation. The pain faded to a twinge.

One of the shamans shouted something, gesturing at Tem.

"Kamzin—I have to go," he said. "We're trying to put out as many fires as possible."

I held on to him for one more second. I didn't want to let go—I didn't want him anywhere near these ghoulish fires, or the witches who had set them. Tem should be at my side. Anything else was wrong.

I set my jaw, forced myself to step back. "Go."

Tem nodded. Then he was gone, charging back into the smoke and the dusky light that filled the street.

"We're almost there," Lusha said, motioning me on. We ran past a temple, as yet untouched by the fire, then came to a towering stone edifice set into the peak of another hill, several stories of pillars and luxurious balconies. Flowering ivy crept over the rails, and in contrast to the stark purity of the emperor's palace, the pillars of this building were painted in vivid reds and golds. I didn't need to ask if Lusha was certain—this was precisely the sort of place I would have expected the pampered shamans of the Three Cities to reside. A grand staircase of white stone loomed before us. It wasn't even the main entrance, for this was an alley.

Lusha led me up the steps, which zagged sharply around a knuckle of rock. There we both halted, for standing in our path was a tall, thin figure dressed in a ragged *chuba*.

"Well," Esha said, his voice quiet as the shadows fell away from him. "You two look familiar."

For a heartbeat, horror froze my limbs. The city below was a tumult of orange and red and darkness, and for a moment, it felt as if the three of us hovered above it all, suspended in midair.

I raised my shaking hands to unleash the star's light.

But before I could, shadow spilled from Esha's hands, quick as lightning, and Lusha and I were engulfed in roiling darkness. I felt it pulling at me, tugging my body this way and that. It was like being buffeted by an intense wind, only the wind had claws and ghostly fists. I flung a hand out instinctively, and light flickered. I concentrated, trying to push the star's light farther, to force the darkness back, but before I could feel any noticeable effect, the shadows rolled away.

Esha stood unmoving, regarding me with anger and calculation. There were other witches here too, circling at a distance.

Lusha.

She lay against the steps, her arm splayed at an odd angle. Esha's magic had flung her backward.

"Lusha!" I fell to my knees, turning her toward me. Her eyes were closed, her face pale. Her arm was broken, clearly. Had she hit her head?

The witches circled, claws clicking on the stone, feathery wings rustling the air. The shadows ebbed and flowed and the wind was laced with ash. Yet all this was mere distraction, as I passed my hand over Lusha's body, searching for wounds, broken bones. Apart from the arm, there was nothing, save a tiny trickle of blood from her mouth. "Lusha." I shook her. Then again, harder.

"The shadows have no effect on you," Esha said. "Let's see if this will."

I looked up. Above me on the steps crouched a monstrous red-toothed bear, snarling and growling. It bared its teeth, which were dark with blood. We weren't the first humans the witch had encountered tonight.

It didn't matter. The only thing that mattered was that Lusha wasn't moving, wasn't breathing. Even Esha, brimming with magic, couldn't frighten me now.

But Esha had done this. I turned to him, my eyes narrowing with something colder than hatred, more fundamental than rage. He wore that odd expression that was not quite a smile, the corner of his mouth upturned in a way that reminded me of River. But River's eyes had never held the malice Esha's did.

"You're a child," Esha murmured. "You've involved yourself in something that has nothing to do with you. You should never have come here."

At that, I felt a tremor of déjà vu. River had spoken that same sentence when we stood on the peak of Raksha. I felt again the anger and frustration of that moment, the feeling that I was challenging not only the witches, but a conflict as ancient and unyielding as a mountain peak. But Esha was wrong—this had everything to do with me. And I had battled mountains before, and won. Esha, standing before me, would destroy everything that I cared about. In a way, he already had. The memory of Raksha melded with my despair to form something white-hot and painfully sharp. With an incoherent cry, I raised my hands, picturing the light soaring from my fingertips like arrows—not at the bear, which drew ever nearer, ready to spring.

At Esha.

Screams rent the air. Even as they did, I summoned more light. *Fallen stars convey power over death*, Lusha had said. Not only the power to raise the dead, but the power to kill. Could I summon that power?

More, I urged. *More*.

The screams faded. But even then, I didn't stop. *More*. The starlight spilled from my fingertips, pale as bone and bright as a hundred suns, beautiful but deadly, painful. I experienced the pain only distantly. I was shielded from most of it—I felt only a throbbing behind my eyes, like snow blindness. The light enveloped everything in its path.

When finally I collapsed, and the light flickered and died, the witches were gone. All but two—the bear lay on the steps only a few feet away, as motionless as Lusha. And on the stairs below lay Esha, his eyes open and unseeing.

There came a cry—two witches in the form of choughs circled the stairs. The birds wheeled once around Esha's body, then fled.

"Lusha," I whispered. Her face was too pale. When I pressed my hand to her throat, I didn't feel the blood moving. But that couldn't be right. Lusha was unstoppable. She could climb mountains and track fallen stars and bend even an emperor to her will.

I shook her again as tears spilled down my cheeks. "Lusha. *Lusha.*"

THIRTY-TWO

LUSHA WAS COLD.

Her hand in mine had cooled some time ago—I couldn't say when. I didn't know how long I had been sitting there with her head cradled in my lap. My legs were stiff, and I was shivering. I felt it distantly, along with the tears drying on my cheeks. Everything was distant, unimportant.

The fires still raged, though it seemed as if some had burned themselves out. Fire burned, shouts sounded in the distance, and no one came. Not River. Not Tem. Not the emperor or his soldiers. We were alone.

Except for Azar-at.

The fire demon had appeared shortly after the witches vanished, hovering at the edge of my sight. At first, I had ignored it. But as time passed, I found that increasingly difficult.

"What do you want?" I said finally. My voice was a croak. It too seemed to come from somewhere outside myself.

Why do you mourn, Kamzin? it said. *Mourning will not help the dead.*

I felt the word like an iron hand gripping my throat. "Nothing can help this."

I can help. I have helped.

I let out a humorless laugh. "How? What have you done for me?"

Heal your familiar, fight the fiangul, the creature recited. *Understand River. Take you to the emperor. All that you have asked, I have done. I can give you what you want.*

I felt cold, as cold as Lusha. "How do you know what I want?"

You want to keep friends safe, Azar-at said. *Friends are hurt. I will help, if you ask.*

"You can't." Another tear slid down my face. I had thought my tears were exhausted. I felt as if I were arguing with the wind, with as little hope for success. "No one can. Not Tem. Not the star. No one."

I will help, if you ask.

"Ask what?" I made a disbelieving sound. "To bring Lusha back?"

As I did before.

"With Ragtooth? He wasn't dead." It tasted like a word in another language. Dead. Lusha was dead.

I gazed at the creature. Its fur seemed more solid, somehow, than it had in the past, its paws larger. But then, that was

Azar-at—the fire demon seemed to have no specific form, only a rough idea of one. But its eyes never changed, glowing like embers roused by the wind.

I remembered Tem's words after Aimo's death. *Whatever it's offering, it isn't life.* The star could bring people back too—but I had seen the result of that. They came back twisted and wrong.

"I would give anything," I said, my voice uneven, "for Lusha. If it were possible. But it isn't."

My magic is beyond the star's magic, Azar-at said. *Beyond human magic. Your sister will be whole again.*

I shook my head, wishing I could block out the creature's words, which crawled through my thoughts like insects, burrowing ever deeper.

I will help, if you ask.

"Then do it." The words were pushed out, desperate. It wouldn't work—Azar-at was lying to me. Nothing could bring Lusha back. She was gone, and nothing and no one mattered beyond that fact. What would Father say? This would break him, and then I would have lost two people I loved.

Father's face drifted across my vision. In the same moment, Lusha drew a gasping breath.

I leaped as if burned. The world seemed to right itself, leaving me breathless and dizzy.

"Lusha!" Tears spilled down my face.

Lusha's eyelids fluttered, and she murmured something. She seemed disoriented, not quite fully awake.

Pain blossomed somewhere near my heart. It was an ominous

pain, pointed and sharp, with a weight behind it that promised worse to come. I felt the star's light flare again, and I instinctively drew on some of its strength, grasping at it as a drowning person grasps at a rope. I pushed back on the pain, and to my amazement, it lessened.

Azar-at made a strange sound I had never heard before, a guttural sort of growl.

"What are you doing?" I said.

You agreed, Kamzin, Azar-at said. *You asked for my help.*

Lusha muttered something. I squeezed her hand, which was warming against mine, no longer the temperature of the stone stairs.

Another stab of pain. It felt as if the pain was pulling at me, drawing me toward some dark place. "How much of my soul are you taking?"

The fire demon's tail flicked back and forth. *Everything.*

"Everything?" Panic gripped me. "You never said—"

You did not ask.

"I—no." The pain dug its claws deeper, dragged me closer to that dark place. "It isn't fair."

It is always fair. It must balance. Your sister's life, in exchange for yours. A soul for a soul.

Dread rose within me, for Azar-at was right. There was a malevolent fairness in what the fire demon demanded. Would I give my life for Lusha's life?

I didn't even have to think about it. Of course I would.

But just because something was fair didn't make it right. I had faced death before, and I hadn't backed down. I wasn't about to start now.

Remembering the reaction it had drawn from Azar-at, I reached for the star's power again, using it to push back against the pain. I didn't know what I was doing, but the star responded readily, and once again, the pain receded.

Azar-at made that eerie sound again. The pain returned, stronger than before.

I do not understand, it said. Its voice in my thoughts was as calm as ever, despite the growls and the brightness in its coal eyes.

Gathering up my strength, I gave another desperate *push*. Azar-at, to my amazement, stumbled back a step.

What is this? The fire demon's growls were constant now. *You agreed—*

"I never agreed to this." I felt almost light-headed at my success, or perhaps it was from the pain still throbbing through my chest.

You cannot break the contract.

There was another horrible tug. I felt the star recoil in terror, even as I clung to it with a desperate intensity. It was the only thing keeping Azar-at at bay, but it was weakening. It had its own great, terrible power, but it couldn't overcome Azar-at's, or the bond between us, harder than iron. The bond that I had agreed to.

Azar-at gave another growl, and I felt something inside me break, as if the rope I had been clinging to had suddenly snapped. I felt a surge of fear that didn't come from me, but from the star. There was a flare of light, and then the star was outside me, no longer girl-shaped, a glittering specter that hung in the air.

"No, please," I said, my voice breaking. "Don't leave. I can't fight Azar-at on my own."

The star flickered frantically. Then it was gone, soaring over the palace. I knew it couldn't escape—it had failed before. But I could no longer reach its power.

So it was going to end like this. The thought hit me dully, as if from a distance. My terror subsided, replaced by an odd sense of disappointment. I had never thought much about my own death, but if I had, it would have involved some feat of bravery, or foolishness, in some distant wilderness or snow-cloaked mountain pass. I would not have imagined it like this, crouched on the stones of a strange city, facing a creature of smoke and fire.

No use in fighting, Kamzin, Azar-at said, its voice as imperturbable as always. Only its eyes, twin fires in the night, gave away its terrible hunger. *Fighting will only bring pain. I do not wish friends to feel pain.*

Lusha would live, and that was all that mattered. Lusha was clever and brave, and she deserved this more than I. I gazed at her face, because that was what I wanted to see last, not the fire of Azar-at's eyes. I hoped she wouldn't be too angry with me when she woke. I swallowed, forcing the tears back.

You care about friends, Azar-at said, its voice almost a croon. *You said you would never hurt them. I understand this. I admire it.*

I froze. "I said . . ."

You made me promise. Never let you hurt friends. I kept my promise.

"Yes, you have, haven't you?" It rose in my mind, a dreamlike thing. The memory of our conversation on the summit of Raksha. It felt like an age ago—another life.

You wished to hurt River. I said: No, Kamzin. Not good. I kept my promise.

"What else did you promise me, Azar-at?" I murmured. My heart thrummed like the wings of a caged bird. "I want to be sure you've lived up to your half of the contract."

Always tell the truth, the fire demon replied. *I have never lied, Kamzin.*

"No," I agreed. "But there was something else. Wasn't there?"

Azar-at was silent. Its tail wagged slower now, its wide, flickering eyes fixed on my face.

"I remember now." I swallowed—I was filled with a desperate hope, so strong it threatened to overwhelm me. "You promised to leave if I asked. To end the contract."

Yes, Kamzin, Azar-at murmured. *Once I have what you owe, I will leave.*

"That wasn't what I said. That wasn't what you promised." My voice grew louder. "You agreed to leave whenever I asked. No matter what."

Azar-at's tail was no longer wagging. *I—*

"No." I was shaking. "I've heard enough. Azar-at, I am telling you to leave." I stood, though my trembling limbs protested. *"Now."*

The creature let out another guttural growl. It seemed to have grown larger—where before its muzzle had reached my waist, now it reached my chest. Words pressed against my mind, but they were strange and disjointed, unlike Azar-at's usual smooth murmur. The creature took a step toward me.

There came the sound of small paws descending the stone stairs. Ragtooth leaped lightly between us, his bushy tail flicking back and forth.

"Ragtooth, get out of the way," I cried. I remembered too well what had happened the last time Ragtooth had challenged Azar-at.

Ragtooth, characteristically, ignored me. Azar-at took a step forward, and Ragtooth's tan fur stood on end. He lowered his chin to the ground in a threatening posture. Then he darted forward and slashed Azar-at across the muzzle.

The fire demon let out another strange sound—a *yip* of pain and surprise. Actual scratches bloomed on its face. After a moment, they faded. Azar-at's stance held a new wariness.

I stared at Ragtooth. Azar-at was a creature of smoke and fire, more substance than either but less than an actual wolf. It wasn't flesh and blood—how had Ragtooth injured a being like that?

My thoughts flashed back to the ghosts on Raksha—Ragtooth had hurt one of them too, and they were *dead*. At the time, I had barely given it a thought.

You see what you want to see, Tem had said.

Azar-at was shaking—but with rage or fear, I couldn't tell. To my horror, the fire demon began to grow again. Steam rose from the damp stone beneath it. The claws of pain tightened, and I fell back, gasping.

As Azar-at grew, a powerful heat wafted off its body. Azar-at had always seemed to possess an internal furnace, as if the creature were flame itself at the core. Now I felt as if I were on an exposed mountain peak at high summer, scorched by the midday sun. Terrified, I moved backward—up the stairs, lifting Lusha by her arms and dragging her with me.

Soon, the fire demon was twice the size it normally appeared, and it kept growing. It pressed an enormous paw onto the railing, as if it meant to leap up the stairs.

"Ragtooth!" I cried, my voice breaking. The fox was circling the fire demon's legs, snapping and snarling, and my heart stopped as I realized that what had happened on Raksha would happen again—only this time, Ragtooth wouldn't recover. Azar-at loomed over me, though it stood lower on the stairs. I would not have been surprised if sparks flew from its glowing eyes. It stepped closer.

Ragtooth's jaw closed on the creature's heel, tearing out a chunk of fur. Azar-at growled, and he was so large now that the sound send reverberations through the stone stairs. Ragtooth leaped onto the railing, his whiskers waving in the wind.

For the wind had picked up. I glanced up at the sky, expecting to see a looming storm, but there was nothing above us but a roof of stars. The wind rose, becoming so fierce that my eyes watered, and I feared Ragtooth would be blown off the railing. But he held firm, seeming completely untroubled. Azar-at, to my astonishment, had fallen back. The creature seemed to be having difficulty holding itself together; like the flame in an old campfire, it was fading, shrinking back into itself. It was not as large as it had been, but it was still enormous: easily twice the size of a yak.

Ragtooth leaped back onto the stairs, and the wind ceased so abruptly I fell backward—I had been bracing myself against the gale without even noticing. Ragtooth snapped at Azar-at, who showed no inclination to challenge him. Some of the heat seemed to have faded from the creature's coal-like eyes, and I could see the stone through its body.

Suddenly, River was at my side, his arm around my shoulders. I caught a glimpse of feathers dissolving into black clothing, yellow owl's eyes melting into River's two-toned ones.

River's eyes flicked over the scene—Lusha's motionless body, Esha on the stairs below. Ragtooth with his fur still standing on end, crouched between me and Azar-at, who towered over us.

"Azar-at." River's voice was quiet. "It's over. Go."

For the space of a heartbeat, the creature seemed to freeze. *You do not command me, River.*

"I'm not commanding," he said. He held the fire demon's gaze. "We were friends once. Or have you forgotten?"

I forget nothing.

They looked at each other for a long moment. I felt afraid to move, or even to breathe.

Azar-at stood. Suddenly, somehow, it was wolf-sized again. I blinked, astonished, for I couldn't recall the precise moment it had happened. Its tail wagged once, slowly. River held out his hand, and I thought for a moment he was casting a spell, but then Azar-at came forward and brushed its snout against his palm. I fell back, repulsed. Then the creature was simply gone.

The pain within me subsided, like a muscle unknotting itself. I sagged against River. I felt a strange sense of confusion, of *lostness*. I searched for the source of the feeling, and found none. Then I realized.

I couldn't sense Azar-at anymore.

"It's done," I murmured.

River's grip on me tightened. I buried my face in the crook of his neck, so filled with relief and exhaustion I didn't think I would be able to stand.

Lusha murmured something. Her eyes were opening, and almost at the same time she began pushing herself up on one elbow.

"Lusha!" I threw my arms around her neck. "Not so fast—you were hurt."

She gave me a look so sharp and familiar that I almost began to cry again. She sat up straight, pushing me away. "What happened?"

I shook my head. "I wouldn't know where to start."

"Esha is dead." River's voice was wondering. "The Fifth Army has arrived, and the witches are retreating. That's as good a place as any."

Ragtooth settled beside me, and I wrapped him in my arms. He struggled, but halfheartedly.

"Kamzin." River's grip tightened. "Look."

I followed his gaze. Through my tear-hazed vision, the sky seemed bright—too bright. The stars were dancing. My head ached as I tried to take it in—the battle we had fought, the city smoking below me, all the wandering light in the sky above.

"What is that?"

River smiled. "Shooting stars."

THIRTY-THREE

THE SKY WAS darkening. The golden glow of sunset was hidden by the trees that surrounded our small campsite, a few hundred yards off the main road to the Arya Mountains.

I shivered—my back, turned toward the campfire, was warm; the rest of me was chilled. I looked forward to leaving the forest behind and returning to the expansive views and blazing stars of Azmiri, perched halfway into the sky. After a week in the palace, I'd had enough of feeling confined. The novelty of servants and fine clothes had quickly worn off, and I had often found myself pulling on my worn, familiar boots and escaping to the emperor's gardens, where you could at least see the sky. I turned, yearning for Tem's familiar presence.

But Tem wasn't there. Tem was with the two royal shamans in our escort, setting up the wards for the night. And after taking us through Sasani Forest, he would return to the Three Cities.

It hurt to think that I was leaving Tem behind. I wondered if it would ever stop hurting.

The Shamans' Council had offered to admit him as a novice. It was a lowly position, junior even to the apprentices, and said more about the snobbishness of the royal shamans toward someone of Tem's upbringing than it did about his abilities. But, in a year, Tem would be able to take the Trials, and after that, there was no doubt in my mind that he would progress rapidly through his studies.

Tem seemed happy. And it wasn't that we weren't going to see each other again—of course we would. But I would no longer see him every day, no longer lie next to him in the grass as the stars appeared, his clothes smelling of rope and yak wool. He wouldn't bend his head over some dreaded assignment from Chirri, explaining the theory in his quiet voice. He wouldn't open the door of his father's hut when I knocked, his face breaking into a broad smile, as if my presence, after all our years of friendship, was still unexpected.

As if drawn by my thoughts, Tem stepped out of the trees. The *kinnika* were looped around his wrist, and he wore the plain brown *chuba* of a novice shaman.

"Need some help?" I said, keeping my voice bland.

"Um . . ." Tem paused, and then he noticed I was smiling. He chuckled, saying, "You could hold the light."

I nodded, whistling for one of the dragons. I placed the beast on my shoulder, and we splashed across the stream. Tem paused and murmured the incantation. After he finished, we moved on.

"I thought you were assisting Dechen?" I said, naming the petite shaman wreathed in so many glittering pendants she clinked when she walked.

Tem sighed. "She was using a silver talisman to set the wards. When I suggested plain bronze, she sent me to tend to the fire."

"The quality of the Three Cities shamans never ceases to surprise me," I said.

"They're not all like that. But too many are." Tem let out a long breath. "All they've known is peace. What do you need with protection spells when you live in the Three Cities, surrounded by the emperor's soldiers? Jewels and flashy tricks will win you more esteem. They'll have to get used to doing things differently now that the witches' powers are unbound."

We moved downstream, stopping by a ring of boulders. There Tem set another anchor for the spell, murmuring the shamanic words with careless ease.

"You can help with that," I said. "You know better than anyone what they're facing."

"I'm not sure they'll listen to me. I'm only a novice. And"—he paused—"I have to be careful."

I didn't need to ask what he meant. Tem's position was a dangerous one. Though the emperor had granted permission for him to train with his shamans, Tem was under strict orders not to reveal his parentage. There were those who would try to kill him if they found out. Witches were even more hated and feared among ordinary citizens of the Empire than they had been before. Even if there were no more attacks, that was unlikely to change any time soon.

"Has he spoken to you?" I said.

"The emperor?" Tem looked surprised. "I don't think he's even looked at me." He paused. "I hope it stays that way."

I nodded. I hadn't told Tem about my own private interview with Emperor Lozong—I was still trying to work out how I felt about it.

"All right," Tem said, after setting another anchor. "That should hold."

"Guess I'll be the one doing this tomorrow," I said. It wasn't easy keeping my voice light.

"You won't need warding spells tomorrow. The soldiers will be ample protection once you're through the forest." His voice held the same careful lightness as mine. "All the same . . ."

He reached into his pocket and drew out a leather cord strung with two of the *kinnika*. The black bell, and the tarnished one, marked *shadow-kin*. When he placed them in my hand, they made no sound at all. The black bell hadn't sounded since Azar-at had left.

Thinking about the fire demon sent a shiver down my spine, and for a moment, I imagined I saw a flash of his fiery eyes from the shadows. But Azar-at was gone—neither River nor I had seen him since the night of the fires. "I can't take these," I said. "You'll need them."

"Something tells me you'll need them more than me," he said, smiling. "I would give you the one I used during the fires, but

Mara said I have to return that to the Elder of Jangsa."

"Mara." I shook my head. The chronicler had left the Three Cities for his family home in a huff, not bothering to say goodbye to any of us. I suspected that Lusha's frequent visits with the emperor had something to do with it.

"According to the royal librarians, those two *kinnika* date from long before the binding spell was cast," Tem said. They're not tainted with the witches' magic, so you won't have to worry about their power failing."

"But those—" I looked at the string of *kinnika* around Tem's neck, which looked strange now, incomplete. "Those will fail?"

"Eventually." His gaze grew distant. "There are hundreds of ancient talismans kept in sealed rooms beneath the libraries. They're faded and crude, and they don't have the same power as the talismans imbued with the witches' magic. But some of the royal shamans are beginning to talk seriously about repurposing them. About resurrecting the forgotten magics that the shamans didn't need to learn when they could rely on stolen power. For instance, I've read several scrolls describing the combined power of fire and ravensbone . . ."

I couldn't help smiling, listening to him talk. Tem caught my expression and blushed. "I mean—I won't be spending *all* my time in the libraries."

"Of course not," I said in a mock-serious tone. "Just that part of the day that falls between dawn and dusk." I paused. "They're lucky to have you."

"They would be luckier if the emperor had never cast the

binding spell in the first place," Tem said. "It didn't just weaken the witches. Shamans have forgotten things they never should have forgotten. Now that the witches are free, they're starting to remember. Now there's . . ."

"What?" I said. "Balance?"

He shook his head slightly. "There is no balance between shamans and witches. Witches have magic in their bones. But that's the way it should be." He gestured to the *kinnika*. "Please take them, Kamzin."

I swallowed. I placed the *kinnika* around my neck, and knew I would never take them off. Not while Tem wore the others.

"I'm sorry," Tem said suddenly.

I gazed at him. "For what?"

"I know I made things difficult," Tem said. His face was flushed, and he didn't meet my gaze. "When it ended between us, part of me always believed we'd have another chance. It was stupid. I always knew it would end up like this."

An ache blossomed in my chest. "End up like what?"

Tem smiled faintly. "With you charging off on some adventure. And me staying behind. Though I never guessed it would be in the emperor's court. You're like the wind—you're meant to be out there, among the mountains and the stars, fighting storms and monsters and anything else foolish enough to get in your way. And I'm . . . well, I'm not."

"Tem." I had to pause, to steady my voice. "You know I'll always love you. Even if it isn't—"

"I know," he said. "You're the most important person in the

world to me, Kamzin. I—" He broke off. "I'll always be there for you. Whenever you need me."

I wrapped him in a hug. Above us, the stars brightened.

"I should check on Dechen's wards," Tem said, pulling back. His eyes were moist, but he seemed calmer. "I don't like leaving it to chance."

I nodded, forcing a smile. "Go."

He went.

Emperor Lozong came to me the day after the Three Cities burned.

I hadn't expected it. After the witches had been routed from the city, the emperor and his entourage had returned to the palace, despite the lingering presence of the sky city. In the banquet hall, a tower of shadow still stood, while apparently the libraries were haunted by a dark doorway that each hour appeared in a different place. Lusha had been summoned before the emperor and his council, where she had remained into the morning. Meanwhile, shamans roamed the Three Cities, putting out fires and hunting for any witches foolish enough to remain behind.

So with no one looking for me, and nothing in particular to do, I had returned to the palace rooms River had chosen for me.

For several moments, I simply sat on the bed, staring at nothing. The beautiful dress that had been made for the banquet was torn and stained, my hands and face streaked with soot. I knew I should do something—wash, perhaps, or tend to the burn on my face that throbbed quietly—but still I sat there. Finally, I rose, and opened one of the windows, though the night was chilly. Then I lay down and slept.

I awoke as I had the previous morning: to a glimmer of light through the shutters, and the sound of birds in the courtyard. I blinked, and for a moment it was as if none of it had happened—the banquet, the mad dash through the Three Cities, the battle with Esha. Everything had changed, and it seemed the world should acknowledge it somehow. A raven croaked in a tree.

"Good morning," said a familiar voice.

I pushed myself up on my elbows. I was only half surprised to see River seated in a chair, his feet propped against one of the bedposts. At some point, he had changed out of the glittering black *chuba* and gloves, but he hadn't returned to his regular courtier's dress. He was clothed as he had been on the journey to Raksha, in a simple gray tunic and worn leather boots. He was not wearing his tahrskin *chuba*.

"Is it?" I leaned against the headboard. Something ached inside me—I couldn't place where.

River stood and threw open the shutters, ignoring my groans of protest. "I suppose it's relative," he said. "The fires have destroyed a third of the city, and the emperor wasn't pleased to learn that another fallen star had escaped his grasp. But he's alive, the Empire stands, and he seems enamored with your sister. I peeked into the council chamber an hour ago. They're still talking. I didn't stay long; it was quite dull. They seem well matched in that respect."

I stared at him. "You didn't let them *see* you?"

"No." He laughed. "The emperor has put a price on my

head—literally. Rather a large one. It's flattering."

"How did you hide, then?" My voice was stern. "If the emperor spots any owls perched on his balcony, goggling at him—"

"Oh, I have a trick or two up my sleeve." He threw himself on his back across the foot of the bed. "I believe this belongs to you?" He reached into his pocket and handed me a rock. Not just any rock.

The star.

I snatched it up. "Where did you—"

"I didn't. It was on your windowsill."

I brushed the star with my thumb. It was warmer than it had been—the same temperature as my own skin.

"If you light it, you'll release its power again," River said. "It appears to be dormant."

I set the star aside. I would deal with it later. "What else did you learn on your spying mission?"

River wove his fingers together and tucked his hands beneath his head. "The witches have retreated, though no one knows where. The emperor suspects the Nightwood—more likely they've gone in all directions. Lusha is to receive some sort of medal."

I snorted. *Of course.* "What about the sky city?"

"It's fading." River looked thoughtful. "Though it may never be completely gone. Magic like that always leaves traces." He looked at me. "Tem paid a visit when you were asleep. And Mara."

I was bemused. "Mara?"

"The servants sent him away quickly enough. He kept

demanding to speak with you—I think he was beside himself, not knowing the full story of what happened. He's used to being at the center of things. I almost bit him."

"*Bit* him?"

"I was a dragon at the time."

I let out a breath of laughter. "How long have I slept?"

"It's almost midday. I thought about waking you. I was getting bored."

I groaned again. I didn't want to get up. The odd feeling had intensified. I rubbed my face and let out a gasp of pain as I brushed the scar where the ember had landed. It wasn't like other burns I had felt.

"Here." River was at my side, gently drawing my hand away. "Let me."

"I thought you didn't have any healing powers." I held myself still as his fingers brushed my cheek.

"I don't." He leaned in so close that I could count each of his eyelashes. "This is different, though."

He chanted no incantation and waved no talisman, but slowly, as his hand moved across my face, the pain in my cheek eased. Or, at least, it no longer throbbed like an infected wound.

"There." He drew back a little, examining me. "You'll have a scar. I can't do anything about that."

"I've always wanted a scar," I said lightly. On the table by the bed was a small mirror, next to a decanter of water and a gilded hairbrush, no doubt placed there by a helpful servant. I lifted it, examining my reflection. The burn was small and round, resting on the edge of my cheekbone beneath my eye. It was darker than an ordinary burn.

River was watching me. I sensed, somehow, that he was about to apologize—for something, or for everything, I didn't know. I realized that I didn't need to hear it.

"How are you at treating stomachaches?" I leaned back into the pillows. "Or whatever I'm feeling now."

There was an odd pause. "Is it a pain you can't place?"

"Yes," I said slowly.

River nodded. "I felt it too, after. It's Azar-at."

"Azar-at?" I felt cold. "He's gone."

"Yes. But it's no simple thing, ending a contract with a fire demon." He absently rubbed the side of his head in that familiar way. "It may be that we're the only people who have ever done it. You were connected, and now you're not. It leaves a mark." His eyes drifted to the scar on my cheek. "One that no one else can see. The pain will fade in a day or two."

We sat there for a long moment as birdsong flickered through the window and the sunlight cast dappled shadows on the marble floor.

"Do you think it . . . grows back?" I said quietly.

River's gaze turned inward. After a moment, he said. "I hope so. But no—I don't think it does."

There was a knock at the door. River disappeared. He fluttered to the windowsill in raven form, settling there in the sunlight, which threw his shadow on the floor tangled in leaves.

"River," I hissed. Was he just going to sit there like a misplaced gargoyle? He merely regarded me with glassy black eyes.

The door opened. To my horror, the emperor himself strode in, all six and a half feet of him, menacing and stark in his white *chuba*. His gaze rested on me, then slid to River.

"One of Lusha's, I presume?" was all he said, before striding in as if he owned the place. Which, of course, he did.

I was too surprised to respond. Then, for clearly it was the right answer: "Yes."

"At least half a dozen have come to her in the last few hours," Lozong said. He took the chair River had vacated, though he did not settle in an indolent posture with his feet on the bed, but rather held himself still with an elbow leaned on each arm, taking up as much space as possible. His presence, blunt and forceful, took up enough space already. "It's an interesting gift, these familiars. Not that it surprises me that they would be drawn to your sister. For that reason, we don't harm them unless given cause."

Lozong regarded me in silence. I felt like an insect beneath his gaze, as if it had a weight and substance other gazes did not. Something deep inside me rebelled against that feeling.

"Well now, I've spoken with your sister," he said. "What do *you* have to say, Kamzin of Azmiri?"

That was all he asked, and then he waited. Clearly, I was supposed to guess the sort of response he expected. I wondered briefly what would happen if I guessed wrong.

"I say my first visit to the Three Cities didn't quite go as planned," I said evenly.

"Your sister feels we should focus on rebuilding the city, rather than chasing after the star you caught."

"You'd do well to listen to her." I said it with heartfelt honesty.

He smiled, and I felt a shiver of relief. "I quite agree." He leaned back, and his scrutiny dimmed to something bearable, though still it was not particularly pleasant. "She said you found it. Oh, she tracked the approximate location, but you were the one who retrieved it from the mountain."

I hesitated. "Yes."

"You're brave." It was a cool assessment, not a compliment. "Stalwart. I'm sure you know what I do with people like you."

Again I felt as if he were testing me, as if there was a correct response and an incorrect one, and a great expanse between the two. "I know you have an opening for Royal Explorer."

At that, he laughed. I didn't risk glancing at River, though I wanted to. I merely waited.

"I like you, Kamzin. Do you know how many people I can say that about?" He paused, and then, as I was about to reply, he said, "Very few. I've come to realize—recently, in fact—that trust can be a very dangerous thing." He regarded me. "But you already know that, don't you? You trusted River, and look how he betrayed us."

I felt about as comfortable being referred to as an "us" by the emperor as I did being told that he liked me. Claws pecked against the windowsill, as River scrabbled at the wood in an attempt at raven-like behavior—or, as I suspected was more likely, as he dismissed Lozong's words with mockery.

"Have you seen him?" The emperor's tone was mild. His gaze was not. "Lusha told me you had no particular relationship with him. But I wonder. The two of you spent a great deal of time together. And River can be very charming, can't he? I confess that I too was taken in by his charms."

I felt my heart speed up. The emperor's voice held the calm of a loaded spring in the moment before release. I didn't trust myself to speak.

The emperor smiled, and it was as if the spring had snapped. "You'll tell me if he does visit you? Or if you ever learn of his whereabouts?"

The words bore only the superficial semblance of a question. "Yes, Your Highness."

"No, no, no," he said. "You will call me Elin, if you call me anything—a childhood nickname, and one few have permission to use. You did help preserve my Empire, after all. And I suspect we may be seeing a lot of each other in the future."

I swallowed. Perhaps because he had unnerved me, or perhaps because I wanted, in some small way, to surprise *him*, the question just came out. "Are you going to ask Lusha to marry you?"

His smile changed. For a brief moment, I caught a glimpse of genuine warmth in his eyes, a hint of what might have been there when he was actually the age he appeared.

"She is very like Iranna." His tone was distant.

He blinked, and reached over to squeeze my hand. "Rest now, Kamzin. You'll have little opportunity for that in the coming months, as I'm sure you've guessed."

I swallowed. Was he offering to make me one of his explorers? I thought so, but he made no move to clarify, merely let his bland words hang in the air, where they assumed an ominous quality. The emperor smiled again, and strode out, his white *chuba* rippling behind him, painfully bright. He seemed to draw some of the light from the room with him, and as the door closed I fell back in relief, welcoming the return of the shadows.

THIRTY-FOUR

WE TRAVELED THROUGH dense forest for the next two days, keeping mostly to the road. Despite this, it was slow going with such a large group and all the gear that entailed.

"Here." Lusha settled at my side by the fire, handing me a bowl of something fragrant with spice.

"What is it?" I said.

She gave a small shrug. "Ask Urma."

I glanced across the fire, where Urma, our personal cook, busied himself with something that might have been dessert, though it was hard to tell with Three Cities food. Everything was laden with sweetness and spice and rare garnishes. It was enough to make me crave even the frequently burned *sampa* porridge of our old rations.

"Tell me again why you agreed to bring a cook."

"I didn't," Lusha said, her voice curt. Her cheeks flushed. "The emperor determined our escort. I had no say in it."

"Of course not," I said, and had the satisfaction of watching Lusha's blush deepen. Though the soldiers who arrayed themselves around us during the day, their armor clanking, and the assistants who snatched things from my hands as we made camp were annoying, I supposed that I should have counted myself lucky. The emperor had been reluctant to allow us to leave at all, given the danger posed by the witches. He had relented only after Lusha agreed to travel with a full guard.

"Just as you had no say in the emperor's planned trip to Azmiri next month," I added.

"That—" Lusha drew in her breath. "That is a ceremonial visit. To honor us—and Azmiri—for protecting the Empire."

I rolled my eyes. I didn't know the specifics of what had passed between Lusha and the emperor. But they had spent much of the past week in each other's company. I would have disliked it more, had I not recognized, on some instinctive level, how closely matched Lusha and Lozong were. It had been evident from the very beginning. Lozong was fearsome and commanding, and I would never cease to be intimidated by him, but many people felt the same way about Lusha. I didn't notice, because I was used to her.

"What about you?" I asked. "Have the dreams stopped?"

Lusha didn't answer immediately. She had told me her sleep had been troubled since that night—though, being Lusha, she wouldn't provide any details. "I'm all right."

"Are you?" Dark circles framed her eyes, and her normally sharp gaze clouded sometimes, as if she had recalled something that troubled her.

"Yes." She smiled at me. "Or getting there, anyway. Don't worry about me, Kamzin."

A thought occurred to me. "What will Yonden think of all this?" I said quietly.

Lusha looked away, but not before I saw the flash of pain in her eyes. I knew how important Yonden was to her—I may have been the only one who did. I also knew that, as a seer, he could never marry. Seers were prevented by fiercely guarded customs even from forming friendships, and his relationship with Lusha had only survived by being kept secret from the rest of the village.

"I don't know," Lusha said finally. "I suppose I'll find out."

I could think of nothing to say to that. I thought of the seer's distant gaze, the long hours he spent charting the futures he glimpsed in the stars, and wondered how much of what had happened he had already guessed. Lusha's gaze was distant. After a moment, she went to help the servant tasked with assembling our tents.

I sat there for a while, gazing into the night. Then I too stood and slipped away—into the darkening forest.

The leaves rustled as a bird or other small creature flitted through the underbrush. I was still within the perimeter of the wards, where there was no need to wonder at unusual sounds. But I kept walking—farther upstream, past the place where the protective magic stopped and the sounds from our camp faded beneath the nighttime forest sounds. The trees parted along the bank, revealing a slash of starry sky.

I paused next to a waterfall, waiting. The wards kept him away too, but even if they didn't, he couldn't show himself when the soldiers were near.

I let out a slow breath. I was happy to have a moment alone. Amid the bustle and clamor of the palace, it had been difficult to find time to think. I scanned the trees. The nights seemed darker since the witches had returned to the Empire, the shadows deeper, more dangerous. I was almost certain it was my imagination. Almost.

I had traveled from one end of the Empire to the other—beyond the Empire. It still felt strange to think it. At times, I wondered if everything that had happened had been an elaborate dream—soon I would awaken in my room crowded with shamanic trinkets, late for my morning lessons with Chirri. I would climb to her lonely hut, gazing down the slope to where Tem grazed the yaks—and beyond, to where the Arya Mountains dissolved into sky, a world of magic and wild places that I would never know.

One of the *kinnika*—I didn't have to look to tell which one—gave a whisper. I didn't start when his hand slipped into mine, but I did feel my heart speed up.

"So," River said, "it seems that your appearance before the emperor's court was a success. Congratulations."

I glanced down at the tahrskin *chuba* I was wearing. It was wonderfully warm without being bulky, and molded itself perfectly to my form. But of course it did—it had been made for me.

Ragtooth had followed River out of the shadows. These days, he was often in River's company, as if he belonged as much to River as he did to me now. Though I suspected this was at least partly Ragtooth's way of making River aware that he was being monitored.

Ragtooth gave my toe an affectionate nip, then began to wash his knee. Since the battle with Azar-at, the fox hadn't demonstrated any unusual abilities—unless gnawing through a pair of new boots in the space of an hour counted as an unusual ability. He sniffed the air, the wind playing through his whiskers, the image of an ordinary, if remarkably scruffy, fox. I shook my head. I wondered if I would ever fully understand what Ragtooth was.

"Did he name you Royal Explorer?" River said.

I let out a short laugh. "No. But Lusha said she'd work on him."

"I'm sure she will."

"I don't need it. Just having this"—I played absently with the sleeve of the tahrskin *chuba*—"is almost too much."

River's grip on my hand tightened. "Kamzin. You deserve every honor the emperor could bestow on you."

"Do I?"

His voice was steady. "Yes."

I wondered at that. I hadn't set out for Raksha to fulfill some noble purpose. Lusha had. Lusha was the one who always thought of the greater good—I had wanted something else. An adventure. A chance. Now I had another one.

I thought of my mother, her face turned to the stars. *The best explorers make the night a little brighter.* I felt a surge of determination.

"So," River said, "where is your first expedition?"

My eyes met his. There was a pensive, almost awkward quality to his expression, as if he were asking an entirely different question.

"West," I said, through the happiness that rose inside me. "Beyond the Drakkar Mountains. The emperor wants a report on the new village by Otinza Falls—its position makes it a target for raiders."

"Sounds dangerous."

"Yes." The happiness brimmed over. "But nothing we can't handle."

He smiled. "True."

My hand tightened in his. "You don't think you'll be missed? You are their leader now, after all."

"Technically." He gave a small shrug, as if the vast powers he had inherited were nothing at all. "No, I doubt anyone will miss me. I don't think we're well suited to courts and thrones and following orders."

"Will they return to the sky city?"

"Some will. It's the safest place for them right now."

I didn't like thinking of the witches' city. I pictured it again on the wind-blasted summit of Raksha, its darkness strengthening as the witches returned, and shuddered. I was glad that River wouldn't be joining them.

"Is this a good time?" he said. "Or should we wait?"

I reached into my pocket, drawing out the star. It looked small and lifeless against my palm, no different from the pebbles scattered across the stream bank. "I don't want to wait any longer. I promised I would help her. I need to keep that promise."

"And this is what she wants?"

I nodded. "I wish we could have done it back in the Three Cities."

River shook his head. He knew as well as I did that it would have been impossible. After all, I had told the emperor that the star had escaped.

I gazed at the star dubiously. "Do you think she's still . . . alive?"

"Let's see." River took it, holding the star with thumb and forefinger. Almost immediately, it began to glow, dark fire gleaning through the cracks and pores of its surface. The light grew brighter and brighter, until I had to look away.

River laughed. "I'd say she's still with us."

I looked briefly, squinting. The star hovered over River's open palm, as if waiting for something. He nudged me.

"I think you should say something."

"What am I supposed to say?" I held my hand in front of my eyes, looking at the star through my fingers.

"I don't know. But she can't leave until you do."

I thought for a moment. "All right. I release you, star. You don't have to stay with me anymore." I paused. "We're going to help you return home."

The star bobbed gently in place, its light flickering. River lowered his hand, and a cloud of shadow rose from the forest floor, lifting the star into the air. It flickered madly, bathing the forest in its pale light. River made a gesture, and the shadows rose higher, until the star was a distant gleam of light. After another moment, I could no longer distinguish it in the tapestry of stars that stretched across the sky.

"Did it work?" I murmured. "Did she make it home?"

River watched the sky for another moment. "Yes."

I leaned against him. He smoothed the hair back from my cheek and kissed me.

"Kamzin?" Lusha's voice drifted toward us.

I sighed. River released my hand.

"It's all right." He was smiling again. "Soon we'll have all the time in the world."

I felt a surge of something heady, a mix of elation and excitement. I saw myself striding over glaciers and through dense, dark forests. I saw sharp mountains and snowy valleys, and vast, open lands framed by stars that glittered like frost.

Now I was heading home. But after that, there was nowhere I couldn't go.

ACKNOWLEDGMENTS

THANKS TO EVERYONE who read this book at various stages of its development (including the earliest, messiest ones) and provided invaluable feedback and encouragement, including Jordyn Alger, Katherine Arden, Amy Chen, Ross Conner, Shannon Grant, Stephanie Li, and Margaret Rogerson. Thanks again to Dr. Lauran Hartley for her insights on Tibetan nomenclature.

Thanks to my brilliant agent, Brianne Johnson, without whom these books would have never seen the light of day, and to my equally brilliant editor, Kristin Rens, who always knows exactly the right questions to ask (I'm convinced this is some sort of superpower). Thanks again to the incredibly talented cover artist Jeff Huang, and to the entire team at Balzer + Bray.

Thanks to the supportive community of debut authors I'm lucky to be a member of, particularly my fellow Vancouver authors, Rebecca Christiansen, Sabina Khan, Rebecca Schaeffer, and Lianne Oelke. Thanks to Catherine Egan, Sarah Glenn Marsh, and Evelyn Skye for championing this series and generally being amazing. Thanks to the bloggers who went out of their way to promote these books, to Cat Scully for her beautiful map, and to the staff at Black Bond Books and the Laughing Oyster Bookshop for their support. Thanks to all my friends and family who supported this series in ways large and small. And, once again, thanks to the trailblazing female mountaineers who helped inspire these books and who have lit paths for others to follow.